Storm Rider

AKIRA YOSHIMURA

Storm Rider

Translated from the Japanese
by Philip Gabriel

HARCOURT, INC.
Orlando   Austin   New York   San Diego   Toronto   London

Requests for permission to make copies of any part of the work
should be mailed to the following address: Permissions Department,
Harcourt, Inc., 6277 Sea Harbor Drive, Orlando, Florida 32887-6777.

www.HarcourtBooks.com

This is a translation of *Amerika Hikozo*. Original Japanese edition
published by Yomiuri Shimbun. English translation rights arranged
through Writers House, LLC/Japan Foreign Rights Centre.

Library of Congress Cataloging-in-Publication Data
Yoshimura, Akira, 1927–
[Amerika Hikozo. English]
The storm rider/Akira Yoshimura;
translated from the Japanese by Philip Gabriel.
p.   cm.
ISBN 0-15-100667-9
1. Heco, Joseph, 1837–1897—Fiction.   I. Gabriel, J. Philip.   II. Title.
PL865.O72A7613 2008
895.6'35—dc22   2003017321

Text set in Minion
Designed by Linda Lockowitz

Printed in the United States of America

First U.S. edition
A C E G I K J H F D B

Storm Rider

Hikotaro sat on the beach, clutching his knees close, and gazed out at the sea. A long, narrow strip of white stretched far away on the gravelly beach, right at the water's edge— the line of shells washed up whenever the surf grew rough.

The early autumn sky was serene, without a cloud. The smell of the sea wafted toward him on the faint breeze. To the left Awaji Island was visible, to the right Shodo Island and two large ships in a row sailing from west to east. Behind them a smaller boat slowly plowed its way through the water.

After his mother died, Hikotaro stopped attending the local temple school and spent most of his time like this, staring out at the sea. Even when it rained, this is where he could be found. What he saw before him was not the sea, though, but his mother's pale, beautiful face. It was hard for him, at thirteen, to believe that she was gone.

He was born August 2 in the third year of Tempo (1837) in the village of Komiya in the province of Harima, on the shores of the Sea of Harima in the Inland Sea. His father died when Hikotaro was still an infant, and he had no memories of him. He and his mother lived alone after that, but several years later his mother, an attractive woman, remarried a man named Kichizaemon from the nearby village of Hamada in Honjo Village. Kichizaemon's wife had died, and he'd been living with his son. Kichizaemon was the captain on a large ship that plied the waters between Hyogo and Edo, and more often than not he was away from home.

Hikotaro felt uneasy at his mother's remarrying, but it turned out his fears were groundless. His stepfather loved him as if Hikotaro were his own child, and was always sure to bring home presents from Edo that were bound to please the boy. His stepbrother too, Unomatsu, was happy to have a younger brother and always looked out for him.

Unomatsu was a happy-go-lucky sort of person and often went out to have fun with friends and didn't come home until late. Worried about his son's future, Kichizaemon had Unomatsu apprenticed to his uncle when he turned sixteen; the uncle was captain of a large vessel that sailed between Osaka and Edo. Unomatsu enjoyed being a sailor, learned his trade quickly, and in three years rose to the rank of second officer.

Whenever Hikotaro's stepfather and stepbrother came back from a voyage, they brought with them the smell of the sea, and after days spent in the brilliant sun and glare of the water, their faces were sleek and tan.

When Unomatsu returned from a voyage, he would regale Hikotaro and his mother with tales of what he'd seen and done, and would go to the neighbors, too, to recount his adventures. Most of the villagers had never set foot in the outside world and were spellbound by his tales. Secretly jealous of his stepbrother, Hikotaro dreamed of becoming a sailor. His stepfather and stepbrother were so manly, he thought, always taking on the sea, traveling to faraway places and meeting fascinating people. And the pay was certainly part of the attraction.

In the spring of his tenth year, Hikotaro told his mother that he wanted to be a sailor.

"Don't be stupid," his mother said.

To rise from common deckhand to captain takes years of grueling training, she told him, and when it storms at sea, life belowdecks is a living hell—the sea shows no mercy when it comes to swallowing up human life. Every time his stepfather and stepbrother left, she prayed they would return safely. "Two people is more than enough for me to worry about," she said, frowning.

"I'd like you to work in a shipping agency in Hyogo," she said. "That's why you have to go to the temple school and learn to read and write and calculate with an abacus."

Thinking that her explanation made sense, Hikotaro applied himself more than ever to his studies at school.

Three years passed, and in the beginning of March Hikotaro's cousin on his mother's side pulled into harbor in his small ship and stopped by the house. He was on his way to Marugame with nine passengers from Edo who were going to visit the Kompira Shrine in Shikoku.

"I'll take you with me," his cousin said.

"My mother won't allow it," Hikotaro replied. "She hates ships." But his cousin promised he would take Hikotaro to the Kompira Shrine and nowhere else. Finally his mother relented and Hikotaro went on board.

When the ship began to pull away, he could barely contain his excitement, for it was the first time he'd ever left his village. They passed right by Shodo Island, the one he could always see from the beach, wended their way among numerous other islands, and arrived at the harbor at Marugame. Hikotaro and his cousin saw the Kompira Shrine, then went to Miyajima, where they visited the famous Itsukushima Shrine.

On the return voyage they dropped off the passengers at Muronotsu, then returned to Hamada. Hikotaro's mother hugged him tight and told him she'd never let him go again.

Later that same day she collapsed. Hikotaro had gone to the neighbors to tell them all about his trip to the Kompira Shrine and Itsukushima Shrine, when a man from the neighborhood ran in and said his mother had taken ill. Hikotaro had just been talking with her and couldn't believe it. He raced home.

His mother was in a coma when he arrived. The doctor was already there and said she'd had a stroke; he'd prepared some medicine, but she had already lost consciousness. Her joy at Hikotaro's return had been too great a strain, and she'd burst a blood vessel. Hikotaro ran to the local shrine to pray, but four days later, on the eighteenth of May, his mother died.

Hikotaro's stepfather and stepbrother were out at sea, so it was left to him, at the age of thirteen, with help from his maternal grandmother, to make the preparations to lay his mother to rest. Following tradition, they laid her body in a large washtub filled with water whose temperature was adjusted by adding hot water (instead of normal bathwater, which started out hot and was adjusted by having cold water added), and as they bathed the corpse for burial, Hikotaro was racked with sobs.

They bound his mother's knees with rope so she was in a sitting position, and placed her in an upright coffin, which was then lowered outside from the veranda. Holding an incense burner, Hikotaro joined the funeral procession.

The procession headed down a path through the cotton fields, where the flowers were just beginning to blossom, to the communal graveyard. The coffin was lowered into the hole that had been dug, dirt was filled in and a large stone placed on top. Hikotaro knelt at the grave and wept loudly.

That night, he joined his relatives as, torches in hand, they went back to the graveyard. This, too, was part of tradition, done to make sure that the deceased had not come back to life and was not tapping on the inside of the coffin. But the grave was silent.

His grandmother and the others sobbed, saying over and over how very sad it was, their hands clasped together in prayer. Hikotaro couldn't say a thing.

Half a month later his stepfather came home. Returning by ship from Edo to Hyogo, he'd received the letter informing him of his wife's death. Kichizaemon was beside himself with grief. He dressed in mourning for the hundred-day period and spent his time shut in his house, lamenting.

Ten days had passed now since the mourning period ended, and Hikotaro's relatives gathered for a meal. His stepbrother had also returned home. Hikotaro couldn't stand being at home now that his mother was gone, and day after day he went to the beach to gaze out at the sea. Sometimes he would make his way down the path through the cotton fields, now covered with white flowers, to the graveyard, where he would kneel for a long while beside his mother's grave.

In the sea to the east the sails of a large ship appeared. A banner with a crimson circle flying from the stern marked an official ship of the Tokugawa shogunate.

Hikotaro heard footsteps, and someone sat down beside him. He didn't turn to see who it was, but he knew it was his stepfather.

Kichizaemon was silent for a while, also gazing out at the sea, then asked, "What do you plan to do, Hikotaro? Your grandmother says she'll look after you, so will you stay at home and attend school? Or would you like to work with me on the ship? You're thirteen now, we could hire you as an apprentice cook." Kichizaemon's tone was serious. Worried about what would become of his stepson, he had clearly thought long and hard about this.

These words caught Hikotaro off guard. He had decided to obey his mother, who so strongly opposed his becoming a sailor, but he couldn't shake the dream of going to sea and seeing with his own eyes the unknown world that lay beyond. The trip that he took on his cousin's ship to visit the shrines had been more wonderful than he ever imagined, and his yearning for the sea had grown.

His stepfather continued. "My ship is owned by a sake brewer in the Sea of Sesshu, a large 1,600-koku-capacity one called the *Sumiyoshi Maru*. I received a letter from the owner telling me to return to Hyogo as soon as the mourning period is over. I leave tomorrow."

Hikotaro turned to his stepfather and said, "Take me with you."

"I see. That's what we'll do, then," Kichizaemon said quietly, looking again at the water. "You'd better go home and pack." He turned and began walking home. Hikotaro stood up and hurried after him.

On the morning of September 13, Hikotaro left his home with his stepfather and paid a visit to his mother's grave. He felt more than a twinge of guilt that he was going against her wish that he not become a sailor, but he couldn't very well live alone. She might worry about him when it was *hell belowdecks,* as she'd put it, but he found the idea of plowing through stormy seas thrilling. On a ship he'd experience new worlds, and his future would open up in ways he could not even imagine.

After they left the graveyard, his stepfather took the road east, joining the Sanyo Highway at Tsuchiyama Village. The road was unbelievably wide and well maintained, filled with travelers and packhorses loaded down with goods, and even palanquins passed by. Drinking it all in, Hikotaro followed his stepfather.

They stopped at Shiotani Village to eat the lunch they'd brought with them, and it was almost sundown by the time they arrived in Hyogo. Hikotaro had been surprised by how lively the town of Akashi was when they passed along the way, but Hyogo was even larger, with crowds of people, draft horses, and heavily laden drays going to and fro. He followed his stepfather to the harbor, where the shore was packed with the warehouses of shipping agencies, the harbor with ships of all sizes.

His stepfather went into a solid building and didn't come out for some time. No doubt he was talking business with another captain.

When he finally emerged, they went to the two-story house attached to the shipping agency. The sailors who would man the *Sumiyoshi Maru* were assembled there, and they expressed their condolences on the loss of his wife.

Kichizaemon introduced Hikotaro as his late wife's son, and the men all turned sympathetic eyes on him as his stepfather went on:

"I can't very well leave him alone at home, so I've decided to have him train as a cook. Don't treat him like a captain's son, though. If he doesn't do his job, feel free to give him a good slap or two."

"So you're going to sea with us? That's great!" a cheerful voice said from the crowd of sailors. They were all men in the prime of life and seemed genuinely pleased that the thirteen-year-old Hikotaro would be joining them.

Finally their boisterous dinner began. The sailors sat in a circle; the young cook, stationed beside a large container of hot rice, ladled out heaping bowls for the men. Hikotaro helped the cook, carrying the bowls to the sailors. Some of the men were drinking as well.

Once the bowls of rice were distributed, Hikotaro's stepfather, who himself was enjoying a cup of sake, turned to Hikotaro and said, "Eat up."

Hikotaro heaped his bowl high and picked up his chopsticks. The gleaming white rice tasted better than any he'd ever had before. If they could always eat like this, he decided, sailors led a pretty nice life.

Soon they were all finished eating, and Hikotaro could see how well ordered their life was. Those who were drinking put down their cups, and they all laid out their futons in the large room. Following the cook's instructions, Hikotaro carried the bowls to the kitchen and rinsed them with water in a large earthen pot.

When he returned to the room, some of the sailors were already snoring. He spread his bedding beside his stepfather, lay down, and quickly fell asleep.

The next morning Hikotaro went on a barge with the sailors over to the *Sumiyoshi Maru*. Cargo was being loaded onto the ship, and fully loaded barges were pulling up alongside, one after the other. In addition to the sake, for the trip to Edo, there were barrels of rice and drinking water for the sailors. While the carrying and loading were going on, they busied themselves inspecting the ship and scrubbing it.

By evening most of the cargo had been stowed, and all the crew, including the captain, Hikotaro's stepfather, stayed aboard.

That night his stepfather and some of the first mates stood at the bow, looking up at the sky and talking. They must be discussing the wind and the weather, Hikotaro decided, and he knew it wouldn't be long before they set sail.

Sure enough, the next morning right after breakfast, his stepfather called out in a loud voice, "Set sail!" and the sailors all leaped to man their posts.

His stepfather stood at the prow and shouted, "Anchors aweigh!"

The anchors were hauled up off the sea floor, and the ship began to rock.

"Raise the sails!" At this command, a sailor began a chant as they turned a pulley, and the huge sail shook as it went up the mast. When it reached the top, it bellied slightly.

The ship slowly made its way forward. Hikotaro felt his heart leap in his chest. He was greatly impressed by how it took only a word from his stepfather for this large ship, heavily laden with cargo, to begin moving.

Their ship left harbor and headed south. The wind was with them, but faint, and their progress was slow, the sails filling, then drooping.

To the left was a row of houses, a town that the sailors told him was Kishiwada. Before them and behind them were other ships also headed south, and Hikotaro could really feel how the sea was a vital highway linking Edo with Osaka and Hyogo. They passed the Kata Straits and continued south.

The cook taught Hikotaro how to prepare meals for the sailors. Another of the cook's tasks on board was cleaning inside the ship.

As the sun began to set, they sailed into Yura Bay, where they anchored. Many other ships were anchored in the same harbor. That night there was a full moon.

The next morning dawned clear with a favorable wind, and the *Sumiyoshi Maru* continued its voyage. Before them lay Hibi Cape, a treacherous place where the tides ran together, but the ship managed to traverse it without incident and set its rudder toward the southeast.

They hugged the shore, but their progress remained slow, and as evening drew near, they anchored in Susami Bay. After leaving this port, they would round the Shiono Cape at the tip of the Kii Peninsula. The cape was exposed to the open Pacific and particularly dangerous because of the rough currents. Hikotaro's stepfather looked long and hard at the night sky.

The next morning a thick layer of clouds covered the sky, but there was a favorable wind, so they set sail. Hikotaro's stepfather stood at the bow watching the water before them, studying the currents and the movements of the clouds.

As they approached the tip of the cape, which jutted severely into the open sea, the waves roared even louder, the ship rolled, and spray drenched the decks. The ship plowed forward, around the tip of the cape, and turned east. It began to rain, with the wind against them for the first time.

They were close to Kumano, so Hikotaro's stepfather decided not to go any farther that day and had them turn the ship into Kumano Harbor. The water there was deep and clear, and that night the sailors took a boat into town in search of women and drink.

The next morning it was still raining, and the wind was still against them, so the *Sumiyoshi Maru* stayed in port.

Two days later a ship about the same size as theirs sailed into port. But it was newly constructed, its masts and deck shining.

"It's the *Eiriki Maru!*" some on board shouted, and they waved to their counterparts on the other vessel.

This ship belonged to Matsuya Hachisaburo, a brewer and relative of Matsuya Matazaemon, owner of the *Sumiyoshi Maru,* who was from Oishi Village in Urahara County in Sesshu—thus the sailors on both ships knew each other well. Like the *Sumiyoshi Maru,* the *Eiriki Maru* was on its way from Hyogo to Edo with a cargo of sake and other goods. The ship came along side and anchored beside the *Sumiyoshi Maru.*

The sailors, bored with waiting days for favorable wind, boarded a lighter with their captain, Hikotaro beside him, and rowed over to the *Eiriki Maru.* Hikotaro was happily surprised to find that six of their sailors as well as their captain, Manzo, who was over sixty, all hailed from his own village. For their part, the sailors were amazed to find Hikotaro, a lad from their small village, aboard the *Sumiyoshi Maru.*

9

His stepfather briefly explained, and Manzo and the others paid their condolences to him on the death of Hikotaro's mother. They looked at Hikotaro with sympathetic eyes and praised him for being able to overcome his grief at losing his mother and for becoming a sailor.

The crew from the *Eiriki Maru* visited the *Sumiyoshi Maru*; the sailors from Hikotaro's village, feeling sorry for him, brought special dishes to cheer him up. After a while they suggested that Hikotaro transfer to their ship. Manzo had often come to his stepfather's home, and Hikotaro also knew the other six sailors well, so he wanted to accept their offer.

When he broached the subject with his stepfather, his stepfather shook his head, saying, "You're too young. You'll just be a burden, and I can't allow it."

Hikotaro conveyed this to the sailors on the *Eiriki Maru*, who in turn told their captain. Manzo came over to discuss it with Hikotaro's stepfather.

"I'll look after Hikotaro myself," he insisted, "so please let him join our ship."

Hikotaro's stepfather repeated that the boy was too young, but he finally gave in to Manzo's earnest entreaties and agreed. In the end he seemed to think that it might be better for the boy to work for someone else than to stay by his side. Also, the *Sumiyoshi Maru* already had a cook, so even though Hikotaro had been helping him, his departure would cause no problem.

Hikotaro gathered his things and took them to the *Eiriki Maru*.

On the morning of September 21 the *Sumiyoshi Maru* remained in port waiting for favorable winds, but Manzo, deciding that the wind had improved, had the *Eiriki Maru* raise anchor. The ship headed north close to the shoreline of Kumano Nada. The new ship had a pleasant woody smell, and its mast was white.

The next day the wind was against them, so Manzo had the ship pull into Kukiura. After that the weather and wind remained poor, and the *Eiriki Maru* was anchored until October 6. Finally on the seventh they could leave port. But again the weather turned bad; they were barely able to make it around Daio Cape, a treacherous spot, and the next day they anchored in Anoriura in Shishu (modern-day Mie Prefecture).

Day after day Manzo checked the weather, and at last, on the morning of the twelfth, he had them raise the sails. They couldn't have asked for better weather as they passed Enshu Nada, sails billowing, and sailed east at a fair clip. Mount Fuji rose up on their left, and Hikotaro, seeing the sacred mountain for the first time, instinctively brought his hands together in prayer.

Their ship gave wide berth to Iro Cape on the Izu Peninsula, cut across Sagami Bay, went around Miura Cape, and entered Edo Bay. Before continuing on to Edo, they entered port at Uraga in Soshu (Kanagawa Prefecture) to go through customs inspection. It was October 15.

After boarding the *Eiriki Maru* in Kumano, Hikotaro had learned quite a bit about the ship. Including the captain, there were seventeen sailors aboard. Those from the same town as Hikotaro were the captain, Yasutaro, Jinpachi, Kiyotaro, Jisaku, Kiyozo, and Asauemon. The cook was a twenty-two-year-old named Sentaro, and Hikotaro worked under him. The cargo they carried was 1,931 barrels of sake, plus soy sauce, sugar, paper, tea, and sundries, which they were to deliver to the shipping agent Nakanishi Shinpachiro in Reiganjima in Edo.

Passing inspection at Uraga, they set sail, arriving off Shinagawa on October 19. They contacted the shipping agent, Nakanishi, and clerks from his agency were dispatched to meet them. One after the other, consignees' boats gathered around the *Eiriki Maru,* and the offloading work began.

The sailors, Hikotaro included, worked without rest. Once they were finished, at the direction of the shipping agency clerks they began loading cargo for the return trip to Hyogo. This consisted mainly of saffron for use in paints and medicine.

When this task was done, Hikotaro and two of the sailors

boarded a lighter and set out for the mouth of the Sumida River. The estuary was crowded with boats of all sizes, the shores packed with warehouses. In the distance they could see Edo Castle.

Hikotaro and the sailors went ashore and walked to see the Sensoji Temple. The streets were lined with all sorts of shops, and there were people everywhere. Hikotaro, amazed by all this activity, clung to the sailors and felt as if he were walking on a cloud. Paying their respects at the temple, they went on to Okuyama, a district filled with acrobats, magicians, archery galleries, and peep-show stalls. They spent the whole day enjoying the attractions, and by the time they returned to their quarters on shore, Hikotaro's face was flushed and his feet were swollen.

The next day they paid a visit to the Kameido Shrine and the day after that went to see some plays. Everywhere they went was crowded with people, and Hikotaro kept feeling that he was floating as he walked. He found it strange that there could be such a place with such great throngs.

The following day they took a lighter back to their ship, where everything was ready for the return voyage. Hikotaro was happy he'd been able to see the sights of Edo and was already thinking about the tales he could tell the people at home. He could picture their surprise and knew he'd made the right choice to become a sailor.

On October 22, the *Eiriki Maru* left the waters off Shinagawa, continued south across Edo Bay, and entered Uraga Harbor a day later. There they took on board 182 straw bags of soy beans, 200 bags of azuki beans, along with walnuts, sardine flakes, barley, and wheat.

While they were anchored in Uraga, Kiyotaro told Hikotaro the frightening story of what he'd experienced eight months before, along with Yasutaro and Iwakichi.

On December 26 of the previous year the three sailors had been on the *Sumisei Maru*, a ship owned by a Kiyaichi Juro, and had sailed out of Hyogo. The captain was a man named Shojiro, and there were fifteen sailors aboard all told.

After they unloaded their cargo in Edo, they took on dried sardines and empty barrels and put in at Mera Harbor in Izu. They set out on the night of February 10, and the next morning a strong north wind began to blow, which soon became a storm out of the west.

"Huge waves bore down on us one after the other, lashing like a waterfall. The ship would be pushed to the top of a wave, only to crash to the bottom. I didn't think we'd make it." Kiyotaro's eyes showed that just the memory was enough to scare him still.

Their rudder finally broke, and they were shot into the open sea like an arrow. The next day the waves had not abated, but off in the distance they spied an island. Shojiro brought the ship to the island, but the waves were too high to allow them to get close enough to shore. He took the ship southeast, and they were finally able to board their lighter and make it to land. The place was Makinawa on Hachijo Island.

The *Sumisei Maru* was blown away, and the men stayed on the island until May 2, when a local official's boat came and took them to Shimoda. Since their ship and cargo were lost, the sailors, including Kiyotaro, were questioned closely by officials, but once the interrogation was concluded, they started working on the *Eiriki Maru* in Hyogo.

"When the weather's good and the wind's at your back, nothing beats the life of a sailor. But let it start to storm, and the sea will swallow people and ships without mercy," Kiyotaro said, fairly spitting out the words.

Hikotaro listened transfixed, and admired Kiyotaro for being brave enough once again to take to the sea after such an experience. He was in awe of Yasutaro and Iwakichi, too, who'd been on the *Sumisei Maru,* for now working on the *Eiriki Maru* apparently without much concern. Hikotaro was determined that he, too, would someday become dauntless like these men.

After the cargo was all loaded, the *Eiriki Maru* set out from Uraga Harbor. The ship sailed south across placid Edo Bay. Ships of all sizes were heading in the same direction, bound for Hyogo or

Osaka, some of them sailing quite close to Hikotaro's ship. He was impressed by how many ships plied their trade along this route.

The autumn foliage on the mountains of the Boso Peninsula was already fading, covering them with a blurry light brown. Near the shore was a scattering of fishing boats.

Once they left the mouth of the bay and reached the open sea, their ship shook a bit more. But unfortunately the wind was from the southwest, against them, and Manzo shouted an order to tack. Their progress was slow, and they could see other ships around them tacking.

Gradually they made their way southwest of Sagami Nada, and Hikotaro watched as the mountains of Izu came into view. The sailors were kept busy trimming the sail while the helmsman worked the rudder.

They had a magnificent view of Mount Fuji to their right. Unlike on the outbound leg of their trip, the peak was now covered with snow, a sublime beauty that made Hikotaro understand why the mountain was holy. Here was a sight, he thought, that only a sailor could fully enjoy.

On the morning of October 28, two days after they'd set out from Uraga, the wind shifted to the northeast and then the east. This was the most favorable wind they could hope for—their sail snapped taut, and the ship quickly picked up speed. The sailors looked cheerful as their brand-new ship plowed through the water. The other ships around them, sails filled, were also making good time.

A break came in the clouds; a clear blue spread over the sky. The sea sparkled, and snowcapped Mount Fuji was sharply etched against the blue background. As the sun began to set, the ship passed Mimaezaki and entered the Sea of Enshu. That night the whole sky was filled with stars.

When you looked at the starry sky from the ship, Hikotaro discovered, it was different than from land—there was a mysterious feeling, as if your body were being drawn up into the sky. The Milky Way flowed thick and broad in the night sky, and Hikotaro couldn't take his eyes off it.

CHAPTER TWO

The next morning dawned clear, without a cloud in the sky.

In that time of year, ships traveling between Edo and Osaka or Hyogo generally cut across the Sea of Enshu and made port at Toba or Anori. They would wait there for good weather and a favorable wind before setting out again, going around the perilous tip of the Izu Peninsula, around the Shiono Cape, to return home in Osaka or Hyogo.

But Manzo said to the crew, a twinkle in his eye: "This good weather will continue for a while. So instead of wasting time putting into port in Izu, let's head straight for the Shiono Cape. The sooner we get back, the happier the owner will be."

This wasn't an unusual step to take, and the sailors all nodded in agreement. The captains of the other ships they could see, both near and far, seemed to have come to the same decision and were headed not for Izu but straight for the cape.

The fine weather held the next day as the *Eiriki Maru* cut across the Sea of Enshu, passed the treacherous Daiozaki Cape, and entered the Kumano Sea.

But now the weather took a turn for the worse, dark clouds covering the sky at sunset, and by eight o'clock the rain began. The ship plowed on toward the southwest as the wind steadily built and the waves became higher and rocked them.

At ten, when they were somewhere off Kumano in Kishu, the

15

weather turned fierce, the wind howling and the rain pounding down. Hikotaro had been fast asleep but woke with the violent lurching of the ship and the howl of the wind. He crawled up from his little quarters just aft of the mast and peered out on deck.

What he saw frightened him terribly, and he turned pale. Out of the dark sea, waves towered above the ship like mountain peaks, crashing down on them, streaming over the deck. Their ship was lifted high by one wave, then a moment later it plunged into the trough of the next. The sails had been taken down, and the thick, bare white mast swayed to the left and right.

Hikotaro's whole body trembled, and his teeth chattered. His mother's words about how life belowdecks could be hell came to him with a new force. The ship was tossed in every direction, pushed up and slammed down, and he was sure it would come apart at any minute. His mother had scolded him, telling him she would never allow him to be a sailor, for this very reason. The image of her floated before his eyes, and he wanted more than anything to cling to her and never let go.

The face of his stepfather also came to his mind. If he'd stayed aboard Kichizaemon's ship, he thought, this would not be happening to him.

Suddenly he could hear the shrill voices of several of the sailors, and a chill went down his spine. "Gods of the Ise Shrine, of the Komoira Shrine, have mercy on us and save us!" This sorrowful prayer rang out over and over again.

A shudder ran through Hikotaro: these normally brave sailors were calling to the gods to save them. Certain that the ship was about to capsize, he threw himself to the deck and joined the prayer that reached him through the roar of the wind, the prayer begging the gods to come to the rescue.

Each time the ship was lifted up high and thrown into the trough of the waves, Hikotaro thought it would be sucked under the sea, unable to rise again.

This terrifying night continued, until around four in the morning, when the rain let up and the wind died down a little, though the waves lost none of their ferocity. He no longer heard the praying.

Noticing that it was growing lighter, he lifted his head. Dawn had broken. He grabbed a part of the ship, clambered to his feet, and looked out at the surging sea. Several other ships were visible; like the *Eiriki Maru* they were speeding west, creaking as they moved, and some of them had lost their masts.

The wind, from the southeast, gradually died down, and by seven in the morning it was only a light breeze.

Manzo shouted the order to raise the sails.

When he heard this, Hikotaro breathed a deep sigh of relief. The waves were still high, but the ship should be able to find a safe harbor somewhere along the coast. The gods answered our prayer, he thought.

The sailors leaped to the pulley to raise the sail. They chanted as they cranked, and the huge sail slowly lifted up the mast.

Hikotaro was looking up at the sail when a blast of wind from the northwest hit them like a demon pouncing.

"Lower the sail!" Manzo yelled, his voice betraying his confusion.

It was no easy task to lower the sail now that it was filled by the strong wind, but if they left it up, the ship would capsize. The sail itself might rip. The sailors strained at the pulley, and finally the sail was back on deck. So that the yards at the top wouldn't be blown away in the fierce wind, they lashed them to the structure with rope.

The ship sped on, propelled by the wind. The towering waves sprayed the ship as they appeared one after the other aft of the vessel, the whitecaps like a monster with fangs bared. Hikotaro crouched beside the battened-down sail. His body plunged, then was flung to the sky. Waves crashed down.

He watched as the thick mast bent to the right, to the left. Above it, clouds raced along at nearly the speed of the ship.

"We're taking on water," Manzo's voice rang out shrilly. Hikotaro realized that Manzo meant that seawater was leaking in.

He watched as the sailors quickly assembled and began working a pump to get rid of the water; some of the men were scooping buckets. The ship was new, but in so violent a storm its joints were starting to loosen, and water was inundating the vessel. The waves pounded the sailors relentlessly as they worked.

Suddenly, from the aft of the ship came a tremendous sound, as if something was cracking. The sailors cried out as one.

Hikotaro looked: the broad blade of the rudder, smashed ceaselessly by the storm, had finally snapped and fallen into the sea. He watched as it was tossed by the waves and floated away from the stern.

Then the ship turned and pitched. Rudderless, it was now unstable and completely exposed to the waves smashing it from the side.

Fearing he would be tossed out into the sea, Hikotaro clung for dear life to the yards. Waves rushed over the ship like a torrent.

"Reverse!" Manzo yelled out.

Hikotaro had no idea what was meant by this but watched as several of the sailors pumping out the water staggered as fast as they could to the bow. No sooner had they arrived at the bow than they threw the two anchors into the sea. Manzo's order, it turned out, was a way of controlling the ship to weather a storm. Once the anchors were dropped, the ship rotated 180 degrees, its stern and bow exchanging places. The shock to the ship from the wind and waves was lessened; this maneuver was a superb way to stabilize the ship.

Hikotaro felt the rolling and pitching stop, but the waves coming from aft were violent, and the sailors continued to work the pump.

The wind began to blow even harder, water flooded the ship in spots, and near noon the transom broke off and floated away. The ship was beginning to sink. With a pained look, Manzo ordered the chief sailors to jettison part of the cargo to lighten the ship.

The sailors cut the ropes that held the sacks of barley and azuki beans and tossed a hundred of each into the sea. Throwing away the cargo the owner had entrusted to him was a hard thing for the captain to bear, but it was permitted in life-and-death situations.

The sea grew rougher still, and the turrets from the center of the ship to the stern broke, one by one, and were washed away.

Manzo stood there, waves washing over him, drew his short dagger from his belt, and cut off his topknot. White hair covered his face, plastered down by the seawater. Seeing what he'd done, the sailors took the dagger from him and one after another cut off their topknots. Hikotaro trembled when he saw this awful sight, these men standing with disheveled hair, and felt that the end had truly come. One of the sailors handed Hikotaro the dagger, and Hikotaro also sliced the blade through his topknot.

Manzo knelt and, hands together, began to pray to the gods, and the sailors joined him in unison. Hikotaro believed that they were all dead men.

It was nearing sundown.

Manzo, head bowed as the waves beat down on him, suddenly clambered to his feet. "Cut the mast!" he screamed, his eyes flashing.

Hearing this, the sailors looked silently at their captain. They'd lost their rudder, and if they cut down the mast, they wouldn't be able to steer the ship at all, and even if the storm subsided, they'd be left as nothing more than a huge piece of driftwood floating on the sea. A doleful look crossed their faces.

The mast was three feet thick and quite heavy. But its height made the ship unstable. The mast, continuously hit by the wind, pulled the ship along at a tremendous speed. Cutting it down was the last possible way to save the ship from capsizing and sinking.

It would be hard to cut down the mast in the dark, so Manzo must have decided to do it while there was still light.

Two sailors approached the mast, axes in hand. Hikotaro watched as one stood upwind of the mast, the other downwind.

The two struck at the mast with their axes, but the fierce wind and waves made them stagger and fall to their knees. They were weak to begin with, and the job didn't go well. Others grabbed the axes, took their places, and the blades dug into the mast. The mast gave a groan and swayed way over in the wind.

There was a terrible sound as the base began to splinter; pushed by the following wind, the mast leaned more. The top was bound by stays to the bow, but Manzo, dagger in hand, quickly severed the stays. The mast toppled with a crash and rolled into the sea.

On their knees, Manzo and the crew watched as the thick mast rose and sank among the huge waves. Hikotaro felt a sob rise up in his throat, and he trembled and clenched his teeth. Raising his head, he saw the mast disappear in the waves.

The ship didn't roll as much now, though the mighty waves continued to lift it up and dash it down.

It grew darker. The storm did not abate, but Hikotaro no longer felt as frightened. His body had grown used to the rolling of the ship, and his mind was a blank. He hadn't eaten for a whole day but didn't feel hungry. The only thing that he noticed was the faint figures of the sailors, seated on the deck, heads bowed.

The wind died down slightly, and after 11 PM it no longer howled. In a hoarse voice Manzo ordered the crew to sleep, with the exception of the helmsman and a lookout. Hikotaro crawled back into his bunk, and as soon as he lay down, he dropped into a deep sleep.

Waking, he lay in bed for a while, opening and closing his eyes. He found it strange that his body wasn't rolling back and forth but was lying still, and for a moment he wondered if he was dreaming.

It was light outside his cabin, and he crawled up to look. A clear blue sky spread out before him, and he blinked his eyes at the bright sunshine. The waves were calm, and the wind had stopped.

He stood up and swept the sea with his eyes. Two other ships without masts were floating in the distance. He tensed when he saw how much debris filled the water. There were broken lighters, barrels, parts of decks, and other pieces of ships—proof of how many had been destroyed by the storm and swallowed by the sea.

Hikotaro stood looking at all this for a while and realized how the *Eiriki Maru*, even though it had lost its rudder and mast, had been fortunate to avoid the fate of these other ships. Still, his ship was a pathetic sight. The mast was gone, now just a jagged stump. The battened-down sail was torn, the transom of the ship had broken off, and all the rigging was destroyed.

Sentaro, the cook, approached Hikotaro and told him to help prepare breakfast. Hikotaro went with him to the galley, near the pulley at the back of the ship. They lit a fire, boiled rice, and made grilled rice balls for the crew. The moment he smelled the rice cooking, Hikotaro was starving and could barely wait to have some. But the rule on board ship was that the crew had to be all served before the cooks could eat, so he ignored his hunger.

Hikotaro and Sentaro placed rice balls with miso paste in bamboo baskets and took them to the captain, then to the rest of the crew. The sailors nearly pushed each other aside to grab their share and hurriedly shoved the rice into their hungry mouths.

Hikotaro and Sentaro went back to the galley, where they could finally stuff themselves.

After their meal the sailors, under Manzo's directions, began straightening up. Some of them fixed a jury-rigged sail to the lanyards. The new sail was only one-fifth the size of the sail on the fallen mast, but it allowed them to creep along.

"All hands on deck!" Manzo called out, and Hikotaro and Sentaro left the galley and went to the middle of the ship. Manzo was standing there, the sailors seated in a circle around him; Hikotaro sat down behind them.

Manzo's white hair was disheveled, but his eyes gleamed with the hard glint of a real captain.

"Many ships are playing with the fish now, but thanks to the protection of the gods we've been able to keep afloat. We're very lucky but owe our lives also to how you all worked together to beat the storm."

The fact was it was thanks to Manzo's long years of experience as a captain, and his decisiveness, that they'd been able—by throwing out the anchors and cutting down the mast—to avoid the fate of so many other ships, and Hikotaro was deeply in awe of the man.

Manzo continued in a grave tone: "We're a bare ship now, and even with this makeshift sail we'll drift. The sea's quite calm now, but there will be another storm, mark my words. This is a brand-new ship, though, and should hold up. As long as the ship stays in one piece, we have a hundred and sixty sacks of rice, so even if we drift for two years, we won't starve to death. Once we make landfall somewhere, there should be a way for us to return home. Let's work together and keep our wits about us."

The sailors nodded at his words, and Hikotaro felt strengthened by what he'd heard.

The ship was slowly drifting to the north. The other ships without masts they'd seen in the distance were gone now, as was the debris.

In the evening, when a strong wind began to blow from the west, Manzo had them lower the makeshift sail, and the ship just drifted with the wind. The sailors all took to their bunks and went to sleep. Today must be the first of November, Hikotaro thought, and shut his eyes.

The next morning the sun shone through a break in the clouds, but the westerly wind was strong and the waves high.

That evening they could see an island faintly in the distance. They didn't know which island it was, but with a makeshift rudder they steered toward it.

The morning of the third dawned clear, the sea calm. The island grew closer, and they were on the leeward side. They saw a large vessel, also without a mast, to the north, but it disappeared.

Slowly but surely the *Eiriki Maru* drew nearer the island, and the men could clearly make out the white waves breaking on the shore. Everyone had his eyes glued to the island. That they saw no smoke meant the island was deserted. It was mostly a series of craggy rocks with a sprinkling of trees.

"Let's bring the ship closer in and go on the island," Seitaro shouted in an excited voice.

"Yes, let's," Yasutaro agreed, and Iwakichi lent his support as well.

These were the three who, at the end of last December, had run into that terrible storm on the way from Hyogo to Edo and had been cast adrift. Later they spied what turned out to be Hachijo Island and went ashore in their skiff. This experience had taught them that it was better to make landfall on an island than drift aimlessly.

Seitaro addressed his fellow sailors in a determined voice. "We're a helpless ship, with no rudder or mast. If we continue to drift, our chances of making it home are slim. The gods' protection has brought us this close to an island. I say we go ashore as soon as we can."

The sailors gazed in silence at the island, their faces indecisive.

One of them finally broke the silence. "Since there's no smoke, it must be deserted, but even if there are people there, we have no idea what kind of people. They might be cannibals who'll murder us all." His voice betrayed his fear, and several sailors nodded.

Another agreed. "Our ship might be helpless, but if we stay aboard, I'm sure we'll run across another ship. We've already drifted quite a bit to the east, so we might very well reach an island we know. We have plenty of food and water, so it's safer to stay with the ship."

Voices rose in support of this opinion.

A heated debate developed between these sailors and Seitaro and the two others who were in favor of landing on the island. No one backed down, and the argument led nowhere.

A low voice was heard. "The ship is under the captain's command, so let's hear what he has to say." This came from Chosuke, the helmsman, who at over fifty was the oldest. The sailors turned to Manzo, who had sat silent throughout the debate.

Manzo gazed at the sailors and calmly said, "Those who want to land on the island should go ahead. You should do whatever you want."

He went on. "If you make landfall, it means you take the lighter to shore and abandon ship. As the captain, though, I can't leave the ship and its cargo, which have cost so much, to the sea. I'd never be able to face the owner of the ship or the consignee. I have a duty to both of them. I'm staying, and if that means dying aboard, so be it."

A deep silence followed.

Again Manzo spoke. "What I just said was my opinion, as captain of this ship. You have parents, brothers and sisters, some of you even wives and children. So your top priority should be to survive and return home. That's what I meant when I said that if you want to land on the island, go. I won't blame anybody who does."

Hikotaro thought that Manzo made a lot of sense.

Once again the sailors discussed whether or not they should make landfall.

"Let's decide by a sacred oracle," Chosuke said.

It was the custom of sailors in such unfortunate circumstances to pray to the gods, draw a sacred lot, and act according to the answer. So Chosuke meant they should let the gods decide.

All agreed. Selected to draw the lot, Chosuke went to the ship's little shrine, where he prayed fervently.

He didn't come out for a long time, but finally, a hardened look on his face, he emerged and came over to the rest of them. They watched him in expectant silence. Chosuke gazed around and said, "The lot says to make landfall."

Seitaro's eyes lit up.

The other sailors said nothing, until one spoke up. "Just to be sure, let's draw lots one more time."

No one objected. Abandoning the ship was a serious matter, so the sailors wanted to be absolutely sure what was the will of the gods.

One who'd taken neither side entered the shrine alone. The captain continued to sit staring out at the sea, his expression showing that he was determined to stay with the ship no matter what the outcome of the divination.

After a while the sailor emerged and said, "The lot says not to land."

The sailors looked at each other. The first lot had told them to make landfall, the second not to. Confusion came to their faces.

Again they debated which oracle to follow, again they were in two camps, one saying that the first oracle was the true will of the gods, the other insisting that the second had to be correct. Their faces flushed now with excitement, now with anger.

The third-oldest member of the crew after the captain and the helmsman was a man named Ikumatsu. He had remained silent throughout but now spoke up to quiet the sailors. "At this rate we'll get nowhere," he said. "I'll draw the final oracle. I'm neutral: either disembarking or staying put is fine with me. Will you agree to follow what the oracle I consult tells us to do?"

The sailors were silent.

Chosuke said, "That's a good idea. Let's make this the last oracle. We'll follow it."

The sailors nodded as one.

Ikumatsu rubbed his hair, which had a sprinkling of white in it, adjusted the collar of his kimono, and went over to the shrine and disappeared inside. The sailors said not a word as they stared intently at the shrine. Hikotaro too watched to see what the outcome would be. Would they land or stay with the ship?

Finally Ikumatsu emerged. The sailors crowded around him, trying to read his expression.

Ikumatsu spoke: "It says to disembark."

A deep sigh arose from the crew. If the will of the gods was to disembark, then that's what they had to do. Even those who'd wanted to stay with the ship now looked ready to leave.

They would need the lighter to reach the island, so the crew went to the center of the ship, where it was stowed. The island might be uninhabited, so they must take provisions. Several of the men began loading sacks of rice into the lighter.

Manzo stood up and said, "You all can go, but as I've told you, I'm remaining with the ship. Don't worry about me."

The sailors looked fixedly at their captain. The oracle told them to land, but Manzo refused to leave the ship. He might be going against the will of the gods, but as the captain he was responsible to both ship and cargo.

When Manzo had finished speaking, someone spoke up. "If the captain's staying behind, so am I." It was Manzo's nephew, Jisaku, the second in command.

The rest of the crew were shaken by this, and some now said they would stay behind with Jisaku and the captain.

The debate fired up again. The last oracle's been cast, some of the sailors said reproachfully, and not doing what it says means defying the gods. Others argued that those who wanted to follow the oracle should do so, that each should do what he wanted.

"Look!" the helmsman suddenly yelled. He was pointing. The sailors' eyes followed his finger, and a loud cry arose among them.

Before anyone had realized it, the island was farther away. The ship had been on the leeward side of the island, and as they debated and debated, the wind had blown them away from land.

Even Hikotaro could tell that they were too far now to row the lighter ashore.

The crew stared silently at the island, and a few plopped down on the deck in despair. The wind had blown them east.

"We should have followed the first oracle and landed," Seitaro said, his voice pulsing with rage.

But the rest of the crew said nothing. Seitaro was right, but it was too late now. They just stared in the direction of the island. A deep silence overcame them.

The wind gradually freshened, and the ship picked up speed. The waves grew higher and sprayed over the bow. The sailors' disheveled hair caught in the wind and blew over their faces, but no one brushed it away.

Evening came on. The island grew even more distant, and by sunset it had disappeared. Prodded by the cook, Hikotaro went into the galley to help prepare dinner.

The next day the wind and waves were fierce, but by evening they died down again. The ship drifted farther east. In the distance they saw another dismasted ship, but soon it too disappeared.

November 9 dawned sunny, with a light breeze from the south. Manzo had them jury-rig a sail so they could head in the direction of Japan. From then until the twelfth they slowly made their way northwestward, but a strong west wind forced them to lower the makeshift sail. Again the ship drifted east. The waves became so fierce they seemed about to overwhelm the ship, so once again the crew had to jettison some of the cargo, throwing overboard a hundred sacks of barley and three hundred sacks of azuki beans.

The fifteenth was sunny, with not a cloud to be seen, and the ship was surrounded by schools of fish. The sailors took bits of dried sardine, put them on fishhooks, and threw them on lines in the water. The fish soon took the bait, and the sailors were able to catch mackerels one after the other. Hikotaro had never had fresh fish before. He and Sentaro cut them into sashimi slices and took them to the sailors. Whatever was left over was salted away.

They had drinking water in barrels, but still the sailors began to gather seawater to use with a device called a ranbiki, which evaporated seawater and then condensed the vapor to make fresh water.

Hikotaro was fascinated by this process. The drops dripped into a barrel, yielding some three cups of potable water. Using the ranbiki, however, required that the sailors burn their precious store of firewood, so they never used it again.

On the morning of the twenty-fourth several large sharks circled the boat. Some of the sailors were afraid, but others insisted it was a good, divine sign. Hikotaro gazed fearfully at the sharks. When one turned its head in another direction, the others all followed suit, and they swam away from the ship.

The good weather continued for days, and the sailors grew bored.

The sky was clear on the first of December, too, when the sailors went to the ship's storage chest of cash, opened it, and took out some coins. With the money they started to gamble at cards. The competition grew intense, the coins changing hands right and left. This went on until late in the afternoon, and then the sailors called it quits.

The strange thing was, those who'd won just walked away, without a second look leaving their earnings lying on the deck. It was such a large amount of money one would have trouble carrying it all, but in any case on a ship like theirs, adrift at sea, it had no value whatsoever.

A lethargy fell over the crew. They would sit vacantly looking out at the sea; some of them curled up and slept. Hikotaro shared this physical listlessness.

December 5 brought another storm. The rain of the last few days had stopped, but a terrible westerly gale blew, and the ship was tossed about on towering waves. Dropping the two anchors at the stern did little to fend off the fierce waves that ceaselessly rolled over the ship, flooding the cabins. The crew took refuge at the stern. It was clear that if this went on much longer, the ship would sink, and the sailors did their best to pump and bail out their vessel.

Hikotaro was tense, aware of the peril. Two of the sailors, though, sat unmoving as the rest of the crew worked like mad to save the ship. The two had sneers on their faces, as if in contempt of those who were bailing. Hikotaro understood that these men had given up.

He had always seen sailors as tough, tenacious people who made their living on the sea, but these two were totally lifeless. This saddened him. He made his way over to the bailers and grabbed a bucket to help.

They worked without eating a bite, then around two in the afternoon the wind began to die down, and by evening it was calm. The sailors worked until late at night, patching up places where the water had seeped in.

On the nineteenth they were hit by a storm whose intensity exceeded anything before, and the ship plowed eastward at a prodigious clip. The two anchors hanging from the bow danced along in the waves, testimony to how fast the ship was traveling. The hull had been breached, and over six feet of water had collected below-decks. While they pumped out the seawater, the sailors stuffed clothes into the cracks to keep the water out.

As the sea pounded down on them, the sailors appealed to the gods, and Hikotaro added his voice to these fervent prayers. The ship made an awful creaking noise each time it was thrust up onto the top of a wave and then slammed down into the trough, and Hikotaro was sure that at any minute it would come apart.

After sunset the wind finally died down and the waves abated. The sailors all wore looks of despair. The creaking noise the ship made was ominous.

"The ship is only a year old, but at this rate it won't last much longer," said one of the sailors, and the rest were silent, their eyes gloomy.

Hikotaro looked at them blankly. He knew that what the sailor had said was true. One more storm was all it would take for the boat—and himself—to be lost beneath the waves forever.

CHAPTER THREE

THE NIGHT OF DECEMBER 20 was bone-chillingly cold, stars filling the clear night sky. The sea was calm but could change drastically when it stormed, baring its ferocious fangs. The hull of the ship had been so battered by the wind and waves that most of its joints were coming apart. Hikotaro looked up apprehensively at the starry sky, then at the ship that lay faint in the starlight.

He went into his cabin and crawled under the covers. Death was very near, he thought—soon his body would sink beneath the waves to join the schools of fish and the thick clumps of seaweed waving in the current. He fell into a deep sleep.

A shrill voice rang out, and he felt the air around him quaver. He'd been dreaming. He could hear footsteps, and he opened his eyes. The night was nearly over, and a feeble light shone in through the crack in the door.

Somebody was yelling. Hikotaro couldn't figure out what the person was shouting about, but it had to be something extraordinary, and he roused himself and sat up in bed. Perhaps the ship was breaking up and sinking.

Sentaro, sleeping beside him, leaped to his feet and flung open the door, and Hikotaro jumped out after him.

It was Yasutaro, from the same village as Hikotaro, who was shouting. He was running all around excitedly. It wasn't unusual for him to be up so early. He was a very pious person, and his habit was to arise alone at dawn, purify himself with seawater, then face west toward his hometown and pray to the gods.

Hikotaro had no idea what he was shouting about. Yasutaro's eyes were bloodshot. He was usually such a quiet person, but here he was shouting like one gone mad.

The other sailors who'd woken up crowded around Yasutaro, asking him what was the matter. He babbled something about a cliff covered with snow, or a castle keep.

"I could see it. I could see it," he said huskily, pointing west.

"*What* did you see?" one of the sailors asked, clutching Yasutaro's shoulder.

Yasutaro repeated that he'd seen a cliff with snow on top, or a castle keep, and again pointed west. The crew all turned to gaze out over the sea, and Hikotaro too.

A loud exclamation arose from the sailors. Hikotaro could see it, too—a black object on the horizon, with something white above it, all set against the dawn sky. It did indeed look like a cliff capped with snow, or a castle keep soaring. Perhaps it was a crag jutting out into the sea, or an island.

"A ship!" one of the sailors cried.

It was a black ship with white sails. Shouts of joy sprung from the whole crew. The ship was heading in their direction from the west. The sun broke over the horizon, and in its light the black hull of the vessel and its white sails were etched clearly against the sky.

Keeping their eyes on the unknown vessel, the sailors exchanged excited words. The ship was different from a Japanese vessel, with many sails hanging from its yards. One of the sailors who'd been to Nagasaki said it must be Dutch.

Moving at a fair clip across the sea to the south, the ship grew closer. The sailors leaped for joy, but then they saw that the ship would pass them, and they shouted, "Save us! Save us!"

If this black ship didn't rescue them, it was certain death. Hikotaro joined in, shouting and waving his hands madly. They could see people on the other ship, but the people were facing away and hadn't noticed the *Eiriki Maru*. The ship plowed on toward the east, showing no sign of approaching.

The sailors shouted till they were hoarse, and one took a torn cloth, tied it to a pole, and waved it. But the black ship, not slowing down, drew away from the *Eiriki Maru*.

Then Hikotaro saw that some of the crew of the black ship had crowded together and were looking in their direction. The crew of the *Eiriki Maru* shouted even louder and waved their cloths even more. They could see people moving about on the other ship, some of them stepping lively. The people had finally taken note of the Japanese ship.

About six hundred yards to the east the ship slowly came about northward and finally stopped. The sailors on the *Eiriki Maru* cheered. The men on the other ship motioned to them, over and over, to come to their ship.

"Let's lower the lighter," some of the sailors said.

Hikotaro looked at Manzo, who was standing at the bow. Manzo had insisted on staying with the ship even when they were in sight of an island. Would he again refuse to leave the *Eiriki Maru*? But Manzo didn't stop them, and walked over toward the lighter himself. Long experience told him that his vessel was irreparably damaged and that it was only a matter of time before it sank.

The sailors hurried to the lighter, which was amidships. Manzo and Hikotaro boarded first, then the sailors loaded clothes and barrels of rice and other things before getting on.

They shoved off and rode the waves up and down. Two sailors grabbed oars and began to row them to the black ship. In their weakened condition, though, they were soon out of breath and made little headway. The black ship had stopped downwind and couldn't fight the headwind to come to them. The lighter had to make its way to the ship.

The sailors strained at the oars, and others took turns, but they got no closer to the ship. Hikotaro was struck by a feeling of hopelessness. The people on the black ship had stopped to rescue them, but when they saw that the lighter couldn't reach them, wouldn't they pick up and go their way? His fellow crewmates must have had the same thought, as their faces showed a rising panic.

Suddenly a terrible cry came from the sailors, and even those manning the oars stopped to look at the black ship.

Ever so slowly, the ship was beginning to move. Hikotaro saw his worst fear realized: the ship was leaving them. It had no obligation, really, to save castaways with whom it had no connection whatsoever. The ship had a destination, needed to resume voyage without wasting any more time.

Hikotaro stared blankly at the moving ship.

Its direction, though, wasn't east; the bow turned west, toward the crew in the lighter.

Despite the headwind, the black ship was approaching them.

"It's beating into the wind," Manzo shouted.

The black ship was using some method, then, to sail against the wind, and indeed it was advancing, white water spraying at its bow. The sailors patted each other on the shoulder in joy, their eyes filled with admiration, too, for the amazing way this black ship was able to sail as it did.

It rapidly drew near, its three tall masts filled with billowing, white sails. On deck the men, dressed in navy-blue outfits, all had their eyes on the Japanese sailors. The black ship now towered over the small lighter.

At the bow of the ship stood a large man who turned and flung them a line. It fell onto the lighter, and the sailors grabbed it and secured it to a post. The line went taut as the lighter was steadily pulled to the side of the ship.

The black ship was as stable as if it had lowered an anchor. With its sails all set, it was hard to imagine how this could be.

Several men leaned out over the side of the ship. One of them, heavily bearded, said something, and another line was lowered. He motioned to the men of the *Eiriki Maru* to use that to pull themselves aboard.

Manzo grabbed hold, got a foothold on the side of the ship, and climbed up. The sailors followed him, one after another, as did Hikotaro.

When Hikotaro finally scrambled up, he saw Manzo and the rest of the sailors kneeling, their heads bowed and hands touching the deck. Their shoulders were shaking as they sobbed. Tears came to Hikotaro's eyes as well when he thought of all they'd gone through. The sailors bowed in gratitude at being snatched from the clutches of death by this mysterious black ship. The image of his mother's face floated before him, and he believed that it was she who'd grabbed his hand and pulled him back to the land of the living.

The sailors clasped their hands together to show their thanks to their rescuers, and Hikotaro did the same, sobbing. With the others, he bowed deeply again and again to show his gratitude.

It was not without fear that he looked at these men. Some of them had red hair, others black. Most had beards. Their eyes were red, blue, or brown, and they wore long pants—he later learned these were called *trousers*—and navy-blue woolen clothes. All had on low boots, except for one, a tall man over six feet; his boots were high, and he seemed to be the captain. The men looked at Hikotaro and the others with curiosity, some of them even smiling.

The ship continued on its way. With the others, Hikotaro watched as the *Eiriki Maru* faded in the distance. Bereft of its mast and stern, the ship looked pitiful, and it was hard to believe that seventeen men had once been aboard.

The *Eiriki Maru* grew smaller and smaller, and finally vanished on the horizon.

Hikotaro and the others were taken to the afterdeck.

The captain brought with him a man of about forty with the strangest head. His hair was all shaved except for a long strand in the center of the crown that he'd braided and that hung down in back.

One of the Japanese sailors who'd been to Nagasaki whispered to the others, "He's Chinese."

The man's face was not like the other faces of the black ship's crew, it was more like that of a Japanese. They eventually learned that the Chinese man was hired to cook meals on the ship and was called a *cook* by the captain.

The Chinese man, who had melancholy eyes, took up a brush, paper, and bottle of ink and at the captain's request began to write something. What he wrote were the characters for "gold mountain." He continued to write, but the sailors only shook their heads, not understanding what he meant by the characters that spelled out "Merika."

After the Chinese had put away his brush, the captain motioned for them to follow him. Hikotaro and the others went with him into a room. This was obviously the galley, and the captain lightly tapped a barrel to indicate that there was water inside, and also pointed to some dried meat and other provisions. The men intently studied the captain's gestures, trying to catch his meaning. Finally it dawned on them that he was telling them that with their crew of seventeen added to his crew of twelve, they'd have to be careful to conserve food and water.

The sailors nodded to show they understood.

He smiled, as if he was satisfied that they understood, and again motioned them to follow. He escorted them to a small cabin outfitted with chairs upholstered with beautiful fabric, and walls and floor of gleaming wood. The captain motioned for them to sit down, which some of them did, though a few remained standing.

A short man entered and laid out a large nautical map on the table. He pointed to many spots on the map, all the while explaining something, but the sailors could only cock their heads in puzzlement. The man then pointed to one large portion of it and said, "*A-me-ri-ka.*"

Four years ago, one of the sailors had been in Uraga when two foreign men-of-war entered the harbor (the *Columbus* and the *Vincennes*) and had heard that the ships hailed from a place called *Amerika*; he told his comrades that *Amerika* had to be the name of a country.

Seeing that they understood, the man again pointed to the

broad expanse of land on the map and then to the floor of the room. The sailors soon understood—the ship they were on was from America.

Next the man pointed to a small island on the map and said, "Japan. Yedo," and pointed to the sailors.

He was saying the name of their country, but they'd never heard that name for their country, and found it hard to believe that their country was so small, and were silent.

Not bothered by their lack of response, the short man rolled up his map and left.

The sailors bowed to the captain and returned to the afterdeck. They sat down and talked over what they'd learned. Knowing the ship was American made them breathe easy, and they started to discuss what the captain had gestured about conserving provisions.

Manzo said that it was only natural that the amount of food and water on board would be limited. One of the sailors, though, looked scared as he asked, "If the voyage takes longer than they expect and they run out of food, won't they try to eat us?"

Hikotaro, too, had heard of cannibal races in foreign lands, and he grew uneasy.

"If you start worrying about that, there'll be no end to it," Manzo said with his customary sternness. "Be thankful to them for rescuing us. We'll have to make do with two meals a day instead of three."

The sailors began talking about the way the ship had tacked against the wind to come alongside their lighter. None of them had seen such a maneuver.

Several, curious about the ship, left the afterdeck and hesitantly made their way forward to the main deck. Hikotaro stayed sitting with the others.

After a while the sailors returned from their tour of the ship. One had been bold enough to approach the helmsman and, using gestures, ask him all sorts of questions. Thinking to ask what the name of the ship was, he asked, pointing repeatedly to the ship. At first the helmsman didn't understand, but finally said something that sounded like "oakland," which appeared to be the name.

Next he asked how long it would take for them to reach their destination. The helmsman laid his head on his bent arm as if sleeping and with his fingers counted out the number forty-two. Which meant it would be forty-two days until they reached their next port.

Nobody could believe this. Japanese boats always kept close to shore, and all the sailors, from Manzo on down, thought the black ship, too, must hug the shoreline. They could not imagine sailing out of sight of land and were certain that they'd be pulling into port in a day or two.

A blue-eyed seventeen- or eighteen-year-old came over to them and indicated that he wanted Hikotaro to follow him. It was clear that he felt close to Hikotaro, who at thirteen was the youngest member of the crew. Hikotaro stood up and went after him.

He was led to a small storeroom that the young man seemed to be in charge of. The young man took a soft piece of food, much like the mochi rice cakes back in Japan, spread some sort of yellowish oil on top, sprinkled some brown sugar on it and motioned to Hikotaro to eat it. Next to Hikotaro he placed a bowl of broth.

The young man had something to do, so he left the room. Hikotaro put the mochi-like piece of food to his mouth, but the smell of the oil was awful and he couldn't eat it, so he stuffed it into his pocket. Hesitantly, he sipped some of the soup with a spoon, and found it delicious. There were beans and salted meat inside, and he drank all the broth.

The young man came back and asked him, through gestures, whether he liked the food, and Hikotaro nodded. The young man smiled in satisfaction. Hikotaro bowed and left the room, and on the way back to the afterdeck quickly tossed the piece of food into the sea. The stink of that oil, though, stayed with him.

As the sun was setting, Hikotaro and the others were led into the dining hall for dinner. They were served boiled potatoes, the same mochi-like food Hikotaro had tried, *butter* (for that's what the yellowish oil turned out to be), salted meat, and coffee. They learned that the mochi-like food was called *bread*. They ate some of the rice they'd brought from the *Eiriki Maru* but didn't touch the butter or meat.

After dinner, quarters were prepared for the sailors, while Hikotaro, the captain of the ship, and four other of the black ship's crew all slept in one room. The captain evidently felt a fondness for the youngest member, Hikotaro, which is why Hikotaro was the only one of the Japanese invited to sleep there. He curled up under the wool futon (a *blanket*) and fell fast asleep.

According to the stars they were making good progress. Before long the sailors were helping out around the ship with various tasks, including Hikotaro, who helped the young sailor who'd given him bread and soup; together they straightened the storeroom. Hikotaro learned that the young man was seventeen, and indicated with his fingers that he was thirteen.

They learned that the man who had shown them the nautical map shortly after they were rescued, the one who had told them the word *Amerika* and that this was an American ship, was the second mate, two down from the captain in the ship's hierarchy.

This short man was very kind to the Japanese sailors and especially nice to Hikotaro. He brought in a large book of maps, sat down beside them, opened it, and pointed to a large piece of land. "*Amerika*," he repeated.

When Hikotaro and the others nodded, he pointed to their destination. "*Ka-ri-for-nia*," he said. They nodded again, and he seemed pleased.

The second mate left the afterdeck, came back with some old clothes, and motioned to Hikotaro to take off his kimono. Hikotaro did as he was told, and the second mate gestured to him that the clothes were now his. He helped Hikotaro into a shirt, a jacket, and some woolen *trousers*. Though the second mate was short, the clothes were still too big for Hikotaro, so the second mate took a white stick of *chalk,* made marks on the clothes, and took them away again.

The next afternoon he reappeared with the clothes in hand and again told Hikotaro to try them on. They were now a perfect fit.

He rested his hand on Hikotaro's shoulder. "Yankee boy!" he said with a smile.

Western clothes, Hikotaro discovered, were much tighter than a kimono, but they were warm and allowed great freedom of movement. He was pleased with the new outfit. His fellow sailors, however, said he looked funny and laughed.

Gradually the second mate began to teach Hikotaro English words. When Hikotaro pointed to water, for instance, and gestured that he wanted to know what this was called, the man replied, "*Water,*" though it sounded to Hikotaro more like *wara,* Japanese for straw. He pointed to features of his face and learned they were called *nose, ear,* and *eye.*

Hikotaro pointed upward and learned the words *sky* and *sun.*

He memorized these and taught them to the others.

On the morning of December 26 they heard an awful scream coming from the forward part of the ship. Hikotaro and the other sailors, who'd been sitting on the afterdeck, jumped to their feet and ran to see. They'd never in their lives heard such a blood-curdling scream.

The sailors came to an abrupt halt. Hikotaro saw a pig, bound by the feet, the Chinese cook beside it flashing a huge knife and slitting the pig's throat. Blood splattered onto the cook's arms and clothes as he sliced away at the pig's thighs.

Hikotaro and the others edged away and returned to the afterdeck.

Having never seen anything like this in Japan, the sailors were pale as they discussed the incident. Many were frightened of these foreigners who could kill a living being so cruelly, and one of them, his voice shaking, said, "If the voyage drags on too long, they might end up tying us up, cutting us into pieces, and eating us."

Hikotaro thought it very likely.

They ran into a storm on December 29. The crew of the black ship struck all the sails, and only one sailor remained at the wheel, the rest of them snug in their cabins napping or reading books. The storm lashed the ship, but no seawater leaked in, and the ship remained completely dry inside.

The Japanese sailors were astonished at how nonchalant the Americans were in the face of the storm, at how sturdy and well built the vessel was.

CHAPTER FOUR

THE STORM PASSED, and the ship again set sail and crossed the sea. The new year came, the fourth year of Kaei (1851).

On the morning of February 2, thick clouds covered the sky, and a strong west wind blew, billowing out the sails as the ship sped forward. The lookout was pointing to something and shouting, and the captain, spyglass in hand, clambered up the mainmast. Hikotaro knew that they must be getting near land.

That night the ship came to a halt, and the next morning, at dawn, it began to move again. The Japanese crew, eager to see land, all got up and stared fixedly ahead of them. The land, at first blurred in the distance, grew clearer as the sun rose. The sailors' eyes sparkled as they drank in the sight, their first glimpse of land in such a long time.

The ship approached the entrance to a harbor. Numerous ships of all types and colors were anchored there, and smaller boats with triangular sails glided in and out between them. One of the sailors heard from an American crew member that this harbor was called *San Francisco.*

Two small boats, pilot vessels by the look of them, approached their ship, and a tall, middle-aged man climbed aboard. He wore a black suit and had a boxlike head covering (a *silk hat*) on his head.

Guided by the pilot boats, the ship entered the harbor and then dropped anchor. A small boat flying a flag and several other boats pulled alongside them, and the people from these vessels boarded. Many were poorly dressed.

Fresh produce was brought on board, and the meals became bountiful. Some of the American crew drank liquor and smoked tobacco. The captain shaved, put on a new set of black clothes and one of those boxlike hats, and went ashore.

Their ship stayed anchored for four days, then they moved farther into the harbor and anchored near a long wharf. Again small vessels hauled up alongside them, and two men with dark clothes and boxhats came aboard. These two were much more refined than anyone who'd come aboard before, and from the attitude of the sailors who escorted them through the ship it was clear they were men of some position.

When the two men reached the afterdeck, they stopped in front of Hikotaro and the others there, and nodded as the second mate explained the situation.

They stepped forward and grasped the hands of the Japanese sailors, and one of them said something that sounded like *hawaiya*.

The Japanese sailors learned later that this was a greeting— *How are you?*—but since it sounded like the phrase *kawaiya*, which means "How charming," they bowed to the men.

The man who'd spoken this greeting to them looked at Hikotaro, pointed to land, and said something. Hikotaro, perplexed, tilted his head to one side, and the second mate gestured to him, pointing over and over to his feet. The crew of the *Auckland* had been to many lands where they could communicate only through gestures and had grown quite good at it, but none were more skilled than the second mate. Hikotaro understood that the man wanted to buy him a pair of shoes and was inviting him to come ashore.

The man looked quite a gentleman, but Hikotaro was afraid and gestured that he would go if the second mate came with him. The second mate nodded, went to his cabin to change into better clothes, then Hikotaro and he got in the small vessel with the two men. The boat pulled away from the *Auckland* and came up to the wharf.

The streets of San Francisco were broad and paved with stone, with sidewalks and carriages running down the street. Most of the houses were stone and were two or even three stories tall. The town was as crowded and lively as Edo. A group of men with black faces approached, and Hikotaro was surprised and frightened.

They went inside a shop with a glass window. The man said something to what appeared to be the clerk of the shop, who proceeded to place several pairs of shoes at Hikotaro's feet. Encouraged by the man, Hikotaro tried them on until he found a pair that fit perfectly. The gentleman nodded and paid the clerk.

They left the shop and went to a bar where the men drank liquor out of long, thin glass cups, while they invited Hikotaro to eat some cake. Hikotaro ate only one, wrapping the others in paper to take back to his crewmates.

The two men stood up, and at the entrance to the bar the gentleman said farewell to the second mate. Hikotaro pointed to his new shoes and bowed, and spoke the American words of gratitude he'd learned from the second mate—*Thank you.* The gentleman smiled and nodded.

Hikotaro and the second mate returned to the *Auckland,* where Hikotaro distributed the cakes he'd brought and told everyone about what he'd seen in the city.

The sailors touched his new shoes and said, "They treat you well—better than us—because you're the youngest." There was no hint of jealousy in their words, however, just happiness that people were being so nice to him.

The weather grew warmer, and the shoreline was filled with flowers in bloom.

Manzo and the rest of the crew allowed their hair to grow back out, tying it in back in a ponytail, but Hikotaro had his hair cut short by the second mate. The second mate and all the American crew called him Hiko, and some of them—because of all the names, Manzo, Kiyozo, Tamizo, and Kamezo, that ended in *zo*— began calling him Hikozo instead of Hikotaro.

Before long the other Japanese sailors were also calling him

Hikozo, and he himself liked the sound of it, so from then on that's the name he went by.

The crew of the *Auckland* were kind to them, feeling sorry that they had to wear such old clothes, and gave them hand-me-downs of their own to wear. Feeling quite self-conscious, the sailors changed into these, some of them receiving shoes as well.

In order to unload its cargo, the *Auckland* tied up next to a large, old ship used as a storage vessel. The crew began transferring the cargo to this other ship, and Hikozo and the others helped. Unloading the cargo took a week, and afterward the captain of the storage ship came aboard and, through gestures, invited the Japanese crew to come to a dance in the town in a few days. He did this, no doubt, to thank them for helping unload.

Two days later the captain of the storage ship came to the crew and told them to wash their faces, shave, and change out of their Western clothes and back into kimonos. The sailors did as instructed, with Hikozo, too, getting out the kimono that he'd put away.

After dinner he and the crew were taken ashore by the captain to a dance hall in a two-story brick building. A friend of the captain was waiting for them and escorted them to the second floor. The room they were brought to was quite large, with seats covered with a beautiful cloth (*sofas*).

They were told to sit down, and when they did, a cry of surprise came from them. In front of them sat some Japanese just like them.

The crew looked at each other and whispered, "Why are they here?"

One of the crew said that the captain of the storage ship must have asked them to dress in kimonos and come here to meet these other Japanese.

A sailor got up to talk to these other Japanese but stopped. It was just themselves reflected in an enormous mirror. They'd never seen or even heard of such a thing—a mirror so big it reflected not only a person full-length but many people at once. Hikozo stared at the mirror, enthralled by his first-ever view of what he looked like.

Suddenly there was a great noise, startling the sailors. They heard a drum and some flutes, so they figured it must be music, but Hikozo and others covered their ears at the loud sound.

The captain of the *Auckland* appeared and led them through a side door into another large room. The room was like the stage of a playhouse, with a curtain hanging in front. A line of chairs faced the curtain, and the captain motioned for them to sit down, which they did. Beyond the curtain they could hear a stir from a great number of people.

The sailors sat there silently, but finally one of them spoke up and said angrily, "That damned captain of the storage ship! He's brought us here to make a spectacle out of us and earn some money."

"So this *is* a playhouse, then."

"That's why they wanted us to change into kimonos."

The sailors talked among themselves, several of them so angry that they jumped to their feet.

Seeing this, the captain of the *Auckland* hurried over and restrained them.

Just then the curtain was drawn and a crowd of faces appeared on the other side. This crowd was standing in a large, candlelit hall, all eyes directed at the Japanese sailors. There were ladies, too, dressed in their finest clothes.

The crowd stared at Hikozo and the sailors on the stage; many turned to people beside them and talked excitedly, and some even laughed. Hikozo and the sailors sat tense in their chairs.

The captain of the storage ship stepped to the wing of the stage and said something in a loud voice to the crowd. He waved a hand, motioning Hikozo and the others to come down from the stage and walk around the hall. The dumbfounded sailors didn't resist, and came down to be among the crowd.

The crowd kept motioning them to approach, and the sailors found themselves scattered around the hall. Hikozo ended up led by a young man. People came over to him, staring at his face and fingering his kimono. Hikozo understood that their great curiosity came from never having seen a Japanese before.

The music quieted down a bit, and the men and women held

hands, their free hand on their hips, and began to dance. Those not dancing enjoyed drinking glasses of liquor and chatting. Hikozo's mind was blank as he followed the young man through the crowd.

A lady of about twenty was next to a stand with legs; on it was a large dial.

The young man who'd led Hikozo took out a silver coin and motioned for Hikozo to put it anywhere on the dial he liked, then spin the thin stick above it. Hikzo did as he was told. The stick spun around the dial, and the tip came to rest on the spot where Hikozo's coin was. The young woman handed him two coins, and Hikozo realized this was a kind of gambling.

The young man urged him to put both coins on the dial, and Hikozo again spun the stick. The stick again came to rest on his spot, and the girl handed him double the number of coins. The young man urged him to put all his money on the dial again, which he did, and sure enough he won again. A small crowd had gathered around them, marveling at Hikozo's luck.

The young man told him to put away his winnings, so Hikozo put the coins in his pocket as they left that place. The man said, "Good-bye," which Hikozo knew was what you said at farewell, and left.

Other people escorted Hikozo around the room. Men and women came up to him, spoke in friendly voices, holding out coins and other metal ornaments, urging him to take them. One woman even took off her ring and made Hikozo take it. He looked around at the other sailors and saw that they, too, were receiving gifts.

Hikozo was happy. It wasn't pleasant to be made a spectacle of, but he figured it was only natural for curious people to want to see these Japanese castaways. Everyone was kind and generous. Some even clasped his hand with their own warm hands. Both of Hikozo's pockets were soon filled with coins and jewelry.

The captain of the *Auckland* gathered the sailors together and took them downstairs to the dining hall. A meal was waiting for them, and Hikozo and the others enjoyed delicious food.

The dancing was still going on, but the sailors were escorted out of the building by the captain and returned to the wharf. The sky was filled with stars, and as the sailors walked along, cheerfully talking, Hikozo could tell that any anger they might have had had disappeared.

The next morning they gathered on deck to lay out and compare all the presents they'd received. Hikozo had received the most: sixty-two silver coins, seven paper knives, twelve rings, and three necktie pins. One of the necktie pins had a sparking stone set in it, which the second mate told them was a valuable gem called a *diamond*.

A few days later the *Auckland*, now completely unloaded, finished preparations for its next voyage. Hikozo and the sailors would have to disembark, and the captain gestured to them to gather their belongings so they could transfer to a ship called the *Polk*.

The next afternoon a boat pulled alongside the *Auckland*, and five sailors and an officer with a sword hanging from his belt came aboard. This was their escort from the *Polk*.

Following Manzo's command, Hikozo and the others knelt on the deck and bowed over and over to the captain and crew of the *Auckland*. These were men who had rescued them when they were on the brink of death, and again and again they expressed, in Japanese, their gratitude. Tears glistened in the eyes of the American captain and crew, and they came forward and shook the Japanese sailors' hands one after the after.

As they got into the boat, Hikozo called out a hearty *good-bye* in English to the second mate, and the mate, himself teary-eyed, said *good-bye*. As their boat heaved away from the *Auckland*, Hikozo and the others bowed to the captain and crew on the deck.

Unlike the *Auckland*, the *Polk* had a hull made of steel, and there were cannons placed around the mast. The Japanese were in awe of the ship as they knelt on deck and bowed in greeting to the officers. Meanwhile the sailors of the *Polk* unloaded the baggage of the Japanese onto the deck.

A very large man appeared, and the officer said something to him. The man motioned to Hikozo and the others to follow him. He led them to their cabin, which had bunk beds. The man carried blankets to them, made the beds, and cleared a space for them to lay out their luggage.

Several times the man pointed to his chest and said, "Thomas."

The sailors, understanding this was his name, nodded, and Thomas gave a warm and gentle smile. He motioned to them that they were not to hesitate to ask him for anything. Hikozo liked Thomas immediately.

The *Polk* was a large ship with three masts, and its interior was spotless. The officers and the men all wore navy-blue uniforms. A flag flew from the stern, but Manzo said that it was a customs-office flag. The crew on board appeared to be customs officials and their subordinates.

Hikozo and the others went up on deck, and the sailors gathered around them, friendly looks on their faces. They motioned to the Japanese to follow them and took them on a tour of the ship. Pointing out everything aboard, starting with the masts and sails, they taught them the English names—*sea, anchor,* etc.

The next day the Japanese were all given uniforms, four pairs of underwear, a thing to wear on your head called a *cap,* and two pairs of boots. The uniforms were wool with gold buttons on the coat. They also distributed boxes to each man, inside of which were spoons and racklike objects they called a *fork.* A sharp object much like what was used to slice sashimi they called a *knife.*

The meals on board were much more varied than on the *Auckland* and of better quality. The officers and crew were exceedingly kind, sometime bringing the Japanese sailors sweets and drinks.

They were being treated almost too well, in fact, and a debate sprang up among them as to what motives could possibly lie behind this. One sailor said that they were being fattened up so the Americans could eat them, but others said that was impossible.

Manzo finally spoke, rebuking his men: "I won't have you speaking ill of those who saved our lives and have been so kind to us."

The sailor who feared they were going to be eaten asked angrily, "But don't you think it's strange? Why are they giving us such special treatment? There must be something behind it."

Manzo turned to the sailor and said in a quiet voice, "They're being charitable to foreign sailors like us, that's all there is to it. They're sorry for us—the way we've drifted into this strange place where we don't even know the language."

Hikozo and the others accepted this. Nothing could be more rude, some of the men said, than doubting the crew of the ship.

No doubt the heated argument arose because they had nothing to do to pass the time. To keep from getting too bored, they had people take them to stroll down the streets of San Francisco, but they soon grew tired of that. In the course of their walks, however, they learned that the city had well over three thousand homes, that nearby lay the fabled Gold Mountain, and that people had come from all over to search for gold.

By now several months had passed since they came to the *Polk*, and they were dying of boredom.

The sailors decided that they needed to do some work and that helping out on the ship would also repay the kindness of the crew.

Once they explained their idea to Thomas, he went to convey their proposal to the captain and officers, who were delighted with the idea. Soon three of the sailors were cleaning the officers' quarters, while Hikozo was cleaning the captain's quarters and doing related tasks. The remaining crew helped scrub the deck.

It was around this time that Manzo began to say he didn't feel well. He was sixty-two. He had no appetite and was so tired he spent most of his time lying down. The ship's physician examined him and prescribed medicine, but nothing seemed to help, and Manzo's manly, tan face grew sallow.

Whenever he was free, Thomas came to their quarters to teach them English. For some reason he was thoroughly taken with Japan and dreamed of someday visiting their country, so he begged them to teach him Japanese. Thomas paid particular attention to teaching Hikozo English, and Hikozo responded by teaching him Japanese.

When they learned of this, two of the older sailors, Chosuke and Ikumatsu, scolded Hikozo. They told him that with the shogunate's policy of exclusion, if he learned a foreign language, not only he but the captain and the entire crew would be severely punished.

This warning frightened Hikozo, and though he continued to teach Thomas Japanese, he stopped trying to learn English from him.

The year ended, and the new year began. A year and two months had passed since they were cast adrift on the *Eiriki Maru.*

The sailors sometimes talked about what would happen to them, but each time they would fall into glum silence. They'd been snatched from death, true, but now found themselves in a distant land with no prospects of returning home. Time would pass meaninglessly, they would get old and die. They would be buried in foreign graves, their bones breaking up and dissolving into foreign soil. A bitter despair filled their faces, and even Hikozo, at night in bed, shed tears when he thought about his homeland.

One of the sailors unexpectedly punched the deck and sobbed. Hikozo looked away and took a deep breath, because he felt like doing the same thing.

At the end of February a large black ship—the *St. Mary*—entered San Francisco Harbor and anchored close to the entrance.

One morning about ten days later, the officers and crew of the *Polk* came to them, pointed to the *St. Mary,* and spoke excitedly, gesturing all the while. Hikozo and the others recognized the word *Japan* among what they said, and watched intently as the men signed that they would be traveling to Japan.

The sailors' eyes lit up. They used the word *Japan,* too, as they gestured their questions. Thomas, who by this time spoke a little Japanese, joined in and with faltering Japanese and gestures explained the situation.

Hikozo knew a little English now, and though it was not easy, gradually understood what Thomas was saying. The head of the harbor customhouse had written to the American government asking how these Japanese castaways should be handled, and a reply had come instructing them to treat them with every courtesy and then have them return to Japan on board a warship. The American government, Thomas explained, was thinking of *shaking hands with* (opening diplomatic relations with) Japan, and to that end was sending Hikozo and the others back.

It took some time for the sailors to grasp this, but when they did, they clapped their hands and leaped for joy. Some couldn't wait and ran into the cabin to gather their belongings. They were excited and in high spirits until late at night.

The next day, the captain of the *Polk*, a large man of about sixty with white whiskers, came to see them. With Thomas interpreting, he addressed them. Thomas used his hands and body to get his points across, and Hikozo and the others watched him fixedly. According to what the captain said, in two or three days the Japanese would be transferred to the *St. Mary*, which would then take them to Hong Kong. The American government was planning to send a fleet to Japan under the command of Commodore Perry, and Hikozo and the others would join this fleet in Hong Kong and return to Japan with them.

When they learned that what they'd been told a few days before was true, the sailors were overcome with joy, and some even wept.

Through Thomas, the captain told them it was hard to say good-bye to them, but he was happy they could return to Japan, and with his large hand he shook hands with them one by one. He bent down where Manzo lay, patted him on the shoulder, and spoke a few words of encouragement to the sick man. Manzo bowed his head deeply.

Hikozo and the crew went to their cabin and gathered their things. In the afternoon the crew stopped by one by one to bid them farewell and shake their hands. Hikozo was grateful to them for their warm feelings.

On the morning of March 11 the *St. Mary* raised anchor and came farther into the harbor, stopping near the *Polk*. In the afternoon two boats were lowered, pulled alongside the *Polk*, and some officers and sailors came aboard—the welcoming committee for the Japanese sailors.

The captain and the whole crew of the *Polk* gathered around

Hikozo and the others, to say good-bye. The captain shook each of their hands again, tears glistening in his eyes. Some of the sailors were crying, and Hikozo felt a warmth swell up in his chest.

The crew helped load their belongings into the boats and then lowered the feeble Manzo, tied to a chair because he was unable to walk. The Japanese crew got into the boats, which then pulled away from the *Polk*. Thomas went with them to see them off.

The *St. Mary* was different from both the *Auckland* and the *Polk*. Twenty-two cannons showed in portholes on both sides of the ship, the crew was large, and Thomas explained to them that the ones with gold braid on their hats were officers.

The Japanese were shown to their quarters, and after they'd stowed their belongings, they went back out on deck to say farewell to Thomas.

Thomas, his cheeks wet with tears, said in English, "*I want to go with you to Japan.*" But then he stepped into the launch and left.

The *St. Mary* was scheduled to set sail the next day, but the wind wasn't favorable, so their departure was delayed by a day. Hikozo and the crew took advantage of the delay to take a boat back to the *Polk* to say their final farewells to the captain and crew.

Several of Hikozo's fellow sailors had a discussion, then went over to the captain and proposed something quite unexpected. Using gestures, Jisaku told him he wanted Thomas to join them on their voyage. They didn't understand English, no one on the *St. Mary* could speak Japanese, and they didn't know anyone on the new ship. With a serious look on his face Jisaku managed to convey the idea that they felt helpless and that if Thomas could go with them, it would be a great encouragement. Hikozo thought this request quite reasonable and hoped it would be granted.

The captain looked surprised and after making doubly sure that he understood what Jisaku wanted, finally nodded. He summoned Thomas.

Hikozo watched as Thomas and the captain talked. When Thomas heard what Jisaku was proposing, he looked happy, but said he couldn't give up his present salary of fifty dollars per month. He thought for a while, then replied that if he could receive the basic salary of a sailor on the *St. Mary,* fifteen dollars per month, he'd go with them.

The captain nodded, went to his cabin, and wrote a letter that he brought back and gave to Thomas. Thomas then took the boat to the *St. Mary.*

Hikozo waited with the sailors for Thomas to return. Since Thomas had said he was willing to take less than a third of his present salary in order to travel with them, Hikozo knew his desire to go to Japan was genuine.

The boat finally returned, and Thomas came up on deck. His happy expression told the story—the captain of the *St. Mary* had accepted his captain's proposal. Thomas handed the captain what appeared to be a letter in reply from the captain of the *St. Mary* and spoke to him with excitement.

Thomas came over to Hikozo and the sailors to tell them he'd be traveling with them, then hurried to his cabin to pack his things. The sailors were overjoyed at the news, and as soon as Thomas returned, they got into the boat with him. Thomas couldn't have been happier, and called out a loud farewell to the captain and crew of the *Polk.*

The next morning, things were busting on the *St. Mary,* with the captain and officers standing on the quarterdeck. One of the officers blew a whistle, and the crew jumped as one to their posts. Hikozo and the Japanese sailors stood in a corner of the quarterdeck watching the proceedings as the ship got under way. A drum and fife played, the anchor chain was pulled up, and at the sound of a whistle the sails on the three masts filled out.

The ship slowly began to move, pointed toward the mouth of the bay. Hikozo felt the excitement rise in his chest. *This ship was taking them back home.* He'd thought that he would end up dying in this foreign land called America, but now he was on his way back to Japan, once again to walk on his native soil.

The warship sailed past the *Polk,* and the captain and men all came out on deck, waving handkerchiefs. Hikozo, sobbing, waved back.

CHAPTER FIVE

THE ST. MARY TURNED to the southwest.

After being lifted aboard, bound in his chair, Manzo became the center of attention for the crew of the ship. Since he was terribly thin and his face deathly pale, they could tell immediately that he was seriously ill.

The captain ordered his men to place Manzo on a stretcher and carry him to the dispensary; Hikozo, the others, and Thomas went along. A tall man of about forty was there, who Thomas whispered to them was the *doctor*, using the English word.

The doctor had Manzo placed on a bunk and, with Thomas interpreting and Hikozo helping out, questioned Manzo about his condition. In a weak voice Manzo explained how his stomach hurt, how he suffered from nausea and had no appetite. The doctor had him strip to the waist and felt his stomach.

After the examination, the doctor washed his hands and silently motioned to Hikozo and the others to follow him. The doctor came out on deck and explained his diagnosis to the men. He made a large circle with his hands and pressed this against his own stomach. Thomas explained that Manzo had a round, hard object in his stomach.

The doctor looked at the sailors and grimly shook his head. Hikozo and the sailors understood that Manzo was too ill to recover, that his death was just a question of time.

After the doctor left them, Chosuke muttered, "Seems like it's stomach cancer."

The sailors were silent.

The *St. Mary* sailed on at a fair clip, and according to Thomas they were headed toward an island called Hawaii. The officers and crew of the ship were all kind to them, providing them with excellent meals and comfortable bunks. The sailors helped the crew scrub the deck and move cargo around.

The sailors started talking with the crew of the ship, little by little learning some English words. Even Chosuke, who'd warned Hikozo not to learn English from Thomas, was starting to use English words like *rice*. When he saw this, Hikozo was determined not only to teach Thomas Japanese but also to learn English from him.

As the days went by, it grew colder. Thomas negotiated with the officers to get a blanket distributed to each of the sailors.

Fortunately they didn't run into any storms, and with a favorable wind the *St. Mary* made good progress. No land was visible, and they saw no other ships along the way. Hawaii, they learned, lay between America and China, and ships put in there to take on fuel, water, and food. The cold finally broke, and the temperature gradually rose.

Manzo lay in a bunk in a trim little cabin, and Hikozo and the men would stop by every day to see how he was doing. Possibly because of the pain in his stomach, Manzo usually wore a grimace, but sometimes he was asleep, snoring, when they visited. At set intervals the doctor gave him medicine to drink, and each time he did this Manzo would bring his hands together in gratitude.

It got warmer, sometimes so warm they perspired. They could see flocks of seabirds in the sky.

On the morning of April 3, they heard the lookout call, and rushed from their cabin.

The captain was standing with the officers near the prow, scanning the horizon with a spyglass. Hikozo and his fellow sailors crowded at the ship's side. Under the dawn sky they could faintly see an island in the distance, and their ship was going in that direction.

Hikozo was excited that their ship had reached this point halfway between America and China, a point he knew put them closer to Japan. After they made harbor in Hawaii, they would probably head straight for China. In his mind floated up the calm scenery of his home village facing the Sea of Harima. He pictured the faces of his stepfather, Kichizaemon, and stepbrother, Unomatsu, and knew that the first thing he'd do when he got home was pay a visit to his mother's grave.

The island, a fairly large one, grew closer, with other islands visible behind it. Mountains rose in the center. Hikozo's eyes were glued to the scene. The island was covered with surprisingly thick greenery, all of it sparkling in the sunlight. The sea was a dark blue, as if dyed indigo, and small boats dotted the shore.

The warship's sails were half lowered as the ship slowed. Along the shore were small thatched huts, and adults and children were visible. In front of the ship lay a harbor carved deeply out of the land, and the ship made for it.

Thomas, who stood nearby, said, "That's Hilo Harbor."

It was eleven in the morning as the *St. Mary* struck its sails and anchored just inside the harbor. There were vessels of all sizes anchored there, with small boats moving in and out among them.

Then Thomas gave a shout. Hikozo and the sailors turned and knew immediately from the hard look on his face that something terrible had happened.

Thomas kept repeating the name Manzo, and used the English word *die*. Hikozo knew what that meant and realized that Manzo had passed away, and he told the other sailors. The sailors paled, left the side of the ship, and raced to the cabin that had been Manzo's sickroom.

Inside they found the doctor and a short sailor standing there. The sailors gathered around Manzo's bed and looked intently at his face. His mouth was half open, the gaps visible where some of his teeth were missing. His eyes were closed, his face a veritable death mask.

Manzo's nephew Jisaku clasped Manzo's arm, hung his head, and sobbed. The other sailors joined him, and Hikozo, too, found himself sobbing, his shoulders heaving. They had nothing but admiration for Manzo and how he'd put his experience and knowledge of the sea to good use when they were hit by a storm, how he'd kept the *Eiriki Maru* from sinking and saved them all from a watery grave. They'd all looked forward to returning home with Manzo, and for him to succumb halfway from home was sad beyond words.

Tears in his eyes, Thomas told what had happened. The sailor in the room with them was bringing in Manzo's meal when he noticed that Manzo was cold. The doctor ran over but discovered that the old captain had breathed his last, probably around dawn.

Chosuke led a discussion of what they should do with the body.

One of the officers came into the cabin, said a prayer over Manzo's body, and then, through Thomas, asked them how they usually buried their dead in Japan. With Hikozo supplementing his gestures with words, Chosuke replied that they dressed the corpse in white and buried it in a barrel or box.

Nodding, the officer left the cabin.

They brought in a large tub, in the traditional way adjusted the water temperature, undressed the body, and washed it in the tub.

Manzo's corpse looked pitiful, his ribs and bones sticking out, his hands and legs as thin as a pestle, and Jisaku wept as he washed it. Afterward, Chosuke used a razor to carefully shave Manzo's face.

The officer came back with a bolt of white cloth. The sailors measured this and sewed it into an outfit they then put on Manzo. Crew members brought over a large wooden box the ship's carpenter had made, and the sailors placed the body inside, along with the customary coins and walking stick. That night they held the wake, taking turns sitting up with the body.

The next morning dawned clear and sunny, the air invigorating.

The captain lent them a boat, which the sailors placed the coffin in. They rowed to shore, accompanied by Thomas and two officers.

There were easily a hundred islanders waiting for them. Their faces were light brown, and all were barefoot. The captain had apparently contacted the town office beforehand, and two officials, both carrying long sticks, made the islanders clear a path for the sailors.

With the officials leading the way, the sailors set off, shouldering the coffin. Next came Hikozo, the officers, and Thomas, and finally all the islanders in what had become a long funeral procession.

The officials finally came to the public cemetery, where a long hole had been dug, evidently at their instructions. The sailors lowered the coffin into the hole, shoveled dirt on top, and placed a large stone on the burial mound. Kiyozo, who had the best penmanship of all of them, took his brush and wrote on the grave marker they'd prepared: *Manzo of Japan, Praise Amida Buddha.* They wanted to add the date of death but had to talk it over among themselves, for during their time in San Francisco they'd grown used to using the Western calendar and couldn't figure out what month and day this would work out to in the Japanese calendar. After much discussion they agreed that it was March 4 of the fifth year of Kaei, and Kiyozo wrote that down on the marker.

The sailors remained standing there after the burial was over. They were reluctant to leave Manzo buried in foreign soil. He had left behind a wife and two sons, and an adopted child.

The officers stood silently but after a time spoke up and motioned to Thomas that it was time to go. Hikozo and the sailors brought their hands together in prayer again and left the cemetery, some of them still crying. Turning often to look back, they trudged with heavy steps back to the town.

In town they were quickly surrounded by people and wandered through it. It was less a town than a scattering of huts, with thick groves of trees heavy with fruit. It was hot, and the people were barely clothed.

In the evening the sailors returned to the warship.

Supplies were already being loaded onto the *St. Mary*. Boats filled with vegetables, barrels of drinking water, fruit, and fuel pulled up alongside the ship one after the other, and the supplies were hoisted up. Some boats had brought chickens and pigs.

Day after day officers and crew went into town in search of more provisions, and Hikozo and the sailors, with nothing else to do, went with them.

Jisaku went to the cemetery, and several sailors went with him, but Hikozo silently went instead with the other sailors to town. Manzo had been from his hometown, a friend of his stepfather, so it was too painful to revisit the grave. Hikozo didn't want to feel that kind of pain.

Everywhere Hikozo and the others went, townspeople tagged along after them. Every time the Japanese turned around to look at them, the locals would avert their eyes shyly, stop, even retreat a few steps. At first they seemed afraid of the Japanese, but everyone remained calm.

Hikozo thought it strange that, except for those who went out fishing, the townspeople seemed to have no occupation at all. Strong-looking young men just squatted outside the thatched huts, watching them as they passed by. The women kept their hair tied back and wore what looked like Japanese *yukata*, minus the *obi*. Hikozo concluded that the land was so amazingly fertile that those who lived here could get by without working.

There was fruit everywhere, and no one scolded the Japanese if they picked some. There were potato fields, too, but unlike Japan, where farmers planted and then harvested the field, here they only had to dig a portion of a field and plant some potatoes there and new potatoes would come out without being tended. They ate coconuts, too. The Japanese learned all this from the local people who swarmed around them, communicating with them through hand signs and gestures.

The town consisted of about two hundred homes surrounded by tall sugarcane, no doubt planted to provide shade. It was about as hot as the beginning of summer in Japan, and occasionally there would be a hard rain, but it would quickly let up and the sun would soon be shining again. Hikozo saw fishermen returning to shore, their boats filled to the brim with fish, proof that the sea was teeming. Men and women would come down to the shore and take the fish without any exchange of money, but the fishermen didn't seem to mind.

After seven days all the supplies had been brought aboard the ship. At dinner they had fried fish.

The *St. Mary* weighed anchor and set sail. Hikozo watched the island fade into the distance. It was unbearably sad to think that they were leaving Manzo behind. From Hawaii, the *St. Mary* headed west.

As Hikozo stood on deck looking out at the ocean, he remembered how they'd been castaways on this same sea, how the *Eiriki Maru* had lost its mast and rudder and drifted farther and farther east. Every day at dawn, Yasutaro would rinse himself with seawater, kneel and face the west and pray to the gods. And now here they were on the *St. Mary,* headed in that very direction, sailing toward Japan. Hikozo's sadness at leaving Manzo behind was quickly replaced by happy thoughts of how, little by little, they were returning.

It was a miracle that they had not lost a single man while they were drifting. Having enough food and water was the main reason, but it was also fortunate that they'd had Manzo to rally around. At any rate, the gods had not abandoned them, and Hikozo felt a renewed sense of gratitude.

Days passed with nothing on the horizon. Sometimes there was no wind at all and the ship barely moved, and once they ran into a storm. Waves lashed the deck, and the ship shook violently. But the crew took it in stride, staying in their cabins playing cards or reading magazines, letting a single helmsman keep the ship steady.

By the Western calendar it was May. Hikozo and the sailors kept busy scrubbing the decks and doing various tasks, impressing the officers with their diligence.

The sailors all studied English conversation with Thomas, who was glad to correct their pronunciation. Every day he came to see

Hikozo to learn more Japanese, and though he had a strange accent, he was able to speak a kind of broken Japanese. He would pat Hikozo on the shoulder and tell him that his English was the best of all.

The voyage was long, with nothing but the sea to contemplate day after day, but the thought that each day brought them nearer to China, and to home, made Hikozo and the others excited.

One day, Thomas said in English, "Hiko, your country's in that direction."

That was toward the north, so Hikozo knew that Japan lay on the starboard side. The horizon was misty, but he held himself still and gazed in that direction, sensing the presence of Japan in the distance. They had a favorable wind at this point and were making good time, the sails so taut they looked like they might burst. Hikozo stood there, not moving a muscle.

As far as the eye could see it was just ocean, but eventually they spied a few islands on the horizon, and they even passed a craggy isle.

The *St. Mary* continued west, and on the morning of May 21 they saw a long shoreline ahead of them. Using the English word, Thomas said it was *China*.

The next day they approached Hong Kong, entered the harbor, and anchored. This island, twenty-eight kilometers around, was under British control, Thomas told Hikozo. American warships often came to the harbor, and right now there was a steamer flying an American flag from its stern and with waterwheel-like objects attached to each side. The coast was packed with small Chinese boats; the streets were packed with people. Hills ranged along the north side of the island, and their slopes ran nearly down to the sea.

Lots of small boats began transporting provisions and fuel to their ship, and Hikozo and the sailors helped the crew hoist this onto the deck. After so many days at sea, Hikozo was struck by how full the harbor was of the smell of human beings.

The next day, two American merchant ships came to port and began unloading and loading cargo.

Their ship pulled up its anchor and, with the land to starboard, sailed until the evening, when they reached Macao, where there was a large paddle-wheel steam frigate, the *Susquehanna*, flagship of the American Far East fleet. Thomas pointed to the flag flying from the ship and said, in English, "It's the flag of Commodore Aulick." Hikozo had never seen such a large vessel before and was impressed by the imposing look of a true man-of-war.

The next morning the captain and officers of the *St. Mary* took a boat over to the *Susquehanna* to pay their respects. After some time had passed, a launch was lowered from the *Susquehanna*, and the two boats together made their way back to the *St. Mary*.

A short, stout man with white whiskers, wearing a naval uniform, climbed aboard the *St. Mary* with the *St. Mary*'s captain, and the crew, all lined up to receive him, saluted. "That's Commodore Aulick," Thomas whispered to Hikozo.

The commodore saluted back and, led by the captain, went down the corridor leading to the captain's quarters. With the commodore visiting them, the atmosphere on board was tense. After a while the captain and he reappeared on deck. The two conversed for a time, then Aulick noticed Hikozo and the sailors standing in one corner of the deck and walked over to them. Thomas saluted, and the Japanese all bowed.

Aulick questioned Thomas about them, and Thomas, standing at attention, explained. Aulick nodded, walked away, and boarded his boat. When the boat set off for the *Susquehanna*, the *St. Mary* fired off a thirteen-gun salute.

Three days later, Hikozo and the sailors were assembled on deck, and one of the officers, through Thomas, told them that they would be transferred to the *Susquehanna*. Thomas explained to them that the American government had decided to send a squadron of warships, under the command of Admiral Perry, to Japan. Perry was on his way to Macao on a warship and would then take the *Susquehanna* to Japan. Hikozo and the sailors, who would accompany him on the *Susquehanna*, would be turned over to the Japanese after the squadron arrived in Japan. Perry had yet to arrive, and they weren't sure when he would, so Hikozo and the sailors would go to the *Susquehanna* now. Meanwhile the *St. Mary* would head to Fiji to negotiate with the natives about an incident in which some Fijians had killed some American sailors, and then return to America.

Hikozo and the others were overjoyed that arrangements had been made for their return to their homeland. They packed their things and the next morning assembled on the deck, belongings in hand and Thomas with them.

The captain and the officers approached them; Hikozo and the sailors got down on their knees, while the oldest member of their group, Chosuke, spoke in Japanese, thanking them for all their kindness. The sailors bowed deeply. The captain said he prayed for their safe return home, and shook their hands.

As Hikozo and the sailors got into several boats, the captain and crew waved good-bye.

Walking on the deck of the *Susquehanna*, the Japanese were astonished at the size of the ship. It was 235 feet long, 41 feet wide, and had plenty of cannon. Hikozo thought about how such a large warship had never been seen in Japan and how surprised his countrymen would be when it arrived.

One of the crew led them to their quarters. The *St. Mary* set sail for Fiji, and two days later the *Susquehanna* left Macao and sailed to Hong Kong Harbor.

One thing that surprised the Japanese after boarding was how ill tempered and unfriendly the crew were toward them. Thomas explained. As the flagship of the American Far East fleet, the ship had long used China as its base of operations. In doing so they hired poor Chinese laborers to work for them, who constantly kowtowed to them to earn their money, and this led the crew to become arrogant in their dealings with them. Hikozo and the sailors, Thomas explained, had the same skin color as the Chinese and similar features, so the crew tended to lump them together with the Chinese and treat them roughly.

The sailors were indignant when they heard this. Since childhood they had been taught that human beings should treat each other with respect, certainly not like animals. It made the sailors angry to think that the crew of the ship should despise the Chinese.

With their own eyes they saw that what Thomas had told them was true. The officers would yell at the sailors, even kick them. The sailors began to cower before them and were eventually driven out of their cabin to take up quarters belowdecks, where it was so hot they could barely breathe.

Some of the sailors wanted to complain to Commodore Aulick, but Thomas dissuaded them, saying nothing good would come of it.

The *Susquehanna* sat at anchor for days, awaiting the arrival of Perry from America.

Whenever the sailors got together, their topic of discussion was invariably their mistreatment on the *Susquehanna*. On the *St. Mary* they had been given rice to eat, but there was no sign of that happening here; the food was worse even than that of the ordinary crew members.

Thomas cautioned them, saying, "Perry will come, and the fleet will sail to Japan, and you'll be handed over to the Japanese government. Just be patient until then."

Boats went back and forth between ship and shore carrying provisions, and Hikozo and the other Japanese sailors were assigned to help in this task. On shore they would load what the Chinese had brought. The Chinese were all servile, and the crew of the ship treated them harshly, which angered Hikozo and the others.

Often the crew would go into town, leaving Hikozo and the sailors squatting by the boat to await their return.

CHAPTER SIX

ONE DAY WHILE WAITING by the boat for the crew to come back from town, Hikozo noticed a man in Western clothes staring at them. This was odd, so he quietly kept an eye on the man.

The man stood there for a while, then came over to them. Warily, Hikozo turned to him.

The man stopped a few steps away and in a low voice asked, "What country are you from?"

Hikozo was shocked, and doubted he'd heard right. It sounded like the man had spoken in Japanese, but they hadn't heard anyone speak in proper Japanese since they first became castaways.

Who could this person be? A Chinese who could speak good Japanese? The man wore Western clothes, but his face wasn't that of a Westerner. His clothes were spotless, his face washed, and he was clean-shaven, with his hair neatly pulled back.

Kiyotaro looked at him in astonishment and answered, "We're Japanese."

The man's eyes welled up; his lips quivered.

"I thought so. I've been watching you every time you come ashore. So you are Japanese after all!"

Hikozo stiffened. There should be no Japanese in Hong Kong. He'd heard that Chinese ships came to Nagasaki every year to trade with Japan. Could this be a Chinese who'd made the voyage and picked up Japanese?

The sailors stared at the man without a word.

The man averted his face slightly and said, "My name is Riki-matsu. I'm from Kuchinotsu in Shimabara, in the province of Hizen."

The sailors called out in surprise, and Hikozo, too, was dumb-founded. The man's hair was cut short, and he wore a Western suit, but if you looked closely, his face was indeed that of a Japanese.

But why in the world would a Japanese be living here in Hong Kong? They themselves had been carried off by fate to a place they expected to be, but this man Rikimatsu looked settled into a life here. He must have been living for a long time in Hong Kong.

Hikozo felt as if he were dreaming. "How is it . . . you're here?" he asked, almost gasping out the words.

Rikimatsu lowered eyes and bit his lip as though trying not to be overcome by sorrow. After a long silence he said, "I'll tell you about that later. And I'd like to hear your story as well. I might be able to help you. But it's getting late, so why don't you come to my house tomorrow? Just ask anyone where the Japanese Rikimatsu lives, and you'll be able to find it. I will see you later." He bowed and left.

Hikozo and the sailors watched as he walked toward the rows of houses. They were so taken aback no one said a word; they just stared at his retreating figure until it disappeared.

The crew of the ship returned from town, and Hikozo and the sailors got into the two boats and pushed off from shore. The sky was a dark red, and the sea sparkled with the same red.

After this the sailors met to discuss Rikimatsu. They never dreamed they would run into a fellow Japanese here, and some of the men said it was divine providence. They were curious to learn why he was living here and eager to let him know all that had hap-pened to them. Rikimatsu had said he could help them, and they wondered if that meant he would help them return to Japan. They decided to pay him a visit the following day.

Excited by this development, they stayed up talking till late at night.

The next morning they told Thomas what had happened and begged him to get permission from the commodore for them to go ashore. Thomas agreed, went to talk with the commodore, and finally came back with the permission. A boat was soon lowered for them, and Hikozo and the others went ashore at the wharf.

Hesitantly they walked along the rows of houses in town. Stalls lined both sides of the road, people jostling them as they went. There was shouting, and the bawling of babies.

Rikimatsu had said that all they needed to do was mention his name and people would point out his house right away, but since none of the sailors spoke Chinese, they couldn't ask directions. They wandered from alley to alley; they tried asking one of the stall owners where Rikimatsu lived, but with a stern look he waved his hand dismissively and turned away.

They had no idea what to do.

Hikozo saw an elderly Westerner approaching. Hong Kong was under British control, so he guessed the man was British.

He stood in front of the man and asked, in English, "Where does the Japanese Rikimatsu live?"

The old man, nodding as if he knew the answer well, replied, "Chinchin shoshu."

When Hikozo looked puzzled, the man brought his hands together as if in prayer, and Hikozo realized he meant a shrine or temple.

The old man added, "Number three house."

Hikozo understood this to mean that Rikimatsu lived in the third house from a temple or shrine. He thanked the man, and he and the sailors set off in the direction in which the old man had pointed.

Along the way they asked people where the chinchin shoshu was, which turned out to be a shrine, and sure enough the third house from there was Rikimatsu's.

They opened the door and announced their presence, and a foreign woman appeared. In broken English Hikozo explained the reason for their visit, and the woman understood and made a gesture of welcome and bade them come in.

Rikimatsu was out, but when he returned, he was happy to see Hikozo and the sailors and introduced the woman. She was

American and turned out to be his wife. She had brown hair and downy, peach-colored skin. The bridge of her nose was high, and her eyes were blue. Hikozo and the sailors were so taken aback that Rikimatsu would be married to a foreign woman that they just stared at the two for a time.

Rikimatsu spoke to the woman in English, and she went back in the interior of the house, her ample hips swaying as she walked. She returned with a tray with sake and cups, which she laid on the dining table, and then brought out all sorts of snacks. The sailors, urged on by Rikimatsu and the woman, began drinking and eating.

Chosuke turned to Rikimatsu and asked, "When you first spoke to us in Japanese, we were so surprised we nearly jumped out of our skins. We never thought we'd meet another Japanese . . . How is it that you came to live here?"

The sailors all turned to Rikimatsu, who said, a dubious look in his eye, "I'll tell you the whole story, but first I'd like to hear how you ended up on an American warship."

Chosuke nodded and related all that had happened to them, from how they became castaways to how they arrived in Hong Kong.

Rikimatsu seemed distressed as he listened to this tale. All the while his wife sat on a chair in a corner of the room.

"You've gone through much," he said, nodding over and over, "and it's sad that your captain passed away, but it's wonderful that all sixteen of you pulled through. The gods were surely with you."

After a silence, he continued, "Now I'll tell you the story of how I came to live here. It all began seventeen years ago . . ."

Hikozo noticed the tears in his eyes. Rikimatsu looked down as he spoke.

In the sixth year of Tempo (1835), Rikimatsu was sixteen and on the crew of an eighty-koku ship captained by a man named Shozo, who was twenty-nine; among the crew were Jusaburo, twenty-six, and Kumataro, twenty-nine. They were sailing off the coast of Amakusa when they ran into a storm, and their ship was damaged and they were blown to the southwest. They drifted for thirty-five days, barely able to survive by eating their cargo of Satsuma potatoes, until they drifted into an island of Herupen (the Philippines) and came ashore.

They thought the island was uninhabited, but then a dozen or so brown-skinned men carrying swords and bows and arrows appeared from the forest and surrounded them. The men threatened them with their weapons, stripped off their clothes, and stole all their tools from the boat. The Japanese were sure they would be killed, but instead the men escorted Rikimatsu and the other sailors to their homes, where they fed them.

"It was a terribly hot place," Rikimatsu went on, "and both the men and women wore only loincloths. They ate mainly potatoes, fish, and the birds they caught. We were petrified that they were cannibals, but they turned out to be surprisingly kind."

They'd been there for some thirty days when officials bearing bows and arrows and guns appeared and took them away. They traveled over heavily wooded, treacherous mountain paths, passed through a deep valley, camping along the way. Leeches were everywhere, dropping off trees to suck their blood.

They took a small boat across a sea, finally arriving at a town called Manila. This area was under the control of a country called Spain, and Manila was the headquarters. Rikimatsu and the other men were next taken by Spanish officials on a ship to Macao, in China. After landing, the officials took them to the front of a house and essentially abandoned them there.

Rikimatsu gazed around at Hikozo and the others, his eyes glistening, and continued his story.

"We were surprised to find three other Japanese living in that house. The officials had left us there because they knew that other Japanese were living there."

The sailors watched Rikimatsu with bated breath. Hikozo could imagine how amazed Rikimatsu and his crew had been to see those other Japanese. The sailors were surprised at this turn of events in Rikimatsu's tale, but no one spoke. Some were so unnerved they couldn't sit still.

Forcing the words out, Seitaro finally asked, "But who were those other Japanese? And why were they in Macao?"

A sadness struck Rikimatsu again, and he looked down. Finally he raised his head and said, "Like me and all of you, they were cast-·aways, blown to unknown parts by the wind." He bit his lip.

Hikozo felt a chill run down his spine as he recalled how they had battled storms, cut their topknots, entreated the gods to save them, toppled the mast. So many times they'd cheated death, to find themselves in this foreign land, like Rikimatsu and the three Japanese he met.

"Those three had been on the *Hojun Maru* out of Owari Province. Their ordeal was far worse than ours, and it made me cry to listen to them tell the tale." Rikimatsu went on to relate what he'd heard from them.

The *Hojun Maru* belonged to a man called Higuchi Genroku from the town of Onoura in Chita County (present-day Onoura, Hama-machi, Chita County, in Aichi Prefecture). On November 11 in the third year of Tempo (1832), the ship, under the command of Genroku's son, Juuemon, set off from Hattori Toba with a load of rice, bound for Edo. It was a 1,500-koku vessel and carried a crew of fourteen.

They were sailing in the Enshu Bay, around the south edge of the Izu peninsula, heading toward Shimoda, when the weather took a turn for the worse, and they were hit by a severe storm. Their rudder broke away, water poured inside the ship, and they had to cut down their mast in order to keep from capsizing. With no way to control their course, they were blown farther and farther to the east.

For fourteen months they drifted, barely surviving on the rice gruel they made, slaking their thirst with sips of rainwater, until they came ashore near Cape Flattery in America. Their captain, Juuemon, and ten others had starved to death, leaving only three survivors, Iwakichi, Hisakichi, and Otokichi.

They were captured by Indians and mistreated as slaves. In that region was the Hudson's Bay Company, a fur-trading monopoly under the auspices of the British government. A man named McNeil, captain of one of the company's ships, the *Llama,* rescued them, and they were put under the protection of the company's trading-post head, a man named McLoughlin.

Figuring that he could use these three castaways to help England open up trade with Japan, McLoughlin took them with him on a ship called the *Eagle* back to London.

"They told me they were taken around the city of London," Rikimatsu said. "Everything they heard and saw there was so different they were overwhelmed."

The British government turned out to be interested in trade more with China than with Japan, so the three Japanese sailors were put on a Hudson's Bay Company ship that sailed around the Cape of Good Hope and ended up in Macao. At the British trade mission they were taken care of by a German missionary named Gützlaff, who worked as an interpreter.

Gützlaff was skilled in foreign languages and, hoping someday to evangelize in Japan, had the three men live with him so he could learn Japanese.

Of the three Japanese, Iwakichi knew only the katakana syllabary, but Hisakichi and Otokichi both knew Chinese characters; Otokichi, the youngest, was particularly able to read the characters well. With his assistance, Gützlaff was eventually able to translate all three Epistles of Saint John from the New Testament into Japanese.

Rikimatsu and his three companions were also taken to Gützlaff and lived together with the three survivors of the *Hojun Maru.*

The powerful American trading company Oliphant had an office in Canton, and its head, a man named King, conceived of the idea of sending these seven castaways back to Japan, and Gützlaff agreed. The two men eagerly made all the necessary preparations, deciding to put the seven Japanese on an Oliphant company ship, the *Morrison,* to take them to Japan.

Rikimatsu and the others were overjoyed and boarded the speedy 564-ton sailing ship, which left Macao Harbor on July 4, 1837 (Tempo 8). The ship's captain was named Ingersoll, and on board were Mr. and Mrs. King, a man named Williams, who was a natural scientist and missionary, a doctor named Parker, and a crew of thirty-eight hands.

On July 12 they made port at Naha, in the Ryukyu Islands, and Gützlaff, who had been on a ship called the *Raleigh*, finally arrived and transferred to the *Morrison*. Since the goal of the voyage was to return the seven castaways, in order not to provoke the Japanese nation they had removed all cannons and Bibles from the ship.

King carried with him four letters written in Chinese to be handed over to the Japanese authorities. The first letter explained how they felt sorry for the castaways and were thus returning them to Japan. The second letter was a simple summary of conditions in America and expressed the hope that Japan would open friendly relations with America. The third letter was a list of presents from the *Morrison*, including a bust of President Washington, a spyglass, and books. The fourth letter stated the wish for trade with Japan and listed the goods that might be included in such trade.

On the morning of July 29, Iwakichi, who'd been acting as lookout, pointed and yelled. He'd spied Mimae Cape, which separated the Enshu Sea and Suruga Bay.

"I can't tell you how happy we were at that moment. We clasped each other's hands, hugged each other for joy." Rikimatsu's eyes filled with tears as he recalled the moment.

They'd traveled back and forth between Edo many times and shouted with joy whenever they recognized part of the landscape as they sailed by. In the evening they passed Irozaki Cape on the south tip of the Izu Peninsula.

On July 30 (June 28 of the eighth year of Tempo), the *Morrison* entered Tokyo Bay and headed for Uraga. Just then a cannon roared, and a pillar of water leaped up from the surface of the sea. The cannon attack continued, so the *Morrison* did not proceed farther toward Uraga but anchored off Nohi Village.

A large number of fishing boats surrounded them at a distance, until finally one small boat pulled alongside them and an old fisherman climbed aboard. Once the other boats saw there was no danger, they drew near their ship.

Many fishermen came on board the *Morrison*. Without any compunction they strode all over the ship, inspecting the masts, touching the boats aboard. King gave them coins, biscuits, and wine, while Dr. Parker examined them and handed out medicine as needed.

King handed a short letter to the man who was the best dressed, a letter that in both Chinese and Japanese said that the Americans would await a visit by the local officials. King and Gützlaff planned to meet with the officials, have them see the seven Japanese castaways, and discuss with them how the castaways should be returned to Japan. The fishermen were in fine spirits by this time and eventually returned to their boats and left.

King and the others scanned the shore with spyglasses, awaiting the arrival of the officials, but there was no sign of them.

A heavy rain began to fall the next morning, right before dawn, and just as it let up, cannonballs rained down on them from the hills on shore. The *Morrison* put up a white flag to indicate it had no hostile intentions, but the attack never let up, with one ball even landing on the deck and bouncing off into the sea.

The *Morrison* had no choice but to pull up its anchor, raise its sails, and retreat. Several ships approached from the rear and began firing on them, and the *Morrison* escaped into Edo Bay. The Uraga commissioner, following the directive issued by the shogunate in the eighth year of Bunsei that all foreign ships, regardless of circumstances, be fired upon and driven away, had attacked the *Morrison* without seeking to know its country of origin or motives for coming to Japan.

With their homeland right before them and confident that they would be repatriated, the seven castaways were sorely disappointed and crouched in sullen silence on the deck.

The *Morrison* headed next for Kagoshima. They chose Kagoshima because King knew about the illicit foreign trade being carried on by the Satsuma Domain and was sure that they wouldn't fire on a foreign ship. The ship sailed west, and early on the morning of August 10 (July 10 by the Japanese calendar), it arrived in Kagoshima Harbor and anchored off Sata Bay.

They lowered a boat from the ship, and Shozo and Jusaburo were transferred to a nearby fishing boat and taken ashore. The people in Sata Bay were astounded to see these two men in Western clothes, but once they heard the story of what had happened to them, they were most sympathetic, and a few of the women even sobbed as they listened.

Finally some officials arrived, and Shozo explained the reason they'd come here, entreating the officials to do whatever they could to help them return home. Before long one very elegant older official arrived, along with his attendants, and Shozo and Jusaburo escorted them all to the *Morrison*. King gave them a letter to the head of the domain, and the officials promised that the domain head would receive it.

The officials told them that the bay was treacherous, with many reefs, so they should wait until a pilot was sent to guide them in. Iwakichi and Shozo then took the officials back and went ashore.

After a while Iwakichi and Shozo returned to the *Morrison* with three officials and a pilot. The officials gave instructions to the pilot and returned to shore. Very timidly, the pilot directed them to the opposite shore, to a place called Okachiyogamizu, and as soon as they'd anchored, he hurriedly left.

Iwakichi and Shozo were overjoyed. When they were ashore, they'd given the officials the names, ages, and birthplaces of all seven castaways and explained the circumstances behind their being shipwrecked. The officials made careful note of all this and praised King and the crew of the *Morrison* for their charity in helping these hapless men. And they expressed their sympathy, saying that the men would definitely soon be able to return home.

When the others heard this, they beamed and were so happy they shouted for joy.

It rained the morning of August 12 (July 22 by the Japanese calendar), the third day after they entered Kagoshima Bay. Sometime during the night the shoreline of Okachiyogamizu became one long military encampment, with banners flying and mounted troops galloping down the streets.

King wasn't sure what this meant, but the castaways sadly informed him, "They prepare for war."

Finally grasping the situation, King gave the order to retreat, and the *Morrison* pulled up anchor and raised sails. Suddenly cannon roared, and puffs of white smoke rose from the encampment. The attack continued but couldn't reach the *Morrison;* the cannonballs made columns of water in the sea.

King and Gützlaff gave up trying to hand the castaways over to the Kagoshima Domain and decided to go to Nagasaki to negotiate their return. Rikimatsu and the others, however, said it would be better to return to Macao, since they could only expect the same reception in Nagasaki. They knew now that under the seclusion policy of the shogunate they were considered criminals and would be kept by force from returning.

King and Gützlaff agreed with them, and the *Morrison* headed back to Macao. The ship sailed past the Taiwan Straits and off the coast of Amoy, and on the evening of August 29 entered the port of Macao. It was raining when they pulled in.

Finishing his story, Rikimatsu wiped away the tears that ran down his cheeks, hung his head, and said no more. Hikozo and the other sailors stared at him wordlessly. Their hearts ached at the pain Rikimatsu must have felt having to flee his homeland when it was right before his eyes.

"And for the last fifteen years you've been here in China?" Jisaku asked, tears in his eyes.

Rikimatsu nodded silently.

"What happened to the others?" Chosaku asked.

Rikimatsu raised his head and said, in a low voice, "Soon after we arrived back in Macao on the *Morrison,* Kumataro fell sick and died. As did Jusaburo."

"He was sick, too?" Chosuke asked.

"He was addicted to smoking opium and grew thin and weak and passed away. Opium is a terrible drug that eats away your flesh and bones." Rikimatsu took a deep breath.

"So only five of you are well..."

"No, Iwakichi of the *Hojun Maru* passed away a short while ago. He was living in Ningpo, married to a Chinese woman, but she was unfaithful to him, and Iwakichi was killed by the woman's lover." Again Rikimatsu took a deep breath.

Hikozo found this depressing. In just fifteen years, three of the seven men had died. Jusaburo's death from opium could only be attributed to the despair he must have felt at being driven away from Japan. Opium must have been his way of drowning his sorrows. Iwakichi, too, had met a pitiful end.

"And the other four?" Chosuke asked.

"Shozo, the captain of the ship I was on, lives close to me. Hisakichi of the *Hojun Maru* lives in Shanghai, both of them with Chinese wives and children. Shozo runs a large sewing company, while Hisakichi, because he's very good with Chinese characters, works in a government office. And I work for a British trading company."

Rikimatsu finally had regained his composure.

"How about the fellow named Otokichi?"

"He lives in Shanghai and is the manager of a British trading office. He reads Chinese characters well, is quite fluent in English, and is married to an Indian woman. He lives a comfortable life."

Hikozo felt admiration for the four survivors and how they'd managed to prevail even in a foreign land.

A deep silence fell over them.

Hikozo had no idea what his fellow sailors were thinking after hearing Rikimatsu's tale. Three of the survivors of Rikimatsu's group had died, and the other four would eventually pass away as well. There was an expression about being *buried in a far-off land*, and that was exactly the fate of these men.

The tale hit close for Hikozo and his fellows, for the same path might well be theirs. These other sailors may even have been more fortunate: at least they'd caught a glimpse, however fleeting, of their homeland. Hikozo was seized by a wave of sorrow.

Kiyotaro broke the silence by asking, "After that, you never tried to return home again?" His tone revealed some impatience.

"You have to understand, they shot at us with cannons," Rikimatsu said dispassionately. "We realized that our country would never accept us. We badly wanted to see our parents and brothers and sisters again, though, so at the very least we thought we'd let them know we were alive and well in a foreign land. Shozo and Jusaburo wrote letters to their relatives."

"Letters?" Kiyotaro said and leaned forward, while Hikozo and the rest of the men looked intently at Rikimatsu.

"This was in June of the thirteenth year of Tempo (1841), five years after we returned to Macao on the *Morrison*." Rikimatsu's eyes searched out the past.

At this time the head of the Dutch trade post at Dejima in Nagasaki, Edouard Grandisson, had completed his term of office, and the newly assigned head of the post, Pieter Albert Bik, stopped in Macao on his way to Nagasaki.

Learning this, Shozo and Jusaburo went to meet Bik, explained their situation, and begged him to carry letters to the officials of the Nagasaki commissioner, which would then be handed over to relatives in their hometowns. Bik felt sorry for them and agreed, and the two men each wrote letters and entrusted them to him.

Finally Bik left Macao on a Dutch ship bound for Nagasaki.

"Why didn't you write a letter?" Kiyotaro asked dubiously.

"Even if that Dutchman gave the letters to officials in Nagasaki, the officials would just tear them up or throw them in the fire," Rikimatsu said, a cynical look in his eyes. "We were criminals, after all. Those letters would never reach their hometowns."

But that is not what happened.

Some intellectuals in Japan at the time began to criticize the government's actions in following the edict to drive away foreign ships and for firing on the *Morrison*. Many were worried that taking such drastic measures would only incur the wrath of foreign countries and drive Japan into a corner, and two scholars of foreign learning, Watanabe Kazan and Takano Choei, wrote a letter criticizing this policy. In response, Inspector Torii Yozo, who was quite antagonistic to these scholars, had Kazan put under permanent house arrest (he later committed suicide) and Choei imprisoned for life. This was the infamous 1839 incident when scholars of Western learning were suppressed.

Afterward the shogunate, concluding that Kazan and Choei's criticism was just, abolished the edict against foreign ships. On July 23, a month after Shozo and Jusaburo entrusted their letters to Bik, the government issued a new edict directing people to treat foreign ships peacefully and to give them water and provisions.

Under these changed circumstances the letters from Shozo and Jusaburo given to the Nagasaki commissioner's office were formally received by Commissioner Yagiyui Senokami and reported to the shogunate.

Jusaburo's letter began: *From: Jusaburo, of Temizusarashi, Sakashita* (Nankan), *Tamana County, Higo Province* (present-day Kumamoto). *To: The officials and attendants of the Nagasaki commissioner.*

Jusaburo knew hardly any Chinese characters at all, so most of his letter was in the katakana syllabary: *With deepest respect I take up my pen,* he began, and went on in faltering prose to describe how they were shipwrecked, floated to the Philippines, and then taken to Macao, in China. He went on to relate how they took the *Morrison* to return to Japan but were fired upon in Uraga and Kagoshima: *The sadness and wretchedness we felt then is unimaginable.* The letter went on to say, *I want more than anything to see my father and mother, and brothers and sisters, again,* but since he was shot at and treated as a criminal, he feared this would cause problems for them. *I no longer wish to return... I've given up this hope,* he wrote, showing he was resigned to his fate.

About his present situation, he wrote, *I lack for nothing,* wanting to reassure his parents and siblings. *This is all I have to say now,* he concluded. *Please do not write telling me to come home.* The letter was addressed to his father, Rinsuke, and older brother, Keisuke.

Being the captain, Shozo knew both hiragana and Chinese characters, and in the opening of his letter used rather flowery characters to write a standard greeting: *It is my fervent hope that this missive finds you all well.*

Just as Jusaburo had done in his letter, Shozo described, in dispassionate prose, how they drifted to the Philippines and were then taken to Macao, in China. Concerning the arrival of the *Morrison* in Uraga, he wrote that the shelling convinced them that *all seven of us should take our own lives,* but since it was decided they would continue on to Kagoshima, they gave up the idea.

In Kagoshima they went ashore and met with officials of the Satsuma Domain, but again their ship was shelled, and with great sadness he wrote, *I couldn't eat a thing for several days, and stayed in bed.*

Concerning the second bombardment, he wrote, *With this attack I resigned myself to the fact that we were criminals and decided never again to return to Japan.* Like Jusaburo, he'd given up.

Next he wrote about other Japanese castaways who had been taken to China and how he wanted to do what he could to help them return to Japan; this, he wrote fervently, was his mission in remaining behind in China.

The letter was addressed to the owner of Shozo's ship, Chaya Kijiro in Kawashiridome in Nakashima Town in Higo Province. Shozo went on to report that he was fine, and he asked that the day they set out from Kawashiri be commemorated as the anniversary of their death. He also asked the owner to apologize for him to his parents for being an unfaithful son.

Shozo also had a wife and children, of whom he wrote, *It will be troublesome for you, but I beg of you to watch over my wife and children. I ask that you please convey these wishes to all of them in my stead.* This ended his letter.

Both of these letters were delivered by the Nagaskai commissioner to their addressees.

The writers never received replies, and both were convinced, like Rikimatsu, that their letters had been simply ripped up by officials in Nagasaki. They had given up expecting anything else.

Hikozo and the sailors detected a gloominess in Rikimatsu and noted that he had not even attempted to send a letter home. Kiyotaro, unable to bear it anymore, spoke up.

"You said you would help us. Will you help us return home to Japan?"

With all eyes on him, Rikimatsu blinked and replied in a determined tone: "If you are set to go home, I will do what I can. But you must understand, this is not an easy task. Just as Japan drove us away, Japan won't take you back."

The sailors watched him in silence.

His expression softened, and he said, "Why don't you just give up the idea of returning and stay here as we have? I can make inquiries at the government office and obtain jobs for you so you can make a living and get married." He looked around at the sailors.

Flustered, the sailors looked at each other.

"How about it?" Rikimatsu pressed them.

Kiyotaro looked straight at Rikimatsu, and managed to say, "We'll think about it..."

The sailors were uncomfortable. One of them said, "I think we should be getting back," and they all stood up, bowed, and left.

They hurried back to the wharf and took the boat that was waiting for them. No one said a word as they climbed aboard the *Susquehanna* and went to their cabin. Then they all began to speak at once.

"I can see exactly what he's aiming at, that Rikimatsu," one said, and others agreed. They joined in criticizing him.

"Giving up—well, that's his choice. He's lonely, so he wants us to settle down here and keep him company."

"He has an American wife, he doesn't want to leave her behind and go back to Japan. There's no way you could go back with a foreign wife. But we're not like him. He's turned into a Chinese." The sailors raised their voices.

Roundly criticizing Rikimatsu, they said, "We'll do whatever it takes to get back to Japan. The gods have kept us alive till now, and their goodness and mercy will surely open a path for us..."

"Let's go home!" they concluded.

CHAPTER SEVEN

LIFE ABOARD THE *Susquehanna* grew indolent.

Perry was to come from America to China, where he would board the *Susquehanna* and then head for Japan. His departure from America had been delayed, however, and the crew of the ship grew restless and bored with waiting.

On top of this, it was terribly hot and muggy, and hard to breathe belowdecks. Going out on deck was little better, for the sun was blazing hot. Many of the crew decided to take boats and spend time ashore. Hikozo and the Japanese sailors would often catch rides with them and search out some shady place under a tree to sit and cool off; they'd become suspicious of Rikimatsu, so they avoided going near his home.

One day they found a shady spot under a large tree on the grounds of a temple and were resting there when an elderly priest came out and approached them, smiling broadly. He motioned them to come inside.

Hikozo and the others stood up and followed the priest into what appeared to be his quarters, a large room with a wooden floor. He offered them pipes to smoke and made tea for them. The sailors bowed in thanks.

Naturally Hikozo and the sailors couldn't understand the priest's words, but time spent walking around Hong Kong had taught them that if they wrote things down in Chinese characters, they could communicate, so Kiyotaro and some of the others began conversing with the priest through writing. They wrote down their desire to return to Japan, and the priest, after inclining his head and thinking about it, finally grasped their meaning.

Through writing and gestures they explained that there was an American warship planning to go to Japan and they would return on that.

The priest waved his hand vigorously in denial. He wrote down his own thoughts, namely, that since Japan drove away all foreign ships, the American warship would be treated no differently. They had best abandon the hope of ever returning to Japan that way.

He urged them instead to travel overland to Canton, some hundred miles northwest of Hong Kong. If they submitted an application to return to Japan at the Canton government office, the office would grant them permission, since China carried on trade relations with Japan. The government should then send them by steamer to Nanjing. Every year a Chinese trading vessel left China for Nagasaki from a port called Zhapu, and the Nanjing government would undoubtedly instruct the Zhapu authorities to allow Hikozo and the others to sail on this trading vessel.

The sailors grew excited at the priest's words. Some of them had been to Nagasaki before and had seen several richly appointed ships, ones the Japanese dubbed China-boats, in the harbor. Since these China-boats came to Nagasaki every year, if they boarded one of these they would definitely be able to land on Nagasaki soil, without any fear of being driven away as the people had been on the *Morrison*.

They asked the priest how they should get to Canton, and he drew them a rough map.

They next asked him if he thought they could get there safely, and the priest replied that he'd issue them a kind of passport. A passport like this issued by a priest was generally honored, and as long as they carried it people along the way should give them food and lodgings.

They begged him to issue them a passport, so the priest wrote out the characters on vermilion paper and handed it to them. They thanked him profusely and left the temple.

They sat down again in the shade of the large tree and began a discussion of the merits of going to Canton. The priest made a lot of sense, and they were certain that if they were able to get a ride on a Chinese trading vessel, they would be able to get to Nagasaki. First they would have to obtain permission from the government office at Canton and Nanjing, but since China and Japan had friendly relations, this shouldn't be a problem.

The one problem was money for the trip. They all had some Japanese money, as well as the coins and valuables the Americans in San Francisco had given them, but they would need to convert this into Chinese currency.

One of the sailors said he'd go see Shozo, the former captain who lived near Rikimatsu, and ask him to exchange their money and valuables for Chinese money. Rikimatsu would no doubt oppose their going to Canton, so the last thing they wanted to do was ask him for help. But some, having only a little money and few valuables, were hesitant about traveling to Canton.

Hikozo had a decent amount of both cash and valuables but didn't like the plan. Thomas had been so kind to him since San Francisco, he couldn't just set off for Canton without saying good-bye.

They talked it over, and nine decided they would make the trip to Canton, the seven others remaining with the ship. They'd stuck together through thick and thin since they became castaways, only now to be setting off in two separate directions. If Manzo were alive, they knew, he would not have allowed this to happen.

The nine sailors who chose Canton set off for Shozo's house, and Hikozo and the six others who chose to stay went with them. They'd been told that Shozo ran a large dressmaking business, and indeed his home was spacious, with more than a dozen workers in the shop area.

Shozo was out on business, but his Chinese wife received them warmly. She was able to converse in broken Japanese, and when she heard that nine of them were heading for Canton, she said they could stay the night and set out the next morning, after exchanging their Japanese money and valuables.

The two groups of sailors said their farewells to each other. The ones staying with the *Susquehanna* might reach Japan first, but whichever group got there first, they promised, it would let the other group's relatives know that their loved ones were alive and well.

"Take care of yourselves!" Hikozo and his group said to those traveling to Canton, then left Shozo's house, went to the wharf, and took the boat back.

It was raining the next morning, and an officer, noticing that nine men were missing, asked them about it. Hikozo replied, in English, "They were invited to stay at a Japanese person's house. They should be back soon."

The rain continued until evening, and at night the moon shone through a break in the clouds.

The next day the sun beat down on the ship. Hikozo and the sailors speculated about how far the Canton group had got by now, one man insisting that they had already arrived.

Just as the day was coming to a close and they were going out on deck to catch the breeze, a small Chinese boat left shore and pulled up alongside the ship. They were astounded to find that on the boat were five of the sailors who'd set out for Canton. The men were barefoot and stripped to the waist.

They grimaced as they explained what had happened. The nine sailors had set out in the rain along the road the priest indicated. Whenever they showed their passport to villagers along the way, people kindly gave them directions. When they got hungry, they stopped at a farmhouse and paid the farmers cash to cook rice for them.

But only gone a couple hundred yards beyond the farmhouse, they found their path blocked by sixty men wielding spades and daggers. The men yelled threats and surrounded them, waving their weapons. They grabbed the sailors' clothes as if to strip them off, and pummeled their heads and backs with their fists.

Fearing for their lives, the sailors took off their Western clothes and boots. All their cash was in a sack, and this too was taken from them. They were left half naked, the thieves barely allowing them to keep their trousers.

The men threatened them again with their weapons, motioning them to go back the way they came, and the sailors beat a hasty retreat. When they could finally gather their wits about them, they saw they were missing four men.

The sun set and the rain let up, so they spent the night outdoors. The following morning they made their way through the hills, where there were no roads, and finally stumbled back into Hong Kong.

Their bare feet were bloody, and as Hikozo and the others were treating their wounds, a second Chinese boat rowed up to their ship. The remaining sailors, looking just as disheveled and pitiful as the first group, were aboard. The men were totally dejected after their experience.

The officers and crew of the ship came over to see why the Japanese sailors were in such awful shape, and Thomas, too, anxiously made his way to them.

When one of the officers asked what happened, Hikozo replied, "They were attacked by robbers and had their clothes stolen." Thomas added a few words of his own. The officers and crew seemed satisfied by this explanation and left. Hikozo and the others gave the nine sailors some of their extra clothes to wear.

This incident made them realize that finding a way home was more perilous and difficult than they'd imagined.

Once they got on the Chinese trading ship, they could make it to Nagasaki, but traveling to Canton meant being robbed of everything they had, even putting their lives at risk. Zhapu, where they could board the ship, now seemed impossibly far away, and a profound despair overcame them.

The only way to return to Japan now was to go with the Perry mission on the *Susquehanna*. They had to put up with the rough treatment they'd been getting from the crew of the ship and stoically wait for Perry to arrive.

Listless days followed one after another. The air lay hot and muggy, and it was hard to sleep at night. Unable to bathe, they developed rashes all over; if scratched, the skin would tear and fester. They jumped into the sea to wash themselves as best they could.

Two months had passed when a ship arrived from America carrying letters and goods for the *Susquehanna* and all the ships in the American Far East fleet.

Hikozo and the sailors were rounded up to unload these goods, and as they worked, they heard all kinds of news from the crew of the cargo ship.

After arriving in China, the Perry mission would head a flotilla of eleven warships. Hikozo and the sailors were dumbfounded by this. Bringing such a huge deployment of ships to Japan meant that America planned to force Japan to accept its demands. The only conceivable way Japan could respond would be with a call to arms, resulting in a full-scale war. And if they were on the *Susquehanna* and got caught in a war, they could forget about ever being repatriated.

The sailors turned pale and said they should avoid taking the *Susquehanna* back to Japan. They went to find Thomas, to see what he thought.

Thomas was just as surprised as they were to hear about the eleven warships and said their concern was understandable. He knew about Rikimatsu and the *Morrison* and how, fifteen years before, they'd been driven away by cannon fire. The *Morrison* was a merchant vessel, with all its guns removed, yet it was bombarded, so there was no doubt in his mind, Thomas said sadly, that when eleven warships showed up, the Japanese would attack them with everything they had.

The sailors were filled with despair.

Hikozo sought out a corner of the deck and sat down, clasping his knees close to him. He could see Rikimatsu's face. Three of the seven castaways who'd been driven away on the *Morrison* were dead, while Rikimatsu and the others had completely given up on seeing Japan again. It looked as if they would all share Rikimatsu's fate and spend the rest of their days in this foreign land, and even Hikozo, the youngest, would end up buried here.

He sat for a long time, head bowed. If only he could see the ocean beside his home village one more time, he thought with a groan. The sun began to set, turning the sea a dark red.

He heard footsteps, and a large man, Thomas, sat down beside him. Thomas put his hand on Hikozo's shoulder.

"Hiko," he began, using his nickname for the boy, "I have something to tell you." He spoke in English as he gazed out at the sea. "I can't stand waiting like this for Perry to arrive."

He had come all this way with them in order to help them get back to Japan. He wanted to go to Japan himself and would be on the *Susquehanna* when Perry arrived, but his patience was running out, and still there was no sign of Perry. And now this news that Perry would be taking eleven warships to Japan. If it led to war, there was no chance that the sailors, let alone himself, would set foot in Japan.

"Hiko," he said in Japanese, "I've decided to go back to America."

California, he went on, was in the midst of the gold rush, and it was a good time to make money. Since he'd given up on going to Japan, California seemed the next-best choice.

"Hiko, why don't you come with me to California? I'll pay your way."

Thomas added that in two or three years Japan was sure to open up to the outside world and allow foreign ships to freely travel. When that happened, Hikozo could go home. But until then, Thomas suggested that he study English in America and absorb Western culture so that when he did return, he could be of use to his country.

"Staying here won't get you anywhere. Come with me to America." Thomas's grip grew stronger, and he pulled Hikozo closer.

Hikozo was stunned by these words. Thomas was a good man, but Hikozo had no intention of leaving his fellow sailors. He'd lived with the fifteen of them so closely, and they'd kept him from being lonely in foreign lands. Leaving them now might be the death of him.

"Come, Hikozo, come with me to America." Thomas looked deep into Hikozo's eyes and nudged him.

Hikozo looked at the bearded Thomas and said in English, "I'm not going." He shook his head.

They'd come all this way to China, and he couldn't bring himself to go back to America. Just the thought of leaving his fellow sailors and living among Americans made him shudder.

"Why not?" Thomas insisted.

"I can't leave the others," Hikozo said, slowly and emphatically, in Japanese.

Apparently expecting this response, Thomas said, "If we take one of the other sailors with us, would you go then?"

Hikozo said *yes,* in English. He knew that none of the sailors would agree to go to America, and he didn't want to hurt Thomas's feelings, so he said yes.

Thomas nodded several times, took his arm away from Hikozo's shoulder, and stood up. Hikozo watched as he slowly walked down the corridor leading to the cabins.

The idea of going to America made Hikozo feel all over again how they'd lost all hope of seeing Japan, and his sadness was so great he felt as if he were sinking to the bowels of the earth.

The next day, as Hikozo stood on deck gazing out at the streets of Hong Kong, Thomas came up to him, put his arm around his shoulder, and said, "Hiko. Kame said he'll come to America." Kame was Thomas's nickname for Kamezo, and this meant that Thomas had persuaded the twenty-four-year-old Kamezo to join them.

Hikozo looked at Thomas in surprise. He'd promised Thomas, so if Kame was really willing to go to America, he'd have to keep his promise and go with him. But he was afraid of leaving the others and going all the way back to America.

Thomas left, but in the evening he came to Hikozo with more unexpected news.

"Tora says he'll go, too." Hikozo was astonished.

Tora was the nickname of Jisaku, who was from Hikozo's village. When he'd heard from his good friend Kamezo that he was going to America, Jisaku sought out Thomas and asked to be taken with him.

Jisaku, aged twenty-nine, was a smart, experienced sailor, and Hikozo, hearing that Jisaku had himself broached the idea to Thomas of going to America, began to rethink his position. Maybe he should go after all.

When Hikozo agreed to go, Thomas's expression relaxed and he said, "I'll get permission from the commodore," and hurried away.

Later that day, after they heard from Thomas that Commodore Aulick had given his permission, Hikozo, Kamezo, and Jisaku reluctantly told their fellow sailors the news.

The other men were shocked. Opinions were mixed, some of the men vigorously shaking their heads, maintaining that it wasn't good for three of them to go out on their own, others countering that it was impossible for the sailors to return home on the *Susquehanna* and that they should go to America and look for other ways of returning to Japan. Their words grew more heated, but eventually opinion started to lean toward the notion that going to America was the only hope they had for ever seeing Japan again.

Hikozo was surprised by the outcome of the debate, and he, Kamezo, and Jisaku went to see Thomas. In a mixture of English and Japanese Hikozo explained the situation to him. Thomas's expression grew clouded; he put his hand on his chin as if deep in thought and left the cabin without a word.

After a while he returned and took Hikozo and the two others to see the rest of the sailors. With Hikozo interpreting for him, Thomas said to all, "Those who wish to go to America, step forward now."

Every man stepped forward.

Thomas spoke again, in Japanese-laced English. Commodore Aulick had given permission for Hikozo and the two others to go but would not allow all of them to leave, for Perry planned to use the handing over of the castaways as a bargaining chip in the nego-tiations with Japan.

"The best I can do is to take three people with me. I don't have the money to take more." Thomas held his hands up.

The sailors turned pale. Thomas said he would pay the fare for the trip, and the fares for Hikozo, Kamezo, and Jisaku added up to a considerable sum. Thomas told them there was no way he could pay for thirteen more people. Realizing it was hopeless, the sailors resigned themselves to remaining behind. They were silent for some time, but once one of them spoke, the rest all expressed their displeasure. If Manzo were alive, they said, he would have encour-aged them to stick together until they could return to Japan and never would have allowed three of them to go off alone to America.

Gradually, though, they had less and less to say. Commodore Aulick had given permission for the three to leave, so their words would change nothing.

"When do you leave?" Seitaro asked Thomas in English.

"Today, right away, we're going to Macao," Thomas said.

There were many foreign trading ships going in and out of Macao, so that's where they would look for a ship bound for San Francisco, he explained. They needed to hurry to Macao.

Thomas turned to Hikozo and the two others who were going and said, "Hiko, Kame, Tora. Pack your things."

Thomas walked away, and Hikozo and the two others went into their cabin, gathered their belongings, and came back out deck.

Soon Thomas returned carrying a large suitcase; he waved to the wharf, and, as if waiting for that signal, a small Chinese boat pulled away from shore and came to the *Susquehanna*.

The other sailors surrounded the three. They didn't say any-thing, but tears glistened in their eyes, and Hikozo felt a warmth rise in his chest. They'd always stuck together, even after Manzo's death, and it wasn't easy for three of them to leave this circle of comrades and just go off. Miserable, Hikozo couldn't look the oth-ers in the eye.

Chosuke spoke up, the words catching in his throat, "You fellows take good care of yourselves." Some of the sailors sobbed, and Hikozo wiped back the tears.

Wordlessly Hikozo's fellow cook, Sentaro, hugged him and sobbed. Hikozo hugged him close.

"Hiko, Kame, Tora. Let's go!" Thomas called out to them.

The small boat had pulled alongside their ship, and the Chinese man at the oars was looking up expectantly. On deck, the officers and crew watched from a distance.

Urged on by Thomas, Hikozo grabbed hold of the rope ladder, with Kamezo and Jisaku following after. Thomas was the last to climb down to the boat.

The Chinese began rowing, and the boat pulled away. Squatting down inside, Hikozo and the others gazed at the *Susquehanna*. The sailors on board lined the deck watching them depart.

"Take care!" a voice called out that sounded like Seitaro's.

Tears welled again in Hikozo's eyes. He had no idea what would happen when they reached America or what fate would befall the thirteen who remained behind. They might never see each other again, and the idea frightened him.

The sailors grew distant, and finally the ship disappeared behind an island.

The little boat made its way west between the islands. The sea was calm. Around sunset they drew near Macao.

Their boat entered the harbor, and Hikozo and the others scrambled up onto the wharf. The three Japanese followed Thomas, arriving soon at a hotel. They were expecting cheap accommodations, but the hotel was nicely appointed. The manager, a Portuguese man named Frank, came out from a back room. Thomas knew Frank, and they greeted each other warmly. When Thomas told Frank about what Hikozo and the others had gone through, Frank looked sympathetic, and approached them and one by one shook their hands and welcomed them.

Hikozo and his shipmates were shown to quite pleasant rooms, then escorted to the dining room. Frank opened bottles of wine, and Hikozo and his companions indulged. The food was well prepared, and Hikozo, used to the rough fare on board ship, felt suddenly well off.

After dinner Thomas went to the harbor to see if any ships were heading to San Francisco, but couldn't find any. He did this day after day, returning exhausted each evening.

He explained to them why he wanted to go to San Francisco. In the western part of America, he said, someone discovered pieces of gold literally sticking up out of the ground, and rumor had it there was gold to be found everywhere you went. One large gold field lay just east of San Francisco, and people had flocked from all over to join the search. Thanks to this, San Francisco was a boomtown, and since the real gold rush was apparently only just beginning, Thomas didn't want to miss out.

Hikozo remembered how the Chinese cook aboard the *Auckland,* the ship that rescued them, had written the words *Gold Mountain* when asked where they were headed. At the time he hadn't understood what it meant.

"The economy's great," Thomas said with a smile, "so you should have no trouble finding work."

Once again Hikozo could feel how kind Thomas was. He'd paid for all three of their fares—no small amount—and this certainly would not profit him in any way. All Thomas cared about was finding a way for them to return to Japan, and he felt sure coming to America improved their chances of doing so. Hikozo was grateful to him.

The three Japanese had nothing to do in the hotel, so they started tagging along with Thomas in his search for a ship to take them to San Francisco. The harbor was full of foreign sailing vessels, and even a few paddle steamers. Every time he ran across a sailor, Thomas would question him about his ship, but none were bound for San Francisco.

A week after they arrived in Macao, Thomas spotted an

announcement posted on the wall of the branch office of a British shipping company. "This is it!" he said excitedly. The bulletin announced that in two days the *Sarah Hooper* would be leaving for San Francisco.

Thomas went right into the small office and soon came out with a tall, young British man.

"We're going to go look at the ship," he said, and Hikozo, Kamezo, and Jisaku followed him to the harbor.

They took a small boat at the wharf, and the British man rowed them out.

The ship was a four hundred-ton three-master. The shipping agent showed them the cabins. The ship was fairly decrepit, the paint peeling off its old wooden sides, and the only cabins available were third-class.

Back at the wharf Thomas said good-bye to the shipping agent and looked for a long while at the ship. Spending a month and half on such an old crate wouldn't be pleasant. Should they look for another ship? But that would take time and extend their stay in Macao, and run up hotel expenses even more. Thomas stood weighing their options.

Finally he strode into the office and purchased tickets for them all, at fifty dollars a head.

"We'll take that old ship," he said reluctantly, but there was amusement in his eyes.

They returned to their hotel and packed their belongings once again.

Two days later, the dawn was sunny and clear. They left the hotel, Hikozo and his mates shouldering their belongings, Thomas with suitcase in hand. Frank accompanied them to the wharf.

They went to the shipping agency office, where the other passengers were assembled. Agency officials led them to the wharf, and they climbed into boats. Frank waved good-bye, and Thomas waved back.

On the *Sarah Hooper*, Hikozo leaned back and looked out at the town of Macao. The faces of each one of the thirteen sailors they'd left in Hong Kong floated before his eyes. He recalled the feeling of Sentaro's arms as he hugged him good-bye. Would these men return to Japan or end up spending the rest of their days in China?

A gong sounded, the anchor clanged upward, and the sails were raised. As the ship began to move, Hikozo sat unmoving, staring at the receding shore.

The sails of the vessel billowed out, and the *Sarah Hooper* left the harbor for the open sea.

CHAPTER EIGHT

T HIRTEEN JAPANESE SAILORS remained on the *Susquehanna*. The ship sailed to Amoy and Macao before returning to Hong Kong and in November voyaged all the way to the Philippines, making port at Manila. In Japan this was already the cold season, but Manila was steamy, with quite a few thunderstorms. The region was controlled by Spain, and Manila was a lively, thriving town.

They anchored there for thirty days, then at the end of December the *Susquehanna* returned to Hong Kong.

Chosuke and the other sailors walked all over Hong Kong. Red strips of paper with the words OUT WITH THE OLD YEAR were sold in shops, and men and women bought these and pasted them on shrines everywhere. On New Year's Day the Japanese went ashore and greeted the new year, the sixth year of Kiei (1853).

In the middle of February the *Susquehanna* again left Hong Kong, this time sailing north along the coast. Seven days later they reached the seven-and-a-half-mile mouth of the Yangtze River and continued upriver to Shanghai.

The next morning numerous small boats pulled up alongside the ship, with merchants shouting out their wares. Before long some of them came aboard and spread fabrics on deck for the crew to look at and touch. The merchants managed to make a few sales to the crew.

One old man, apparently in charge of all the merchants, walked over to the group of Japanese sailors and in English said, "Are you Japanese?"

When Chosuke replied that they were, the man said, "There's a Japanese who lives here. His name is Otokichi."

Chosuke had heard from Rikimatsu in Hong Kong that two castaways—Otokichi and Hisakichi—lived in Shanghai.

Chosuke and the others wanted to meet Otokichi and in broken English asked the old merchant for the address. The man took up a brush and paper and drew a simple map for them. The sailors received permission from the officers to go ashore and catch a ride with some of the crew who were going to town.

The town was divided into sections, and at the entrance to each section were a gate and guards. When Chosuke showed one of the guards the map and gestured that they were looking for Otokichi's house, the guard nodded and set out before them. Finally he stopped and pointed to a building beside the road and turned back.

The sailors were dumbfounded and looked at each other. The building was huge, three stories, in a spacious yard surrounded by a wall. The windows had glass panes—quite unusual—and behind the building were several storehouses. Could the guard have pointed to the wrong house?

They hesitated for a time, then timidly passed through the gate, opened the front door, and called out.

A well-dressed, elderly Chinese man came to the door, and Seitaro wrote down on a piece of paper that they were Japanese and wanted to meet Otokichi. The old man nodded and went back into the house; soon he emerged with a squat, middle-aged man with clipped hair and wearing a Western suit.

He looked at Seitaro and the others and said, in Japanese, "I'm Otokichi."

The sailors were relieved, but when Chosuke began to introduce their group, Otokichi interrupted, saying, "Please come in. We'll talk inside." The sailors followed him inside.

They were brought into a large room whose beauty amazed

them. There was solid, shiny furniture, and birdcages that were obviously made of gold. Beside this room was a large greenhouse with a riot of unfamiliar flowers.

Otokichi invited them to sit down, and they did, in colorfully embroidered chairs.

"I'd heard that a dozen Japanese were in Shanghai. So that was you?" he asked.

Chosuke replied, "Yes, we were in Hong Kong."

A woman with large eyes and tanned skin came in, followed by several Chinese women—servants, by the look of them—who brought in tea and placed it on the table.

"This is my wife," Otokichi said, introducing the doe-eyed lady. She wore a flowery suit and had deeply etched features.

"She was born in India," Otokichi said, and the woman smiled and bowed. "Tell me how you came to be in China," he went on, looking around at the sailors.

Urged on by Chosuke, Seitaro related the whole story, how they were adrift and rescued by an American ship, then taken from San Francisco to China. And how their captain Manzo had passed away, and how Hikozo and two others went with Thomas back to America, leaving the thirteen of them behind.

Otokichi nodded as he listened, and when Seitaro was finished, he said, the sympathy showing in his eyes, "You've been through a lot. Yet you've managed to survive."

He fell silent for a time, then said, "For me it began twenty-one years ago..." He told how he and the others on the *Hojun Maru* were shipwrecked and made castaways, and all that happened to them afterward.

"Of the three of us who survived," he said pensively, "Iwakichi was murdered, so it's now just Hisakichi and I here in Shanghai."

Seitaro, looking around the room, spoke up and said, "You seem to be doing quite well for yourself. If you don't mind my asking, how do you make a living?" His question was on all the sailors' minds.

Otokichi settled back in his armchair. There was amusement in his eyes as he explained. His house was owned by a British company that traded with China, and he was the general manager of their branch office. He was in charge of about thirty men and purchased all sorts of goods in China and shipped them to Britain. He had seven servants.

Seitaro and the others were astounded and again stared at the furnishings. A man like this, who'd risen from castaway to prosperous businessman, was someone they felt they could trust; that the British trading company had put him in charge of a branch office only added to his reliability.

Seitaro spoke in a low voice to Chosuke, then turned to Otokichi and said, "When we told the man we met in Hong Kong, Rikimatsu, that we wanted to return to Japan, he said it wasn't possible and told us to stay in China, find wives, and settle down. But we want to go back to Japan. Can you help us?" There was pleading in his voice, and the other sailors waited intently for the man's response.

Otokichi held an important job and was living well, married and fully settled in China. He didn't seem to want to return to Japan and was satisfied with his present life. Thus the sailors expected his reply to be no different from that of Rikimatsu.

Otokichi said, "When I was on the *Morrison* and they fired at us and drove us away, I gave up the idea of ever returning to my country. That was my fate, and I accepted it. Afterward, though, I was struck by a thought—that it was now my task to help other Japanese who'd suffered like me as castaways to find a way to return to Japan . . ." He took on a decisive look.

The sailors didn't move a muscle, all eyes trained on him.

Otokichi regarded them and said in a firm voice, "I will do whatever I can to help you."

Joy filled the sailors' faces, and some even had to fight back tears.

"But how can we get home?" Seitaro asked.

"As you know, there's a Chinese trading ship that goes to Nagasaki once a year. It transports all kinds of Chinese products to

Japan, then returns loaded with Japanese products. If you can obtain passage on that ship, you'd be able to get back to Japan."

"But where is the ship?"

"There's a port south of here called Zhapu. You need to negotiate with the officials at Zhapu for permission to take that ship, which means that you must leave the *Susquehanna*. So the first thing to do is ask the captain for permission to leave."

The sailors looked at each other and nodded.

"Well, then, we'd better get back to the ship right away and talk to the captain," Seitaro said in a spirited voice, and stood up.

The other sailors politely nodded to Otokichi and hurried outside.

They talked as they walked to the ship. The commodore of the Far East fleet, who'd been on the *Susquehanna* since they themselves first came aboard, had recently returned to America because of illness, so they would have to ask the new captain, Commander Buchanan. They'd often talked with Aulick, but Buchanan was someone they'd seen only from a distance.

"Seitaro," Chosuke said, "you go speak to him." Seitaro was the one among them who could communicate best in English.

When they returned to the ship, Seitaro told one of the officers that he'd like to see the captain, and he went together with Chosuke to the captain's quarters.

"We wish to leave this ship," Seitaro told Buchanan, who was seated.

"Why?" Buchanan asked with a frown.

"We want to stay and work here," Seitaro replied, the lie springing to his lips.

Buchanan shot them a stern look and spoke quickly in English. Seitaro didn't catch much of what he said but understood the gist of it, which was that the Americans were not about to change the plan to escort the sailors to Japan on this ship.

After this Seitaro knew it would do no good to plead his case further, so he bowed to the captain, and he and Chosuke left.

The other sailors were discouraged by the news and began to discuss ways to overcome this obstacle. They felt indebted to America—it had been an American ship that rescued them, after all—and weren't about to run away from the ship without the captain's permission.

"Let's find out what Otokichi thinks," one of the sailors said, and the others agreed.

They decided to send Seitaro to visit Otokichi and crowded the deck watching him go ashore at the wharf and disappear among the rows of houses.

After a while Seitaro and Otokichi appeared on the wharf and rowed back out to the ship in a small Chinese boat.

Otokichi went up to one of the officers and in fluent English requested a meeting with the captain; the officer nodded and led him and Seitaro down a corridor to the captain's quarters. The other sailors gathered close together to await Seitaro's return.

A long time later, Otokichi and Seitaro appeared in the corridor.

"The captain has agreed to let four of you leave the ship," Otokichi said. "I'll say good-bye for now but will negotiate again for the other nine." He added that he would take the four sailors with him now.

They selected who the four would be. These men went into their cabin, gathered their belongings, came back on deck, and got into the boat with Otokichi.

Seitaro told the remaining sailors how Otokichi had dealt with the captain. First he demanded in fluent English that the captain release the Japanese castaways. To this the captain replied that the plan was to take the sailors back to Japan as part of the Perry mission, thus he couldn't allow anyone to leave. Not backing down a bit, Otokichi argued that the captain should show mercy on these men and let them go free, and at last the captain relented.

"What an amazing fellow," Seitaro said in awe.

The nine sailors on the *Susquehanna* discussed what they should do next. Otokichi had promised to come back to speak further with Commander Buchanan, but most doubted that he would be successful. Perry, when he finally arrived, planned to use the castaways as pawns in his negotiations with the Japanese. If Buchanan released all nine, he would be punished for disobeying orders, so he wouldn't give in, no matter how much Otokichi argued.

The sailors felt they were at a turning point. If they could leave the ship, they might be able to board a Chinese vessel for home, but as long as they stayed with the ship, the chances of their ever setting foot on Japanese soil again were slim.

The more they discussed the situation, the more they saw themselves with only one option left: jumping ship.

"They will keep closer watch on us from now on," Seitaro said, summing up the opinion of most of them, "so let's slip out tonight." He went on to suggest how they should make their escape. Late at night, when the crew was asleep, they would quietly come up on deck and lower a boat. When he found out they'd escaped, Buchanan would send a search party, but Shanghai was so packed with dwellings there was little chance they'd be found.

"Bring only a few things with you. Go get ready," Seitaro said, his eyes glistening.

The sailors went back into their cabin.

Seitaro talked with Chosuke about what to do after they escaped from the ship. They were relying on Otokcihi, so they would have to go to his place and follow his instructions. Certainly he had already taken the four sailors in the original group back to his house.

But it would be dangerous to head straight for Otokichi's— Buchanan, suspecting that Otokichi had instigated the escape of the nine, would begin the search at his house—so they must split up into small groups and lay low for three days, after which they would assemble at Otokichi's in the middle of the night.

Evening fell, and they ate dinner. Fortunately, the sky was covered with thick clouds and the darkness was palpable. They gathered their belongings and lay on their bunks.

Suddenly there was a loud noise outside, and the sailors looked at each other. It was the sound of machinery starting up. Occasionally the crew would test the steam engines, and they thought that's what it might be, but they could hear the paddle wheels on both sides of the ship slowly begin to turn.

"We're leaving!" one of the sailors yelled.

Seitaro, his face pale, leaped out of bed and ran from the cabin. The sound of the paddle wheels grew louder, and the sound of the water as the paddles slapped it. The ship was definitely moving.

Seitaro finally returned to the cabin. "They're going to watch the battles up in Nanjing," he blurted, his face pale. By battles, he meant the Taiping Rebellion. Rumor had it that the rebel forces would attack Shanghai, and the city was in an uproar.

The sailors knew that the rebellion was a consequence of the Opium War, which took place thirteen years before. Britain harvested opium from poppies in India, one of its colonies, and smuggled it into China, leading to a drain of silver from China. This became a huge political, economic, and social problem, and the Chinese passed strict laws prohibiting the smuggling of opium. The British, claiming this restricted free trade, dispatched its navy, attacking first the coast of Canton, then Tianjin, Shanghai, and Nanjing; China surrendered and signed the Treaty of Nanjing. The treaty opened five ports, including Shanghai, and forced China to give Hong Kong to Britain and pay reparations. After this China became almost a British colony.

The Manchu Dynasty lost its authority after concluding the treaty, and a man from the majority Han Chinese named Hong Xiuquan raised up an army to wrest the government from the Manchu and return it to the Han Chinese. He started out with a three-thousand-man peasant army, but soon this had swelled to a hundred thousand, and on March 29 they attacked Nanjing and made it the capital of their Taiping Paradise on Earth.

News of the fall of Nanjing had reached Shanghai a few days previously, and the *Susquehanna,* as flagship of the United States Far East fleet, was going to Nanjing to take stock of the situation.

The Japanese sailors were devastated. Their plan of slipping away in the middle of the night was now impossible. They fell silent, sitting glumly on the floor, some of them taking to their beds.

Meanwhile from outside came the regular beat of the engine and paddle wheels.

The ship left the harbor and slowly went up the Yellow River, but often had to stop and wait because of the dense fog, and the waiting could last even a whole day and night. To the sailors the broad expanse of the Yellow River looked like the ocean.

As they drew nearer to Nanjing, they saw countless warships along the banks of the river. The ships flew colorful banners and flags, and their crew members brandished swords and fists menacingly in their direction. The *Susquehanna* came to a halt, and Buchanan and the other officers trained spyglasses on these military vessels.

They must have come to some decision, for the ship turned around before it reached Nanjing and headed back down the Yellow River. Seitaro asked the crew where they were going; back to Shanghai, he was told. The sailors were overjoyed.

At Shanghai, the ship dropped anchor in the evening, the whole voyage having taken a week.

Learning of their return, Otokichi came out to see them the next morning. Wanting to discuss matters with Buchanan again, he and Seitaro went to the captain's quarters.

Otokichi had presents he gave to Buchanan, and again spoke with him in fluent English. He told him how very grateful the Japanese sailors were for having been rescued by an American ship and brought here to China. Allowed to go ashore freely, they could have run away at any time, but they did not, knowing this would sully all the goodwill the Americans had shown them.

"If you have even a little feeling for them, let them go," he argued ardently.

Buchanan repeated that Perry planned to take the castaways back to Japan. But Otokichi didn't give in, saying that on humanitarian grounds it wasn't good to keep the men restricted like this, that Buchanan should have mercy on them and grant their petition.

Buchanan was silent for a while, gazing out the portal as if mulling this over. Otokichi's passionate appeal finally seemed to have a struck a chord. He turned to Otokichi and said, "All right, I will let them go. On one condition—that Sentaro remains on the ship."

Otokichi felt it was terrible to ask Sentaro to stay alone on the ship and again pleaded with Buchanan to let all the sailors go.

"I have compromised as much as I'm going to. If you won't accept my condition, then this conversation is over," Buchanan said, his face bright red with anger.

Otokichi knew it made no sense to ask anything more, so he agreed to Buchanan's terms. Buchanan wanted to keep Sentaro, no doubt because he was the youngest and a skilled cook.

Otokichi and Seitaro left the captain's quarters and went to the afterdeck, where the rest of the sailors were gathered. The sailors listened intently as Otokichi, his expression hard, told them the result of his negotiation with the captain.

"I feel really bad for Sentaro, but this is the best we can do. He'll stay behind on this ship, but I'm sure that someday he'll find a way to return home. Eventually the *Susquehanna* will sail for Japan, and he may very well be handed over to the Japanese side. I pray that the gods will give him good fortune." It pained him to speak these words in front of the very man they were abandoning.

Otokichi looked around at the other sailors and quickly added, "The other eight of you should go back with me immediately, before the captain changes his mind. Gather your belongings..."

Sentaro, his face pale, stood rooted to the spot. The others couldn't look him in the eye and said nothing.

"Hurry up," Otokichi said roughly. At this, the sailors slowly made their way down the corridor to their cabin.

When the sailors emerged, their belongings in hand, their faces were drawn. One approached Otokichi and asked, "Are you sure we can't take Sentaro with us?" His voice was pleading, the words broken.

"I promised the captain. You must accept it," Otokichi said emphatically.

They turned to look at Sentaro, who just stood there.

Sentaro's features contorted, tears in his eyes. Suddenly he turned away from them and half ran down the corridor toward their cabin. Sobs burst from some of the sailors.

"Let's go," Otokichi said, and walked to the rope ladder hanging from the side of the ship.

CHAPTER NINE

SHANGHAI, UNDER BRITISH control, was in a state of alarm. Rumor had it that the Taiping rebels would soon attack the city. The British commander of the city's garrison had placed four thousand troops on the six-yard-high, seven-and-a-half-mile-long wall that surrounded the city, and had 250 cannons at the ready.

The eight Japanese sailors joined the four others at Otokichi's house, and they all were armed by their host with axes and spears to guard it. In the event that the rebel forces did invade the city, Otokichi had a small boat ready so they could make their escape.

Before long they learned that the report that the rebel army was about to attack Shanghai was a deliberate piece of disinformation put out by the rebels, and that the rebel army was actually heading toward Beijing. The confusion in the city eventually subsided.

On May 4 (March 27 by the Japanese calendar), a steam frigate flying the American flag pulled into Shanghai Harbor. This was the *Mississippi*, outfitted with a great number of cannon. The word on the streets of Shanghai was that Commodore Perry, head of the mission to Japan, was aboard, and that he would soon transfer to the *Susquehanna*, flagship of the fleet. From shore the sailors could see numerous small vessels pulling up alongside the *Mississippi* unloading coal and provisions, and barrels of drinking water.

The next day an officer from the *Susquehanna*, accompanied by several guards, came to Otokichi's. Otokichi took them inside and talked with them for a long while, and finally the officer and guards left.

The sailors learned that when Perry found out that the only Japanese castaway still on board was Sentaro, he was very upset. Buchanan ordered an officer and men to go to Otokichi's residence and demand that the twelve sailors return to the ship.

"I told him it was unacceptable," Otokichi said, "that people they let go should be forced to return. The officer told me there's a man on board who's accompanying Perry named Williams who can speak a little Japanese, and he wants two or three of you to come back for a while." Otokichi screwed up his mouth. "It's a lie. Once you are back, they'll hold you there. I told him the sailors didn't want to return, and rejected his offer."

The sailors smiled at this.

The officer and guards from the *Susquehanna* visited Otokichi's house again. The sailors concealed themselves in a back room.

Finally the Americans left, and the sailors came out to the large room to learn what had transpired. Otokichi, seated on a chair, said, "This time they said they want *me* to accompany them to Japan. Since I speak English, they want me to serve as interpreter in their discussions with the Japanese. And they said that if I wish to be repatriated, they'll do what they can to hand me over to the Japanese side..." He smiled wryly and went on: "I turned them down, saying I have a job here and no time to do what they propose. I don't think they'll be back, but we can't relax."

The sailors finally looked relieved.

Life at Otokichi's agreed with them. Otokichi's Indian wife was kind to them and took great pains to cook food that agreed with them, steaming rice the way they liked it.

Again they repeated to Otokichi their desire to return to Japan and their hope that he would help them attain that end. Otokichi agreed and took them to see the commander of the Shanghai garrison, with whom he was quite close.

When they entered the commander's spacious office, Otokichi handed him some presents, then in fluent English explained the sailors' background and asked for his help to get them back to Japan. The commander greatly sympathized with their plight and said he would divert to Japan a British ship that had entered Shanghai Harbor, but Otokichi said no, there was every reason to believe that the Japanese would refuse them entry; it would be better for them to take one of the Chinese trading ships going to Nagasaki. The commander agreed immediately and promised he would have some of his officials escort them as far as Zhapu.

When Otokichi interpreted the commander's words for the sailors, they put their hands together reverently and bowed repeatedly in thanks. There was a definite spring in their step as they left the garrison.

The sailors prepared to depart at a moment's notice. Once they reached Zhapu, they would have to get permission from the officials there to board a ship, and since the sailors wouldn't be able to handle these negotiations themselves, Otokcihi and his wife decided to join them.

Finally a messenger came from the British commander telling them he'd made ready two riverboats they were to take the following evening. Otokichi went to the harbor to secure a boat for himself and his wife.

The next evening the sailors, wearing sedge hats, followed Otokichi to the harbor and, along with the officials who were coming with them, boarded the two boats. The boats headed south, with the boat carrying Otokichi and his wife following close behind. The mist was thick, the boat lights blurry. The sailors huddled together and fell asleep.

The mist was still thick the next day and their progress was slow, and in the evening they pulled into Lake Ping and spent the night in the boats. The next day the mist had cleared and they continued along the shore; around noon they arrived in Zhapu.

Otokichi and the officials went to the local government office to explain why they'd brought the castaways with them. Zhapu Harbor faced Hangzhou Bay, and the seawater was clouded and muddy.

Otokichi and the officials returned, and with them was a Chinese official, who said, "We will come for you very soon. Please wait here..."

Surprisingly the man spoke to them in Japanese with a Nagasaki accent; apparently he often went on the trade ships to Nagasaki. The sailors' eyes sparkled as they realized the close connection between the two port towns of Zhapu and Nagasaki.

When the official came again, the sailors, Otokichi, and his wife went on shore. Zhapu was a lively port town with many shops lining the streets, and homes with large storehouses. The sailors were taken to a meeting hall, an assembly hall for merchants, and ushered into a large room there.

The official told them sternly, "It is forbidden for you to leave this room. Those who do will be punished."

Otokichi said, "You've been put under the care of the owner of the Chinese ship that will be going to Nagasaki. They say the ship sets sail in June or July. Please take that back to Japan."

The sailors bowed deeply to Otokichi and his wife.

Otokichi and his wife took lodgings in town and came to the assembly hall every day to see them. But after four days they had to return to Shanghai with the officials they'd brought along.

"Be well," Otokichi said when they parted, the tears shining in his eyes, and the sailors, too, shed tears. Otokichi and his wife then left the room.

The sailors lived in the large room without taking a step outside. A guard stood watch just outside the door, as if they were in jail. The food wasn't good, but they didn't mind. They were given two meals a day, one in the morning, one in the evening, both of which included rice, though of terrible quality. The side dishes were oily and smelled bad.

Thus they spent their days, clinging to the hope that the Chinese ship would leave in June or July.

Every time the Japanese-speaking official came to see them, they asked him when the ship would sail, and every time he gave the same answer: "Soon."

In June, he told them, "There's no ship going out this year."

The sailors were so discouraged they couldn't say a thing. If the ship wasn't going to sail, they should have stayed with Otokichi and enjoyed the good food and treatment he afforded and waited a year to come to Zhapu.

Summer passed and cold autumn winds had begun to blow when, one day in October, the official told them that seventeen Japanese castaways had been sent to Zhapu. Sure enough, that evening a group of men in Japanese clothes and topknots came into the room. The sailors expected that these men would all be sailors as well, but some were samurai, wearing the standard long and short swords. The samurai were from the Satsuma Domain in southern Kyushu.

The samurai, at the order of the domain, had set sail from Kagoshima on a ship captained by a man named Hira Zaemon, bound for Okinawa. When their work there was finished, they left Okinawa on June 10 for the return voyage to Kagoshima but ran into a terrible storm; their mast snapped, and a howling east wind blew them all the way to the mouth of the Yellow River. There they were taken into custody by officials and moved to Suzhou, where they stayed for sixty days. During this time two of the men contracted malaria and died, leaving seventeen. They told the Chinese they wished to return to Japan, so they were sent to Zhapu.

Chosuke and the sailors were happy to have these new companions, and from this day on, all twenty-nine shared the room.

At the end of the year one of the Satsuma sailors died of influenza. When the officials learned of this, they sent a party of ten petty officials and a doctor banging a gong as they entered. The doctor carefully examined the body. Apparently they had the suspicion that the man had been killed in a brawl, but satisfied that this wasn't the case, they left.

The official who spoke Japanese brought in a large oblong box. The Satsuma sailors placed the corpse in the box and tearfully carried it out of the assembly hall. Ropes were tied around the casket and a pole passed through these, and the casket was then carried by two Chinese. The sailors of the *Eiriki Maru* followed behind the sailors from Satsuma. This was the first time in months they'd been outside since coming to Zhapu.

They passed through the town and ascended a hill where there was a graveyard with small headstones. The Chinese dug a hole, lowered the casket into it, and covered it with dirt and then stones. Nearby was a temple whose sign identified it as Tenson Temple. They all went to the temple, where they made an offering of a hundred mon. A priest came out and went to the graveyard, where he recited sutras while beating a wooden drum. He wore a gray robe and looked just like a priest in Japan. The service done, they headed back to the assembly hall.

The sixth year of Kaei (1853) ended, and on New Year's Day they had unexpected visitors: Otokichi and his wife. Otokichi told them since they had heard no news about the castaways of the *Eiriki Maru* taking a Chinese trading ship to Nagasaki, they'd grown worried and came to see what was happening.

The sailors never thought they would see Otokichi and his wife again; they wept and were thankful yet again for the couple's kindness to them.

They were particularly worried about Sentaro, the cook who'd been left behind on the *Susquehanna*. Otokichi said that last June Perry had taken the steam frigates *Susquehanna* and *Mississippi*, along with sailing frigates, from Shanghai and arrived in Uraga, in Japan. Instead of driving the four warships away, the Japanese had peacefully welcomed them.

Sentaro had most definitely been on the *Susquehanna*, Otokichi reported, but he didn't know whether or not Sentaro had been handed over to the Japanese. Further, he told them that last August 5 the Shanghai garrison had fallen to an attack by the Taiping rebels, but no civilians had been injured.

As Otokichi gave them the food he'd brought, he said, "A Chinese ship will definitely travel to Nagasaki this year. I pray you'll be able to return home."

Although the samurai from Satsuma had had to relinquish

their swords, their manner was still overbearing, and they were more openly upset than the others at being held in confinement. When February came, they couldn't endure it anymore and said, "All of you come with us. We're going into the town," and they left the assembly hall.

Afraid of them, the guards didn't try to stop them, and the sailors of the *Eiriki Maru* followed the samurai, walking all over town, then returning in the evening. This became a daily event, all of them going into town, even seeing plays before they returned.

The main street in Zhapu was paved with stones, and the roofs of the houses were all tiled. There were shops that sold woodblock prints and fans from Edo, and one could really feel that this was a port that had connections with Nagasaki. Chinese had the custom of binding the feet of their women to make the feet tiny, and the sailors often saw upper-class women, unable to walk by themselves, supported on either side by servants.

The sailors walked wherever they wanted in the town, but on the evening of February 22 they noticed that they were missing Iwakichi. They thought he might have returned alone to the assembly hall, but instead they found a note he'd left behind, and they realized he'd run away. In the note he wrote that there was no prospect of returning home, the food was terrible, and he feared he might die of illness, so he would try to find employment with an Englishman and discover his own way home.

Seitaro spoke with Chosuke, then reported what had happened to the two chief clerks who worked for the owner of the Chinese ship. The clerks told the owner but did not notify the Zhapu town office.

Officials would inspect them from time to time, and when they discovered Iwakichi's absence and reported it, an investigation was begun, the two clerks who failed to notify the office were arrested and thrown into prison, and the owner of the ship was ordered to search for Iwakichi. The owner dispatched men everywhere, and eventually Iwakichi was discovered working in a business managed by an Englishman. The English, though, had such power that Iwakichi, in one of their countrymen's employ, couldn't be brought back, and the shipowner took the loss, falsely reporting to the authorities that Iwakichi had died of an illness.

The two clerks were given a hundred lashes, and that was the end of the affair. The crew members from the *Eiriki Maru* remaining in the assembly hall were now down to eleven.

In May they were overjoyed to hear that two trading vessels would be going to Nagasaki that year. Indeed, on June 23 an official came to tell them that the castaways from Satsuma and the crew of the *Eiriki Maru* would be put on two separate ships and travel to Nagasaki. The sailors made preparations to leave and waited for the day of departure.

Finally the head of the town office, accompanied by other officials, came to the assembly hall and gave each man a farewell present of two cakes and one fan.

On the morning of July 8 the Satsuma castaways, including the samurai, left the assembly hall to board, at the officials' directions, a trading vessel called, in the Japanese reading, the *Hori*. The sailors of the *Eiriki Maru* learned that the ship they'd be taking was called the *Genho*.

The sailors went to the town office to pay their final respects to the head official. In turn he presented each of them with a bag of white sugar and cakes, and the sailors were taken to the harbor.

Despite their happiness at being released from confinement and on their way home, they were worried about one of their number, Yasutaro. Since the evening of the third he'd shown symptoms of malaria, with chills and a cycle of high fever, the fever breaking after he sweat terribly, then rising again. His companions had to support him, as he could barely walk. They were accompanied by an interpreter who spoke the Nagasaki dialect; he told them that the *Hori*, bearing the Satsuma castaways, had set sail early that same morning.

Reaching the harbor, they rowed out to the *Genho* on small boats. The ship was brightly painted and flew colorful banners and flags. It was large, thirty-six yards long and nine in width, and boasted one large cannon and six smaller ones to fight off any pirate attack. The crew of the *Eiriki Maru* were taken to one of the many cabins belowdecks. A great deal of cargo was loaded onto the ship, and officials and merchants who were going to Nagasaki came aboard, carrying their own luggage.

Two days later they had a favorable wind, and the *Genho* set sail from Zhapu. Apart from the castaways the Chinese crew numbered 108.

The ship sailed east. The sailors stood near the side, looking out at the sea ahead of them, knowing that over the horizon lay their homeland, and their eyes sparkled with anticipation. At night they gazed upward, enchanted by the full moon.

The fourth night after they set sail, an unexpectedly luxurious banquet of food and drink was sent to their room. The dumbfounded sailors asked why and learned it was a farewell gift from the captain. They enjoyed the sake, which they hadn't had in a long while, along with all the food, and shouted and clapped their hands, overjoyed at their good fortune.

From the position of the stars they could tell that they were on course toward the east, but on the evening of the eighth day of their voyage the weather took a turn for the worse. The next day the rain and wind became even fiercer, and the ship was tossed about by terrible waves. It was swiftly borne on the noticeably stronger tide.

Most of the merchants were prostrate with seasickness, but the Chinese crew, accustomed to storms, took it all in stride. In the evening the sea was still rough, but next morning they could make out land to the east. The sailors stared steadily at the land, knowing it had to be Japan.

The crew began bustling around the ship, which despite the waves plowed its way toward land. The *Genho* made it into the harbor at Hatori in the Satsuma Domain. It was the morning of July 22.

The town was thrown into excitement by the unexpected arrival of the Chinese ship, and the local officials dispatched a messenger to Kagoshima. Soon officials from the foreign-affairs section of the domain arrived, along with others, and rowed out to the ship. They learned that the *Genho* had pulled into Hatori seeking refuge from the storm, and ascertained that there were eleven castaways from the *Eiriki Maru* on board.

The *Eiriki Maru* crew begged the Satsuma Domain officials to treat Yasutaro, who was sick with malaria, and the officials agreed and dispatched a doctor to the ship. The doctor who examined Yasutaro told them that the illness was beyond his powers, and recommended that they take him to Nagasaki for treatment, since there were many skilled doctors there. He left without prescribing any medicine.

The next day the weather improved, and the day after that they had a favorable wind, so the local officials directed forty small boats to tow the *Genho* out of the harbor and into the open sea.

The *Genho*'s sails filled in the wind, and it headed north, making port on the twenty-fifth in Oe, in the Amakusa Islands in Higo Province.

They set sail again the next day and waited for the tide to turn off Kaba Island in the Goto Islands, and soon after they anchored, Yasutaro passed away. Sadly, this was the day before they were scheduled to pull into Nagasaki.

They prepared a coffin on the *Genho,* and the sailors, sobbing, placed the body inside. That night they held a wake, and the Chinese joined in lighting incense for the repose of the dead man's soul.

The next morning the ship left Kaba Island and headed east. The lookout at Nomozaki Peninsula at the entrance to Nagasaki Harbor spotted their ship and started a signal fire; he sent a message to the sentry outpost at Koseto inside the harbor, and they in turn contacted the Nagasaki magistrate's office.

The *Genho* slowly made its way into the harbor and came to a halt near the mouth. A boat with the commissioner's officials and a Chinese interpreter rowed out to the *Genho* and conducted the usual inspection, taking down the names, addresses, and ages of the ten remaining castaways and examining Yasutaro's corpse.

After the inspection, at a sign from the officials a number of small boats approached and tied two thick towlines to the *Genho*. The boats lined up in two rows, and at another signal the rowers in them all began rowing. The *Genho* slowly moved farther into the harbor. The sailors of the *Eiriki Maru* beheld the dark green that covered the hills and the houses that drew near.

The ship came to a stop, threw out the anchor, and then gongs and drums rang out to celebrate their safe arrival.

The next day at eleven in the morning, the sailors of the *Eiriki Maru* came ashore, accompanied by officials of the Nagasaki commissioner, along with the owner of the Chinese ship and two others, and made for the commissioner's office.

At the office the sailors were given lunch, and enjoyed miso soup for the first time in a long time.

The owner of the ship, Wang Yang Quan, and the other Chinese with him were made to stay in Shirasu while the sailors were questioned by the local superintendent and police. The interpreters included the chief Chinese interpreter, Egawa Toyojuro. The sailors of the *Eiriki Maru* were interrogated about their stay in China, the reasons they were brought to Nagasaki, and the circumstances behind their making port in Hatori Island in the Satsuma Domain.

Next, to make certain that none of the sailors had become Christian, they were made to perform the apostasy ritual of stepping on sacred pictures, and then each man was questioned about his age, place of birth, etc. They were questioned further about how they became castaways and ended up in China. Yasutaro's corpse was taken off the *Genho* and temporarily buried in the graveyard at Daionji Temple.

The doctor assigned to the commissioner's office gave the men a physical examination and concluded that, with the exception of Asauemon and Jinpachi, all the sailors were ill. Kyosuke in particular was suffering from a severe case of beriberi, and the doctor paid special attention to him.

The men were kept in a detention center and found that the

castaways from Satsuma who had sailed on the *Hori* two days before them were being kept there as well.

Before their interrogation the sailors of the *Eiriki Maru* had talked together to get their stories straight and to conceal that they'd been to America. They'd been cautioned by the Chinese that, with Japan's banning of Christianity, if it came out that they'd been to America, they would be executed. Thus the sailors all maintained that after their ship was wrecked, they drifted to China.

But, at the commissioner's office the officials learned from the owner of the *Genho* and his companions that the sailors had been rescued by an American ship and had spent time in San Francisco. The sailors were called many times to Shirasu for questioning, and under such intense grilling they couldn't keep the lie going, and eventually the truth came out.

At the detention center Kyosuke's condition worsened. The physicians, Yoshida Ryosen and Kouri Kenzo, did what they could to treat him, but at 3 AM on the morning of September 5 he passed away. He was thirty-six.

The nine surviving sailors were given permission to accompany Kyosuke's body to the graveyard, and they carried the coffin to the Zenrinji Temple and buried it as the priest recited the sutras.

The commissioner, through the Osaka commissioner's office, got in touch with the owner of the *Eiriki Maru*, Matsuya Hachisaburo, and also requested a copy of the ship's manifest from the shipping agent in Edo, Nakanishi Shinpachiro, thus ascertaining that much of what the sailors had told them was indeed true. Thus ended the investigation. It was the end of September.

The sailors were treated quite well by the commissioner's office. They were free to smoke and were allowed a hot-tub bath three times a month. They were fed well, too, which they were especially grateful for.

When they learned that there was a shrine in Nagasaki dedicated to the god of the sea, Kompira Daigongen, they asked to be allowed to pray there to give thanks for their safe return. The commissioner gave permission, and on October 13 the nine sailors, accompanied by some officials, paid a visit to the Kompira Shrine and made an offering of fifty sen that had been given to them by the commissioner's office.

On October 15 they also visited Daionji Temple and Zenrinji Temple, where Yasutaro and Kyosuke were buried, to pray for the repose of their souls.

The commissioner's office wanted to return the sailors to their hometowns as soon as possible and contacted the domains they were under, urging them to come take charge of the men.

The first to arrive to take charge of the sailors was a samurai from the Tottori Domain named Murase Yahyoe. Murase found lodgings in Nagasaki, then went to the commissioner's office to claim Yotaro, who was thirty-one now. Yotaro hailed from Nagase Village, Kawamura County, in Hoki Province (modern-day Tottori Prefecture), part of the Tottori Domain. After Murase had taken care of all the formalities, on November 14 he left Nagasaki together with Yotaro.

Five days later an official of the commissioner's office from the Himeji Domain, Akaishi Kumahachi, arrived in Nagasaki with nine others, including minor officials and village headmen. Asauemon, thirty-eight now, who lived in the same village as Hikozo, along with Seitaro (aged 32), Jinpachi (43), and Kiyozo (37), were all born within the boundaries of the Himeji Domain, and the headman from each of their villages had come.

Yasutaro, who had died the day before they anchored in Nagasaki, was from the same domain as Seitaro and the others, and they all went to the Daionji Temple, where he was buried, and made an offering of incense and flowers there. Accompanied by Akaishi, they left Nagasaki for Himeji on November 23.

Tokubei (aged 34) and Tamizo (29) departed to their respective domains, leaving only Chosuke (52) and Ikumatsu (41). Both were from the Settsu Domain (modern-day Hyogo Prefecture). On November 27 the reign-era name changed to Ansei, and the New Year (officially the beginning of the second year of Ansei) came with no one coming to claim these final two sailors.

On January 15 they visited the Zenrinji Temple and prayed before Kyosuke's grave. That day was a holiday in Nagasaki, and drums and gongs rang out over the city. On January 23 the headman of Chosuke's village, Kobe, named Yohei, and the elder of Ikumatsu's birthplace, Futatsujyaya Village, Yasabei, arrived in Nagasaki, and on the twenty-seventh the two sailors left Nagasaki.

In their hometowns the sailors were feted by many people, were invited to various places to talk about their experiences as castaways, and received all sorts of presents. Some of the domains wrote down these experiences. They were particularly interested because the sailors had actually set foot in America, which the domains had read about only in imported foreign books.

For instance, one of the sailors, Yataro, was invited by the Tottori Domain to relate in great detail his tale of being shipwrecked, being taken from San Francisco to China, and then returning to Nagasaki. This was written down in a book, *Tales of a Castaway from Nagase Village,* by a samurai of the domain, Okuda Masatada.

Because Yataro had ridden on a steamship, something no other Japanese had ever done, and because, as a sailor, he'd observed the vessels carefully, in March of the second year of Ansei the domain appointed him a petty official of their domain school, the Shotokukan, and he was given the right, as a samurai, to carry swords and have a last name; he took the new name of Saeki Bunta. The head of the domain, Ikeda Yoshinori, son of the head of the Mito Domain, Tokugawa Nariaki, was extremely interested in foreign countries, and when he was at the Yoshioka Spa for the water cure, he invited Yataro to join him and tell him all about his castaway experiences, as well as circumstances in America and China. These talks were taken down in a book, entitled *Records of a Castaway,* by the domain samurai and Confucianist Hori Shojiro.

The four sailors from Hikozo's hometown, Asauemon, Kiyotaro, Jinpachi, and Kiyozo, arrived in Himeji on December 18 of the first year of Ansei and were housed near the castle. Their relatives hurried to see them, crying in joy when they were reunited. The domain continued to interrogate them, but once this was completed, they returned to their hometowns in the middle of February.

The nine surviving members of the *Eiriki Maru,* then, all returned safely home but lived thereafter under some restrictions. The national seclusion policy allowed them to talk about their experience as castaways, but they were forbidden to discuss with ordinary people their experiences in foreign lands. They were also forbidden ever to take a ship again on the sea, so that they could not again visit a foreign country. This was a severe blow to their ability to earn a living, for the only trade they'd ever known was being a sailor. They were forced to seek other employment.

At the end of April that year Seitaro received a letter from Akimoto Yasutami, a samurai of the Himeji Domain and instructor at the National Learning Institute of the domain. The letter informed him that one of his colleagues, Isshiki Kenryu, and others were very interested in hearing from Seitaro about the conditions in foreign countries he observed while a castaway, and they would like Seitaro to travel to Himeji to speak with them. Traveling expenses were enclosed. Akimoto was a scholar of the Japanese tradition, but while stationed in Edo he'd familiarized himself with Western books and was fascinated by the products of Western civilization.

Seitaro thus traveled to Himeji, along with Asauemon, Jinpachi, and Kiyozo, and met with Akimoto. Akimoto took them to the domain school, where they met Isshiki Kenryu and talked with him about conditions in America and the construction of the sailing and steam vessels they'd been on. A samurai named Sugao Nobutani acted as secretary, taking notes, and after five months of dialogue this was compiled into a record entitled *Strange Tales from East and West.*

Seitaro and the others were given an honorarium, and returned home, but two months later, on November 6, a second letter arrived from Akimoto.

With Western ships appearing off the shores of Japan, the

shogunate saw itself in crisis and felt keenly the need for its own Western-style ships; two years before, in May of the sixth year of Kaei, it had granted a request made by the Satsuma Domain to start construction on a large-scale Western-style warship named the *Shouhei Maru.*

A month after this, Perry arrived in Uraga with his fleet of four warships, and the country was forced to open itself to the outside world. Feeling even more now the need for a modern navy, the shogunate rescinded its law banning the domains from constructing large-scale vessels. The shogunate's first Western-style ship to be completed was the *Houou Maru,* finished the next year, in May of the seventh year of Kaei. Further, after the Russian frigate the *Diana,* which came to Japan with Putiatin on board to negotiate relations between the two countries, had run aground and sank, a Western-style ship was constructed with help from Putiatin and his crew in the village of Heda in Izu Province.

Under these circumstances, Akimoto felt the great need to construct a Western-style sailing vessel and petitioned the domain's daimyo, Sakai Tadateru, for permission to do so. Tadateru himself was enthusiastic about organizing the military along Western lines and immediately granted Akimoto's petition.

Akimoto was familiar with Western-style sailing ships from books but wanted to make use of the knowledge Seitaro and the others had gathered while actually riding on these vessels. In his second letter he told them that the lord of the domain had ordered him to construct a Western-style sailing ship and wanted to know what the construction costs would be, so he, Akimoto, asked Seitaro and the others to come to Himeji to begin consultations with them.

Seitaro and his three friends set off right away for Himeji, and it was decided that they would be engaged, under Akimoto's direction, in the constructing of the ship. The men were also accorded the samurai privileges of having a last name and carrying swords, and each received an annual stipend. Seitaro took the name Honjou Zenjirou, Kiyozo the name Hamamoto Kihei, Asauemon the name Yamaguchi Youemon, and Jinpachi the name Kimura Jinpachi.

121

Seitaro, being the most knowledgeable about ship construction, was put in charge of the carpenters, while Asauemon was put in charge of procuring building materials, and Jinpachi and Kiyozo were put in charge of the laborers.

Using Akimoto's books on Western shipbuilding, Seitaro and the others began construction of the ship at Murotsu. They assembled the finest ship carpenters and blacksmiths and set to work.

Because constructing a Western-style ship and a Japanese ship were so different, many things perplexed the carpenters, and Seitaro had to carefully explain to them. This frequently brought the work to a standstill, but by the end of the following year the basic construction was complete, and in the fifth year of Ansei they were in the final stages. Toward the end Jinpachi died of illness, and his body was buried in the Rengeji Temple, part of the Bodaiji Temple complex.

The ship was launched on June 25 and was named the *Hayatori Maru.*

The *Hayatori Maru,* an official ship of the domain, was taken out for test runs many times, and on September 16, with Seitaro as captain, Kiyozo as navigator, and Asauemon at the helm, completed its maiden voyage to Edo, with a cargo of a thousand sacks of rice, thirty bales of cotton produced in the province, and baggage for domain samurai who were stationed in Edo. The ship safely arrived in the waters off Shinagawa and headed back to Himeji. After this it continued to ply the waters mainly between Himeji and Edo until the fourth year of Meiji.

With the domain lord's permission, Akimoto planned to build a Western-style ship larger than the *Hayatori Maru,* and in the second year of Bunkyu, with the help of Seitaro and the others, he constructed a new ship, named the *Jingo Maru.* This ship completed its maiden voyage to Edo on January 8 of the fourth year of Bunkyu, loaded with 2,500 sacks of rice. Kiyozo was the captain for the voyage.

The *Jingo Maru* performed well and continued its voyages into the Meiji period.

Seitaro, Asauemon, and Kiyozo took turns as captain of the two vessels and mastered the art of piloting Western-style ships. The survivors of the *Eiriki Maru* were forbidden to go to sea again, but as employees of the domain, these three were exceptions, taking to the sea in their Western-style ships.

The Himeji Domain experienced great turbulence during the unsettled period at the end of the shogunate, but Seitaro and the others continued piloting their ships as the Meiji period began. Seitaro passed away on December 5 of the eighth year of Meiji, Asauemon on February 11 of the eleventh year of Meiji, and Kiyozo on January 29 of the seventeenth year of Meiji.

When they landed in Nagasaki on the Chinese ship from Zhapu, they were questioned at the commissioner's office also concerning Hikozo, Jisaku, Kamezo, Sentaro, and Iwakichi. As a result of this interrogation it was recorded officially that Hikozo, Jisaku, and Kamezo, who'd accompanied Thomas back to America, "set sail on an American merchant ship, and their whereabouts are unknown." Concerning the cook Sentaro, the record said, "Remained on American vessel, whereabouts unknown." And concerning Iwakichi, who'd run away, the official report read: "After disappearing, he grew sick and died."

CHAPTER TEN

So what became of Sentaro, who stayed behind on the *Susquehanna*?

Left in Shanghai because he was the youngest among them, only twenty-two, he regretted his youth and was devastated by the turn of events. He stayed in his cabin and just sat there on his bunk, hands clasped around his knees. Seeing this, the crew members brought him food, but he barely ate a bite.

The sailors felt sorry for Sentaro and tried to comfort him, urging him to eat something. Finally he responded to their earnest concern. He resigned himself: if fate decreed that he be a castaway, be rescued by an America ship and taken to China, it decreed likewise that he remain alone. He'd have to carve out a path for himself from here on. To symbolize his resolve, in a common Japanese tradition he renamed himself: Senpachi. The sailors affectionately dubbed him Sam Patch.

Perry arrived in Shanghai on the steam frigate *Mississippi* on May 4 (March 27 of the sixth year of Kaei) and transferred to the *Susquehanna*. As we have seen, he angrily ordered the captain of the ship, Buchanan, to bring back the Japanese sailors, but since negotiations with Otokichi came to naught, Perry had to make do by taking Senpachi with them.

The *Susquehanna* and the *Mississippi*, along with the *Supply*, left Shanghai on May 16, heading for Naha in the Ryukyu Islands, and were joined by the sailing ship the *Saratoga*. They set off to survey the Ogasawara Archipelago, then returned to Naha and set off in July for Japan proper. The *Susquehanna* towed the *Saratoga* behind it, while the *Mississippi* towed the *Plymouth.*

After leaving Shanghai, one of the sailors, named Jonathan Goble, became particularly close to Senpachi. Goble was a man of deep faith who dreamed of becoming a Baptist missionary and hoped someday to spread the Gospel in Japan. He felt great affection for the well-mannered and bright Senpachi and hit upon the idea of having him help him in missionary work in Japan.

The four-ship fleet headed across the Pacific toward Edo Bay. Senpachi had made the same trip many times in the *Eiriki Maru,* and the scenery along the shore made him tearful.

On July 8 (June 3 of Kaei), the fleet entered Edo Bay, stopped in the waters northeast of Uraga, and dropped anchor. Uraga was the last port the *Eiriki Maru* had left, and tears sprang to Senpachi's eyes as he gazed at the houses of the town.

But he also feared that, as with the *Morrison,* which Rikimatsu and Otokichi had been aboard, they would be driven away by a cannon barrage. There was no sign of this happening, but when domain troops, with muskets and spears in hand, surrounded the ships in their small boats, Senpachi trembled in terror.

Rikimatsu and Otokichi's words came back to him—that castaways were considered outlaws by the Japanese and could never return home—and Senpachi was afraid to look at the Japanese warships from the deck and hid below the deck.

Negotiations between the American fleet and the Japanese began, with Japanese officials coming aboard the *Susquehanna* many times, but Senpachi had no idea what they discussed.

Six days later, Perry and some three hundred sailors, marines, and even a military band took boats to shore and held talks with the Japanese at a place called Kurihama. Senpachi could see the camp enclosures spread out along the shore, the flags and banners flying, the multitude of armed soldiers. Many warships lay anchored off shore as well, and Senpachi trembled with the thought that a battle was about to begin.

Perry and his men returned to the ships from Kurihama, and the next day the fleet continued farther into the bay.

Senpachi was summoned out onto the deck by the officers.

"Sam Patch, what is that thing?" one officer asked, pointing toward the broad mouth of a river.

The object in question was a channel marker. Senpachi indicated, with broken English and gestures, that it was a stake that marked the main channel in the river. The officers seemed to understand what he was trying to tell them.

He spent an uneasy day below deck, coming out only at night. The whole shore was one big military encampment, with a line of glowing bonfires. The night air, though, was unmistakably that of his homeland, and he breathed it in deeply. The stars, too, were different from the stars in foreign lands, shining bright and clear in the night sky.

Ten days after arriving in Edo Bay the fleet lined up and proceeded out into the open sea and headed west.

Senpachi was sure this was his last glimpse of his homeland, but Goble came up to him and said, consolingly, "We will come back next year."

The Perry fleet returned to Naha, then on to Hong Kong, Canton, finally anchoring in Macao.

Just as Goble had said, the fleet, now with three additional ships—the steam frigate *Powhatan* and the sail frigates *Macedonian* and *Vandalia*—planned to return to Japan, and just after the new year it left Macao, went to Naha, and on February 13 (January 16, the seventh year of Kaei), one after the other the ships entered Edo Bay.

The fleet went deeper into the bay, stopping off Haneda. This action made the shogunate feel threatened, and they responded to what they perceived as a heavy-handed attitude by agreeing to open meetings, this time at a village called Yokohama.

In the negotiations that preceded the meeting, Japanese officials, including Kayama Eizaemon, police supervisor of the Uraga commissioner's office, came aboard the *Susquehanna* often, accompanied by interpreters, and in the course of their meetings Captain

Adams informed Kayama that their crew had a Japanese known by the name Sam Patch.

Kayama, greatly surprised by this news, said he would like to meet the man. Adams promised, "We'll comply with your request in two or three days."

According to Kayama's diary, he met Senpachi (Sam Patch) on February 7 (according to the Japanese calendar), when he and fellow police supervisor Nakajima Saburosuke went on board the *Susquehanna*.

When Senpachi appeared before him, Kayama wrote, "He was dressed in an American outfit, his hair was cut short, and he looked like someone from that country."

Of the meeting between Senpachi and Kayama and Nakajima, the account in Perry's book states:

> According to the agreement, Sam Patch was brought forward and presented to the Japanese officials, and no sooner did he behold these dignitaries than he prostrated himself at once, apparently completely awe-stricken. Sam had been frequently laughed at during the voyage by his messmates, and teazed [*sic*] by statements of the danger to which his head would be exposed on his arrival in his own country, and the poor fellow possibly thought his last hour had come. Captain Adams ordered him to rise from his knees, upon which he was crouching with the most abject fear, and trembling in every limb. He was reminded that he was on board an American man-of-war perfectly safe as one of her crew, and had nothing to fear; but it being found impossible to reassure him while in the presence of his countrymen, he was soon dismissed.

S. Wells Williams, the interpreter who accompanied Perry, wrote in his book *A Journal of the Perry Expedition to Japan, 1853–55* the following about this incident:

> While on board Sam Patch was brought before him [Eizaemon] and questioned a little as to his antecedents, but the poor boy was in such a paroxysm of trepidation that he hardly

knew what he did or ought to do. Prostrate on the deck, he murmured some incoherent words, and could not be induced to stand up, so terrified did he become under the stern eye of Yezaimon [sic] who hardly deigned to look at him.

Despite these "incoherent words," Senpachi did respond to the Japanese questions, and according to their records, "His name was Kurazo, age 23, born in Aki Province (Hiroshima Prefecture)," and he had been a cook on the *Eiriki Maru,* was shipwrecked, rescued by a American ship and taken to San Francisco, then taken to China and left there on a warship as the only Japanese sailor remaining.

Senpachi couldn't shake from his mind what had happened to Rikimatsu and Otokichi sixteen years before, in the eighth year of Tempo, when the *Morrison* was driven away from Japan by cannon fire. If those two, on an unarmed merchant vessel, were treated as if they had committed grievous crimes against the laws of the country, then surely someone like himself, on a heavily armed warship, would be thought of as a criminal whose crimes were unforgivable—thus his fearful prostrations when confronted with Kayama and Nakajima, and why he gave a false name, Kurazo, when questioned in order to keep his relatives back in Hiroshima out of trouble.

Naturally Senpachi wanted nothing more than to return to Japan, and to his hometown. But if he was handed over to the authorities, he was sure he'd be executed, another reason he trembled with fear.

Captain Adams and his officers were quite surprised at Senpachi's actions in front of the Japanese officials. To their mind Senpachi, who drew a monthly salary of nine dollars, was one of their sailors, and having him act so fearful in front of the Japanese was an affront to the dignity of the fleet, so they made him withdraw quickly from sight.

The American fleet left Edo Bay and proceeded to Shimoda, one part of the fleet heading to Hakodate.

On June 21 (May 26 by the Japanese calendar), the chief interpreter, Moriyama Einosuke, who had traveled to Shimoda, submitted a request to the fleet's interpreter, Portman, that Senpachi be turned over to the Japanese. Moriyama was a Dutch interpreter but had learned to converse in English from a Ronald McDonald, an American sailor who had rowed ashore from an American whaling ship on the shores of Rishiri Island in Ezo (Hokkaido) and who was then taken to Nagasaki.

The American fleet's position regarding Senpachi was firm: if Sam Patch wanted to be repatriated, then they would hand him over, on the condition that the Japanese authorities issue a written promise not to execute him. Moriyama insisted that executing him was the furthest thing from their minds; they only wanted to return this poor fellow to his hometown.

"Then please come to the ship tomorrow and discuss things directly with Sam Patch," Portman said.

The following day Moriyama came to the ship, along with officials from Shimoda. Portman, again emphasizing that it all depended on what Sam Patch wanted, brought him out on deck. Again Senpachi lay prostrate on deck, trembling in fear.

Moriyama approached Senpachi and knelt beside him. "The situation has changed," he explained. "We won't punish you. Please go back to your hometown, to your loved ones." But Senpachi's forehead remained pressed against the deck.

"The American fleet say they will turn you over right away. So let's get in the boat and go to the commissioner's office." Moriyama's words were gentle and reassuring.

Senpachi crawled backward, away from Moriyama, and shook his head emphatically.

"What's wrong? There's nothing to be afraid of," Moriyama insisted, but Senpachi continued to tremble and shake his head.

Portman, standing next to them, said, "He doesn't want to go ashore, so we can't force him to."

Moriyama stood up and with a sad look gazed down at Senpachi and said, in English, "I guess there's nothing we can do about it." He left the ship with the commissioner's officials.

Three days later the American fleet left Shimoda and returned to Canton by way of Naha. Their duty done as part of the Perry mission, the ships all left China and one by one sailed back to America. Jonathan Goble, after arriving in New York and leaving the marines, took Senpachi with him to his hometown of Wayne.

Goble then left Wayne and moved to Hamilton, in New York State, and entered Madison University, a Baptist school, and had Senpachi enroll as well. Senpachi, though, proved not fluent enough in English to keep up and had to withdraw; he entered the employ of Goble, who had meantime married. During this period, at Goble's urging, Senpachi was baptized by Pastor Hezekiah Harvey at the Hamilton First Baptist Church, thus becoming the first Japanese to receive baptism in the U.S.

In 1859 (Ansei 6), Goble was ordered to Japan as a missionary, and left for New York with Senpachi, and left New York on the *Baltic.* After stopping in San Francisco and Hawaii, they transferred to the *Zoe* for the trip to Japan, arriving in Yokohama on April 1 (March 11 of the seventh year of Ansei). Their arrival came only eight days after the assassination of the senior government minister Ii Naosuka, in the so-called Sakuradamon Incident, and the country was in an uproar.

Senpachi's citizenship became an issue in Japan, with the American consulate and the Kanagawa commissioner's office contending over this; the conclusion was reached that he would be treated as an American citizen. Having feared he would be executed, Senpachi was relieved to learn that there would be no problem as long as he was an American.

Senpachi always kept up his appearance as an American, wearing Western clothes and keeping his hair cut short; he never spoke in Japanese and insisted on going by the name Sam Patch. He moved in with the Goble family on the grounds of the Jufuji Temple.

Dr. and Mrs. Ballagh of the Reformed Church, who had come to Japan, were also living in the temple. Senpachi left Goble and entered Ballagh's employ as a cook. Later he moved with Ballagh to the foreign settlement in Yokohama and in 1866 (Keio 2) went with Mrs. Ballagh back to America.

Mrs. Ballagh introduced Senpachi to a Warren Clark, who had been invited to Japan to be a professor at the Shizuoka Gakumonjo School, and in the third year of Meiji Senpachi accompanied Clark back to Japan. The school was divided into youth and children's sections, and among the pupils in the children's division was Tokugawa Iesato, who succeeded to the head family of the ruling Tokugawa Shogunate. The professors included Nakamura Keitaro. Clark was given a monthly salary of three hundred dollars to teach physics, chemistry, language arts, and geometry.

Clark at first lived with Senpachi in the Ren'eiji temple, but built a two-story Western-style house on the grounds of the former Sunpu Castle and moved there; Senpachi lived in an adjacent one-story dwelling. The reason he lived apart from the Clarks was that by this time he was married.

Clark and Senpachi were more like close friends than employer and employee. Senpachi looked after Clark and cooked delicious meals for him and his wife, and both Clark and his wife had great affection for Senpachi, as shown by the fact that they built a house for him next door to them.

In December of the sixth year of Meiji, Clark moved with Senpachi and his wife to Tokyo to become professor of science at Kaisei School. It was during this time that Senpachi contracted beriberi, which was prevalent at the time, and at Clark's recommendation the following year Senpachi was admitted to the Tokyo Municipal Hospital, where many foreign doctors were employed.

On July 23 Clark and his wife set out on a trip to Kyoto, and while they were away Senpachi slipped out of the hospital and went to their home: he wanted to straighten up their house before their return.

Clark was surprised when he came home and put Senpachi back in the hospital, but his condition worsened, and he became extremely ill because of the damage done to his heart by beriberi. Clark came often to see Senpachi in the hospital, but on October 7 Senpachi was in critical condition, and he died the next day. He was forty-three.

There was a Christian burial service, where a missionary named Thompson presided and spoke of Senpachi's experiences as a castaway. The coffin was placed inside a horse-drawn hearse. Nakamura Keitaro, the former colleague of Clark's at the Shizuoka Gakumonjo School, sympathized deeply with Senpachi's plight and offered his own ancestral burial plot at the Hondenji Temple in Otsuka for his burial.

After the funeral service the procession took off, with Nakamura, Clark, and Senpachi's wife following the hearse in rickshaws. People along the road stared with curiosity at the combination of a hearse and foreigners following it.

The hearse and rickshaws proceeded through the streets of Tokyo, arriving at the grounds of the Hondenji Temple. A Christian service had already been held, but a Buddhist funeral service was now held too, as part of the procedure for burial within the Buddhist temple grounds. The coffin was carried into the main hall of the temple, the priest chanted the sutras, and the participants made offerings of incense. Clark wasn't pleased, as a Christian, with this type of funeral service, though in his book *Life and Adventure in Japan* he wrote, "This was the only occasion when I was favorably impressed with the solemnity of a Buddhist ceremony."

The ceremony over, the coffin was buried in the cemetery.

Nakamura himself placed a headstone at the grave, on which was carved, in his own calligraphy, the words THE GRAVE OF SANPACHI-KUN. Senpachi had always gone by the name Sam Patch, and Nakamura didn't know which characters to use to write out his real name, so he just selected ones that phonetically sounded out the name and that meant simply "three-eight." The *kun* affixed to the name on the gravestone, a familiar yet polite suffix used with men's names, Nakamura added to indicate the respect he felt for all the trials and suffering Senpachi had endured.

Clark soon left his post at Kaisei School and the following March returned to America. Afterward he owned a farm in Florida, which he called Shizuoka.

CHAPTER ELEVEN

IN OCTOBER OF 1852 (Kaei 5) Hikozo, Kamezo, and Jisaku left Hong Kong with Thomas on the English ship *Sarah Hooper.* Hikozo was fifteen, Kamezo twenty-four, and Jisaku twenty-nine.

Hikozo felt guilty about leaving the other sailors behind in China and returning to America. Kamezo and Jisaku, too, no doubt felt they'd betrayed their companions, but Hikozo thought that going to America was no guarantee they'd be repatriated, and that those left behind in China might very well be the ones who found a way to return home. In his heart he felt the three of them were fated to wander aimlessly in a foreign land, tossed about at the whim of fate.

The decrepit *Sarah Hooper* made slow progress, giving off high-pitched creaks each time it was pounded by the waves. When the seas grew calm, though, it drifted quietly on the currents.

Hikozo and the others spent most of their time in their cabin, not saying much, with only Thomas upbeat about their prospects when they reached San Francisco. He insisted he'd find them all good jobs.

After a fifty-day voyage the ship reached San Francisco.

Once they'd anchored, Thomas asked Hikozo to watch their belongings as he and Kamezo and Jisaku went ashore. Hikozo was worried that he would be left behind on the ship, but three hours later they returned.

Thomas told him that at the wharf he'd run across the *Frolic*, a revenue ship, and had met two old acquaintances who were members of its crew, Lieutenants Carson and Wilkinson. Carson and Wilkinson had been officers aboard the revenue ship *Polk*, the ship that Hikozo and the other castaways had been transferred to when they first arrived in San Francisco on the *Auckland*, the ship that rescued them. The lieutenants were pleased to see Kamezo and Jisaku again. When Thomas explained to the two lieutenants why they'd returned to San Francisco, they pledged that they'd do all they could to help.

"Let's go ashore and see them," Thomas said, and trundled his large suitcase under his arm as Hikozo and the others followed him off the ship carrying their belongings. The three Japanese followed Thomas to the *Frolic*.

When Carson and Wilkinson, both tall men, saw Hikozo, they called out and gave him a hug. Hikozo remembered again how the whole crew of the *Polk* had been so kind to them, and he breathed a sigh of relief to meet these old friends once again.

Thomas told the lieutenants he'd be taking Kamezo and Jisaku into town to find work for them and asked them to look after Hikozo. Hikozo guessed from this that it would be hard for Thomas to find him a job, because of his age. The two lieutenants agreed.

Thomas said to Hikozo, "I'll be back as soon as I can," and left with Kamezo and Jisaku for town.

The lieutenants spoke with the captain and got Hikozo a position as errand boy for the *Frolic*. The pay was next to nothing, but Hikozo devoted himself to his tasks, which included assisting in the kitchen and making sure the ship's stores were in order.

Despite his promise, Thomas didn't return for a long time, and Hikozo grew uneasy. The lieutenants and the others on board treated him kindly, but he grew lonely, and he'd often go out on deck to scan the city in hopes of seeing Thomas returning. It was the first time since he'd become a castaway that he was left alone, and he felt how very difficult that was in a foreign land.

At dawn one day in the middle of December he felt the ship swaying and heard high-pitched yells above deck. He leaped out of his bunk and was surprised to find the sails full and the ship headed toward the mouth of the harbor.

Flustered, he raced to ask Lieutenant Wilkinson where they were going.

Monterey, the lieutenant answered. He explained that the captain had been ordered by the head of revenue to sail to that town, about eighty miles away.

Hikozo was frightened. What if they never came back to San Francisco and he never saw Thomas, Kamezo, and Jisaku again?

The ship sailed on and anchored the next day at its destination. Two days later they set sail again, for Kathleen Island, and Hikozo became even more uneasy. He asked Lieutenant Wilkinson, "Is this ship ever going back to San Francisco?"

"Of course," the lieutenant replied, looking puzzled as to why such a question would even be raised. Hearing this, Hikozo finally calmed down.

The *Frolic* stayed at anchor for three days at Kathleen Island, went on to San Diego, and two days later returned to Monterey.

It was Christmas Eve, and some of the sailors got drunk and fought, and blood was shed. One sailor in particular caused a scene, yelling drunkenly and thrashing about, and the captain ordered him to be held down and put in chains. Hikozo, stunned, could only watch.

The ship left port the next day and returned to San Francisco. When they arrived at the wharf, Thomas, who'd been waiting for them, came aboard.

"I'm glad you're all right," he beamed, shaking Hikozo's hand. It turned out that the newspapers had reported the *Frolic* lost at sea in a storm. They had, indeed, run into a storm on the way from Kathleen Island to San Diego, and it had made Hikozo seasick.

When he saw Thomas again, Hikozo was struck with the fear that if he stayed on the *Frolic*, he'd be taken away somewhere again, and he said, "I want to get off this ship."

Thomas frowned. Kamezo and Jisaku were both employed now as cooks, Kamezo on the surveying cutter *Ewing* at sixty dollars per month, Jisaku at seventy dollars per month on the revenue cutter *Argus*. But Thomas had yet to find a position for Hikozo.

"To tell the truth, I used up almost all my money to pay our passage from China to San Francisco," Thomas told him. "I wouldn't be able to feed you if you went ashore." He looked at Hikozo entreatingly and asked him to stay a little longer until he could locate work for him.

"I understand." Hikozo nodded and watched as Thomas left the ship.

I must be strong, Hikozo told himself. Fate had brought him here to America, where he had no parents or relatives to rely on. From the moment he'd left his shipmates in faraway China, he had only himself to depend on, and he couldn't expect anyone to come to his aid. He would have to take whatever came his way.

Hikozo worked diligently as errand boy on the ship. He ate things he'd never had in Japan—beef and pork—and even started to use butter, the smell of which he used to hate, on his bread.

The new year came, and the days grew cold. The *Frolic* remained in San Francisco, performing customs inspections on newly arrived foreign ships.

Eventually the weather grew warmer, and spring flowers blossomed on shore.

A dispute arose at this time among Lieutenants Carson and Wilkinson, the other officers, and the captain concerning Hikozo's wages. The officers said it wasn't fair to barely pay Hikozo, who worked harder than any American, but the captain refused to listen. When the officers insisted, the captain finally agreed that Hikozo was working hard but that since he only spoke broken English, he should be thankful they were feeding him.

This incensed the two lieutenants, and they sent a messenger to bring Thomas to the *Frolic*. The lieutenants advised Thomas to take Hikozo away; when Thomas told them he didn't have the means to support him, the lieutenants said they would take care of his living expenses. Thomas agreed, and Hikozo paid his respects to the captain and crew and left the ship.

Thomas was acquainted with Lieutenant Pease, captain of the *Argus,* the ship Jisaku worked on, and suggested they go there first. Hikozo happily followed, since this meant he would see Jisaku, who came from the same village and whom he hadn't seen in a long time.

Jisaku looked well, his face having filled out since Hikozo last saw him. He held out his hand like an American and shook Hikozo's hand. Lieutenant Pease came out as well, shook Hikozo's hand, and had a pleasant chat with Thomas.

Pease nodded as Thomas explained the situation, and said, "I'll find a job for Hiko. Until then both of you can stay aboard." Lieutenant Pease then turned to Thomas and asked him to work as master-at-arms on the ship at a monthly salary of fifty dollars. Thomas, who had not been successful in finding employment for himself, was overjoyed and thanked Pease many times.

Three days later, as promised, Lieutenant Pease found a position for Hikozo, at twenty-five dollars a month, in a large boardinghouse. But the Chinese cook there was mean to Hikozo for some reason. Hikozo could put up with it, but when Pease found out how he was being mistreated, he found a position for him at another boardinghouse, this one run by a woman and her daughter.

This boardinghouse was small, with a handful of boarders who were all gentlemen of quality. The work was easy, and the salary was thirty dollars per month. Hikozo happily devoted himself to his duties.

About a month after he'd settled into his new job, Thomas came to visit him and invited him to the *Argus* to see Jisaku again. Hikozo asked for permission from the mistress of the boardinghouse and went with Thomas. Lieutenant Pease had been called away by the head of revenue for San Francisco and was not aboard, so Hikozo, Thomas, and Jisaku chatted on deck, awaiting his return. It was a hot day, but the breeze felt cool. Jisaku asked Hikozo about his new job, and he replied that he was quite happy with it.

Pease finally returned, accompanied by a young man.

Hikozo was startled when he saw the man, who had black hair pulled back and wore a Japanese kimono. A short sword hung at his waist, and he held a large bundle wrapped in a furoshiki cloth.

Jisaku looked at Hikozo fearfully. "I knew we shouldn't have left China to go back to America. The other sailors must have got to Japan and told the officials we went to America." His voice trembled as he spoke. "That man must be a shogunate official—that's why he has a sword—and I'll bet he's come to take us back to be punished!"

Jisaku was a very sensible man, so Hikozo became tense with fear.

Lieutenant Pease walked over to them and, glancing back at the other man, said, "We have another Japanese castaway on our hands. His ship was adrift near Tahiti, and a ship transporting fruit picked him up and brought him here."

The man had been taken first to Sanders, the head of revenue, and after an exchange of gestures and signs they concluded he was a Japanese castaway, but they could get nothing more from him. Knowing that the *Argus* had a Japanese cook, Jisaku, Sanders summoned Lieutenant Pease to his office. He ordered Pease to take the man to the *Argus* and have Jisaku, who could speak some English, act as interpreter and find out more about how the man had been shipwrecked.

When Hikozo heard the man was a castaway, his fear disappeared, and Jisaku, too, was relieved.

Lieutenant Pease said, "It's wonderful that Hiko's here, too, as well as Tora [Jisaku]. And Thomas, you speak some Japanese, so I'd like the three of you to find out the details of this man's story."

It made Hikozo homesick to meet a fellow Japanese so unexpectedly, and he and Jisaku approached the man. The man regarded them with a hard expression, then bowed deeply. Hikozo realized that with their short hair and Western clothes, they must look like Americans to him.

When Jisaku spoke to him in Japanese, the man's eyes went

wide in surprise. Apparently he thought Jisaku was an American able to speak the language fluently.

When Jisaku introduced himself and Hikozo, explaining how they'd been rescued by an American ship and then returned to San Francisco via China, the man fell to his knees, put his hands together in supplication, and touched his forehead to the deck. Over and over he said, "I beg of you to help me."

Jisaku knelt by the man's side and said, "There's nothing to be frightened of. The captain of the ship just wanted to know what happened to you, and so he brought you here to meet us, since we're Japanese."

Hikozo added, "The captain and crew here are all very kind."

Finally the man seemed to relax, and got up.

Hikozo and Jisaku took the man to Thomas's cabin. They sat on a bunk across from the man, while Thomas sat on a chair. Jisaku asked some questions, and the man finally revealed how he came to be a castaway.

His name was Yunosuke, age twenty-two, born in Itagai Village, Iwafune County, in Echigo Province (present-day Itagai, Yamakita Township, Iwafune County, in Niigata Prefecture). At the age of nineteen he became a crew member on the *Yahata Maru*, a seven-hundred-koku vessel owned by a man named Zentaro from Neya Village (Neya, Yamakita Township). Last year, in April, the *Yahata Maru* traveled to Etorofu Island, where it picked up a load of salted trout. It set off from Matsumae on September 1 for the voyage back to Niigata with a crew of twelve.

The captain of the ship, Kumajiro, planned to make port in Dewa Province (present-day Yamagata and Akita prefectures). They had only a small cargo of rice, and since rice was far cheaper in Dewa Province than in Matsumae, he planned to lay in a stock there. They had good weather for three days, but once they were out of the Tsugaru Straits, the wind died down completely, and the current swept them east of the straits and into the open ocean.

On the fourth day out, in the afternoon, a sudden northwest wind blew up; it grew stronger, until they were in the midst of an awful storm. Huge waves crashed down on the ship; they lost their rudder, and the stern of the vessel was torn to pieces. Buffeted by the wind, the *Yahata Maru* was swept eastward by the current. The sea pounded the ship, and the sailors scrambled to bail out water. Kumajiro, certain they were about to sink, ordered the mast cut down.

The weather cleared, but with no rudder or mast the *Yahata Maru* was helpless and carried farther by the current. On the ninth day they ran out of what little rice they had and had to survive on salted trout. The sailors were able to gather a bit of rainwater to drink and rinsed the trout in seawater before eating them, but the salt remained and they suffered terribly from thirst.

They'd been drifting for two months, suffering from hunger and thirst, when the first crew member died, on November 28. It was the helmsman, Katsunosuke, and they buried his pitifully emaciated body at sea; on December 5 a second man, Nishinosuke, drew his final breath.

The new year came, and that morning the owner of the ship, Zentaro, lay cold and lifeless. He had owned three ships that plied the waters between Niigata and Matsumae. On February 2 Kumajiro died, then on the twelfth Tatsunosuke, and on the twenty-sixth Jirokichi. In March Iwajiro passed away, then the cook Ichibei, in April Yujiro and Sokichi, then on May 2 Iwakichi died, and after that Yunosuke was left the lone survivor.

His throat was terribly swollen from eating only salted trout, as were his lips. He gathered rainwater and used the ranbiki device to filter seawater, but his condition deteriorated to the point where he couldn't drink anything.

On May 14 he fashioned a harpoon, speared a passing dolphin, and with his last ounce of strength hauled it aboard, but found his throat was so swollen he couldn't swallow any of the meat.

On June 17 he began to drift in and out of consciousness, and lay prostrate on the deck. He heard the faint sound of a boat coming up alongside, then saw foreign men peering down at him. They lifted him and put him in their boat and took him to their sailing ship. This was the American cargo ship *Emma Parker.*

Hikozo, in English laced with Japanese, related Yunosuke's tale to Thomas, who at his desk wrote down the whole account.

As Yunosuke told his tale of one sailor dying after another, Hikozo had to wipe away tears. Tears rolled down Jisaku's cheeks as well, and even Thomas had to blow his nose often. When Yunosuke finished, silence filled the room for a time. Clearly Yunosuke had been miraculously snatched from the jaws of death.

The captain entered the cabin.

"I've never heard a more terrible story," Thomas told Pease tearfully, and passed him his notes. Pease read the notes with a grim face and took a deep breath.

"It really is a terrible tale. They went through hell," he muttered, tears in his eyes. He went over to where Yunosuke was sitting and gently patted his shoulder.

Pease had been ordered by Sanders, the head of revenue, to report to him on the story behind Yunosuke's becoming a castaway, so he asked Hikozo, who was able to converse in English, and Thomas to come with him. Together with Yunosuke, furoshiki bundle in hand, they left the ship.

On their way to the revenue office they passed a clothing store, and with Pease's permission Hikozo went inside. The rough outfit he'd been wearing since China was beginning to wear thin in places, and he felt embarrassed to meet the head of revenue in such wretched apparel. He selected a navy-blue wool frock coat, vest, and trousers and paid twenty-two dollars for them. It was more than he planned to spend, but he was happy since it was his first time using the money he'd earned. He changed into the new clothes then and there and looked at himself in the mirror. He barely recognized himself.

The revenue office was a three-story stone building near the wharf, and when they went upstairs, Pease pushed open a thick door at the top. A bearded, broad-shouldered man in his fifties sat behind a large desk, and he urged them to take seats. This was Sanders, the head of revenue.

Sanders began to read the notes that Pease handed him. A young woman in a white apron brought in tea and quietly left.

He looked up, and was silent for a while. He turned to Yunosuke and said, his eyes pained, "Physically, how are you now?"

Hikozo translated, and Yunosuke, bowing deeply, said, "Thanks to all of you, I'm very well now."

Glancing over the notes again, Sanders questioned Yunosuke about several points. Unable to catch all the English, Hikozo turned to Thomas for help, then translated the questions for Yunosuke, and Yunosuke's replies.

Sanders asked Yunosuke what he had wrapped in the furoshiki, and they laid the contents out on the table. There were Japanese coins, one each of gold, silver, and copper, and Sanders and Pease, curious, turned them over in their hands. There were also a plaque with the name of the ship on it, a crepe de chine cloth, and a ship's compass in a box, which particularly caught the eye of Sanders and Pease. They were fascinated by these things, and as they exchanged a few words in low voices, they glanced at Yunosuke from time to time.

They discussed Yunosuke. Pease proposed that the man's clothes and living expenses be paid out of public funds. Sanders replied, "We must do everything we can for castaways," and directed that Yunosuke be put under the care of the *Argus*.

As they stood to take their leave, Sanders pointed to Hikozo and said something to Pease. Thomas, who was listening, turned to Hikozo and in faltering Japanese said, "The revenue chief says he wants you to live in his house." He went on in English: "He wants you to go to school and receive an education."

"That's a wonderful idea," Pease said, his eyes sparkling, and urged Hikozo to accept.

Hikozo, confused by the sudden proposal, replied that if the lady who owned the boardinghouse he worked at would give her permission, he'd be happy to accept. "Leave the lady to me," Pease said with a smile.

After they left the revenue office, Hikozo parted from the others and returned to the boardinghouse.

He told the owner about Sanders's proposal and said he'd like to quit his job. The lady looked troubled. Not wanting to let Hikozo, a diligent worker, go, she said she'd raise his salary to forty-five dollars a month if he stayed in her employ.

Hikozo thanked her for her kindness but said it wasn't a matter of the salary. He wanted to receive an education, and this was a chance he couldn't let pass by. The lady understood, and thanked him again for his faithful service to her.

Having quit his job at the boardinghouse, on June 15 Hikozo began work at the revenue office. Pease and Thomas came by that day, and Thomas told him what his duties would be. Hikozo was to attend to the revenue chief's needs, making sure his newspapers and letters were in order; after explaining all the things that had to be done, they left.

In addition to his duties at the revenue office Sanders ran a private bank together with an investor named Branam. After Sanders showed this bank to Hikozo, in the evening they returned to Sanders's home, a place surrounded by beautiful flowers. Hikozo took up residence there.

In the mornings he went with Sanders by carriage to the revenue office, and after a day's work would return home with him, have supper, and sleep in his comfortable bed. His life now had changed so completely that he felt he'd become a real gentleman overnight, and he spent every day happy and content.

The story about Yunosuke spread and ended up as a feature story in the *San Francisco Times*. The reporter interviewed Pease, and the article began by saying that the *Emma Parker*, on its way to Tahiti recently, had run across a foreign ship adrift, and a solitary survivor on board, at latitude 28°50′, longitude 158°40′.

The article went on to say that the cook on the *Argus* (Jisaku, in other words) "was a Japanese who had also been rescued in the past and who helped by interpreting to clear up various points. One sailor on a patrol vessel, named Thomas, also understands a little

Japanese, and with the help of both men we were able to ascertain the following."

After this were the details of Yunosuke's story, how twelve men had been set adrift, with only one surviving. The name of the owner of the vessel, Zentaro, came out *Jin-tha-ro* in the English article, while the captain's name, Kumajiro, was spelled *Koo-ma-gi-ro*.

Concerning Yunosuke himself the article stated, "He appears an intelligent man, and seems amazed by everything around him. He's recovered from the terrible ordeal he went through, and has completely regained his health."

The article also described Hikozo, in the following way: "Besides the cook mentioned above, there is also a fifteen-year-old Japanese boy [his actual age was sixteen by this time] who was rescued three years ago," who was with Pease. The article mentioned some of the things Yunosuke had with him, and concluded with a description of the compass: "It's a finely wrought instrument that has only 24 graduations on it. Twelve of these have marks on them."

Hikozo had one of the employees at the revenue office read the article to him, and was embarrassed to hear that he'd been mentioned in the newspaper.

CHAPTER TWELVE

I~~N~~ THE MIDDLE OF JULY, Sanders announced that he wanted to take Hikozo back east, where his wife was living in their home. Hikozo and he boarded a merchant ship out of San Francisco and arrived in New York. The harbor was crowded with countless steamships and sailing vessels, the shore packed with buildings, some five stories high.

Two-horse carriages awaited the passengers at the wharf, and Hikozo joined Sanders on one of these and went into town. The wide roads were all lined in stone, the sidewalks crowded with men and women, and on both sides of the road, like a castle wall, towered an unbroken line of tall buildings. Seeing Hikozo gazing around at everything, Sanders said that New York was the business capital of America and boasted a population of eight hundred thousand.

Their carriage came to a stop in front of a five-story stone building, the Metropolitan Hotel. Hikozo was astounded at how beautiful everything was inside. The floor was covered with soft carpeting, and there were marble pillars and splendid chandeliers hanging from the ceiling.

Sanders registered at the front desk, and then a black man carried their luggage and escorted them to a room on the fifth floor.

The room included a bedroom, bathroom, and toilet, and a large mirror on the wall. There were glass windows with gauzy flower-patterned cloth (curtains) that made Hikozo feel he was seeing flowers through mist.

Sanders said he was going to send a telegraph to inform his family, who lived two hundred miles to the southwest, in Baltimore, that he would be returning the next morning, and he took Hikozo down to the basement.

There Sanders wrote something on a piece of paper and handed it to a man in a black suit. The man nodded, sat in front of a machine next to the wall of the room, and, running his eyes over the paper, lightly moved his fingers in a tapping motion. A *click-click-click* filled the room.

After they left the room and were walking back up the stairs, Sanders said that in twenty minutes he would receive a reply by telegram. Sure that there was no way a reply could come that quickly, that Sanders must be joking, Hikozo smiled to himself.

But sure enough, twenty minutes later a man from the front desk came and handed Sanders a slip of paper. Sanders read it aloud:

Pleased at your safe arrival in New York. Everyone is fine here. We'll clean the house and meet you at Baltimore Station tomorrow.

Hikozo was struck dumb. He could hardly believe it—how in the world could a telegram fly faster than any bird?

The sun was setting, and the room grew dark. A black boy came, went over to a lamp next to the wall, and turned a brass pipe with three holes in it. Gas rushed out, and the boy struck a match and lit it. The light was much brighter than any candle, and looking out the window Hikozo could see that, with all the lamps lit along the street, it was as bright as daytime outside.

They went to a large dining hall, which was also bright with gas lamps, and Hikozo and Sanders dined together.

The next day they took a carriage to New York Station. Sanders told Hikozo they would be taking a steam train. At the station they found a locomotive with a smokestack and a great number of passenger cars attached. Hikozo followed Sanders into one of these. Inside were seats on either side of an aisle, and he and Sanders sat down.

After a while they heard blasts from the locomotive, and the train began to move. Slow at first, it gradually picked up speed, until the people working in the fields outside raced by like birds in flight. The train shook, but not enough to prevent a person from reading.

The locomotive made many short stops, and finally at noon, in the midst of a broad, treeless plain, they came to a halt. In brick buildings nearby people were selling food, and Hikozo and Sanders got off the train, purchased bread and meat, and ate lunch.

After an hour the train fired up again and resumed its journey. Sanders leaned against the window and fell asleep.

The train pulled into Baltimore Station. As they alighted from the train, sure enough, as Sanders had said, his brother-in-law was waiting with a carriage, and Hikozo now knew for sure that Sanders hadn't been joking. He didn't know how words written on a slip of telegraph paper could fly that fast but was convinced that America possessed awe-inspiring machines.

Hikozo climbed into the carriage with Sanders. When they arrived, they passed through an iron gate and into extensive grounds full of trees. The house itself was a two-story stone structure surrounded by beds of flowers.

As the carriage pulled up to the front door, Mrs. Sanders, along with a number of servants, came out to greet them. Sanders had already written to her about Hikozo, and with a warm look in her eyes she beckoned him to come inside.

During the time he spent at the Sanders's residence, Hikozo learned more about Sanders's personal life. The couple had no children and lived alone, but three years ago Mr. Sanders left Baltimore for San Francisco, which was booming, and with Mr. Branam opened a bank by pooling their funds.

He had come home to prepare for a business trip to Russia. Taking note of all the uses ice was being put to—in cooling and in helping reduce the high fevers of sick people—he'd hit upon the idea of purchasing large quantities of ice from Russia and had negotiated to be the sole importer of Russian ice. To do this, though, he would first need to quit the very busy post of revenue head. Thus he'd returned to Baltimore in order to travel to Washington, the seat of government some 110 miles southwest of his home, where he planned to hand in his resignation and secure a passport for travel to Russia.

"Hiko," Sanders said, "I'll take you with me to Washington."

Washington, Hikozo knew, was the equivalent of Edo, where the shogun resided, and just hearing that made his heart leap with excitement. Working for Sanders had opened up his world in new and exciting ways, and he knew he was experiencing far more than Jisaku and Kamezo back in San Francisco. Sanders began to prepare for the journey, and Hikozo, too, packed a bag.

Two days later, they took a carriage back to Baltimore Station.

As they waited there, a steam locomotive, billowing smoke, pulled into the station and came to a stop. Hikozo followed Sanders into one of the passenger cars and sat down. The train began to move and picked up speed.

Suddenly it struck Hikozo that he might be the very first Japanese ever to ride in such a conveyance. As far as he knew, the only Japanese in America besides himself were Jisaku, Kamezo, and Yunosuke. They were on the *Argus* and the *Ewing*, at anchor back in San Francisco, and wouldn't have the opportunity to ride in a steam locomotive. He thought about how dumbfounded the villagers back in Hamada would be if he went back and told them about this adventure.

How strange that someone like himself, a mere cook on the *Eiriki Maru*, was now sitting in a carriage pulled by a steam locomotive, on his way to the nation's capital. As he looked outside at the scenery, he felt he was in a dream.

Broad farm fields stretched out along the railroad tracks all the way to the horizon, without any mountains or even small hills visible. Occasionally, on the arable land, he could see clumps of trees, but that was all. Only a few farmhouses dotted the landscape, which meant that each farm was huge.

The train pulled into the Washington station in about two hours. They took a carriage to the Arlington Hotel. The hotel was an imposing six-story brick structure, and their room was on the third floor. It was a beautiful room, with a toilet and bath attached.

The next morning, after breakfast, Sanders said, "I'm going to see the president now."

"President?" Hikozo had never heard the word before.

"The head of our country," Sanders explained. "I'll take you with me."

Hikozo shrank back at these words. In Japan the head was the shogun, who lived in Edo Castle. He was such an exalted person that ordinary people never saw his face, the kind of person whose very presence would make one tremble.

"I don't want to go," Hikozo said, frightened.

"Don't worry. I'll be with you," Sanders said.

Hikozo seemed to have no choice, so he nodded.

He took his best suit of clothes out of his suitcase and changed, then stood before the mirror and combed his hair. They left their room and got into a two-horse carriage in front of the hotel.

The carriage proceeded down the street, the horses' hooves clicking against the stone pavement. They went down Pennsylvania Avenue, along a low stone wall, until they came to a gate, which they passed through, then they stopped in front of a white, two-story building. Sanders got out, walked up the stone steps to the front door, and knocked.

A man just past middle age, dressed in black, opened the door, and Sanders proffered his calling card. The man took the card, politely asked them to wait for a moment, and disappeared inside. After a short while he returned and said, "Please come in," motioning them inside.

He led them to a high, thick door, opened it, and went inside, then offered them seats and disappeared again. The room was at least fifty mats wide, with another room of equal size farther in. In that room a fortyish man was puffing away on a cigar while talking with two other men, apparently guests of his.

Hikozo found it all exceedingly strange. Sanders had said they were going to visit the *head of our country,* and Hikozo had imagined such a man's residence as a grand citadel; other than its size, this building differed little from Sanders's Baltimore home. The gate was iron but quite ordinary, and there were no sentries—one just drove one's carriage inside the grounds. With the *head of the country* you'd expect a great number of servants, but there was no sign of any, and no guards either.

Hikozo looked at the man in the far room as he conversed with his guests. The man was obviously the head of this household, but he wore a plain dark suit and didn't look at all imposing. Had he misheard Sanders's words?

The guests stood up and shook the man's hand, came toward them, nodded at Sanders and Hikozo, opened the door leading to the entrance, and left. The man they'd been conversing with stood up and motioned Sanders into the far room, and Hikozo followed.

Exchanging a few words with Sanders, the man shook his hand. Turning to Hikozo, Sanders introduced him, explaining how he was a Japanese castaway who'd been rescued and whom he'd brought from San Francisco. The man seemed surprised to hear this, questioned Sanders, and approached Hikozo and shook his hand. The man was of medium height, with a gentle look, apparently a very pleasant gentleman.

He motioned for them to take a seat; Sanders sat down, but Hikozo withdrew and stood in a corner of the room. As he stood looking out the window at the Potomac, Sanders and the man conversed. They talked as equals, and again Hikozo found it hard to believe that the man was the leader of all America. In Japan even a minor official would be more imposing, more dignified, and certainly would never shake hands with a sixteen-year-old former ship's cook like himself and ask him to take a seat. A laugh occasionally arose from Sanders and the man, and, as was his habit, apparently, the man slapped his knee as he laughed.

Their business concluded, Sanders motioned to Hikozo, who left the window and came over to stand by him. The man turned a gentle eye on Hikozo and said something to the effect that since he was so young, if he went to a government-run school at public expense he could be of great service.

Sanders replied, "I plan to put him in school at my own expense," turning down the man's offer.

Nodding, the man again shook Sanders's hand, then Hikozo's, and the two of them exited to the waiting carriage.

As the carriage left the gate, Hikozo asked, "Who was the man you were just speaking with?"

"The president," Sanders replied. "The highest leader in America, equivalent to the emperor in Japan. His name is Franklin Pierce."

As he bounced along in the carriage, Hikozo still couldn't believe that the man he met held such an exalted position. The man lacked dignity, not to mention guards and servants. His way of living was too plain and humble. In Japan, even ordinary officials had attendants, and one had to go through all sorts of ceremony to approach them, while it would have been impossible for him to even catch a glimpse of the face of a daimyo, let alone the shogun.

President Pierce had accepted Sanders's resignation as head of revenue for San Francisco. He'd also agreed to issue him a passport for Russia, and Sanders picked it up at the appropriate office. His tasks all taken care of, Sanders and Hikozo took the train back to Baltimore.

He began to prepare for his trip to Russia, and even after the New Year was still busy writing letters and getting documents in order. He would have liked to take Hikozo with him but decided it would be better for the boy to stay home and attend school.

To Hikozo, Sanders was like a father, and it made him sad to part from him.

Sanders left on January 17. Hikozo watched as his carriage disappeared down the driveway.

Three days later, he was taken by Mrs. Sanders's younger brother to begin attending a Catholic school, where he was enrolled and entered the dormitory. There were 150 to 160 pupils in the school, some who commuted, some who lived in the dormitory. There were a headmaster and teachers, one teacher in charge of each class. The teacher in charge of Hikozo's class was Mr. Waters.

At school they studied English reading and writing, astronomy, geography, arithmetic, and music. Able only to converse and write some rudimentary letters, Hikozo was at first overwhelmed, but Mr. Waters kindly kept him after class to tutor him. Hikozo was grateful to him, and even after returning to his room he continued to review his lessons.

His classmates were all younger than he and very kind to him. Japan wasn't included in their geography textbook, and the boys, curious about Hikozo's homeland, crowded around him during recess to talk with him. They also helped him with his lessons.

Being with them every day, Hikozo made great strides in speaking English, while his reading and writing slowly but surely improved.

Classes ended in June, and summer vacation came and the dormitory students all went home, including Hikozo, who returned to the Sanders home. The weather was blazing hot.

Every summer the Sanderses escaped the heat by traveling to a farm run by Mrs. Sanders's mother, and Hikozo went with them by carriage to this farm, seven miles away on a high plain. Tilled fields stretched as far as the eye could see, and the farm had fifty cows and twenty-five horses, with forty blacks working there, as well as other men and women.

Mrs. Sanders's mother was over eighty but spry and very much in charge of the farm. When Hikozo paid his respects, she said, "You're very welcome here," and shook his hand. Her hand was soft and warm.

The next day one of the servants brought a cup with white liquid and ice cubes floating in it, as well as sugar, and urged Hikozo to drink it.

"What is it?" Hikozo asked, and the servant pointed out the window to the cows far off and said, "Cow's milk."

Hikozo waved a hand in front of his face and grimaced. In Japan the meat of animals was considered unclean, and drinking animal milk was out of the question. Since he refused, the servant returned the cup to its tray and took it from the room.

The servant apparently reported this to the lady of the farm, who soon appeared, with the servant, again with the cup on the tray.

"When a baby's mother can't give milk, they use cow's milk to feed the baby. It's very good for you, so drink up." Her words were insistent, almost an order.

Not wanting to disobey her, Hikozo picked up the cup, closed his eyes, pinched his nose shut, and drank. The liquid went down his throat. He opened his eyes. The drink was better than he'd imagined, and he drank it all down.

"How is it?" the old lady asked, looking intently into Hikozo's eyes.

"I had no idea it was so delicious," Hikozo said, to which she replied, "I'm so pleased!"

On the first Sunday after arriving at the farm, the whole family went to church, and they took Hikozo with them. The old lady and the family went by carriage and had Hikozo follow them on a horse.

A black servant brought around a large, chestnut horse, and Hikozo, trembling in fear, helped by the black man, mounted. With the black servant holding the reins, the horse followed the carriage. Hikozo enjoyed watching the farm from horseback and the gentle undulation as the horse moved.

Two months went by, and Hikozo and his family left the farm to return to their home in Baltimore, and he began the new term at school.

Sanders had meanwhile come back from Russia. He reported to them that he'd won the sole distributorship for Russian ice for the whole West Coast and had also been appointed paymaster for the Russian naval forces assigned in San Francisco.

In order to take up this appointment he had to return to San Francisco and planned to take Hikozo with him.

Fall was deepening, the leaves turning beautiful colors.

Their departure was set for November 1, and Hikozo submitted his notice of withdrawal from school and returned to the Sanders home from the dormitory. The time in school had seemed so short, yet he'd vastly improved not only his English conversation but also his ability to read and write the language.

Mrs. Sanders was a devout Catholic, and three days before they were to depart, she told him something quite unexpected. Before he left Baltimore, she wanted him to be baptized.

Having left Japan when he was thirteen, Hikozo wasn't aware of the shogunate's prohibition of Christianity. To him Christianity in America was just the country's religion, as Shinto and Buddhism were in Japan. Mrs. Sanders had been so kind to him, paying twelve silver coins a month to allow him to study at school, so Hikozo accepted her request without protest. Mrs. Sanders, overjoyed, took Hikozo in a carriage to the church.

A gentle-looking priest came out, nodded as he listened to Mrs. Sanders, then escorted Hikozo into a small, boxlike room, where he asked him some questions, which Hikozo politely answered.

When they'd finished, the priest took out a book (the Bible) and began reading the names of people written in it, asking Hikozo to choose his baptismal name from these. Hikozo was flustered. The names were all foreign to him, and he had no idea which to choose. Americans nicknamed him Hiko, but he thought of himself as Hikozo and saw no need for a baptismal name.

The priest, starting to get impatient, pointed to one spot and said, "Joseph," and looked at Hikozo.

This name was different from the others he'd read—it sounded gentle and familiar, somehow. Realizing this must be one of the customs of the church, Hikozo knew he should go along with it. He said, "I think that will do."

The priest nodded, brought Hikozo up to the altar, and had Mrs. Sanders stand beside him. The priest sprinkled Hikozo with holy water and in a solemn voice said he baptized him as Joseph. Hikozo and Mrs. Sanders worshipped at the church, then took the carriage home.

When Sanders heard from his wife about the baptism, he said, in a low voice, "So—you're now Joseph Hiko."

For dinner that night they had some special dishes Mrs. Sanders prepared to celebrate the baptism. Before they ate, Mrs. Sanders put her hands together and prayed, and Hikozo followed suit. Praying with them made him feel peaceful, as if he'd finally settled into life in this vast country.

Joseph Hiko, he whispered to himself.

CHAPTER THIRTEEN

On the morning of November 1, Hikozo and Sanders went to the Baltimore Station and took the train back to New York.

They stayed at the Metropolitan Hotel and waited for a steamer for San Francisco. They had to wait for days until a suitable ship was available. Hikozo was glad to return to San Francisco, for he had happy memories of the place where he first set foot on American soil; also, his fellow crew members from the *Eiriki Maru,* Jisaku and Kamezo, were there, as well as his good friend Thomas.

Their ship entered San Francisco Harbor on November 28, and Hikozo settled into Sanders's home there.

The next day he went down to the harbor, where he met Thomas, then Jisaku and Kamezo. They all commented on what a fine young gentleman he'd become, how both in dress and the way he carried himself he'd become completely American. In Hikozo's eyes, too, Jisaku and Kamezo now fit right into life in this foreign country.

When Hikozo asked how Yunosuke was doing, the answer took him by surprise.

Yunosuke had found a job working on a storage ship in San Francisco. A merchant and shipowner, Silas Burrows, became very interested in him after reading the feature story about him in the newspaper. Burrows did a lot of business with China by ship, and hit on the idea of delivering Yunosuke back to Japan. It was such an unexpected opportunity that Yunosuke burst into tears when he heard of the plan.

Burrows knew that ten months earlier the Perry fleet had again gone to Uraga and had concluded a treaty of friendship between Japan and the United States, and that two ports, Shimoda and Hakodate, were now open to outside trade. Burrows was already planning to take his sailing ship, the *Lady Pierce,* to Hong Kong and thought he would stop at Shimoda on the way and let Yunosuke off there. He had Yunosuke transferred from the storage ship to the *Lady Pierce.*

The *San Francisco Times* reported how kind and generous Burrows was in planning to repatriate Yunosuke free of charge. When Jisaku and Kamezo learned about this, they doubted that Japan would actually accept Yunosuke when he arrived at his homeland. Japan and America might have concluded a treaty of friendship and opened Shimoda, but the ink on the treaty was barely dry, and it was questionable whether the Japanese would welcome the *Lady Pierce.*

The *Lady Pierce,* with Yunosuke aboard, left San Francisco Harbor on April 15, with eighteen aboard: Burrows; the owner, aged sixty; his son, aged fifteen; a Dutch interpreter named Berry; the captain; and a crew of thirteen sailors and a cook. The ship stopped at Hawaii, where it took on coal, water, and provisions, then continued west.

At 10 AM on the morning of June 17, people in Edo Harbor saw a foreign sailing vessel, its sails filled with a strong southerly wind, quickly enter the harbor, and they reported this at once to the Uraga commissioner's office. The vessel passed Uraga and finally anchored. The commissioner's office immediately dispatched a boat that carried Sasakura Kiritaro, police supervisor in charge of foreigners, and Hosokura Toragoro, along with the interpreter Tateishi Tokujuro. This foreign ship, of course, was the American merchant vessel *Lady Pierce.*

Through Berry, Burrows told the officials that there was a Japanese castaway on board and that his purpose in coming to Japan was to bring this man back to his homeland. Accompanied by the captain, Yunosuke came out on deck. As soon as he came face to face with Sasakura and the others, he prostrated himself. The Japanese official taking notes described Yunosuke in this way: "His head is shaved bald, and his clothes are those of the other place" (i.e., America).

Sasakura questioned Yunosuke about his background, and his reply, also noted in the record, said he was "Yunosuke, twenty-three, born in the Year of the Tiger, in the domain of the Uesugi clan in Itagai Village, Iwafune County, in Echigo Province [modern-day Niigata Prefecture], a sailor on the *Yahata Maru*, owned by one Zentaro."

Since the only two ports open to foreign vessels by the friendship treaty were Hakodate and Shimoda, Sasakaura directed them to make for Shimoda. However, since there was a strong wind against them, it was impossible for them to leave Edo Harbor, so they had to stay put for the time being. The commissioner's office sent a special courier to inform their counterparts in Shimoda of the impending arrival of a foreign ship.

The next day the wind and rain were too strong, so the *Lady Pierce* remained at anchor.

The day after this, the rain stopped and the skies cleared, but the southerly wind showed no sign of abating, and the ship was lashed by waves. They were getting low on drinking water, so Burrows applied to the officials to supply them with water, but when they made inquiries in Edo, they were commanded not to comply since the treaty allowed for supplies to be given to foreign ships only in the ports of Shimoda and Hakodate. Burrows repeated his request, pleading for water, and the commissioner's office reluctantly gave them twenty barrels of water, three hundred chicken eggs, a bag of sweet potatoes, and 120 bundles of firewood.

On the twenty-second there was finally a favorable wind, so the *Lady Pierce* was able to leave Edo Harbor for the open sea.

Two days later, the *Lady Pierce* again entered Edo Harbor and anchored off Uraga. His suspicions aroused, Sasakura went out again to the ship. Burrows told him that they'd tried to approach Shimoda, but with no wind and swift currents, they were unable to enter the harbor and had to turn around.

The captain requested a pilot on board to guide them, and the commissioner agreed and had Usui Shinpei and Tsuchiya Eigoro of his office, plus three sailors familiar with the route between Edo and Shimoda, put on board. The next day, the twenty-fifth, at 8 AM, the *Lady Pierce* once again raised anchor and left Edo Harbor.

The ship made good progress, reaching the sea just outside Shimoda Harbor, but again the wind died, and they came to a halt. The commissioner ordered eighteen rowboats to fasten lines to the ship, which they then towed into the harbor. It was past noon when the *Lady Pierce* anchored.

The commissioner's office dispatched the police supervisor Gohara Isaburo and the interpreter Hori Tatsunosuke to the ship. The Uraga commissioner had received a report on the purpose of the ship's visit, and Gohara conveyed to Burrows the gratitude of the commissioner for going so far out of their way to bring a castaway home.

Gohara wanted to meet Yunosuke, and Burrows brought him. Yunosuke prostrated himself, his forehead pressed against the deck. In a gentle voice Gohara told him not to fear, that they would most definitely take him back. Yunosuke, bereft of words, sobbed aloud.

Burrows asked to be allowed to go ashore and see the town. The treaty had a provision allowing Americans to walk in a seven-ri (approximately seventeen-mile) radius around the town of Shimoda, so the magistrate gave his permission. However, he told them the conditions: they should purchase nothing, enter no homes, and when they heard the temple bell toll 6 PM, they were to head back to their ship immediately.

Agreeing to this, Burrows got into a boat with his son, the captain, their interpreter, and Yunosuke and went ashore. Accompanied by police official Saito Sonoshin, they rested at the Ryosenji Temple, then strolled about the town, and finally hurried back to their ship in order not to violate the curfew.

The next day, Isa Shinjiro, administrative head of the commissioner's office, came on board the *Lady Pierce* with an interpreter and secretary to question Yunosuke more closely.

Yunosuke stated how he had been a sailor on the *Yahata Maru*, which was wrecked and drifted until he was the only one of twelve crew members still alive, how he was rescued by an American ship and taken to San Francisco. This was all taken down at great length in the official record of the interrogation.

Yunosuke also related that he was the son of a farmer named Juzaburo and had lived with his parents and younger sister, but his father died of an illness when Yunosuke was eight. Since he was too young to become the head of the family, his aunt took a husband, who then became the family head. When Yunosuke became an adult, he felt bad about having his aunt's family take care of him, so he left home at age nineteen and became a sailor on the *Yahata Maru*.

Crying, Yunosuke entreated Isa Shinjiro, "I want to see my old mother and sister again as soon as I can, and I beg you to be merciful and allow me to return quickly to my hometown." This statement was also recorded in the record of the investigation.

The next day Yunosuke was handed over from Burrows's keeping to the care of the commissioner's office.

Burrows said, "Yunosuke has long wanted to wear proper Japanese clothes again. I'd like to see him in those clothes, too, and request that I be allowed to." He said this in English, which his interpreter Berry put into Dutch, which Hori Tatsunosuke then put into Japanese for Isa.

Isa agreed, and took Yunosuke with him as he left the ship.

Isa's questioning of Yunosuke continued after they arrived at the commissioner's office. Afterward, they allowed him to bathe and have his forelocks shaved and hair done up in a chonmage topknot. They decided that it would reflect badly on Japan to have Yunosuke's rough appearance represent the way Japanese dressed, so he was given an expensive kimono and cloak, and a narrow-banded obi sash with an undersash, so he looked like a typical high-born gentleman.

The commissioner's office invited Burrows to the Ryozenji Temple, where Isa brought Yunosuke. When Yunosuke was brought before him, the American tearfully said, "How splendid!" over and over, gazing deeply into Yunosuke's face as he shook his hand in a strong grip.

To express their thanks to Burrows, the commissioner's office wished to give him whatever items he was in need of, but the ship lacked nothing, so Burrows was presented with ten sacks of rice and wheat, porcelain, and fabrics. In return he gave the commissioner's office books, maps, liquor, and sweets.

His goal in Japan now accomplished, Burrows decided to head for Hong Kong, where he had business. The commissioner's office allowed Burrows, his son, the captain, and the interpreter once more to meet Yunosuke at the Ryozenji Temple. Yunosuke, in English, tearfully thanked Burrows for all he had done, and Burrows, also with tears in his eyes, gave Yunosuke a farewell hug.

The next morning the *Lady Pierce* set sail and disappeared over the horizon.

The officer in charge of handling the *Lady Pierce* was Gohara Isaburo, but the official in charge of protocol was Isa Shinjiro, so it was he who dispatched the official report of the handling of the matter to the commissioner of foreign affairs in Edo.

Once the *Lady Pierce* had departed, Isa's role was over, but he still took a great interest in Yunosuke, which he also noted in his report to the foreign-affairs commissioner, praising the sailor in the highest terms, writing, "The man is exceptionally intelligent, as different from an ordinary seaman as day is from night," praising also his humble nature.

What especially caught Isa's interest was Yunosuke's knowledge of the "American language." In addition to being able to read and write Japanese, Isa noted, Yunosuke was also "able to some extent to understand American writing."

Hori Tatsunosuke was of course able to converse and even read and write fluently in Dutch, but his knowledge of English left something to be desired. Isa ordered Hori to question Yunosuke in

English, which Hori did, falteringly, to which Yunouske promptly replied in English. At the Ryozenji Temple, when Hori and Burrows had spoken together in English, whenever Hori couldn't quite catch Burrows's meaning, Yunosuke added a word of explanation. Isa had also observed Yunosuke freely conversing with crew members on the *Lady Pierce.*

Isa called in Hori and asked him whether he thought Yunosuke would be of help as an English interpreter.

Hori replied, "With some training I believe that he would soon be of use," adding that Yunosuke had an outstanding grasp of English and freely admitting how his help had been invaluable in helping him understand Burrows.

At the time the only Dutch interpreter really able to understand English conversation was Moriyama Einosuke. He had learned English conversation from an American of Indian descent, Ronald McDonald, who had washed ashore in Japan.

Knowing all this, Isa thought Yunosuke's language skills should be put to use and in his report to the foreign-affairs commissioner wrote that Yunosuke had "for the past two or three years been abroad (in America)," and asked for instructions as to whether or not to send Yunosuke to Edo to act as an "American interpreter."

Isa urged Yunosuke to accept a post as English interpreter, but Yunosuke begged to be allowed to return home as soon as possible, and the foreign-affairs commissioner, sympathetic to his wish, turned him over to the Uesugi family, the head of the domain that included his hometown, and Yunosuke went home.

Hikozo, who like Jisaku and Kamezo had no idea that the Japanese had taken Yunosuke back in Shimoda, was sure that he would never be allowed to land in Japan.

He'd heard that with the treaty of friendship between Japan and America the two ports of Hakodate and Shimoda were now open to foreign ships, but he thought these were merely items in a treaty that wouldn't be put into actual practice, or at least not right away. The stance of the Japanese government—the way they fired on the *Morrison,* with Otokichi and the other castaways on board, to chase them away—surely couldn't change overnight. Even if Yunosuke wasn't fired on, Hikozo couldn't imagine that they'd let him in the country. Most likely the castaway was put off in Hong Kong, Hikozo concluded, and taken care of by Rikimatsu or someone like him.

Hikozo began working at the bank that Sanders and Branam owned, helping around the office. Near the end of that year, at Sanders's recommendation Hikozo entered a commercial school run by an Englishman and took classes in reading and composition, as well as accounting.

Soon after the New Year of 1855 (Ansei 2), Hikozo read a small article in the *New York Times* of the previous October about the *Lady Pierce*. He was astonished. According to this, when the *Lady Pierce* anchored in Shimoda in Japan, the officials there were quite surprised to find the castaway Yunosuke on board, and received him with great happiness. The officials and townspeople were deeply grateful to the owner of the ship, Burrows, for bringing Yunosuke back to Japan without asking for any recompense. Burrows was also quoted as saying, "Bringing a castaway back like this does much more to help friendly relations with Japan than sending any official mission."

Hikozo took the paper immediately to Jisaku and Kamezo; when he read the article to them they looked at each other in amazement. They found it hard to believe but didn't think that newspapers lied, so Hikozo and the others knew now that the Japanese government's policy on foreign countries had changed drastically.

They wanted to find Burrows and ask him for more details, but the reporter had interviewed Burrows while the *Lady Pierce* was heading toward New York, its exact whereabouts unknown.

After they'd calmed down a bit, the three of them talked it over. If Japan accepted Yunosuke, it surely would let them return. The question was how to return. They'd have to be patient as they searched for a way. Smiles came to all three of their faces.

Now that he knew there was hope he could go home, Hikozo calmly applied himself to his studies. Thanks to Sanders's kindness, he was fortunate enough to be able to go to school, and since it seemed like he'd be in America for a while yet, he figured he needed to make a living on his own. To survive in American society he'd have to be able to read and write English well, besides learning the intricacies of business. If he could return to Japan, now that the country was open to the outside world, the knowledge he'd acquired in America would serve him in good stead. Hikozo was eighteen now and prudent enough to start giving careful consideration to his future.

Unfortunately, though, he had to give up being a student in November of that year. A financial panic occurred in San Francisco and other areas, and the bank that Sanders ran with Branam had to suspend payments and close up. Sanders, worn out trying to raise funds, said to Hikozo, "I'm very sorry, Hiko, but I can't pay your tuition anymore."

Fortunately, a friend of Hikozo's, the son of a businessman, sympathized with his plight and paid his tuition so he could continue in school. His friend's father, though, was soon caught up in the recession, and at the end of March Hikozo finally had to withdraw from school for good.

He went to see Sanders to ask for help in finding a job. Sanders was running a business with his friend but didn't have the resources at the time to hire anyone new, but he did find a position for Hikozo at the Macondray Company.

Hikozo began working on April 5, commuting from Sanders's home. The company was a large commission firm with four partners that received goods on consignment from all over the world. Many people worked under the manager, and the place was quite lively. Hikozo enthusiastically went to work, helping with a variety of tasks around the office. By autumn he felt comfortable in his job, and one of the partners, Mr. Cary, took a liking to him and sometimes invited him out to eat.

Jisaku, now able to converse freely in English, left the revenue cutter *Argus* and went to work at Wells Fargo in town, while Kamezo left the survey vessel *Ewing* to work on a merchant ship that sailed between San Francisco and China. He hoped that on this ship he would find an opportunity to return to Japan someday.

Hikozo often met Jisaku, and made friends with an American named Van Reed. Reed worked in a trading company, and his dream was to go to Japan and do business with the Japanese. To this end, he had Jisaku and Hikozo tutor him in their native language.

THE YEAR 1857 (ANSEI 4) saw Hikozo, confident now at his job, enjoying life.

Spring was over and the days were getting warmer when Senator Gwin visited the company. Hikozo had been introduced to the senator before, when Sanders was the chief of revenue and Hikozo worked in the revenue office.

Hikozo wondered why the senator was paying him a visit, a question that was answered when the senator said, "I'm going to Washington on very important business, and I'd like to take you with me. This will definitely work to your advantage."

"I'm happy working here at the company," Hikozo demurred, "and don't want to quit. Mr. Sanders has been more than kind to me, and I can't go against his wishes. You'll need to talk things over with him."

Gwin nodded and left. Afterward he sent a letter to Sanders, who showed it to Hikozo. The letter urged Hikozo to come to Washington to obtain a post as a clerk at the State Department. With the knowledge about America this experience would give him, Hikozo could be of great service when he returned to Japan. His not being a citizen might present a stumbling block but should not prove an insurmountable obstacle. The letter was dated August 3, 1857, and signed William M. Gwin.

After Hikozo read the letter, Sanders said to him, "Hiko, I think it best that you go with the senator to Washington. A whole new future might open up for you."

Hikozo nodded. "I'll do whatever you think is best."

Sanders sent a letter to Gwin giving his approval, and Hikozo began preparing for the trip to Washington.

He first went with Sanders to see the manager of his company to submit a letter of resignation, then visited Jisaku and Van Reed as well to say good-bye. They held a farewell party for him, and though he enjoyed the wine, he felt sad to leave these friends.

On September 20 Gwin came to collect Hikozo, and they boarded a ship that sailed out of San Francisco. Gwin told him that he had a house in Washington and that Hikozo needn't worry about anything since his wife would see to his needs.

They arrived in New York on October 7, and Hikozo and Gwin took separate rooms at the Metropolitan Hotel.

The next morning a middle-aged woman, judging by her attire obviously a woman of quality, appeared at his room, accompanied by a tall gentleman. This was Mrs. Gwin, who'd come up from Washington.

She said, "Please go with this gentleman to get a suit of clothes made for you."

"I brought a change of clothes with me," Hikozo replied, "so please don't go to any trouble on my account."

Mrs. Gwin insisted that since Hikozo was going to meet some highly placed people in Washington, his present clothes were not suitable. She turned to the tall man and said, "Take him to a fine tailor and shoe store and see that he's fitted for a suit, shirts, and boots." Hikozo couldn't ignore her kind intentions in presenting him with these things, so he followed her instructions.

He left the hotel with the man and went to Broadway, where at a tailor shop he was measured for a suit; next they went to a shoe store where they purchased boots. The whole bill came to seventy-five dollars, which the gentleman paid. Before he set out for Washington with the Gwins, Hikozo went to the tailor to pick up the suit that was ready for him.

The next morning he took a carriage with the Gwins to New York Station. On the way he thanked the Gwins for the suit and shoes.

A steam locomotive took them to Washington, and a carriage waiting at the station took them to the Gwins' residence, a beautiful two-story dwelling on a large plot of land, surrounded by a thick stand of trees. Hikozo was given one room to use. The house was filled with maids and manservants.

About a week later, a letter Sanders had written to Gwin concerning Hikozo was published in the local newspaper. This letter related how at age thirteen Hikozo, a cook on a Japanese ship, had been cast adrift and rescued by an American vessel, taken for a time to China, then back to San Francisco, and how he'd gone to school and was now working in a commission firm.

Why did Gwin publish the letter in a newspaper? Clearly he wanted to arouse interest in Hikozo among influential people in Washington before they even met him.

As Gwin had hoped, the article caused a stir. America and Japan might have concluded a treaty of friendship, but for Americans Japan was an unknown country, and they'd never set eyes on a Japanese before. According to Sanders's letter in the newspaper, a twenty-year-old Japanese man, whose baptismal name was Joseph Heco (for this was how Hikozo spelled it), was now among them.

Everyone was excited by this news, and hordes of people visited the Gwins to meet this young man; they shook his hand and showered him with presents. Hikozo was also invited to dinner parties, where he wore his new suit of clothes and boots. People all turned a curious eye on him, shook his hand, and peppered him with questions. He sipped wine and answered their questions with a smile.

On the morning of November 25, Gwin took him by carriage to the State Department. They entered an enormous building, and after passing through a series of doors, a robust man in his fifties came out to greet them. This was General Cass, the secretary of state, to whom Gwin introduced Hikozo. General Cass said he'd read all about Hikozo in the newspaper, and greeted him warmly.

Next they were shown into the office of William Hunter, acting undersecretary of state and chief clerk, and Hikozo was introduced to him. Gwin wanted these men in high positions to become aware of who Hikozo was, a task he accomplished, as both were pleased to meet him.

After they left the State Department, Gwin took Hikozo to the White House.

They had an appointment, so they were shown at once into a large reception area. Four years earlier, Sanders had taken Hikozo to meet President Pierce, and at the time Hikozo, noting the spare lifestyle of the man, hadn't completely understood the high position the president occupied. Now, though, he knew full well that the president was the highest political leader in the land. So, about to meet Pierce's successor, President Buchanan, Hikozo could barely contain his nervousness.

A large man in his seventies, dressed in black, sat behind a solidly built desk, and when he saw them coming toward him he stood up and walked over to greet them. One of his eyes was bad, and he held his head tilted at an angle.

President Buchanan shook Gwin's hand, and as Gwin introduced Hikozo, the president nodded and extended his hand, and Hikozo introduced himself and shook the president's large hand. The president invited them to take a seat, and sat down himself; Gwin sat opposite him, while Hikozo remained standing.

Gwin began with the purpose of their visit. Japan had now opened itself to the outside world, and America would be having numerous diplomatic and trade missions with this land. If Hikozo could take a post as clerk in the State Department and gain first-hand knowledge of the workings of the American government, when he returned to Japan he would be of great service to the United States. "I'd like to see him employed by the State Department," Gwin added, "and ask your help in obtaining the position."

The president nodded and said, "I'll discuss it with the secretary of state. If there is an open position, I would be happy to appoint your young friend."

Their business concluded, Gwin thanked the president. They shook hands all around, and Gwin and Hikozo exited the White House.

On the way back, riding in the carriage, the thought struck Hikozo that it must be highly unusual for a Japanese to have shaken the hands of two presidents, Pierce and Buchanan, as he had done. He didn't realize that he was the first Japanese ever to meet an American president let alone two.

The cold weather continued, as Hikozo stayed in Gwin's home, doing secretarial tasks—putting newspapers in order, filing letters, even sometimes, at Gwin's direction, writing short letters in reply to ones he'd received.

No word came from either the president or the secretary of state, and even after the New Year came, there was no word from them. Gwin said nothing about the matter.

As before, Hikozo had many visitors, and he became acquainted with many people in the capital. One person in particular he got to know well was Lieutenant John M. Brooke. Lieutenant Brooke planned to survey the uncharted coasts off China and Japan and take soundings to measure the depth in the Pacific Ocean. Naturally government support was a necessity in such an undertaking, and the lieutenant was confident that since it would eventually profit his country, such support would be forthcoming. He promised Hikozo that when his survey became a reality, he would appoint Hikozo as the expedition's clerk and use his good offices to help Hikozo get back to Japan.

Hikozo was overjoyed at this unexpected proposal and entreated him to allow him to join the expedition.

He was growing tired of living with the Gwins. He'd come all the way to Washington on the promise of a position as clerk in the State Department, but months passed with no reply, and the chance of success seemed more and more remote. The secretarial work he did for the senator was too trivial to bother over.

He was also a bit dismayed by Senator and Mrs. Gwin's lifestyle. They were quite well off, with extensive plantations in the South and countless slaves. Mrs. Gwin was a mainstay of Washington high society, often holding balls and dances. She fairly threw away money on expensive clothes and jewelry but was cold toward her servants and paid them poorly. Hikozo was promised thirty dollars a month, not much more than what a servant received, and he wanted to find a position that would pay better.

On February 15 he went to Gwin's office and asked to be let go. Gwin, a blank look on his face, nodded and casually said, "I'll give you fare back to San Francisco."

Hoping to join Lieutenant Brooke's expedition, Hikozo didn't want to go back to San Francisco but planned to wait in Baltimore for Brooke's directions. The Sanderses lived in Baltimore and could be counted on to welcome him warmly and assist him. He also had plenty of friends and acquaintances there, and surely through their good offices he'd find some sort of employment to tide him over.

When he told Gwin this, the senator said, "That's a good idea. I'll write a letter of introduction to the collector of the Port of Baltimore. I'm sure he'll help you find something, even if it's a temporary position." He quickly wrote the letter and handed it to Hikozo. In it he said that Hikozo was an intelligent young man of good character, hardworking and honest, and that it was his wish that the collector secure a position for him.

Hikozo decided to leave the next morning and asked that he be paid his monthly salary. Gwin agreed and gave him a written statement of accounts. The total salary from the previous September to the end of February came to $150, from which he subtracted $55 for meals for the five months, leaving $95. On top of this, $75 was subtracted to pay for the new suit and boots Hikozo received, leaving him a mere $20.

Hikozo was dumbfounded. He'd been taken away—indeed,

almost compelled—to leave his job at the commission firm, a job he thoroughly enjoyed, put to work for five months, and all he ended up with was twenty dollars! He had met many friendly, kind Americans but never anyone as cold as Gwin, though the man was a United States senator.

Without a word he took his twenty dollars and left.

The next morning he went to Washington Station and took a train to Baltimore. Arriving at Baltimore Station, he searched for the collector's office, met him, and handed over the letter.

The collector read it and said, "Unfortunately we don't have any vacancies at present, so I can't offer you a position." He handed the letter back.

After he left the collector's office, Hikozo was incensed. Gwin had no authority to order the collector to do anything; he had written this pointless letter merely out of a sense of guilt over paying Hikozo so little. Hikozo felt a loneliness sweep through him like an icy winter wind.

He couldn't afford to take a carriage, so he walked the long road to the Sanders home, buffeted by the wind as he struggled with his heavy suitcase. He finally arrived at the front door of this home he knew so well. He knocked, and the door was opened by a manservant who looked at Hikozo and then ran back inside. Exhausted, Hikozo dropped his suitcase at his feet.

Footsteps sounded inside, and Hikozo was surprised to see Mr. Sanders come out along with his wife. Sanders spread his arms wide and gave Hikozo a big hug. Mrs. Sanders was delighted to see him. Sanders, an arm around Hikozo, led him into the living room.

Hikozo hadn't expected Sanders to be there. Sanders told him that he'd settled his business affairs in San Francisco and returned home.

Hikozo sat down and told them all about his time with Gwin.

Sanders shook his head and said, "That's the kind of a useless fellow he is. He makes promises and then never carries them out." He fairly spat out the words. "But I can't tell you how happy I am to see you here again, in my very own home!" he went on, tears in his eyes. "Please consider this house your own and stay here as long as you like."

Hikozo, himself tearful, thanked Sanders deeply. His own father had died when he was young, so he had no memory of what he looked like, and though his stepfather, Kichizaemon, had treated him like his own son, Hikozo felt that his real father was this man seated before him, who'd always treated him so affectionately and with such concern for his future. Mrs. Sanders, too, was a warmhearted person, and Hikozo felt completely at ease in their home.

The immediate problem was that he'd used up almost all his money. Of the twenty dollars Gwin had given him, he'd used all but two on traveling to Baltimore and other expenses. The Sanderses would provide meals, of course, but with no cash he was stuck where he was.

He thought to ask Sanders to help him financially but realized he shouldn't. Sanders had said he'd settled his affairs in San Francisco, but what this really meant was that he'd gone bankrupt. From whispered conversations between the couple Hikozo gathered that Sanders, a victim of the financial panic, had started a small company to recoup his losses, but this too failed. Forced into liquidation, he had returned to Baltimore.

Hikozo asked among his group of friends and acquaintances in Baltimore to find a job, but Baltimore itself had been badly hit by hard times, and work was not to be found.

Signs of spring began to appear, with flowers blooming in the flower beds, but Hikozo was in a gloomy state.

One morning he received a letter from a T. C. Cary in Boston, someone he'd never heard of. The letter stated that he was the father of the Mr. Cary who was one of the partners in the Macondray Company Hikozo worked for after leaving school in San Francisco. The younger Mr. Cary had often invited Hikozo out to eat, and Hikozo had grown quite attached to him.

According to the letter, the younger Mr. Cary was off on business in China and had expressed his concern about how Hikozo was faring. He said that if Hikozo was in need of funds, his father should send them, payable on his account. The son didn't know Hikozo's exact whereabouts but said that if his father sent the letter in care of Mr. Sanders, it would surely reach Hikozo.

Hikozo was astonished that Mr. Cary, his former employer, had worried about him so much that he'd sent a letter to his father about him from halfway around the world.

He wrote an immediate reply to T. C. Cary. He thanked his son for worrying about him, and the father for forwarding the letter, adding that as far as money was concerned, he would take advantage of their generous offer. Hikozo felt a warm glow at this touch of human kindness.

His good fortune continued when he received a letter from Lieutenant Brooke on June 1.

The letter stated that the navy had officially approved Brooke's expedition to survey the coasts of China and Japan, that Hikozo would be appointed clerk of the expedition, and that Brooke would see to it that Hikozo was taken back to Japan. Hikozo read the letter over and over. With Japan now open to the outside world, he might very well—like the castaway Yunosuke—stand on his native soil once again.

He felt a rush of joy course through him, and he bounced around the room, letter in hand.

The letter went on to say that the expedition planned to assemble and depart from San Francisco, with more information to follow in a later letter. In a postscript the lieutenant added, he assumed that Hikozo would be traveling to San Francisco to join them there.

Realizing that he'd need a fair amount of money to cover the passage to San Francisco, Hikozo wrote to the elder Cary, explaining the situation and asking for a loan. The reply came with a bank draft enclosed. Mr. Cary's letter stated that if Hikozo needed more, he had only to ask. Hikozo wrote back a reply thanking Mr. Cary for the bank draft.

He showed the letter from Lieutenant Brooke to Sanders, who with his wife was delighted that Hikozo's dream would finally come true.

Hikozo made preparations to leave soon, but after dinner Sanders made an unexpected remark that alarmed him. Sanders was of course aware that Yunosuke had been allowed back in Japan, but with a concerned look he said, "In your case, Hiko, something else worries me."

The Japanese government continued to ban Christianity, and even though the country was open to the outside world now, there had been no reports that this ban was lifted. Frowning, Sanders said, "My wife regrets now having taken you to a Catholic church and having you baptized."

Hikozo felt the blood rush from his face. When he was baptized, he figured it was only natural that, living in America, he become a Christian, which is why he followed Mrs. Sanders's suggestion. Afterward he heard about how evangelizing Christianity in Japan was forbidden, and stories about people in Japan being forced to trample on boards carved with the image of Christ in order to prove they weren't Christians. They said that the first thing the returned castaways were grilled about was whether or not they had become Christians in their time abroad. Yunosuke must have been questioned about the same thing in Shimoda and compelled to step on the sacred image.

Hikozo had received baptism in a Catholic church and been given the baptismal name of Joseph Heco. It might be possible to conceal this fact, but if some visiting American happened to let the secret be known, he'd surely be sentenced to death for breaking the ban.

"I've given this some thought," Sanders said quietly, "and I think it would be best if you were naturalized."

"Naturalized?" Hikozo had not heard the term before.

"It means taking American citizenship. If you're an American, you should have no problem entering Japan even though you're a Christian."

Hikozo didn't know what to say. He felt strongly he was a Japanese, born and bred, that his real name was Hikozo, not Joseph Heco. He had no desire to become an American.

"What do you think?" Sanders said, gazing into his face, but Hikozo was speechless.

It was something he'd never considered. Of course, he was more than grateful for being rescued by an American ship and for being so warmly taken care of by Sanders and many other Americans. But he'd never once imagined himself becoming an American.

Unnerved, he blinked. The image of his mother's face rose before him. If she were alive and heard this news, she'd faint from the shock. She'd lament his decision to give up being a Japanese; it would be a blot on their ancestors' names. She might even take her own life at the news.

Hikozo stood and paced the room. Who would have thought that getting baptized would cause so great a problem?

Sanders came over to him and laid a hand on his shoulder.

"Hiko. Everyone in every country is the same. Citizenship isn't a major issue. Your taking American citizenship won't change the fact that you're Japanese. You're worried about this because Japan was a closed country. But things have changed—it's not closed anymore."

Sanders paused, watching Hikozo intently.

"What's important now is getting you back to Japan. If you become naturalized, everything will go smoothly. Why don't you sleep on it tonight?" He patted Hikozo's shoulder, walked away, and quietly left the room.

That night Hikozo lay in bed, pondering. Sanders hadn't said much, but it made perfect sense. Sanders himself was the citizen of a country that had thrown its gates wide open to the world, so it was easy for him to say that citizenship was not a major factor. But was that really the best way to consider the issue?

Your taking American citizenship won't change the fact that you're Japanese. This remark touched him to the core. He might have his hair cut short in the American fashion, wear Western clothes and boots, and eat American food every day, but he was still the same Japanese man he'd always been.

With the Japanese government ban on Christianity, becoming naturalized might well be the safest way to return to Japan. Ever since Hikozo showed him the letter from Lieutenant Brooke, Sanders had been racking his brain to make Hikozo's dream come true. He cared about Hikozo as if Hikozo were his own son. The most important thing, he'd said, was getting back to Japan. Indeed, that was the one hope Hikozo had cherished since his shipwreck, and now, after all these years, it was about to come true. No matter what the sacrifice, he must get home.

I'm going back to Japan! he shouted inside himself.

Tears welled up in his eyes, and his whole body trembled.

The next morning, after breakfast, Hikozo told Sanders he had decided to be naturalized.

"That's wonderful. Everything will go smoothly now," Sanders said, repeating his words of the night before, nodding for emphasis.

Sanders had already looked into the procedures for becoming naturalized, and told Hikozo they'd be going to the Baltimore district court. Mrs. Sanders, when she learned that her making Hikozo get baptized was proving an obstacle to his return home, had become quite depressed, but once he declared his intention to take citizenship, she looked relieved.

Hikozo changed into street clothes and got into a carriage with Sanders. The carriage drove down the streets of the city, coming to a stop in front of the district court. Inside, Sanders spoke with the clerk of the court, a Mr. Spicer. Spicer nodded, stood up, and returned with some documents that he placed in front of Sanders and Hikozo.

Sanders signed the part calling for a guarantor, while Hikozo filled in the name Joseph Heco in the column for the applicant. Spicer left the room with the documents. The two men waited. All the while Hikozo kept repeating to himself: *Though I'm taking American citizenship, I'll always be a Japanese. It's just a necessary step to get me home.*

Spicer returned and said, "Your application is accepted. Here's your certificate. I hope you'll be a good, conscientious citizen of the United States of America." He handed the certificate to Hikozo; it was signed by both Spicer and United States District Judge Gill.

Spicer offered his hand, which Hikozo shook, as did Sanders.

As they boarded the carriage that had been waiting for them, Hikozo thought about what had taken place, and was surprised at how simple it had been.

"I'm very happy, Hiko. There will be no problem now," Sanders said, his eyes fixed on the road ahead.

When they returned, Hikozo placed the certificate in one of his bags.

An official document arrived from Lieutenant Brooke appointing Hikozo as captain's clerk of the expedition. The opening of the letter stated that this was an official appointment made by the secretary of the navy, adding that Hikozo should take the mail ship departing New York on July 5 for San Francisco and report in as soon as he arrived. The letter was signed Lieutenant Brooke, leader of the expedition.

Hikozo felt the tears welling up at Lieutenant Brooke's kindness toward him. This appointment was his ticket home.

A postscript from Lieutenant Brooke said that he and his officers and crew would be preceding Hikozo from New York to San Francisco and that he'd left instructions with his younger brother, who worked in Customs, to help Hikozo obtain passage on a ship; Hikozo was to rendezvous with his brother.

Excited, Hikozo went to Sanders and showed him the letter.

"Congratulations," Sanders said, giving Hikozo a hug and a pat on the back. As he let Hikozo go, tears glistened in his eyes.

With his departure imminent, Hikozo went to say good-bye to various friends and acquaintances. He went to see them one by one, thanking them for all their kindness to him, and to wish them farewell. They held a round of farewell parties and teas for him.

To make the steamer leaving on July 5, Hikozo needed to board a train leaving Baltimore on the evening of the third. On the evening of the second, Sanders held his own farewell dinner, where Hikozo enjoyed the dishes Mrs. Sanders prepared especially for him, and wine as well.

After dinner he sat across from Sanders and had a nice talk with him, puffing on a cigar.

"Tomorrow's the big day, and there's just one more thing I want to tell you," Sanders said quite formally.

He began by saying that he had not been able to give Hikozo the kind of education he'd hoped to. He talked about how, when he visited President Pierce, the president had suggested placing Hikozo in a public university. What he meant was putting Hikozo in West Point, but Sanders said no. Though West Point provided an outstanding education, it was too narrowly focused; it would be better to attend a private university, where Hikozo could study a broader range of subjects, which would serve him in good stead later in life.

"My bankruptcy meant we had to cut short your education, which I regret very much." In a pensive tone he continued: "I've written a letter to you about my thoughts. I'd like you to read it only after you're on the train."

The next morning, Hikozo checked his bags, packed the minimum amount of things in his trunk, only what was essential. In the afternoon he said good-bye to all the servants, while his luggage and trunk were loaded onto the carriage.

The train to New York was at 5 PM, so Hikozo and Sanders left by carriage thirty minutes earlier. Mrs. Sanders and the whole domestic staff came out to see him off, and Hikozo bid them all farewell and waved as the carriage began to move.

On the way to the station Sanders said, "Here's the letter I spoke of last night," and handed Hikozo a thick envelope.

At the station he gave Hikozo a hearty handshake and said, "Farewell, my boy. I'll be praying for you."

Hikozo felt a warmth rising in his chest. In this foreign land Sanders had taken care of him even more than a real father would have, seeing to his education and daily needs. A wave of sadness struck Hikozo when he realized he might never see this kind old gentleman again.

The departure time came, and Hikozo boarded the train and leaned out the window. The train began to roll out of the station, and Sanders, his eyes bright with tears, waved his hand for all he was worth, and Hikozo waved back. Soon Sanders's figure faded into the distance and disappeared.

Hikozo settled into his seat and opened the envelope.

The letter was surprisingly long, starting with the period five and half years before, when they first met in San Francisco, covering Hikozo's entrance into school, Sanders's bankruptcy, the unfair treatment Hikozo received at the hands of Senator Gwin, and how happy Sanders was when Hikozo returned to his home in Baltimore. Sanders wrote how he always felt like a father to Hikozo, and that Hikozo had always repaid this by being honest, honorable, loyal, and grateful, highly trusted and respected by his friends and all who knew him.

The letter ended with the expression of Sanders's regret at parting with Hikozo but said that thoughts of Hikozo's bright future cheered him. "From the bottom of my heart I pray for your prosperity and future happiness," he wrote.

When he finished reading the letter, Hikozo hung his head and sobbed. He was overwhelmed by how much Sanders cared for him.

He thought of how Sanders had no children of his own. Back in San Francisco, when he was the collector, when they first met and he took Hikozo into his home, Sanders must have felt the young boy was like his son. As they grew to know each other more, this feeling deepened. His wife, too, came to look on Hikozo as her own child. The letter contained more love toward him than one might expect to find in a letter from a parent to a child.

Holding the letter, Hikozo wiped at his tears.

CHAPTER FIFTEEN

Hikozo arrived at three the next morning at New York Station and went to the Metropolitan Hotel, where he took a room. After breakfast he went to the Customs House to meet Lieutenant Brooke's brother.

As Lieutenant Brooke had written in his letter, his brother knew all about Hikozo. He gave him $300 that the navy had provided for his trip, and instructed him to board the steamer *Moses Taylor*. The fare to San Francisco was $300 for first class, $200 for second class, $150 for third. Hikozo told him he'd go by second class.

The lieutenant's brother was kind enough to go to the office of the president of the Pacific Mail and Steam Ship Company, the firm that owned the *Moses Taylor*, to request that it make an exception and issue Hikozo a first-class ticket for the price of a second-class one. The president, however, wouldn't bend the rules and refused this request.

Hikozo thanked the lieutenant's brother for his kindness and returned to the hotel.

The *Moses Taylor* was set to depart the next day, but since this was the Fourth of July holiday, the departure was delayed a day. On the appointed day Hikozo went to the harbor and boarded the ship. As he stood on deck and gazed down at the streets of New York as the ship began to move, he thought that this was the first step in a journey that would—after all those years—take him home.

Just then a loud voice called out: "Hiko! Is that really you?" A man in a captain's uniform came toward him and shook his hand. This was McGowan, the first officer on the *Polk*, the ship that Hikozo had been transferred to after being rescued and brought to San Francisco. It turned out that he was the captain now of the *Moses Taylor*.

McGowan left Hikozo for a short time, but once the ship was safely out of the harbor, he returned and invited him to his quarters. He knew that Hikozo was holding a second-class ticket, and called in the chief purser and directed him to prepare a first-class cabin for him.

McGowan reminisced about their times together, asked Hikozo what had transpired in his life since they last saw each other, and listened intently as Hikozo responded. The ship was scheduled to travel to Aspinwall, where passengers bound for San Francisco would then take a train over the isthmus of Panama and board the *Sonora* for the final leg of the voyage.

"The captain of the *Sonora*, Bobie, is a good friend," McGowan said. "I'll go with you to Panama and introduce you."

Under Captain McGowan's careful watch, the voyage was smooth. Hikozo was able to take his meals at the captain's table, the best seat in the ship, and the food and service were outstanding. He enjoyed his cabin and comfortable bed, and after breakfast he strolled the deck and gaze out at the sea.

At dawn the next day they reached Aspinwall. Hikozo had breakfast with McGowan and afterward went ashore and boarded the train, which took them across the isthmus.

The steamer *Sonora* was anchored in the harbor, and McGowan took Hikozo to it and introduced him to Bobie, the captain.

"Please do everything you can to make his trip a pleasant one," McGowan said to his friend.

"I'd be happy to. Leave everything to me," Bobie replied, happy to help out.

McGowan waved and got off the ship, and returned to his own vessel, anchored in Aspinwall Harbor.

Captain Bobie called in the chief purser, introduced him to

Hikozo, and ordered him to prepare the finest cabin for him. The purser nodded, and Bobie escorted Hikozo to a first-class cabin.

The *Sonora* left Panama Harbor, heading west, then turned north. Hikozo dined at the chief purser's table, second in rank from the captain's, and the fare was as delicious as it had been on the *Moses Taylor.* Both the captain and the chief purser were very much interested in Hikozo's having been a castaway from Japan, and he was often invited to the captain's quarters to talk about his experiences.

Soon the other first-class passengers, having heard about Hikozo from the captain and chief purser, began to come over and greet him in a friendly way. Whenever Hikozo strolled on deck, a circle of other passengers would form around him. After dinner, people often invited him to join them for a drink and to relate all his adventures.

The passengers were eager to learn more about Japan and the Japanese. All they knew was that Japan was an island country in the Far East that Perry's expedition had visited, and they were convinced it was quite primitive. Hikozo explained how the country was divided into han, or domains, each of which was ruled by a daimyo, and how the shogun ruled over them all. Hikozo's listeners were impressed that Japan had a political structure not unlike that of the United States, with the president as its head.

When they asked him about schools in Japan, Hikozo replied that there were small private schools, called terakoya, all over the country, and that over half the Japanese were literate, a statement that the passengers found incredible. They just couldn't believe that Japan was such a culturally advanced country.

Hikozo became very popular, and he enjoyed the time spent with the other passengers.

The ship continued north, and after a smooth voyage Hikozo could see San Francisco off the bow of the ship. The *Sonora* anchored in the harbor on July 29.

Hikozo took a room in a hotel and, as Lieutenant Brooke had instructed him, went to the naval dockyard at nearby Mare Island

and reported to Brooke, who was busy getting his ship fitted out as a surveying vessel.

The lieutenant was happy to see him and asked him to wait in the city until they were finished outfitting the ship, at which time he would come get him.

Hikozo returned to the city and went to the Wells Fargo Company to see his old shipmate Jisaku, who was employed there. Jisaku was overjoyed to see him and, as if he'd been waiting all this time to tell him this news, related the following unexpected story.

On June 4, nearly two months before, the collector's office had informed them that a British vessel, the *Caribbean,* had arrived in port with what seemed to be a dozen Japanese castaways aboard, and Jisaku was asked to ascertain if they were indeed Japanese. Van Reed, who worked now at a trading company and was able to speak some Japanese, was also asked to investigate, and came to see Jisaku.

Not sure what to believe, both were escorted by a customs official to the ship.

The castaways were brought out on deck, and Jisaku knew at once that they were Japanese. They had on filthy, torn kimonos, tabi and zori sandals, and their hair was done in a topknot.

Hands placed on their knees, they bowed deeply to Reed and Jisaku, clearly thinking that Jisaku, too, must be an American. When he began speaking to them in Japanese, their eyes went wide and they were struck dumb for a moment. Jisaku told his own story as a castaway and explained how he'd come to be working here in San Francisco.

The customhouse needed a written report on these men, so starting on this day, Jisaku went several times to the *Caribbean* and together with Van Reed listened to the sailors' tale, then reported it in English to a customs clerk, who wrote it down in an official record.

These sailors were the crew of the *Eiei Maru,* captained by Shichisaburo from Handa Village, Chita County, in Owari Province (present-day Handa, Handa City, in Aichi Prefecture). The ship had set sail from Handa on November 2 of the previous year Ansei

4 (1857), with a cargo of rice, sake, vinegar, miso, mirin, lumber, tiles, and sundries. They put into port at Kishu Obama (present-day Obama, Toba City, in Mie Prefecture), had a favorable wind early on the morning of the thirteenth, and set off again toward Shimoda, but then ran into a strong westerly wind. They were lashed by rough waves, their rudder was destroyed, and they could no longer maneuver. Tossed about by the wind and waves, the ship was in danger of sinking, so they cut down the mast and tossed much of the cargo overboard.

The dismasted ship was carried farther and farther east. They had 660 sacks of rice so were in no danger as far as food was concerned and could slake their thirst somewhat by gathering rainwater.

The fifth year of Ansei dawned, and the ship continued to drift, buffeted at times by storms. On April 7, after five months of drifting with nothing but the sea visible all around them, they spied a white sail on the horizon but coming closer. This was the British merchant vessel *Caribbean,* which rescued all twelve sailors, including Shichisaburo.

The *Caribbean* was on its way from China to San Francisco. In addition to its cargo it was crowded with some five hundred Chinese aboard, but the ship's captain, Captain Winchester, saw to it that room was made for the castaways in the crew's quarters. The captain was kind to them, providing them with clothes, hats, and boots; he made sure they were well fed, and came often to check on how they were doing. He recommended that they cut off their top-knots, but Shichisaburo refused.

The ship entered San Francisco Harbor on July 15 (June 5 of the Japanese calendar), and the Chinese all debarked and the cargo was unloaded.

When Jisaku went to see the castaways, a reporter for a local newspaper went with him. The reporter was quite interested in their story and wrote an article about it that was reprinted in the *New York Times.* Jisaku handed Hikozo the article.

The article took up a good portion of one page and began by relating Jisaku and Van Reed's visit to the *Caribbean* and their meeting with Shichisaburo and the others. It went on to describe in detail the condition of the castaways. Their appearance was presentable, the article said, "the majority of them with ordinary features, while a handful were quite handsome." Their kimonos and tabi and zori sandals were introduced as exotic items, and the article mentioned how their topknots were different from the queues worn by Chinese.

Captain Winchester, interviewed, said, "These men are neat and orderly.... They've tried to make themselves useful around the ship, and I've been impressed by their agility [when they help trim the sails]." Naturally the Japanese sailors did not know English, but the captain remarked that through gestures and signs they were able to communicate and that "through their expressions as they listened to our queries" it was clear they were able to grasp most of what was being conveyed to them.

The Japanese crew took with them from the *Eiei Maru* a compass, ceramics, a musical instrument (a samisen), many books, and a cat. The article went on to list particulars about the ship's captain *Chiszab* (Shichisaburo), age thirty-eight, with a wife and two children and his parents still alive. The first mate, Daizo (the newspaper spelled it *Dhidho*), was listed as thirty-five, married, his parents also still alive and well.

"I'd like to meet these men," Hikozo said, raising his eyes from the paper.

"They're not here now," Jisaku replied as he took it back from Hikozo and folded it. "The *Caribbean* took them north with Chinese and other foreigners who are going to work the gold mines. Captain Winchester said they'd be back in San Francisco by the middle of August."

"I wonder if they'll really come back," Hikozo said worriedly, looking intently at Jisaku.

"I wouldn't worry about that." Jisaku explained why. The article about the *Eiei Maru* castaways had drawn quite a reaction among the citizens of San Francisco, who were sympathetic to their desire to return home. With the treaty of friendship now concluded between America and Japan, the repatriation of these men would deepen the friendship between the two countries, and with their firsthand experience of America they would be able to strengthen mutual understanding. In fact, a signature campaign had begun among the citizens to petition the government to return the men to Japan; a petition addressed to President Buchanan had already been sent to Washington.

Captain Winchester, one of those backing the campaign, assured Jisaku he would bring the crew of the *Eiei Maru* back to San Francisco.

Hikozo was relieved to hear that and waited at his cheap lodgings for directions from Lieutenant Brooke, sometimes going out to Mare Island to see how the refitting of the surveying ship, the *Fenimore Cooper,* was progressing. The *Cooper* was a former pilot ship, a small schooner of ninety-six tons belonging to the navy.

Hikozo often met Jisaku and Van Reed but couldn't see his friend Thomas, who was off in the gold fields, or Kamezo, who worked on a cargo ship that sailed along the California coast.

The days were blazing hot, with occasional thunderstorms shrouding the city.

The *Caribbean* returned on August 19. Hikozo went with Jisaku to the ship and met Shichisaburo and the others. He was hit by a wave of nostalgia when he saw that the men still had their hair done up in topknots. They were all freshly shaved and appeared clean and neat.

Hikozo went many times after this, alone, to the *Caribbean* to see the crew of the *Eiei Maru*. He tried to cheer them up by telling them about Yunosuke, the castaway who'd taken an American ship to Shimoda and been welcomed back by the Japanese.

A reply to the petition came from President Buchanan, but it was less than they had hoped for. The president wrote that he could not dispatch a special ship to take the castaways back to Japan but would provide for their fare once they found a suitable vessel for the return trip.

The citizens involved in the petition campaign met several

times to discuss the matter, finally deciding that since the *Caribbean,* the ship that had originally rescued them, would be heading for Hong Kong, it could also take them to Japan. Hikozo, however, wondered whether they'd be able to make their way that far.

On September 20, a message from Lieutenant Brooke told him that the refitting operation was done and he should make preparations to transfer to the ship. Two days later the *Cooper* arrived in San Francisco Harbor, and Hikozo went aboard.

On that very same day the *Caribbean* left San Francisco with the twelve Japanese castaways, and Hikozo anxiously watched from the deck of the *Cooper* as the other ship left the harbor.

The *Caribbean* sailed west across the Pacific, arriving in Hong Kong on October 4 of the fifth year of Ansei. There Shichisaburo and the others went ashore. A British man who could speak Japanese took care of them, and when they went to the local government office there, they found Rikimatsu, the former castaway, who interpreted for them. According to the written record left by one of the *Eiei Maru* crew, a sailor named Tokutaro, "This man [Rikimatsu] seemed to despise Japan" and still held a deep-seated grudge for being driven away while on board the *Morrison.*

On October 14 the crew of the *Eiei Maru* left Hong Kong on a British steamer, which made a port of call in Fuzhou, arriving in Shanghai on October 27. In Shanghai they were taken care of by Otokichi, the former castaway of the *Hojun Maru.* According to a contemporary account of castaways, Otokichi was living the wealthy life of a rich daimyo.

On November 11 their ship left Shanghai bound for Nagasaki and arrived on the fourteenth. The British had gone to great pains to repatriate these twelve men, their purpose being to improve relations between Japan and Britain.

The following day the castaways were handed over to the Nagasaki commissioner. They were treated well by the officials and taken to stay at the Taishoji Temple rather than the usual holding facility. Each was in turn handed over to samurai from their home provinces, except for Shichisaburo, who, on July 25 the following year, just before he was to return home, succumbed to the epidemic of cholera then sweeping Nagasaki.

Meanwhile the *Cooper,* with Hikozo aboard, continued across the Pacific, carrying out depth measurements of the ocean as it went. It arrived in Honolulu on November 9 and anchored in port for a time for repairs and maintenance.

Hikozo enjoyed going ashore and strolling around the town, but on the twentieth he heard from Lieutenant Brooke that an American whaling vessel, the *Hobomac,* had arrived in port carrying some Japanese castaways. Hikozo, greatly surprised to hear that there were castaways in Hawaii, had a boat take him over to the *Hobomac.* The castaways were named Kantaro and Kihei.

According to them, on December 10 of the previous year (Ansei 4) they had left Edo on the three-hundred-koku vessel *Shinryoku Maru,* which hailed from Kamesaki Village, Chita County, in Owari Province (present-day Kamesaki, Handa Village, in Aichi Prefecture). The ship had a crew of five, including the captain, a man named Genya.

On the way back to Owari they ran into a storm and were set adrift; in February of the following year (1858) they were rescued by the American whaling ship *Chas. Philippi.* Along the way they came across another American whaling vessel, the *Hobomac,* and the latter being shorthanded, Kantaro and Kihei were transferred to it. They worked on this vessel until they arrived in Hawaii. The *Shinryoku Maru* was spotted because of the recent influx of American whaling ships using Hawaii as their base of operations.

Kantaro and Kihei put their hands together in supplication, begging Hikozo, now fluent in English, to help them to return to Japan. Hikozo, himself going home, searched his thoughts for a way to make their wish come true.

Since coming to Hawaii, he had made the acquaintance of the attorney general of the Hawaiian Kingdom, a man named Bates, so he approached him in this matter. Bates told Hikozo that he'd heard that a Dutch vessel, the *Godean,* was planning to stop in Nagasaki on its way to China, and he took him to the ship. Hikozo asked the captain of the vessel to take Kantaro and Kihei with him as far as Nagasaki, and the captain was happy to oblige.

The next day Hikozo and Bates went to the *Hobomac* to ask its captain to allow Kantaro and Kihei to leave the ship. Quite pleased with the two honest, hardworking men, the captain accepted Hikozo's proposal. Kantaro and Kihei shed tears of joy when they heard the news, bowing repeatedly to Hikozo and Bates.

The two sailors boarded the *Godean* and set off for Nagasaki. They arrived there on January 28 of the sixth year of Ansei and were handed over to samurai representatives of their home provinces.

The number of whaling ships in the harbor continued to increase, until there were some fifty moored there. Their hunting grounds being frozen over in the winter, the ships were waiting until spring in the warm waters of the Hawaiian Islands.

Hikozo heard that yet another Japanese castaway was aboard one of the vessels in port, and he went to meet him. He met the captain first and told him he'd come to see the Japanese man, to which the captain replied, "Oh, you mean Tim? That's him," pointing to the one scrubbing barrels of whale oil.

Hikozo approached the man and said, "I'm a Japanese, and my name is Hikozo. I heard there was a Japanese on board, so I came over. What is your name?"

The man's eyes were fearful, and he got to his knees. Hikozo had spoken to him in Japanese, but since he was wearing a naval uniform, complete with brass buttons, as well as a naval cap with gold stripes, the man couldn't believe Hikozo was really a fellow countryman.

When Hikozo explained that he had once been a castaway and was now on his way back to Japan on a naval ship, the man calmed down. Hikozo asked him how he came to be rescued by a whaling vessel, and the man, still kneeling before him, said his name was Masakichi, and told his story.

Masakichi was from Awaji Island and had been a sailor on the *Sumiyoshi Maru*, a six-hundred-koku vessel that sailed between Awaji and Kishu (present-day Wakayama Prefecture). The captain of the ship was Yoshisaburo, and he had a crew of only three, including Masakichi.

After taking on a load of tangerines in Kishu, they were on their way to Ise when, on October 21 of the third year of Ansei, they encountered a storm. The ship, damaged, began to drift. Being a vessel that always stayed close to shore, it carried a few provisions, and the men suffered terrible hunger. First the other crew member died, then the captain, leaving only Masakichi.

Masakichi himself was near death when he was picked up by a passing whaler. Once he regained his health, he worked with its crew and finally arrived in Hawaii.

"As I said," Hikozo repeated, "I'm a Japanese just like you. Please stand up."

Masakichi clapped his hands together in supplication and said, "Please, I beg of you, sir. You said that you are on the way to Japan aboard an American ship. Take me with you." He bowed over and over.

Hikozo regarded the man. From his hometown he used to gaze across the water at Awaji Island, this man's home, and this memory made him all the more sympathetic to Masakichi's plight.

"Please, sir. I beg you." Prostrate before him, Masakichi put his hands together again.

If he left Masakichi behind, Masakichi would surely stay in Hawaii until spring, when he would be put back in service working on a whaling ship. He might very well spend the rest of his life as a crew member on a whaler without ever finding an opportunity to return home.

"I can't promise anything, but I'll give it some thought," Hikozo said, promising to return again, and left the ship.

As he walked back to the *Cooper*, Hikozo pondered the situation. The *Cooper* was a small vessel, with a total of twenty-one on board: Lieutenant Brooke, the first officer, an engineer, himself as chief clerk, and a crew of seventeen including a cook. That was the limit, and there was no room for another person.

Hikozo's health wasn't that good at this point: he had suffered from seasickness during the typhoons and storms they'd encountered on their way from San Francisco. And in Hawaii he'd had terrible indigestion. He didn't feel like getting on a ship again any time soon and wanted to stay in Hawaii for a while to recover.

He hit upon the idea of having Masakichi take his place as chief clerk. Being named chief clerk was just a generous gesture on Brooke's part to allow Hikozo to return to Japan. Wouldn't he just as easily accept Masakichi in Hikozo's place, seeing how much the man longed to return to Japan? Hikozo felt sure that the kindly lieutenant would see things this way.

As soon as he returned to the *Cooper*, Hikozo told Lieutenant Brooke his idea.

Brooke listened quietly and then said, "I agree. It's not easy for me to say good-bye to you, Hiko, but I think we should help that poor man return to Japan."

Hikozo went to see the captain of the whaling vessel Masakichi worked on to ask him to let Masakichi go.

"Tim's an excellent worker," the captain said, "and popular with the crew. It's hard to let him go, but this is an excellent opportunity for him to return to his country, and I won't stand in his way."

Masakichi was so happy he shed tears when he heard the news, and Hikozo escorted him to the *Cooper*. Lieutenant Brooke agreed to hire Masakichi as an apprentice sailor at a salary of twelve dollars a month.

The *Cooper* sailed out of Honolulu.

Hikozo greeted the New Year, 1859 (Ansei 6), in Hawaii. He was finally feeling his old self again.

He was surprised that he'd run across so many Japanese castaways in Hawaii—Kantaro and Kihei, and then Masakichi—all three of whom had been rescued by American whalers.

Hikozo himself had been fortunate to be rescued and then be aboard various American sailing and steam vessels, and he knew that they could voyage in the open sea with no problem. Japanese ships, in contrast, were meant to hug the shore. When a storm hit and a Japanese ship was washed out to sea, it invariably suffered so much damage that it became impossible to steer.

Until recently there had been few foreign ships in the Pacific, which meant that once a Japanese vessel lost its mast and rudder and was adrift, the crew members were fated to run out of food and starve to death, and the ship would eventually become waterlogged and sink.

The spinning industry had started in England and was now going strong in America, and manufactured silk cloth was being shipped across the Atlantic and around the Cape of Good Hope to the new market in China. Before long, the advent of large sailing vessels meant that people were crossing the Pacific, directly from the American West Coast to China; with steamships, this commerce only increased. The ship that originally rescued Hikozo, the *Auckland,* was on its way back to San Francisco from China.

As a result, the demand for whale oil, used as a lubricant for spinning machines and as lamp oil, increased tremendously, and so the number of whaling vessels from many countries also increased. Soon large herds of whales were discovered off the coast of Japan and elsewhere in the Pacific, and whalers hurried to these new hunting grounds.

The majority of these ships were American, and with Hawaii as their base they plied the Pacific in search of their prey. Thus it was much more likely now that Japanese castaways would be rescued by these ships and that the rescued sailors would be taken to Hawaii.

Whaling ships came into port one after the other, and Hikozo realized it was not so strange that he'd run across three Japanese castaways.

Early in March a clipper, the *Sea Serpent,* arrived from San Francisco, bound for Hong Kong. It had many well-heeled passengers aboard, and Hikozo was delighted to find among them his old friend Van Reed.

Reed was amazed to find Hikozo here in Hawaii on his way to Japan, and when he'd learned all the details, he strongly urged him to join him on the *Sea Serpent*. Reed was on his way to Japan via China.

Hikozo had only $120, not enough to ride on such a luxurious vessel. Racking his brain for a solution, he went to consult an influential local man, Mr. Hanks, whom he'd got to know in his time in Hawaii, about how he might manage the fare. His idea was to borrow money and return it when he was back in Japan.

Hanks listened, then told Hikozo that he knew the captain of the *Sea Serpent* well. "Leave this to me," he said.

Still anxious about whether things would work out, on the twelfth Hikozo went to the ship. Unexpectedly, Hanks was waiting there for him. He handed him a first-class ticket, and when Hikozo offered to pay for it, he wouldn't hear of it and said, "The captain's agreed. Here's something I want you to read when you're aboard." And he handed him a letter.

Hikozo, amazed at his good fortune, thanked Hanks and shook his hand, and boarded the ship with Van Reed.

Once on deck, he opened the letter. As he read it, tears coursed down his cheeks. Hanks wrote that he had told his friends about Hikozo and his financial difficulties in getting home, and they had collected enough money for the purchase of a first-class ticket.

The ship's sails filled out, and the vessel began to move. Hikozo looked out at the dock. The short, stout Mr. Hanks was standing there, and Hikozo leaned over the railing and gave a big wave with his hand. Hanks spotted him and waved back. All the days Hikozo had spent in America came rushing back to him. He'd been sustained only through the kindness of many people, starting with Mr. Sanders—and now in Hawaii by the warmhearted Mr. Hanks.

Brushing back his tears, he continued to watch as Mr. Hanks's figure shrank in the distance.

The voyage on the *Sea Serpent* was pleasant. Even on days when the sea was rough, Hikozo never felt in danger because of the size of the ship, and this time he wasn't plagued by seasickness. He spent every day with Van Reed, and at night they'd enjoy drinks in the salon. The first-class cabins were clean, the beds comfortable.

Japan had just been opened to foreign trade from June of that year, and Reed was on his way there to do business. He was of the opinion that despite the booming trade with China, doing business with Japan, a newly opened country, offered far better prospects. For Hikozo the notion of finally treading his native soil with his good friend was a stroke of unexpected good luck.

The ship continued its smooth way across the ocean, finally arriving in Hong Kong Harbor at 12:30 PM on the afternoon of April 6.

Hikozo went ashore and enjoyed walking around, rediscovering the town. The town was much livelier than when he'd last been there, seven years ago. The harbor was filled with countless steamships and sailing vessels, and there were quite developed facilities along the shore. The *Sea Serpent* stayed at anchor for some time to load and unload cargo.

Eleven days later, the captain of the ship, Whitmore, invited Hikozo to join him on business to Canton, and Hikozo accepted. They took a small boat to Canton, and when they arrived, the captain went to the British consulate. China was by this time nearly a British colony, and the captain was visiting the consulate to smooth the way for his business.

While the captain spoke with consular officials in the parlor, Hikozo walked toward the exit, thinking to stroll in the gardens, when he suddenly came to a halt. A man was entering the consulate, and when Hikozo saw his face, he let out a shout. For his part the man stood stock-still, his mouth open in surprise. His hair was cut short, and he wore a Western suit.

"Hikozo!" the man gasped. It was Iwakichi, one of the original crew members of the *Eiriki Maru*.

The two men stood silent for a while, staring at each other.

"Why are you here?" Iwakichi asked in English, and then, realizing who he was talking to, switched to Japanese and repeated the question in a high-pitched voice.

Hikozo gave a quick summary of how he'd come to be in Hong Kong.

But as he excitedly told the tale, he found himself unable to look Iwakichi in the eye.

When Hikozo, along with Jisaku and Kamezo, had gone with Thomas to America, they'd left behind Iwakichi and the other twelve crew members of the *Eiriki Maru* on board the *Susquehanna*. This was seven years ago, and finding Iwakichi here in Canton meant that the rest of the crew must also still be stranded in China.

After Hikozo finished speaking, Iwakichi said in amazement, "Were you really in America that long? It's a wonder that you could come back to China."

Hikozo was afraid to ask the next question. The faces of each and every sailor they left behind on the *Susquehanna* floated before his eyes, and the sad looks in their eyes as they watched him pull away from the ship.

"What happened to the others?" he finally managed to ask.

Suddenly, Iwakichi was shaken. "They left Sentaro alone on the *Susquehanna*," he said in a low voice.

Sentaro, the ship's cook, had helped Hikozo in so many ways when he was an apprentice cook.

"Why just him...?" Hikozo intently watched Iwakichi's light brown face.

"You remember Otokichi, don't you, that fellow with the Indian wife? He said he'd put us on a Chinese ship to Nagasaki and got the captain of the *Susquehanna* to let him take us off the ship. But the captain insisted that Sentaro stay on board, and he did, the poor fellow. He was crying when we left. I wonder what's become of him."

Iwakichi looked away.

Hikozo was thunderstruck. His chest tightened, thinking of how sad Sentaro must have felt to be abandoned by his fellow sailors. How did he spend his days, Hikozo wondered, among the American crew, almost completely unable to communicate with them? Maybe he fell into despair and took his own life. Hikozo could see Sentaro's face, with its gentle eyes.

"What about the others?" he asked.

Even if Otokichi got them off the ship, most likely they had no way of getting home and wandered around China, hungry, like stray dogs. Or might they even be dead?

"We all followed what Otokichi said, about getting us on a Chinese ship, and went to Zhapu Harbor. That's where the trading ships to Nagasaki leave from, but we waited and waited, and the ship didn't leave."

Iwakichi avoided Hikozo's eyes, his face distorted with the memory.

"This country's been torn apart by war for a long time, and they haven't been thinking much about trade. Otokichi knew the ships wouldn't leave, and he tricked us. I decided to come back to Shanghai." Iwakichi eyes flashed with anger.

Hikozo was depressed by what he'd heard. They'd gone through the hell of being adrift at sea, then had been rescued by an American ship and taken to San Francisco, and finally to China. Through all this the crew had stuck together, but first he, Jisaku, and Kamezo went back to America, and then Sentaro was left behind. Finally even Iwakichi found himself apart from his fellow sailors. After the death of their captain, Manzo, who'd always kept them together, their unity had disintegrated.

"Why are you here at this consulate?" Hikozo asked.

Iwakichi wore a trim Western suit, and his short hair shone with pomade. He seemed to be managing well. "I worked a long time for a British trading company but then was asked to work as interpreter for the consulate." Iwakichi's expression turned proud as he went on.

Mr. Alcock, the British consul in Canton, had been appointed consul general to Japan and had taken notice of Iwakichi. Iwakichi was fluent in English by this time, he told Hikozo, and Alcock came up with the idea of taking him to Japan to act as his interpreter.

"Thanks to the British, then, I'll be able to go home. Seitaro and the others were smart to strike off on their own. When I wound up in Shanghai, by the way, I changed my name to Denkichi so no one could find me. The people at the trading company call me Dan Ketch, or Dan for short. Here at the consulate, too, that's what they call me." Iwakichi's face softened.

When Hikozo worked as a cook on their ship, he'd never been able to figure out what kind of person Iwakichi was. The man always seemed lost in thought, was short-tempered, and kept to himself. It was certainly in keeping with his character to go his own way. At any rate, it was wonderful that he'd been hired by the British consulate and would finally be able to realize his dream of returning to Japan.

Captain Whitmore, finished with his talk with the consul, came out of the room.

"Well, I hope to see you again," Hikozo said to Iwakichi in English. The latter, in good English, replied, "I look forward to that, too."

Hikozo left the consulate with Captain Whitmore.

"Who was that?" Whitmore asked as they walked.

"He was one of the crew I was with on the ship when we were castaways."

At this, Whitmore stopped, shook his head in disbelief, then began walking again.

The *Sea Serpent* remained at anchor in Hong Kong Harbor, and Hikozo stayed on board with Van Reed.

About two weeks later, Denkichi (Dan) came to visit Hikozo. He told him he was in Hong Kong accompanying Mr. Alcock, who was on the way to take up his post in Japan.

"Mr. Alcock says he'd like to meet you, and wants me to bring you to him. So could you come with me?" Denkichi asked.

Hikozo agreed, and went with Denkichi to the hotel where Alcock was staying. Denkichi knocked on the door of the room, and Hikozo followed him inside.

Denkichi turned to a tall man who'd just arisen from a chair and said, "I've brought Hikozo with me," and in a dignified tone introduced Hikozo, then left the room.

Alcock shook Hikozo's hand, thanked him for coming, and offered him a seat. Prefacing his question by saying that he'd heard some of the details from Dan, he asked him about his life in America. Hikozo summarized his experiences, touching on the education, insufficient though it was, that he received through the kindness of Mr. Sanders, and his experiences working in a consignment firm.

Nodding as he listened, Alcock occasionally voiced his surprise at what he heard. His eyes evinced a great interest in how well Hikozo spoke English.

Hikozo stood up and was about to take his leave when Alcock said, in a quiet voice, "What would you think about becoming an interpreter in the consulate in Japan?"

Hikozo had guessed why Alcock called him here, and politely gave two reasons for declining the offer. The first was that Denkichi had already been hired as an interpreter, and if Hikozo were hired, Denkichi would lose his position; even if Denkichi weren't asked to resign, Hikozo could imagine how poorly he would be treated. The second reason was the deep gratitude he felt to all the people in America who'd been kind to him, and to the American government, which had always been good to him in all his dealings with it. He thought it best not to decide on a job until he was back in Japan; after his arrival he could choose a suitable position based on what the American representative there directed him to do.

"I understand completely. You're entirely correct," Alcock said, not at all annoyed by being turned down. Again he shook Hikozo's hand.

Hikozo bowed and left.

The *Sea Serpent* was scheduled to begin the voyage back to America on May 6, and before he left the ship, Hikozo made the rounds, saying farewell to the captain and crew. His friend Van Reed and he, at the invitation of a Mr. Speiden, U.S. naval storekeeper for Hong Kong, stayed at the latter's home.

On May 10 the steamship *Powhatan* arrived in port, and Speiden, who had gone to meet the ship, returned with good news. Promoted from consul general to United States minister to Japan, Townsend Harris was in Shanghai and would soon be taking the *Mississippi* to Japan. Four years earlier, in Ansei 2 (1855), he had been appointed the first consul to Japan, and a year later, accompanied by the interpreter, Heusken, arrived in Shimoda, concluded the Treaty of Shimoda, and went to Edo as well and concluded a trade agreement between the two nations. Harris, however, had fallen ill and returned to Shanghai to recuperate. Hearing that Hikozo was hoping to return to Japan, the captain of the *Powhatan* offered to take him to Shanghai, where Harris was.

Hikozo went to thank the captain for his kindness and requested and received permission for Van Reed to accompany him.

On May 17 the *Powhatan* left Hong Kong, and Hikozo gazed out at the receding city. Since he had taken U.S. citizenship, there was no reason for Harris to refuse his request to travel with him to Japan, and once again he was grateful to Sanders for looking out for his welfare. Sanders had told him everything would work out— and he was right. After making a stop in Ningpo, the *Powhatan* arrived in Shanghai on May 27. They saw the *Mississippi*, flying the American flag, anchored there, and Hikozo grew excited at the thought that this was the ship that would finally make his dream come true and take him, finally, home.

Two days later he and the officers of the *Powhatan* went over to the *Mississippi* so the captain could obtain permission for Hikozo to board their ship, and also so that Hikozo could meet Mr. Harris.

When he heard about Hikozo's background and desire to return to Japan, Captain Nicholson of the *Mississippi* replied that he would be pleased to have Hikozo on his ship. Finally having the means to return home in his grasp, Hikozo felt a tightening in his chest and tried to keep from sobbing.

The captain took him to Mr. Harris's cabin. There they found a man with a long, white beard and a rather pinched look on his face, wearily occupying an armchair. Captain Nicholson briefly told Hikozo's story, and Harris, nodding as he listened, motioned to Hikozo to take a seat.

Hikozo sat across from him, and Harris asked him many questions about how many years he'd been in the United States and what sort of life he'd led. The man's face was expressionless, but his eyes shone with interest at what he heard.

When Hikozo mentioned that he'd been naturalized as an American citizen, Harris gazed at him in silence for a while, then said, "Please bring me the original certificate. And a copy as well..."

A tall man with a white beard entered the cabin. Nicholson told Hikozo that this was Mr. Dorr, newly appointed as consul general to Kanagawa, and Hikozo shook hands with him. Harris told him that Hikozo was a Japanese but a naturalized American citizen and that he'd be traveling with them on the *Mississippi* to Japan.

Dorr spoke in a low voice to Harris, all the while glancing in Hikozo's direction. Finally he turned to Hikozo and asked, "How would you like to be the official interpreter for the consulate?"

Taken aback by the sudden proposal, Hikozo looked over at Harris, who said, "You'd be perfect for it."

"I really would like you to be our interpreter," Dorr said, and Hikozo then nodded his assent.

Hikozo left the cabin and the ship and returned to the *Powhatan*. He couldn't have been happier. Being hired as an official interpreter for the consulate, to return home as a government employee—the thought made him want to shout for joy, and he paced the deck in his excitement.

The next morning he visited Harris again, with his original naturalization certificate and a copy in hand.

"When we arrive at Kanagawa," Harris said sternly, "I must show the local magistrate this copy and convince him that you're an American citizen and not a Japanese."

Hikozo agreed this was the best way to avoid any problems with the Japanese accepting him back. Leaving the *Mississippi*, he went ashore to the Heard Company to visit Mr. Dorr, who was staying there. Dorr welcomed him warmly, and they decided on his compensation as an interpreter and other matters. The pay was more than Hikozo had expected, and once again he relished his good fortune in being hired.

After leaving the Heard Company, he stopped, realizing there was someone he needed to see: Otokichi.

According to Denkichi, Otokichi had had the twelve remaining crew members of the *Eiriki Maru* leave the *Susquehanna,* and he took them to Zhapu so they could take a Chinese vessel to Nagasaki. Denkichi alone left Zhapu, but what had happened to the eleven he left behind? Otokichi would surely know, and Hikozo was eager to meet him to find out news about them.

Otokichi, now the manager of a British trading firm, was known to everyone as Ottosan, and Hikozo had no trouble finding him. He lived in a magnificent house, and when Hikozo showed up, Otokichi welcomed him into his living room.

Otokichi answered Hikozo's questions, telling him that the eleven sailors had been taken by Chinese ship to Nagasaki, where they were handed over to the commissioner.

"I heard from people on the Chinese ship, though, that Yasutaro succumbed to illness just before their ship entered Nagasaki Harbor, and that a sailor named Kyosuke died while they were in Nagasaki." Hikozo nodded at this sad news, but he was relieved to hear that the rest had safely made it home. He'd always felt guilty going to America with Jisaku and Kamezo, leaving the others behind, but now that he knew that they'd made it to Japan, these feelings no longer burdened him.

"Don't you feel like going back to Japan?" Hikozo asked hesitantly.

"No, I'm fine here. I have a wife and children now, and I can't leave my business. Just like Rikimatsu, I'm fated to become part of the soil here in China." His smile was sad.

Hikozo wordlessly bowed to his host and left.

On June 13, he and Van Reed, baggage in hand, transferred from the *Powhatan* to the *Mississippi.* Van Reed, now able to speak Japanese well, had used the practical business experience he'd gained in San Francisco to get appointed as chief clerk of the American consulate in Kanagawa. Hikozo was not only happy to be traveling to Japan with his old friend but also pleased by the prospect of their working together.

Two days later the engines of the *Mississippi* fired up, and they steamed out of Shanghai. As Hikozo stood on the deck and looked ahead, he was filled with deep emotions. Nine years had passed since he was a castaway. Standing on the deck of the vessel that would take him home, he felt as if he were floating.

The ship set its course east. Hikozo and Reed walked the decks together, and at night they were invited to Consul General Dorr's cabin and enjoyed drinking and talking.

In the evening two days after leaving Shanghai (May 17 of Ansei 5), their ship arrived at the mouth of Nagasaki Harbor and anchored. The sky was covered with thick clouds, and there was no starlight, and all they could see in the darkness were the indistinct shapes of hills surrounding the harbor. The clear night air brought with it the scent of the sea and of trees. This was the smell of his native land he'd not experienced for years, and Hikozo felt refreshed, washed clean by this fragrance that filled his being.

That night he was again invited to have drinks with Dorr. As the liquor began to take effect, he grew more voluble and even tearful.

The next morning he arose early and came out on deck. His breath was taken away by the brilliant green of the hills and islands sparkling in the morning sun—the kind of beautiful scenery he'd never seen in America or China.

Black smoke billowed from the ship's smokestack, and the ship slowly began to move forward. They passed by an island, and as they entered the harbor proper, the town of Nagasaki was laid out before them. Different from a Chinese harbor, the town looked orderly and neat, and when he saw the tiled roofs, tears sprang into his eyes.

The ship drew closer to the town and then threw out its anchor.

"How wonderful! It's a beautiful town," Reed, standing beside him, said in admiration.

Inside the harbor were many ships, including warships flying Russian and British flags. The harbor was dotted with fishing boats, and people and palanquins moved back and forth on paths along the shore. When Hikozo saw these palanquins, he knew he was finally home.

CHAPTER SIXTEEN

S OON AFTER THEIR SHIP anchored, a small boat came from shore and pulled alongside. Three men boarded, officials from the commissioner's office and an interpreter. The officers greeted them. The Japanese officials took down information in a notebook and left.

Next a boat from the British warship rowed over to the *Mississippi*. Two officers had come to pay their compliments to the Americans and shook hands with the officers of the *Mississippi*. The British ship turned out to be the *Sampson*, with Mr. Alcock aboard, bound for Kanagawa. Hikozo knew that Denkichi, hired to be interpreter for the British consulate, must be there as well, but though he scanned the deck of the ship, he didn't catch sight of him.

Captain Nicholson of the *Mississippi* came up to Hikozo and said, "While we're in Nagasaki, I don't want you leaving the ship . . . And you shouldn't speak to any of the local people." He gave a Hikozo a stern look to underscore his orders.

The *Mississippi*'s mission was to escort Mr. Harris, the newly appointed minister to Japan, safely to Kanagawa, and Hikozo's identity being known at this point might lead to complications that would delay the minister's taking up his post.

Hikozo replied that he would obey.

Several small boats approached their ship, and local merchants selling various antiques, vegetables and fruit, and other goods came aboard. Hikozo was forced to listen in silence as they spoke in Japanese. They had a Nagasaki accent, but it still thrilled him to hear his native tongue.

The *Sampson* left port, and the *Mississippi* left soon after, on May 24. The ship went through the Akamazeki Starits (present-day Shimonseki), continued out into the Pacific, and arrived in Shimoda. There they found Mr. Heusken, Harris's attentive clerk-interpreter, who'd been waiting for Harris's arrival, and he joined them on the ship.

The ship left Shimoda and on the last day of May arrived in Edo Bay, anchoring off Kanagawa. The *Sampson* anchored nearby.

Officials from the Kanagawa commissioner's office boarded to ask the standard questions, then left, and on June 2 Sakai Okinokami Tadayuki—both Kanagawa commissioner and commissioner of foreign affairs—came to pay his respects to Harris and to Dorr.

Harris asked Hikozo to join them, and he stood there facing Sakai. Harris explained that Hikozo was a Japanese castaway but had now taken U.S. citizenship, and he requested that Hikozo be treated as any American citizen would be. Sakai gazed silently at Hikozo and through his interpreter replied that he accepted this.

The next afternoon several officers of the warship came to Hikozo and said they wanted to go ashore to do some shopping and asked him to accompany them. Hikozo agreed, and they took a boat to the village of Yokohama.

Hikozo stared for a moment at the ground beneath his feet. *After nine years*, he thought, *I'm finally home*, and was overwhelmed.

He proceeded with the officers into the village. According to the treaty of commerce, tomorrow would mark the official beginning of trade between Japan and the outside world, and in anticipation of this buildings were going up—a customhouse and other government buildings and official residences, as well as consulates of various nations. All sorts of newly constructed shops lined both sides of the broad avenue. The village was filled with the sounds of carpenters at work with saws, planes, and hammers.

Hikozo escorted the officers to the customhouse, where they exchanged their dollars for Japanese currency, and then the officers began to make the rounds of the shops. Hikozo helped them select items and interpreted for them. The shopkeepers were astonished to hear him speak to them in Japanese. They didn't seem to understand what he really was, this Japanese in Western clothes. For his part, Hikozo grew tearful at hearing Japanese everywhere he turned, and was overjoyed to freely converse again in his native tongue.

On June 5 they moved into Honkakuji Temple, which had been leased as the new American consulate in Kanagawa. Here Mr. Dorr would take up his post.

A boat was lowered from the *Mississippi* with Minister Harris, Mr. Dorr, Captain Nicholson, and other officers, as well as Hikozo, as interpreter, and Van Reed. They came ashore in Kanagawa, walked through Yokohama Village led by a government official, and arrived at the temple. Since the temple had already been designated to them, there were no priests to be seen.

Inside the temple precincts stood a large pine tree, which the Americans trimmed so they could hang an American flag from it. The Japanese commissioner's officials and footmen watched in silence.

The Americans opened some champagne they'd brought along for the occasion, poured it out in glasses, then all sang the American national anthem. Hikozo joined them and toasted their new consulate. The party entered the main hall of the temple and had lunch. The menu included fish, boiled chicken, roast duck, vegetables, cakes, and wine.

From that day on Hikozo lived in the temple with Mr. Dorr and Van Reed. The temple was on a beautiful hill and commanded a wonderful view of Kanagawa Bay and Yokohama Village.

Harris opened the new American ministry in the Zenpukuji Temple in Azabu, while British General Consul Alcock set up his consulate in the Tozenji Temple in Takanawa. In addition to performing his duties at the Kanagawa consulate, Hikozo found himself often shuttling back and forth to the ministry in the Zenpukuji Temple to help procure furniture, and well as to interview local people for positions as cooks and cleaning staff.

As he diligently went about these tasks, Hikozo had many opportunities to deal with the commissioner's officials and with merchants, and as a matter of course he became well known in the community. They learned that he'd lived for a long time in America and been educated there, spoke English fluently, and was an American citizen. He was at home in Western clothes and moved and gestured like an American—shrugging his shoulders, winking, etc. People also found it unusual how foreigners called him by his foreign name, Joseph Heco. Hikozo began to sense he was the center of attention every time he walked down the street.

On June 22 he was on his way back from the Yokohama customhouse, where he'd exchanged some money, when someone called out to him from behind. He turned around to find a merchant he knew who ran a large shop in Yokohama Village.

The man came over to him and told him that the captain of a vessel that transported goods from Hyogo to Edo had heard that his younger brother had come to Kanagawa from America, and he wanted to check to see if this could be true.

"The captain said he heard the man coming back from America was born in either Kishu or Harima. May I ask where were you born?" The merchant gazed intently at Hikozo.

"In Harima," Hikozo answered.

"The captain said he himself was from Harima. Do you have an older brother?" the merchant asked.

"I have an older stepbrother. He's a sailor." Hikozo felt his face stiffening.

His stepbrother, Unomatsu, had been a chief navigator for a merchant ship, and it was perfectly possible that now, nine years later, he'd become a captain. This could indeed be his brother, though of course there were countless sailors from Harima, many of whom had no doubt become captains of vessels transporting Nada sake to Edo.

"What do you think? Would you like to visit this man? Or would you prefer that I bring him to see you in the consulate?" The merchant gazed at Hikozo.

Hikozo shook his head. He was hoping eventually to make it back to his hometown of Hamada, Honjo Village, to see his stepfather and stepbrother, but meeting his stepbrother a mere month after he set foot in Japan seemed too swift, unnatural. His crewmates on the *Eiriki Maru* had returned home, and surely there were other castaways returned from America. Most likely it was one of these other returnees that this captain had heard about.

It would be terribly disappointing for the captain to take time out of his busy schedule to come all the way to the consulate only to discover that Hikozo was not his brother. Hikozo himself was busy but not bound by any fixed duties, so he decided that it was better for him to make the effort to go meet the man.

"Where is the captain staying?" Hikozo asked, and learned from the merchant that he was in Shinagawa, at the home of the manager of a local shipping agency. This was situated in an area of inns and other accommodations in Shinagawa and was, according to the merchant, very nearby, only eleven miles from Kanagawa.

"Let's go, then," Hikozo said. "Please take me there, tomorrow if it's convenient..."

Hikozo returned to the consulate and related the story to Dorr and asked for the next day off.

Dorr was happy to grant him leave. "That's fine," he said. "I'd like you to go. If this man really is your brother, you should invite him to the consulate."

Hikozo gave a servant a letter to take to the merchant asking him to hire two palanquins and bring them to the consulate the next morning.

The next morning dawned bright and sunny, and as promised, at 8 AM the merchant showed up in a palanquin. He reported that he had sent a letter the day before to the captain asking him to stay at home today.

Hikozo got into the palanquin the merchant brought for him,

and the two set off from the Honkakuji Temple. Since becoming the official interpreter for the consulate, Hikozo had mostly walked when he had business outside, and this was the first time in his life that he'd ridden in a palanquin. At first he found it cramped, but soon enjoyed looking at the sea out the right side as he swayed down the road.

They passed a row of inns and teahouses in Kawasaki, crossed the Tama River on a ferryboat, and arrived at the area of Shinagawa where lodgings were concentrated. The merchant had their palanquins stop in front of a solidly built house. He pointed out a man there, saying this was the captain he'd spoken of, and the man stopped and regarded Hikozo.

Hikozo knew it was Unomatsu. He was dressed as one would expect a captain to be, but the face was the same as ever.

Unomatsu, though, seemed disappointed, as if he thought this was the wrong person. He turned to the merchant, an awkward expression on his face, and back again to Hikozo. Hikozo was sad that his stepbrother didn't recognize him, but it was understandable. Hikozo had been only thirteen when he last saw Unomatsu, and nine years had passed. Hikozo's features had become those of an adult, and besides he now had a mustache and a beard. Unomatsu last saw him as a youngster in a kimono, and here he was an adult in a Western suit, a bow tie, and black boots.

Hikozo bowed and said, "Where is father now?"

Unomatsu said nothing.

To make Unomatsu believe this was indeed his stepbrother, Hikozo blurted out, "How is grandmother? Sakubei next door must be getting on in years by now—is he still alive? I'm sorry to say that Manzo, father's friend who was the captain of the *Eiriki Maru,* passed away while we were in the Hawaiian Islands."

As he spoke, Unomatsu's eyes grew wider, and Hikozo could feel that he was beginning to believe. Still, doubt remained in his eyes as looked Hikozo up and down.

Hikozo related his experiences, how after being a castaway he lived for a long time in America, how his desire to return home had come true when he landed in Kanagawa, and how he was now employed as interpreter for the American consulate.

"That's why I look the way I do, with short hair and these foreign clothes," Hikozo said, glancing down at his outfit.

Unomatsu finally relaxed.

"You've changed so much, I didn't recognize you. So it really is you, Hikotaro!" he said, using Hikozo's childhood name.

Hikozo nodded over and over.

Now convinced, Unomatsu came closer and said, "Grandmother is dead. And this year is the seventh anniversary of our neighbor Sakubei's death."

"Is father well?" This is what really concerned Hikozo.

Unomatsu looked away. "He had a stroke three years ago, in the spring, and passed away without regaining consciousness," he said.

Silently Hikozo nodded. He thought of the long nine years he'd been away, and it pained him that he was never able to repay the kindness his stepfather had shown him.

"The sailors who were shipwrecked with you all came back to the village, and their families cried and cried, they were so overjoyed. The whole village was excited for a while. But then we learned that you and Jisaku had gone to America and nobody knew what happened to you after that. We gave you up for dead. Yet here you are . . ."

Unomatsu burst into tears. Hikozo, too, was overcome and wept.

The lady of the house came out and urged them all to come inside.

Unomatsu wiped away his tears with a cloth; then he, Hikozo, and the merchant entered the house. The woman brought out refreshments, and Hikozo was able to spend some quiet time in conversation with his stepbrother. Unomatsu had served on the ship his uncle captained until last autumn, when his uncle also got sick and passed away, after which Unomatsu was asked to assume command of the vessel.

When they'd paused for a while, Hikozo asked, "Why don't you come to visit the consulate?"

Unomatsu hesitated but then said, "I guess as your older brother I should go to thank the gentleman you're serving under."

When he heard this, Hikozo could sense how Unomatsu felt about him as his older brother, the weight of duty and responsibility on him now that he had assumed the position of captain of a merchant ship.

The head of the household arranged for three palanquins, and Hikozo set off with Unomatsu and the merchant.

As he swayed back and forth in his palanquin, Hikozo felt it was all a dream—to have his stepbrother right here with him. Since his brother captained a ship that sailed between Hyogo and Edo, he'd thought that perhaps someday they'd be able to see each other again, but to meet him like this so soon after coming back to Japan was nothing short of miraculous. Tears again welled as he gazed out at the sea.

The palanquins carried them past the Kanagawa inn district and stopped outside the main gates of the Honkakuji Temple. The merchant said there was business he had to attend to and rode off in his palanquin for Yokohama Village.

Hikozo pointed out to Unomatsu the American flag fluttering from the pine tree, and told him, as they went inside the main hall of the temple, that they did not need remove their footwear.

Hikozo went to Mr. Dorr's office, and when he announced he'd brought his stepbrother to pay his respects, Dorr stood up and came out to the main hall.

"Very pleased to meet you," Dorr said, introducing himself. He smiled and held out his hand as Hikozo translated.

Unomatsu stared at the consul's large hand, then turned to Hikozo and asked, uncertainly, "What does he expect me to do?"

"In America," Hikozo explained, "when people are introduced, they clasp each other's hand. Just the way we bow."

Unomatsu grasped the consul's hand.

The consul asked him to sit down in a chair and Hikozo to bring in some illustrated newspapers, drawings, and landscape photographs to show him. Unomatsu's eyes went wide when he saw these, and he mentioned the things that Seitaro and the sailors of the *Eiriki Maru* had brought back to their village. These consisted only of several old newspapers and some glass bottles, but people came from far away to view the unique items.

Unomatsu's amazement at the things Hikozo showed him was so great that the consul presented him with the illustrated newspapers and handed him some dollar bills and silver and copper coins from his own pocket.

"These are presents from the consul to you." When Hikozo said this, Unomatsu blushed, stood up, and bowed repeatedly in thanks.

Dorr, in fine spirits, said to Hikozo, "Why doesn't your brother stay here in the consulate a couple of days?"

When this was conveyed to Unomatsu, he thanked Dorr for the offer but, gathering himself together, said, "I'm afraid I have my work as a captain to consider and must return to Shinagawa today." And he bowed again.

When this was translated for the consul, he said he understood perfectly and asked Hikozo to get dinner ready early. Anticipating that Unomatsu would have difficulty using a knife and fork, Hikozo made sure a pair of his own chopsticks were set out for him.

As they ate, Unomatsu asked detailed questions about each dish before hesitantly tasting it. Some dishes he had no comment on, but some he pronounced delicious.

After dinner Hikozo called for a palanquin and gave Unomatsu a photograph, one of himself and Van Reed taken in San Francisco. Unomatsu looked back and forth between the photograph and Hikozo, marveling at the resemblance.

The palanquin came, and Unomatsu left.

Later that evening, Hikozo sat in his room mulling over the events of the day. He'd been able to meet his stepbrother and learn about the death of his stepfather so quickly. Of course, he and Unomatsu were not related by blood. The only place he could call home was the sea around Harima, and though he'd returned to his homeland, he felt alone.

On top of this, as a member of the consulate staff he was

troubled by the intense antagonism that had grown up between the foreign diplomats and the shogunal government.

With the trade treaty between Japan and foreign countries, Kanagawa had been made an open port, but since it was near the busy main Tokaido Road, the shogunate feared that if the foreigners built their settlement there, fights would break out between them and the Japanese. The shogunate thus built a commissioner's office and customhouse in Yokohama Village to the south, in the hope that this area would become the permanent foreign settlement. Harris opposed the plan, contending that the settlement should be near the Tokaido Road, accusing the Japanese in the strongest terms of trying to isolate the foreigners as they did with the Dutch in Nagasaki. Alcock seconded this notion and ignored the shogunate's requests and set up his consulate in the Tozenji Temple in Shibatakanawa, while Harris set up his mission in the Zenpukuji Temple in Azabu.

Dorr agreed completely with Harris and went to the Kanagawa commissioner's office to pay a visit to Hori Oribenokami (Toshihiro), the Kanagawa commissioner and commissioner of foreign affairs, to lodge a protest, taking Hikozo along as interpreter.

Very calmly Hori explained the shogunate's position. Within Japan there was a radical faction that opposed opening the country and wanted nothing more than to drive all foreigners out, which made it extremely difficult for the government to guarantee the safety of foreigners near such a busy thoroughfare as the Tokaido Road. Hori went on to emphasize that with its excellent harbor Yokohama Village was far more suitable for the foreign settlement than the shallow waters off Kanagawa.

Dorr responded, saying, "The treaty stipulates quite clearly that Kanagawa is where the foreign settlement will be. Surely you haven't forgotten this," pressing home the point.

Hori calmly said, "Yes, Kanagawa is stipulated as an open harbor, but Yokohama Village is within the boundary of Kanagawa, so this is not in violation of the terms of the treaty. For a number of reasons it's best for the settlement to be in Yokohama Village."

Dorr found it hard to refute the magistrate's logic. "This point will require further study," he said and stood up.

This was the first time Hikozo had been so close to a high official of the Japanese government, and he was tense. Hori sat there on his folding stool, his eyes fixed on Dorr, never once glancing at Hikozo. There was an unshakable dignity to the man, as his face never once betrayed his emotions. This commissioner was the exact opposite of the American presidents Hikozo had met, Pierce and Buchanan, who had both been outgoing and friendly, but Hikozo had to admit he had great respect for Hori.

America possessed numerous steam warships with cannon and other formidable armaments. Naturally Hori was aware of this and surely felt Japan was a weak little nation by comparison. Still, he never hesitated to express his views, logically laying out his points to Dorr, a man fully conscious that his nation was by far the more powerful of the two. Hikozo looked in admiration at Hori as he interpreted, sensing how sharp the man was. It was no wonder, Hikozo concluded, that Dorr found himself on the losing end of the argument.

Not long after this, Hikozo learned how very correct Hori's ideas were.

A Mr. Hall, head of one of the larger American trading companies, had planned to follow Harris and Dorr's advice and build his office in Kanagawa, but after surveying the surroundings purchased a site in Yokohama Village instead and began building there. Dorr tried to interfere, but Hall insisted that the harbor facilities in Yokohama were much superior to those in Kanagawa.

The other merchants, one after another, built their offices in Yokohoma—Jardine and Matheson at the number 1 dock, the Dent Company at numbers 4 and 5 along the shore road.

Dorr was dejected, but Hikozo was heartened by this turn of events. Merchants, always on the lookout for what would give them an advantage, had simply come to the conclusion that Yokohama was preferable as a port and had begun moving there and trading there. And neither the minister nor the consul could prevent this.

With the trading companies moving to Yokohama, the number of foreigners living in Kanagawa declined sharply. Only Harris and Alcock insisted on staying in Kanagawa, as did a few missionaries. Hikozo found their insistence on staying near the Tokaido Road amusing.

Whenever he had some free time, he liked to walk around Yokohama Village. The streets were lined with foreign shops displaying all sorts of goods from each country, with rifles and pistols for sale. The village was lively, with lots of foreigners strolling the streets, and Hikozo was struck by the illusion that he was walking in a foreign country, not Japan.

In that very same village of Yokohama, on July 27, a murderous attack took place.

The Russian warship carrying Admiral Muravyov of the Siberian fleet entered Edo Bay and anchored off Shinagawa. Two sub-lieutenant cadets, along with three sailors, went ashore to arrange for provisions, and were walking around Yokohama making the necessary purchases. Around six in the evening, as they were coming out of a greengrocer's, a samurai approached them and suddenly drew his sword and began slashing. The man was obviously a skilled swordsman: one sailor died instantly, one lieutenant was wounded and collapsed, while two sailors who were injured ran back in the greengrocer's. The samurai quickly left the spot.

Yokohama was thrown into an uproar, and officials from the Kanagawa commissioner's ran to investigate. They found at the scene the broken-off tip of the sword, nine and a half inches long, a samurai haori cloak, and a single sandal. The body of the dead sailor and the wounded men were taken to the Russian officers' temporary quarters, where a Japanese physician attended to the wounded man, but the wounds were grave and the man soon breathed his last.

When news of the incident reached the American consulate from the commissioner's office, Hikozo and Dorr, each armed with a pistol, hurried to the Russians' lodgings.

Postmortem examinations were done by the commissioner's

officials and the doctor, under the eyes of officers from the Russian ship who'd rushed to shore from the warship, and Hikozo shuddered at the sight of the two bloody corpses. As the doctor examined the wounds, a clerk took down the information: the sublieutenant had sustained a wound fourteen inches in length, running from his right shoulder down to the left side of his back, a wound nearly a foot in length down the left side of his back, as well as a cut to his left thigh. The sailor who died instantly had sustained cuts to his head, face, and both shoulders, and one of his arms had been sliced cleanly off. That the tip of the sword had broken off was evidence of the ferocity of the samurai's attack.

At dawn Hikozo and Dorr returned to the consulate. Dorr composed a letter to Harris, reporting that they'd investigated the scene and warning American citizens in Yokohama to be on their guard. The reaction in the foreign community was close to panic, and people made sure to carry guns with them at all times and not to go out at night.

The two wounded men were taken to the Russian ship, while the two corpses remained at the Russian officers' quarters. Being summer, it was necessary to inter the bodies quickly, and on July 29 at 4 PM a contingent of marines and Hikozo and Dorr joined the funeral procession. The coffin was buried in the precincts of the Sotokuin Temple in Yokohama.

The next day Admiral Popov, accompanied by his adjutant, visited the American consulate. The admiral reported with a frown that he had tried to negotiate repeatedly with the Kanagawa commissioner but, without a competent interpreter, was getting nowhere. The talks were held in English, but Popov's young Russian interpreter knew only a scattering of Japanese, and the commissioner's interpreter wasn't sufficiently well versed in English, so they were having trouble understanding each other.

"If Hiko doesn't mind, perhaps he can be of service to you," Dorr said, looking over at Hikozo. "I'd be glad to," Hikozo replied.

The admiral, happy to hear this, asked him to help out.

Two days later an officer came to escort Hikozo to the Russian ship to consult with Popov. After this, they went ashore to the residence of the Kanagawa commissioner.

Hikozo, the admiral, and his adjutant were shown into a large hall and took seats on chairs, then the Kanagawa commissioners Mizuno Chikugonokami (Tadanori) and Sakai Okinokami (Tadayuki) appeared along with inspectors and other officials in charge of investigating the incident. The two commissioners sat down across from Hikozo and the Russians.

The meeting began with Popov, Hikozo interpreting, who asked how the search for the perpetrator was progressing. The commissioners replied that they were doing their utmost, searching everywhere for the man, but had not yet had any luck.

"We've confiscated the items left at the scene by the perpetrator, and we'd like you to take a look at them," one commissioner said, and commanded an official to fetch them. The official disappeared into another room and emerged with a bundle wrapped in cloth, which he laid on a table.

When the cloth was untied, they saw the sword tip, the cloak, and the sandal. Popov examined all these carefully. The cloak was covered with blood, and it was conjectured that the attacker had discarded it, fearful that he might be questioned about all the blood on him.

Popov again asked them to do everything to find the culprit, and the commissioner assured him that they would do everything in their power under the law to arrest and execute the man.

With this the meeting drew to a close.

Some time after Hikozo had returned to the consulate, an officer came at Admiral Popov's command and took him again to the ship. Another meeting had been arranged, this one on the ship, and soon after Hikozo came aboard, Sakai and six commissioner's officials arrived.

Again Popov asked the Japanese to do everything they could to arrest the perpetrator, and again Sakai replied that they would do everything in their power.

Lunch was served, and as they ate, Hikozo, Popov, and the officials discussed how this matter would be resolved. They ended their discussion, and at three in the afternoon Sakai and the officials left the ship.

Popov invited Hikozo to stroll around the deck with him, and as they walked, Popov said, "I wonder if the commissioners and their men are seriously trying to locate and arrest the man who did this. What do you think?"

"I believe they're doing their best," Hikozo answered, speaking his mind.

Popov nodded and said, "They do seem earnest, and I'd have to say that I agree with you." He linked arms with Hikozo. "Hiko, thanks to you we've been able to find out quite a bit from the commissioner. I'd like to thank you, so please tell me if there's anything you'd like to have—anything at all."

"I'm glad to have been of service," Hikozo said. "You needn't give me anything."

"Don't say that," Popov said. "I'll prepare something for you."

Hikozo walked for a while more with Popov, then said goodbye and left the ship.

The next day he went out with Dorr, and when he returned, Van Reed reported that in his absence Admiral Popov had stopped by with a gold watch he asked to be given to Hikozo. It was in appreciation of all Hikozo's efforts on the Russians' behalf. Hikozo was very grateful to Popov for being so conscientious, and he happily accepted the gift.

After this the Russians and the shogunate continued their negotiations through written communications, and Hikozo heard of the conclusions reached. The Russians demanded the following of the shogunate:

1. That shogunal officials come to the Russian warship and apologize in person.
2. That the Kanagawa commissioner be dismissed from office.

3. That when the perpetrator is arrested, his execution be witnessed by the Russian officers and sailors.
4. That a monument be built over the graves of the slain officer and sailor, and that these be maintained in perpetuity.

On September 1 the shogunate accepted all four conditions, removing Mizuno Chikugonokami as Kanagawa commissioner and Kato Ikinokaminoriaki from office, transferring Mizuno to the post of commissioner in charge of foreign warships, and Kato to the post of commissioner in charge of building and construction.

Thus the incident of the attack on and murder of Russian naval personnel came to a close. By this time autumn was already in the air.

CHAPTER SEVENTEEN

More and more merchants and traders began arriving in Yokohama from China and other countries, and the foreign settlement grew. Business flourished, with all kinds of deals taking place.

Early in October an official came to the consulate and asked Hikozo to accompany him to the commissioner's office. "There's something we'd like to ask you," he said. He didn't go into any details, and Hikozo had misgivings as he set off with him.

The official in charge came out carrying a bound document and sat down opposite Hikozo. "This is a copy of a written report sent from the Hakodate commissioner to Edo," he said. "It's a record of an investigation into a castaway who was in America."

Hikozo grew nervous when he heard this, and he looked intently at the official.

The official opened the cover, and as he began reading the first lines, Hikozo let out a low groan of surprise. It was the record of an interrogation of a man who, the official said, "was a castaway in America hailing from Honsho Village in Banshu (Harima Province) by the name of Jisaku."

Jisaku! When Hikozo came to Japan in June, he'd left Jisaku and Kamezo back in America. Kamezo was working on a ship and away from San Francisco when Hikozo set sail, but he'd been able to see Jisaku, who was working for a trading company, and had felt very sorry and sad to leave him behind.

Hikozo listened carefully as the official read, to learn what sort of investigation of Jisaku had been carried out.

The Matter Concerning the Return of a Passenger on an American Ship Recently Docking at Hakodate, the official intoned. So Jisaku had taken an American ship to Hakodate.

The document gave Jisaku's birthplace, the fact that he was the older brother of a farmer named Shichizaemon, and that he was thirty-seven years old. That his detention began on April 19 of this year meant that he'd been handed over to the commissioner's office from the American ship. He'd been released on May 3, meaning that the commissioner's investigation of him had taken place in that interval.

The record went on to state that after drifting on the *Eiriki Maru* Jisaku had been rescued by an American ship, taken for a time to China but then returned to San Francisco. Hikozo's name was recorded there, along with Kamezo's.

The Hakodate commissioner's office had confirmed the facts of Jisaku's disappearance on the *Eiriki Maru* with the Himeji Domain, in whose jurisdiction lay Jisaku's village, as well as with the Osaka commissioner's office, which had jurisdiction over the ship, and had concluded that his testimony was accurate.

The record included an inventory of items Jiskau had with him: "a head covering, tight-sleeved clothing, leggings, and shoes," using a phonetic character for the word *shoes*. Hikozo knew they meant a hat, a coat, trousers, and boots—so Jisaku had been dressed as an American when he arrived.

The silver coins with him were exchanged at the commissioner's office for Japanese money. One of the councilors investigating him offered to purchase a "silver *koffu*" from Jisaku for a high price; Hikozo knew they meant a silver *cup*.

Finally the report said that since Jisaku wanted to return to his home village, where his mother and brother were, as soon as possible, the Hakodate commissioner suggested turning him over to representatives of the Himeji daimyo, Sakai Utanokami, and awaited instructions.

When the official finished reading the report, Hikozo let out a deep sigh. He'd been worried about Jisaku, left behind in America, and was overjoyed to hear that his friend had followed him across the ocean to arrive in Hakodate.

The official spoke again. When Hikozo first arrived in Kanagawa with Harris and Dorr, he'd submitted a document to the commissioner explaining that as a cook on the *Eiriki Maru* he'd been shipwrecked and had stayed in America before coming to Japan. In the record of the investigation of Jisaku it stated that Jisaku had been employed by the *Eiriki Maru* and was shipwrecked on a return voyage from Edo. Thus the official presumed that these were one and the same ship.

"Is that true?" he asked Hikozo.

"Yes," Hikozo replied.

Hikozo told him how he, Jisaku, and Kamezo had gone back to America from China, and how Jisaku had worked for many years in San Francisco; as he related this, it was all taken down by a secretary.

"What sort of life did this Jisaku live in America?"

"At first he was hired as a cook on a ship, and later got a job with a merchant house. He was an earnest person, held in high regard by Americans, and had good relations with them."

"How about his being a Christian?"

"I never heard that he was."

Hikozo realized that being a Christian was indeed a hindrance to being allowed back into Japan, and was thankful again to Sanders for his wisdom in recommending that he become a U.S. citizen.

"Thank you for your trouble. I was requested by Edo to question you concerning Jisaku." The official politely bowed.

"No, I should thank *you*," Hikozo said, and stood up. Now that the investigation of Jisaku seemed finished, he should be going back to his hometown. Hikozo could imagine how pleased he'd be, and was pleased for his friend.

Most of his former shipmates from the *Eiriki Maru* had arrived in Nagasaki on a Chinese merchant ship and had then gone back to their respective hometowns. The one sailor who'd disappeared in China, Iwakichi, had changed his name to Denkichi and under the name of Dan had returned to Japan as the interpreter for the British minister Alcock. He was no doubt living at the British mission at the Tozenji Temple, though Hikozo had yet to meet him again.

But what had happened to the one sailor left behind on the *Susquehanna*, the cook Sentaro? And what of Kamezo, alone now in America? Was he still well? Hikozo was greatly concerned about these two.

The next day the consulate had a visitor, and when Hikozo went out to see who it was, he called out a loud greeting and strode over to shake his hand. The visitor was Lieutenant Brooke, the man who had got him started on the road back to Japan, and Hikozo felt an eternal debt of gratitude toward him.

Lieutenant Brooke told him he was still on his surveying expedition and presently surveying the Japanese coast. His ship was anchored off Kanagawa, and he'd come ashore to pay his respects to Mr. Dorr.

Hikozo took Brooke to Dorr's room and introduced him, explaining how he'd come to know the lieutenant. Brooke and Dorr had a nice talk as the lieutenant related how their surveying work was progressing. Brooke said he was pleasantly surprised at how much natural beauty there was in Japan, and with a sparkle in his eye described how moved he'd been when he saw Mount Fuji from his ship.

Brooke said he'd like very much to invite Dorr and Hikozo to his ship, and Dorr happily accepted the invitation.

One thing worried Hikozo, though. Was Masakichi—or Tim, as he was known—the Japanese castaway who'd taken his place in Hawaii, still on board the *Cooper*? After they finished their talk, the lieutenant stood up, shook Dorr's hand, and took his leave. As Hikozo saw Brooke out to the grounds of the temple, he asked, "How's Tim?"

The lieutenant stopped and turned to look at Hikozo.

"He's well," he replied. "In fact, there's a favor I'd like to ask of you in regard to him. I have an appointment with the commissioner tomorrow afternoon at two. I'd like to hand Tim over to them, but could you be present with us then?"

Hikozo nodded. "Of course, I'd be happy to..."

"Well, then, let's meet at the Yokohama dock at one thirty tomorrow afternoon." The lieutenant shook Hikozo's hand and walked out the main gate.

The next day Hikozo explained the situation to Dorr, who gave him permission to take the time off, and he went to the dock at the appointed hour. The boat from the *Cooper* was already at the dock, with some sailors aboard, and the lieutenant and a man with darkly tanned skin.

"Masakichi," Hikozo called out, walked quickly over to him, and took his hand.

Masakichi's eyes glistened, and Hikozo wordlessly bowed.

He walked in the lead, and Masakichi followed, wiping his tears. Hikozo, too, turned teary as he thought about the joy this man must be feeling—being the only one on his ship to survive starvation and now, at last, to finally stand on his native soil.

Hikozo announced their business to the guard outside the commissioner's office, and the guard went inside. Soon an official Hikozo was familiar with came out and bade them enter.

They were escorted to a room and waited there awhile, then the commissioner, Niimi Buzennokami Masaoki, entered with his chief officials and others. Hikozo introduced the lieutenant to him, Niimi asked them to sit, which Hikozo and the lieutenant did. Maakichi remained kneeling on the floor, his hands touching the floor and head bowed in a pose of utmost respect.

The lieutenant began by saying, "We've come to hand over to you this Japanese man Tim. We've brought him because he wishes to be repatriated. Tim is a very sincere fellow and worked very hard on my ship as an apprentice sailor."

Hikozo added that Tim was the name the Americans called him, that his real name was Masakichi, that he was born on Awaji Island, that the cargo ship he worked on was cast adrift, and that he alone survived to be rescued by an American whaling vessel and taken to Hawaii.

The commissioner's clerk took all this down, and then the commissioner directed several questions to the prostrated Masakichi. Masakichi, his head lowered throughout, replied to these.

"We'll investigate the details with him at the commissioner's office," the chief official said in a gentle tone, and the questioning ended.

Hikozo turned to Lieutenant Brooke and explained, "The commissioner's office will accept Tim. In other words, he'll be repatriated."

The lieutenant nodded, pulled out a cloth bag from his bag on the floor, stood up, and handed this to the chief official. He said that there was $230 inside. Tim had worked very hard on the *Cooper*, and these were his wages for the voyage.

Brooke looked at Niimi and said, "I'd like you to exchange this money for Japanese currency and give it to Tim. This is compensation for his diligence, and he has a right to it."

Hikozo interpreted this, and Niimi, a gentle look in his eyes, said, "Indeed, we'll be sure that's done."

"Thank you," Brooke said, the emotion evident in his voice. "Your kindness is much appreciated."

Niimi said, "I am grateful from the bottom of my heart to you for taking such good care of one of my countrymen, and for bringing him safely home."

When Hikozo interpreted this, Brooke said, "It's wonderful that things have turned out so well," and he bowed several times.

The meeting was over, and Hikozo and the lieutenant stood up.

Hikozo went over to Masakichi, still with his hands pressed in supplication against the floor, knelt beside him, and rested a hand on his shoulder. "You'll be able to go home now. I'm very happy for you," he said, then stood up and followed the lieutenant from the room.

Hikozo never saw Masakichi again, but a thorough investigation took place at the commissioner's office. They confirmed that his birthplace was Kinami Village, Tsuna County, on the island of Awaji (present-day Hokudan Town), that he was the third son of a farmer and had become a sailor. The full account of the wreck of the *Sumiyoshi Maru* was recorded, and how Masakichi had alone survived and been rescued.

The commissioner's investigation turned up nothing suspicious, so he was transferred to Edo and handed over to the Edo mansion of the Tokushima daimyo, under whose domain Masakichi's village lay. The domain conducted its own interrogation, hearing his testimony into the details of how he became a castaway, how he nearly starved to death, and how he worked on both the whaling vessel and survey ship. This testimony was all noted down, and the complete record of the inquiry was sent to Tokushima.

Masakichi was escorted back to his home village, and when he arrived, his relatives, who'd given him up for dead, were overjoyed.

Two months later a messenger came from the domain to escort him to Tokushima. The domain had a great interest in this ordinary sailor who'd had such extraordinary experiences. The domain had no one who was able to use English, and decided that Masakichi, who could now freely converse in the language, was fully qualified to be an interpreter. The domain also determined that, having worked for so long at whaling, he had abundant knowledge of Western sailing vessels and that his experience in both whaling and surveying would be invaluable to them.

The domain appointed Masakichi to samurai status, and he was allowed the privilege of having a family name and carrying the two swords of the rank. He decided, since he'd been called Tim by the Americans, to choose characters for his last name that could, in one reading, be pronounced *Tenmu*—a close approximation of *Tim*—but would normally be pronounced Amage. His entire new name thus became Amage Masakichi.

He became a domain interpreter, as well as captain of the Western sailing vessel, the *Tsusai Maru*, that the domain constructed. He married the second daughter of Kiba Kashichiro and fathered one son and two daughters. In the second year of Bunkyu (1862) he was dispatched by the domain to Yokohama to purchase a Western sailing ship.

After the Meiji Restoration he worked in whaling in Hokkaido, and passed away at the age of sixty-two from illness, in the twenty-fifth year of Meiji.

Clear, sunny days continued, and though it snowed on the morning of December 6, the snow soon ended and the air was dry again.

Around this time the Kanagawa commissioner's office was busy with people streaming in and out, with many mounted samurai and shogunal officials traveling back and forth between the commissioner's and Edo Castle. During discussions for the conclusion of the U.S.-Japan Trade Treaty it was proposed that Japan send an official mission to the United States. Minister Harris warmly welcomed the proposal, and the shogunate was now busily preparing to make this mission a reality.

Selecting those who would go on the mission proved difficult, but in the end the shogunate appointed Niimi Buzennokami Masaoki, the commissioner for foreign affairs and Kanagawa commissioner, as head of the mission, Muragaki Awajinokami Norimasa as assistant head, with Oguri Bungonokami Tadamasa as superintendent officer. The entire mission would be taking the American warship *Powhatan* to the United States, while the shogunate's steam vessel *Kanrin Maru* would accompany them on the journey.

Since this was the very first official mission to be sent abroad, various chief officials of the shogunate, from senior councillors on down through superintendents, their bosses, the financial commissioner, and the commissioner for foreign affairs, held numerous meetings, handing down directives to the Kanagawa commissioner as a result. Messengers scuttled back and forth from Minister Harris to Dorr at the consulate as arrangements for the trip were finalized.

Finally the *Powhatan* arrived in Kanagawa, and Hikozo and Van Reed spent busy days procuring and finding storage facilities for the coal needed for the voyage.

In the meanwhile the survey ship *Cooper* had unfortunately run aground on shoals during a severe storm and, being deemed unfit for sailing, was put up for sale at auction. Lieutenant Brooke and the rest of the crew, bereft of their vessel, were left to find some merchant ship for passage back home, but when Brooke heard about the mission to America, he made a proposal, through the America mission, to the shogunate. The Japanese at the helm of the *Kanrin Maru,* the ship that would accompany the *Powhatan,* were instructors at the shogunate's naval training facility, but naturally they had never crossed the Pacific Ocean before. Brooke proposed that he and his crew accompany them and help them navigate the waters.

The Japanese officers who were to pilot the *Kanrin Maru* were fiercely opposed to this, saying that they were confident they could make the voyage without any outside help. The shogunate, however, partly because of Harris's recommendation, accepted Brooke's proposal. It decided that as the captain of a surveying ship Brooke was familiar with all the waters between Edo Bay and San Francisco and that nothing could be more desirable than having him and his crew help guide their ship.

The *Kanrin Maru* and the *Powhatan* were set to depart in the middle of January.

The end of the year came, and they celebrated the beginning of the New Year, Ansei 7 (1860). The Japanese shops in Yokohama were decorated with traditional pine and bamboo ornaments, the whole district quite festive.

The sunny weather continued, the morning of January 8 dawning typically bright, crisp sunlight streaming into the grounds of the American consulate at the Honkakuji Temple.

After breakfast, Consul Dorr passed some documents to Hikozo, ones he said he'd just been handed by officials from the Kanagawa commissioner's office, and asked him to translate these into English. A steady stream of written requests and reports concerning the upcoming mission were coming into the consulate at this time from the commissioner's, and it was Hikozo's task to translate them into English and show them to Dorr. These documents mainly arrived either early in the morning or late at night, so Hikozo was certain this new document was another that concerned the upcoming mission to America.

But when he opened it and ran his eyes over it, he felt the blood drain from his face. The short missive reported that the Japanese interpreter attached to the British mission had been attacked and killed the previous evening.

Iwakichi's face came to Hikozo's mind—his crewmate on the *Eiriki Maru*. Hikozo had run across him by accident in Canton, where Iwakichi was hired as interpreter by the British consul assigned to Japan, Mr. Alcock, then lived at the British general consulate (which five months later was promoted to the status of British mission) in the Tozenji Temple in Takanawa.

Could it be Iwakichi, or was the murdered man someone else, another Japanese well versed in English who'd been hired by the mission?

"Is something wrong?" Noticing how pale Hikozo had become, Dorr was anxious.

"The interpreter for the British mission was murdered last night. A Japanese." Hikozo replied.

"You think it's Dan?" Dorr asked.

Hikozo had spoken to him of Denkichi, and Dorr knew how he'd come to work in the British mission.

"I wonder...," Hikozo muttered, and said he'd like to go to the commissioner's office to learn the details.

Even if the victim was Japanese, he was an official interpreter for the British mission, so Dorr knew that this murder involved the entire diplomatic community. He agreed: it was vital to ascertain everything possible about the incident.

Hikozo hurriedly changed clothes and left the temple grounds. The road was dry, and the sea to his left sparkled in the sun. He walked quickly along the road.

Confusion reigned at the commissioner's office. In the midst of preparations for the mission to American had come this news that

230

the British mission's official interpreter had been murdered, and it happened in their jurisdiction.

The murder of a Russian naval officer and sailor had been followed in October by the murder of a Chinese employee of the French legation who wore Western clothes and had no doubt been mistaken for a foreigner by samurai from the radical faction that wanted to exclude foreigners from Japan. These had all become international incidents, ones the shogunate was still struggling to resolve—and now this additional attack was sure to provoke a protest in the strongest terms from Ambassador Alcock.

Hikozo told the officials that he'd come on order of Consul Dorr, and requested that they tell him the details. The official in charge soon appeared and agreed to explain to him all that they had gathered from reports of the attack.

"What is the name of the interpreter who was murdered?" Hikozo asked. The official glanced down at the documents in his hand.

"He was known as Dan. His Japanese name was Denkichi, and he was well versed, apparently, in the British tongue," the official replied.

Hikozo stared at the official without speaking a word. His worst fears had come true. He remembered how happy Denkichi had been when he learned he'd been hired as interpreter for Alcock. The poor man had finally returned home to Japan only to meet this cruel fate.

As he read over the report, the official related the details of the incident. At around five the previous evening Denkichi had gone outside the gates of the British mission at Tozenji Temple; there he'd run across some little girls playing battledore and shuttlecock, and he joined them for the fun of it. A single samurai suddenly appeared and approached him from behind. The man unsheathed his short sword and plunged it into Denkichi's back, then slowly walked away.

Denkichi staggered toward the gate, trying to make it inside the compound, and a passing guard noticed him and ran over to help, but Denkichi fell to the ground, face up. The doctor assigned to the British legation rushed out and treated him, but the sword had pierced all the way through to the left side of his chest, and he soon expired.

Officials from the legation as well as guards dispersed in all directions to find the culprit, but it was soon dark and they returned empty-handed. According to witnesses, the samurai had white hair and was in his sixties.

That night the Kanagawa commissioner, Hori Toshihiro, was informed of the attack, and late at night he went to the legation, accompanied by his attendants. He expressed his condolences to the chief secretary, Heusken, and they discussed how to deal with the incident.

Hikozo, hearing this account, left the commissioner's in low spirits.

Why would Denkichi be murdered? If the murderer was a samurai of the faction that wished to drive all foreigners from Japan, why would his wrath be directed at a Japanese who worked for a foreign legation? But if it was, then someone like Hikozo, who'd taken U.S. citizenship and worked for the American consulate, might also become a target.

This faction loathed foreigners, he'd heard, and had sworn to drive every one of them from the country. While in America, Japanese castaways were treated with great kindness, and Hikozo had even been able to go to school and be educated and live a comfortable life. Those who wished to expel foreigners were narrowminded and prejudiced to an extreme. Hikozo felt a tremendous anger toward the samurai who had cut down Denkichi.

Returning to the consulate, he reported to Dorr on Denkichi's death.

"This country's insane," Dorr commented, and Hikozo took a deep breath. Dorr seemed to find the Japanese uncivilized and ignorant, and Hikozo felt ashamed.

Dorr wrote a letter of condolence to Ambassador Alcock.

All kinds of reports concerning the incident came into the American consulate and the commissioner's office.

The morning after the murder Alcock wrote a letter of protest to Wakisaka Yasuori, senior councillor in charge of foreign affairs, demanding that the instigator of the crime to brought to justice. Wakisaka replied that he'd issued a strict order to arrest the man, but at present they had no clues.

As Hikozo mourned his friend, some unexpected news reached him. A week or so before the incident, one of the Kanagawa commissioners, Mizoguchi Sanukinokami, had gone to the British legation and talked with Chief Clerk Heusken. The reason for Mizoguchi's visit was Denkichi.

At first Denkichi had very humbly performed his role as official interpreter, but had gradually started to act different. Alcock and the entire staff of the British mission had assumed an arrogant attitude toward the shogunate, treating with great haughtiness even the highest officials who paid them a visit, and before long this attitude affected Denkichi. Despite his humble background as a sailor, he began to feel that, with his official position as legation interpreter, he, too, had the full might of the British Empire behind him, and he began dressing like an English gentleman—wearing the latest fashions, carrying a pistol at his waist, and puffing away on a cigar.

The shogunate had dispatched some two hundred soldiers to guard the British legation, their own troops as well as troops from the Kouriyama and Nishio domains. Denkichi treated them all with contempt, angering the guards and provoking quarrels. At every quarrel, he would puff himself up and say, menacingly, "I'll have you know I'm the official interpreter for the British legation." Afraid of the reaction of people in the legation, the guards would usually back off.

Even outside the grounds of the legation Denkichi's actions began to draw attention. Commoners were not allowed to ride horses, but Denkichi, taking advantage of his position, proudly trotted down the streets on the back of a Western horse, sometimes even breaking into a gallop. Whenever he ran across samurai from the various domains on the street, he'd act quite haughty, and often an angry exchange of words ensued.

Denkichi's unrestrained behavior grew more and more noticeable. He began a sexual liaison with the daughter of the owner of a teashop called the Miura-ya near the legation and spent many a night there, drinking sake while the women attended to him into the wee hours. People frowned whenever they saw him striding down the street, and many stepped off the roadside as soon as they saw him. His bad reputation preceded him everywhere.

The Kanagawa commissioner's office, in fact, feared for his safety, predicting that someone from the faction for expulsion of foreigners might target him. His being attacked and killed would become an international incident, affecting relations between Britain and Japan. The commissioner's office couldn't keep quiet about this problem, so Mizoguchi visited the legation to warn them.

He talked at length with Heusken about Denkichi's conduct, urging him to dismiss the man immediately from service at the legation to avert an attack.

Hikozo heard all this from an official from the commissioner's office, which felt that since it had gone to the trouble of dispatching a high official such as Mizoguchi to give warning to the legation, it had discharged its responsibility.

From an official he knew well Hikozo learned more about the unpardonable behavior of Denkichi, and Hikozo felt very sorry for him. After Denkichi disappeared in China, he was able to hide himself by working for a British merchant in Shanghai, though undoubtedly he was treated coldly there. The British, flaunting their overwhelming power, saw China as a colony of their empire, and the people who worked at the merchant's treated the Chinese roughly. Denkichi was Japanese, but to the British merchants he looked like another Chinese, and they surely abused him. After putting up with this cruel treatment, he unexpectedly found himself employed by Alcock as the legation's chief interpreter and was able to return to Japan. The Japanese he came in contact with began to defer to him because of his position, which led to him to becoming more and more overbearing himself.

Dorr reported back to Hikozo on the atmosphere inside the British legation after Denkichi's death. Heusken had dismissed Mizoguchi's warning out of hand, but Alcock and the rest of the legation staff were well aware of Denkichi's behavior and had been shaking their heads over it for some time.

Alcock himself expressed his anxiety about this in a book he wrote entitled *The Capital of the Tycoon*:

> I had for some time been under the conviction that danger was at hand in some shape.... I was even seriously meditating sending him out of the country, for his own sake, though his knowledge of the Japanese made him very useful, if not necessary to me, in the first months of our location.... I felt, nevertheless, that a more discreet and better-tempered man than he had any pretensions to be would have been insecure.

Alcock admitted that Mizoguchi's warnings were well founded, writing, "He had received a distinct warning that it was determined to take his life," also revealing how accurately he'd observed Denkichi's personality with the following words: "He was ill-tempered, proud, and violent."

News of Denkichi's death soon spread throughout Edo, and those familiar with his behavior remarked that they were not surprised that he'd been killed.

One samurai serving the Choshu Domain at their residence in Edo, one Kaura Kogoro, had long noted Denkichi's behavior, and in a letter to Kijima Matabei of the Hagi Domain he severely criticized Denkichi, writing that he "was a very insincere fellow" and that "under the umbrella" of British power he "looked down upon our empire." At the end of the letter he noted that Denkichi's murder "served him right."

Alcock, while believing that Denkichi's death was unavoidable, ordered that his funeral be one that expressed the prestige of Britain, one befitting an official interpreter for the British legation. Interment was to take place at the Korinji Temple in Azabu, with Alcock and the entire staff of the legation in attendance. He insisted that the Kanagawa commissioners, Mizoguchi and Hori, both attend.

The day of the funeral, the tenth, was sunny. Denkichi's coffin was transported to the Korinji Temple, and a magnificent funeral service was held. Many priests intoned sutras, and Denkichi's posthumous Buddhist name, following tradition, was carved on his gravestone.

After the service the coffin was taken inside the temple graveyard and buried. Denkichi was forty-one.

CHAPTER EIGHTEEN

In the midst of the trouble over Denkichi's murder, the Kanagawa commissioner's office, under directives from the shogunal cabinet, turned its attention to preparing for the Japanese mission to America.

On January 14 a note came from the commissioner's office requesting Hikozo's presence at the office together with Lieutenant Brooke, who would be piloting the *Kanrin Maru*. Hikozo agreed and set off for the commissioner's with Brooke.

Takemoto Masatsune, chief of documents for the shogunate, came out to greet them and expressed to Brooke how grateful the shogunate was that he had accepted the post of piloting the ship for them. Hikozo interpreted this for Brooke, who said it was a great honor that he was delighted to accept.

Takemoto said they would like to express their gratitude by way of some presents, and had his retainers bring a plain wood tray. On the tray rested a dagger with a silver handle, and embroidered silk cloth. Brooke's eyes sparkled in delight, and he thanked Takemoto many times.

The *Kanrin Maru* was scheduled to depart four days afterward, so the next day Hikozo took a lighter out to the ship to say farewell to his friend Brooke.

At this time he was introduced to the commodore of the *Kanrin Maru*, Kimura Yoshitake, commissioner of battleships, the captain of the ship, Katsu Awa, and their interpreter, an officer named

Nakahama Manjiro. Hikozo had heard about Manjiro, how he was a former castaway that the shogunate was employing in the important post of interpreter.

Manjiro was from a fisherman's family in Tosa, and at the age of fifteen his boat had been blown off course, and he landed at a deserted island (Torishima). Six months latter he was rescued by an American whaling vessel piloted by a Captain Whitfield and taken to Hawaii. Afterward he landed in New Bedford. Whitfield, who'd grown fond of the boy, saw to it that he received an education in school, in English and mathematics. Later Manjiro learned navigation and surveying. He eventually became a crew member of a whaling ship and in 1846 returned to Hawaii, from where in January of the New Year he made landfall in the Ryukyu Islands and finally reached Nagasaki.

Recognizing his skills not just in English but also in navigation and surveying, the Tosa Domain put him in their service; later he was put in service to the shogunate to translate English documents, and also to serve as instructor at the naval training school and to teach modern whaling techniques.

Manjiro, known as John Manjiro, had heard about Hikozo. "I understand you went through the same sort of terrible experiences I did as a castaway," he said. "Let's both do our best to work for our country." He gave Hikozo a firm handshake.

Manjiro was thirty-four and had real presence about him. Hikozo, ten years younger, was in awe of him.

Hikozo heard that the *Kanrin Maru* had set sail from Uraga on January 19, bound for San Francisco. Three days later, the seventy-seven members of the Japanese delegation to the United States left Yokohama on the American warship *Powhatan*, also bound for San Francisco. At long last things grew quiet in Kanagawa.

Sunny weather continued for a time, but when February came, it started to snow more often than not. Even so, it was a warmer winter than usual; the snow soon changed to sleet and then rain.

At the end of February Hikozo tendered his resignation to Dorr. He knew his prospects for the future would be limited as long as he remained in service at the consulate, and he wanted to be free to travel his own path. A month before he'd received a letter from a friend in San Francisco, a businessman who proposed that they open a joint venture in Japan. Hikozo was inspired to do this and felt it best to leave his post in the consulate if he wanted to go into business.

Dorr was surprised and tried his best to dissuade him, relenting only when Hikozo promised to offer his services free of charge as interpreter whenever the need arose.

Hikozo found that he'd accumulated a fair sum of savings, enough to live on if he lived modestly, and he proceeded to move out of the consulate to a small house he rented in Yokohama Village.

It was snowing heavily on the morning of March 3, and Hikozo, who felt he was coming down with a cold, was in bed when a messenger arrived from Dorr carrying a letter from the consul. When he opened it, Hikozo found the surprising news that the Regent Ii Kamon no kami Naosuke had just been assassinated in Edo. Dorr requested that he come immediately to the consulate.

The snow had stopped by the time Hikozo reached the consulate.

Dorr was pale as he showed him an urgent message he'd received from Harris. The message related how, while on his way to Edo Castle some ronin samurai ambushed Ii's party and cruelly cut him down at Sakurada Gate of the castle. At Dorr's request Hikozo stayed over at the consulate.

One letter after another arrived from the British legation. The shogunate told Harris and all the foreign representatives in Japan that Ii was only slightly wounded and in no danger of dying. But other reports from reliable witnesses were coming from Edo that the band of samurai had made off with Ii's severed head. Finally on the last day of March the shogunate publicly announced Ii's death, their previous statement obviously intended to hide the fact that the regent had been slain.

Dorr was very fearful when he learned that the regent of the shogunate himself, heavily guarded at the time, had been murdered by members of the faction demanding that all foreigners be removed from Japan. Ii had supported the open-door policy, thus incurring the wrath of the faction. But with the kind of protection provided a man of his stature—a cabinet official of high rank—the attackers should never have found an opening to him.

Thinking about the great hatred of these men, Hikozo shuddered.

The ever-cautious Harris announced that he would not be leaving the legation compound, and Dorr, too, severely limited his own trips outside the consulate grounds. When he absolutely had to venture forth, he always made sure to carry a sidearm with him. Taking the hint, Hikozo, too, took to carrying a pistol.

Near the end of that month a report reached them that another foreigner had been murdered in Yokohama Village. Hikozo didn't know all the details but heard that the captain of two Dutch vessels that had come into port was walking around the shops in Yokohama with his retinue when a samurai suddenly began slashing at them from behind. Two men fell to the ground, dead. According to eyewitnesses, beside one of the Dutchmen lay a cap and a severed arm.

This incident only increased the fears of the foreign community, and no one went out after dark.

The assassination of the regent Ii led the shogunate to change the era name from Ansei to Man'en.

The Kanagawa commissioner's office decided, in order to dispel the gloom that had overtaken Yokohama, to hold the annual festival of the Bentensha Shrine on June 2 to celebrate the first anniversary of the opening of the port and ordered the festival to be bigger than ever before. To accomplish this, local parishioners of the shrine had geisha leading floats around the town's streets and had them dance on a stage. Foreigners came to enjoy the spectacle and were welcomed by the Japanese.

On September 22 the American ship *Hartford* came into port with Commodore Stribling aboard. Dorr held a ball for the commodore and his officers. All the Americans in the settlement were invited, and the party, which Dorr also planned as a means of cheering up the local resident Americans, was a resounding success.

On the morning of September 28 the American warship *Niagara* entered Edo Bay, anchoring at about 11 AM in the waters off Yokohama Village. On board were Niimi Buzennokami and the first official mission to American that he had headed, now returned to Japan.

Together with the consulate's clerk, Van Reed, Hikozo went out by boat to the *Niagara,* where they met Niimi and the second in charge of the mission, Muragaki Norimasa. With Hikozo interpreting, on behalf of the consul Reed expressed his happiness at their safe return.

Niimi replied that he wished Reed to convey to Dorr that they had a most pleasant trip and were warmly welcomed wherever they went in the United States. Niimi then told Hikozo he wished to convey their appreciation to the captain, officers, and crew of the *Niagara* for their many kindnesses during the voyage. Hikozo, with Niimi and Muragaki, approached the captain and officers, who were standing nearby, and as Niimi spoke, he interpreted his words. The captain smiled broadly, and Hikozo conveyed his reply back in Japanese.

After Hikozo and the others left the ship, the *Niagara* sailed on, anchoring off Shinagawa. The next day Niimi and his retinue bid farewell to the captain and crew and took boats to shore. As they moved away, every single sailor climbed up the rigging, the captain and officers lined the deck and gave three cheers, waving their hats, and a seventeen-gun salute was sounded, the echo of the cannons ringing out.

This scene was described far and wide among the residents of Kanagawa, and Hikozo heard how some of the sailors were so sad to say good-bye to their Japanese friends that they shed tears. Hikozo could only hope that this news would reach the ears of the faction against foreigners and somehow soften, even if only a little, their intense hatred.

Three days after the mission to America returned, an official from the commissioner's officer came and, in a very polite tone, requested Hikozo to accompany him back to the commissioner's.

Wondering what it could all be about, Hikozo changed his clothes and went with the man.

He was waiting in a room when the investigating official and scribes entered and sat down facing him.

The official placed some documents on the table and asked, "Do you happen to know a man named Kamegoro?"

Hikozo inclined his head, searching his memory.

"You don't know him?" the official said, surprise on his face. "He claims he lived with you in San Francisco. He said there was another fellow as well, by the name of Jisaku..."

Hikozo cried out in surprise. This had to be Kamezo! It wasn't unusual for people to take on a new name: the murdered Iwakichi, for instance, had taken the name Denkichi, and he himself had become Hikozo instead of Hikotaro. Kamezo had been nicknamed Kame by the Americans, so he must have kept that and added the other part, becoming Kamegoro.

"Yes, I know him very well. His name was originally Kamezo." As he said this, Hikozo wondered why the officials would be talking about Kamezo in the first place.

"Ah, so you *do* know him," the official confirmed. "This man was on board the ship that brought back Niimi Buzennokami and the mission from America. He's being investigated in Edo as we speak."

Hikozo's mouth fell open. At first he couldn't believe his ears— that Kamezo had finally come home.

As the official read through the document, he explained further. On its way back from America, the *Niagara* had stopped in Hong Kong on September 10 to take on coal, water, and provisions, and in the meantime Niimi and others in the mission went ashore.

They left Hong Kong on the eighteenth, but a day earlier a Japanese man came out to the ship on a Chinese boat. He was carrying a letter of introduction from an American and asked to speak with Whitman, the interpreter on board. When Whitman came to see him, the man introduced himself in fluent English as Kamegoro.

He said that he was born in Mukunoura in Geishu (modern-day Mukunoura-cho, Innoshima City, in Hiroshima Prefecture) and that ten years ago he'd been shipwrecked on the way back from Edo, the boat running into a storm off Kumano Nada and then drifting; he was then rescued by an American merchant ship and taken to San Francisco. They were seventeen men all told, but their captain passed away from illness in Hawaii while they were being taken to China. Kamegoro said that he, Jisaku, and Hikozo had returned to San Francisco, where he'd worked as a cook on a ship.

After returning to San Francisco from a long voyage, he discovered that both his friends had already gone back to Japan—Hikozo to Kanagawa and Jisaku to Hakodate.

Left behind, Kamegoro searched like one possessed for a ship that might take him to Japan. When he learned that a merchant vessel would be traveling to Hong Kong, he appealed to the captain to take him aboard. The captain agreed, and Kamegoro was hired as one of the crew, arriving fifty days later in Hong Kong. When he found out that the *Niagara* was in port with the Japanese mission to America, he hit upon the idea of seeing Whitman and asking that he be allowed to ride back with them to Japan.

Whitman was sympathetic to Kamegoro's plight and conveyed his request to Niimi, who agreed to meet him. Whitman escorted Kamegoro to see him, and when he came before Niimi, Kamegoro fell to the floor and began to wail. One of the retainers began questioning him in a gentle voice, and choked with tears, Kamegoro related his story.

Moved, Niimi asked the captain of the *Niagara* to take Kamegoro on board. The captain had no problem with that but was opposed to handing him over directly to Niimi's custody. According to American law, in handing over castaways it was first required that the captain receive a written petition addressed to him from the local American consul. Since Kamegoro had not followed this procedure, the captain maintained that he couldn't hand him over to the Japanese authorities. Niimi kindly repeated his request, but the captain wouldn't budge.

As a result of much discussion it was agreed that after reaching Japan Kamegoro would be handed over by the captain to the

American ambassador, who would decide what was to become of him. When they landed in Shinagawa, therefore, Kamegoro was detained at the legation, and then the legation handed him over to the local officials.

"This fellow is now undergoing investigation in Edo. Does his statement accord with the facts as you know them?"

"To the best of my knowledge, it's correct," Hikozo replied.

Leaving the commissioner's office, Hikozo walked down the road in high spirits. Jisaku had landed in Hakodate, and now Kamezo was in Edo. Niimi's kindness had led to Kamezo's repatriation, and as Hikozo recalled the man's face at their meeting four days before, he vowed to thank him from the bottom of his heart at the first opportunity.

Soon the investigation of Kamezo would finish, and no doubt he'd be able to return to his hometown of Mukunoura. Hikozo could picture how overjoyed the man's family and relatives would be.

In a cheerful mood Hikozo worked with various foreign and Japanese merchants, acting as interpreter at their business negotiations, receiving proper compensation for his services.

The leaves on the trees turned, then the colors faded, and the air was filled with falling leaves as the temperature began to drop. The autumn sky was blue and clear, women crowded the shore collecting shellfish, and the sea was dotted with fishing boats. The sunny weather continued, but it was chillier than in years past. The first snow of the year fell on November 15, and Yokohama Village was covered with white.

On December 5 the sky was clear, but it was terribly cold.

That evening Hikozo enjoyed some wine that Dorr had sent him and went to bed. In the middle of the night he woke to the sound of knocking at his front gate. He opened the door to find a Japanese employed by the consulate standing there; the man said that something urgent had come up and they needed him.

Wondering what it could be about, Hikozo strapped his pistol to his waist and, lantern in hand, hurried after the man. Lights were on at the consulate, and ten or so officials from the commissioner's office, with their minions, were on the grounds, their faces stern.

When Hikozo went into Dorr's room, his lamp lit up the consul and Van Reed sitting there.

"Mr. Heusken has been attacked. He's severely injured."

Hikozo was at a loss for words.

He'd met Heusken once, when the ship he'd taken back to Japan from Shanghai with Harris stopped in Shimoda to pick Heusken up, but hadn't seen him since.

"How did it happen?" Hikozo could barely ask.

Dorr told him what had happened. On July 19 the Prussian delegation led by Count Eulenburg arrived in Shinagawa on a warship and requested to conclude a treaty with the shogunate, and negotiations ensued.

Hoping to make use of the services of Heusken, who was not only an interpreter but well versed in the situation in Japan, Count Eulenburg appealed to the American legation, and Harris was happy to comply. Heusken began commuting to the Akabane Guest Quarters in Shiba, where Eulenburg was in residence, and, together with the Japanese interpreter Moriyama Einosuke, collated the Japanese and English clauses of the treaty. When they had completed this task, Eulenburg and those with him expressed their deepest appreciation to Heusken for all his hard work.

Harris had forbidden all legation personnel to be outside at night and directed Heusken to return each day before sundown. However, Heusken, as he worked with Eulenburg, made a habit of coming back after dinner, after 9 PM. On the night of December 5 he left the guest quarters at this same time.

He was on horseback, accompanied by three mounted officials. They trotted down the road toward the legation, the officials all holding lanterns, one man in front and two bringing up the rear. Four stewards, also carrying lanterns, ran alongside them. Heusken carried only a whip and was unarmed.

At a point about halfway to the legation the road narrowed,

and at this place seven samurai leaped out and attacked them. They knocked down the lanterns the officials were carrying, knocked down the stewards, and began slashing at Heusken. Injured, he was able to escape on horseback, but after two or three hundred paces he was so weak he had one of the stewards help him down from his horse. He walked a few steps and collapsed.

His horse was injured on its haunch, so the stewards tied it to a fence, then removed a shutter from a nearby house and placed Heusken on it and carried him to the American legation.

When he learned of the incident, the head of the Kurume Domain, Arima Yoshinori, dispatched the domain physician; in addition the Prussian delegation immediately sent over Dr. Lucius, and the British legation sent over Dr. Myburgh. Heusken had been deeply cut from stomach to waist, his intestines exposed, and the doctors valiantly sewed him up and treated his wounds, but he had lost so much blood his eyes were vacant, and his pulse got progressively weaker.

Heusken said he wanted some wine, and after he'd drunk some, in a weak voice he thanked all who'd helped him and then fell asleep.

"What do the doctors say?" Hikozo asked, staring at Dorr.

Dorr shook his head several times. "They hold out no hope," he muttered.

Just then an official from the commissioner's office knocked on the door.

"Mr. Heusken passed away at midnight," he reported with a bow. Hikozo interpreted this for Dorr.

Dorr clasped his arms tightly about him, hung his head, and was silent for a long time.

Hikozo knew how much Harris cared for Heusken and could imagine his grief at learning of his death. Harris had said that he loved Heusken as his own child, and had spent his whole diplomatic life with him. Dorr, knowing this, was stunned by Heusken's death.

He finally raised his head. "Damn those Japanese scoundrels," he said, his eyes flashing with anger.

From far off they heard a cock crow.

Hikozo stayed the night in the consulate. Officials from the Kanagawa commissioner's office came often to the consulate with further news about the incident, and each time Hikozo was called on to interpret for Dorr.

Heusken's death shocked the foreign diplomatic community, and though they roundly condemned the shogunate, Harris's reaction was relatively calm, which surprised Hikozo. Harris held that the incident had nothing to do with the shogunate, declaring publicly that he was certain of the shogunate's sincerity and good intentions in upholding the treaty. He also requested that the shogunate pay condolence money of ten thousand dollars to Heusken's parents, an idea the shogunate immediately acted upon. Thus they avoided an international incident.

Heusken's funeral was held December 8, with Dorr heading to the American legation to attend. The shogunate feared that if Harris and the many foreign diplomats who attended the funeral joined in the procession afterward, they risked being attacked by rogue samurai; their cautions, though, fell on deaf ears: Harris was adamant that they accompany the body of his beloved companion. The funeral procession was thus a long one.

Ambassadors and consuls from various countries, along with officers from the nations' warships, joined the procession, each group carrying its country's flag. On the Japanese side foreign commissioners were in attendance, as well as many other officials and soldiers. The funeral procession started at the legation and ended up at the Korinji Temple.

The casket was taken to the burial grounds and interred. Father Girard led a ceremony that followed the rituals of the Church, and a military band played hymns. Then a large number of Buddhist priests chanted sutras, Harris gave a short speech of thanks to all who came, and the funeral was over.

Hikozo heard about the funeral from Dorr after he returned to the consulate. Dorr was so morose he looked like a different person. The foreign diplomats and staff that attended the funeral obviously feared that they might suffer the same fate as Heusken.

Both the British ambassador, Alcock, and the French ambassador had set up their legations in Shiba in Edo, but thinking the danger too great there, they planned to move their missions to Yokohama.

"I'm afraid to go out even during the day, let alone at night," Dorr said, his face pale.

CHAPTER NINETEEN

As 1861 COMMENCED, the days were often snowy.

Hikozo had moved out of the consulate back to his home in Yokohama Village and could keenly sense how upset the local foreign merchants and their families were over the murder of Heusken.

Not long after, a Japanese merchant was attacked on the road at night and killed. People said that this man had grown wealthy doing business with foreign merchants. To the faction advocating expulsion any merchant who profited through dealings with foreigners was a traitor to the country and deserved to die.

On the night of January 29 a fire broke out in Yokohama. It started in a Dutch merchant's horse barn and soon spread to neighboring homes and warehouses. Not knowing if it was accidental or an act of arson, the foreigners in town, fearing that the faction would take advantage of the confusion to attack them, shut themselves up in their homes; not a single foreigner rushed to help.

The fire spread quickly. The Kanagawa commissioner's officer dispatched a fire brigade to battle the blaze, while a contingent of armed troops from the warships landed to guard the vicinity.

On February 19 the reign name changed from Man'en to Bunkyu, and not long after this an official from the commissioner's, with his retinue, came calling at Hikozo's home.

"At the commissioner's office we are all concerned about you," the official said sternly.

He explained that though Denkichi had been known for his rough language and behavior, they believed it was the fact that he was employed by the legation that led to his murder. The cooks and servants at the legation all maintained a Japanese appearance, wearing kimonos and having their hair in a topknot. Denkichi, in contrast, kept his hair cut short and wore Western attire, including boots. It was believed that his Western appearance incurred the wrath of the faction.

"The office knows quite well how restrained you've always been in your behavior," the official went on, "but you are employed by the American consulate, and with your Western haircut and clothes you are like Denkichi." The official stopped at this point and looked intently at Hikozo.

"We know for a fact that some samurai have been talking about you as a target, saying they'll cut you down," he went on. "That's why we're concerned for your safety."

Hikozo knew they weren't just trying to frighten him. He had indeed been feeling in mortal danger.

Local officials were subjected to a wave of protests from the legations and consulates each time there was an attack, the official explained, and the Japanese were at a loss as to how to respond. If something were to happen to Hikozo, on top of what happened to Heusken, Dorr and Harris would be outraged and demand of the shogunate a complete accounting.

"Therefore," the official said, withdrawing a document from his breast pocket, "we would like you to adhere strictly to the following: one, that you will not ride a horse; two, that you will not go near the Tokaido Road; three, that as much as possible you will remain within the foreign settlement in Yokohama; and four, that you will never go out after sunset."

Putting away the document, the official warned that the samurai were particularly enraged when commoners, who were not allowed to ride horses, did so, and that one of the factors that lead them to murder Denkichi was the way he often trotted through town on horseback.

"I hope I've made myself clear," the official said, and Hikozo nodded.

Relaxing a bit, the official added, "The world's getting to be a dangerous place, so please be doubly on your guard." He then left with his retainers.

Hikozo sat there, not moving, staring at the wall. The official had said there were people targeting him, and Hikozo knew this was a fact, not mere rumor. His fervent wish for years was to return to his homeland, and now here he was, back on Japanese soil— only to find the peaceful country he'd dreamed about filled with mortal danger.

If he wore a kimono and let his hair grow out and put it in a topknot, perhaps the samurai wouldn't attack him. The long years in America, though, made him feel more comfortable in Western clothes, and he couldn't bring himself, at this late date, to go back to traditional garb. In the first place, he was an American citizen, a reality that wouldn't change no matter what his appearance. He spoke English, his gestures were those of a foreigner, and Japanese indeed considered him a foreigner. He had to face the fact that he was no longer really a Japanese but an American. He decided that the officials were right: if he wanted to keep on living, he should never go out at night and always remain within the foreign community in Yokohama.

The thought sent a chill through him, as if he were standing in a wilderness with a wintry wind lashing at him.

The cherry blossoms had all scattered, and each day grew warmer.

The sunny weather continued in May, with an occasional thunderstorm. The seas were filled with fish at this time of year, and fishmongers threaded their way among houses shouldering yokes heaped with platters of fresh fish and shellfish. Hikozo was busy every day interpreting in business negotiations between foreign merchants and Japanese. The trees were brilliantly green, and one peaceful day followed another.

On the night of May 24 a great commotion occurred in the

Japanese community in Yokohama. A comet with a long tail appeared in the northwest sky, and people ran outside to see it. Comets were thought to be portents of armed uprisings or great natural disasters, and the people stared at it with fear in their eyes.

In the middle of the night the comet disappeared beyond the mountains to the north, but its afterglow lit up the northern sky as brightly as if the moon were rising from behind the hills.

For the next two days the comet stayed in the star-filled sky, its long tail lighting up the night. Hikozo, too, went out to gaze up at the sky. On the evening of the twenty-eighth the comet made its way to the upper reaches of the sky, and he found it genuinely eerie.

The next morning he heard noise outside and people's voices. It turned out that the previous evening samurai had attacked the English legation in the Tozenji Temple in Takanawa in Edo. The Japanese merchants, their faces pale, kept talking about how the comet that appeared every night had indeed foretold this incident.

When he heard this, Hikozo stood stock-still, his face drawn. Until now attacks on foreigners had taken place on open roads— never before had samurai dared to invade the grounds of a foreign embassy. And this attack took place in the British legation, whose ambassador had always been rather high-handed toward the shogunate, so there was bound to be a diplomatic crisis.

But was Alcock himself unharmed by the attack? He must have been the samurai's target. If he was killed, the British would undoubtedly mobilize their forces and take military action against Japan. In that sort of scenario, Britain would throw its considerable military resources into the campaign, take no time at all to overpower the militarily inferior Japan, and place the country completely under British control—as it had done in China, which was now almost a British colony.

During his time in China Hikozo had become familiar with the despotism of the British, and felt this incident would lead to something very ugly. He remembered the unearthly light of the comet.

Had Alcock been spared or not?

Hikozo knew that Dorr would be receiving the latest reports, so he hurried to the American consulate. The consulate at Honkakuji Temple was under close guard by stern soldiers who had been dispatched by the shogunate. When Hikozo spotted the chief clerk, Van Reed, standing in the main hall, he approached him and said, "I heard the British legation was attacked. Is the ambassador all right?"

"It was a close call, very close. He's safe, thank God," Reed replied, agitated. "A narrow escape," he added in Japanese.

Reed's accent was a bit off, but overall he'd become quite versed in the language and was able to serve as the consul's interpreter. In response to Hikozo's questions, he explained what had happened, lacing his English with the occasional Japanese word. He liked to throw in Japanese words to show how much of the language he knew.

The night before, at about 10 PM a band of samurai had broken into the British legation. Later investigation revealed there were fourteen of them. The shogunate had assigned some two hundred men to guard the legation, but it appears that most of them were asleep and taken by surprise. The ones who did notice the intrusion yelled that outlaws had broken in and woke the others, and a sword fight ensued. Alcock was asleep in a back room, but his young interpreter and clerk woke him, and he loaded the revolver he carried for self-defense. Another clerk, Oliphant, staggered into the room, wounded on the arms and neck, followed by Morrison, the consul to Nagasaki, whose face was covered with blood from a cut on his forehead.

The guards put up a good fight, killing two of the samurai and wounding another, whom they captured. Three of the samurai, badly wounded, ran from the legation grounds to a teahouse in Shinagawa, where they disemboweled themselves. One legation guard and a groom were killed, with the total of dead and wounded on both sides coming to twenty-three.

"Fortunately the ambassador wasn't hurt. It was very frightening, though." Reed grimaced and shook his head a number of times.

Dorr was out of the consulate at the time, having gone, after the incident, to the American legation in the Zenpukuji Temple in Azabu. The commissioner's office had sent guards to accompany him, and Dorr himself was armed with a revolver.

The shogunate, badly shaken by this attack, dispatched guards to all the foreign legations and consulates, with extra troops stationed at the American consulate. All through the night the consulate was under heavy guard.

Van Reed related how ever since the murder of Heusken, Dorr had been jumpy and had taken to wearing a loaded pistol, which he even put next to his pillow at night. When Dorr heard how Heusken's intestines spilled from his body when he was cut down, he became extremely fearful of Japanese swords, which were razor-sharp. Shuddering, he often said he'd rather be shot than cut by a samurai sword.

"They frighten me, too," Reed said in Japanese. "Samurai swords scare the wits out of me."

Hikozo had heard many stories of criminals being beheaded at a single stroke of a sword. Samurai practiced swordsmanship constantly, and it was said that their swords could cut through flesh and bone in a second. If a bullet struck you in a vital organ, you'd die instantly, but that was nothing compared with the agony of dying by a sword. It was no wonder, Hikozo thought, that Dorr was frightened.

Reed began speaking quickly in English. These expulsion faction samurai, he said, hated all foreigners and didn't attack on the basis of personal enmity. To them Western clothes were the enemy, and since the only ones wearing Western clothes were foreigners, they attacked anyone who wore them.

"Both of us, Hiko, wear Western clothes. Which means that we're both a target. We must be extremely careful." Reed's eyes glistened.

Hikozo nodded and said, "Well, then, I'll see you later." He shook hands with Reed and left the temple.

He hurried down the road through the foreign settlement in Yokohama. He had a pistol at his waist, but a sword might tear into you faster than a bullet, he thought. Suddenly seized with the fear that a samurai might leap out and draw his sword, he stiffened and nearly ran the rest of the way home.

Day after day there was no rain, and even June, a normally rainy month, was clear and sunny. In neighboring villages the fields grew dry and cracked, and people were said to be performing rituals to pray for rain. Wells in Yokohama dried up, and many families went out in search of water.

Officials often came to see Hikozo and pass along disquieting news. Apparently some samurai had sneaked into Yokohama from Kanagawa, some of them coming ashore at night by boat.

"The commissioner's office is taking every precaution," one official told him, "but we can't very well arrest samurai just because they look suspicious. It's dangerous out here at night, and I hear rumors that people are targeting you, so please be careful." The official scowled to underscore his words and hurried away.

Hikozo felt his spirits sink. Ever since the samurai attack on the British legation he'd been filled with an unbearable fear. That the samurai had pushed their way into the heavily guarded legation showed how deep their hatred of foreigners was.

As the official had said, someone like himself, a naturalized U.S. citizen, working at the consulate, dressed in Western clothes, must surely be seen by these men as an unforgivable traitor, someone who deserved to be executed.

The official had warned him many times not to step outside the foreign settlement, but with the incident involving the murder of the Russian officer and sailor in Yokohama Village, the settlement itself wasn't safe. Hizoko not only didn't go out at night, he avoided going out during the day as much as possible. The samurai might disguise themselves as ordinary citizens and attack him, and he began to size up any man approaching him on the street and tried to keep his distance.

In the evening he shut all his doors tight and would sit barely breathing, his pistol by his side. Sometimes he'd anxiously check to make sure the pistol was loaded.

Hikozo felt like escaping to some distant place, but the faction samurai were all over the country, and no matter where he went, he could be attacked. That he was a Japanese wouldn't matter to these samurai: they would never tolerate a person like him, a Japanese Christian with a Western name.

A dog's bark at night was enough to throw him into a panic. Thinking that someone was creeping up on him, he'd grip his pistol tightly and try to be as quiet as he could. He couldn't sleep, and he had no appetite.

The days continued terribly hot, with no hint of rain.

The thought of returning to America crossed his mind. His long-held dream of returning to Japan had come true, but now his native land seemed a death trap. In America he had many friends, and he needn't fear for his life there. Maybe that was the place for him. He paced his room. Fluent in English, he would have no trouble making a living if he went back to America.

The only person close enough to understand his feelings was Van Reed. Reed would see the position he was in and give him the best possible advice.

Hikozo strapped on his pistol and left his house. He walked down the dry road, enveloped in the intense heat. The air shimmered, and he watched as an ox ahead of him struggled under the heavy burden tied to its back.

The grounds of the consulate were noisy with the screech of cicadas. He found Reed sprawled in a chair in the main temple hall. Hikozo stepped into the main hall and sat down in a chair opposite him.

"How are you feeling?" Reed asked in Japanese. "No heatstroke, I hope?"

Hikozo thought it funny to hear Reed use the Japanese term *heatstroke* and realized how very haggard he must appear. He said nothing, just looked out at the greenery in the temple compound.

When they were in San Francisco together, Reed knew how eager Hikozo had been to return to Japan. He knew, too, how overjoyed Hikozo was to be able to join the Harris mission and take the *Mississippi* to Nagasaki. How would Reed react to the news that his friend was thinking of returning to the States?

Hikozo faced Reed.

"I'm sure you'll be very surprised to hear this coming from me," Hikozo said in English, "but I'm thinking of going back to the U.S."

Indeed, Reed was taken aback.

Hikozo told him how officials often visited him to warn him about rumors that he would be attacked. Like Denkichi, he was a target of the faction samurai, and if he stayed in Japan, it was only a matter of time before he, too, was murdered on the street. He couldn't live like this anymore and thought his best option was to go back to America. Hikozo's eyes were cast down as he spoke, and Reed stared at him intently.

"You're the only one I could talk with about this. I'd like to hear your thoughts." Hikozo looked up at him.

Reed was quiet for a time, thinking. Finally he spoke, his expression showing how painful it was to say this: "It's a difficult problem. I understand completely that you feel you're in danger. There's no guarantee that you won't be murdered like Dan.

"Actually I've heard too from an official that you're in an extremely bad position," Reed went on, frowning. "The officials admit that there's not much they can do to protect you."

Hikozo nodded, and made his decision.

"I'm going back to the States," he said, almost muttering the words.

Reed looked at him. Outside the cicadas screeched.

"Yes, that might be the best course of action. You're a very capable, intelligent person. I'm sure that once you're back in America, things will go as smoothly for you as they did before."

"I appreciate your advice," Hikozo said. He turned again to gaze at the trees.

Reed stood up and paced the main hall, finally coming to a halt in front of Hikozo. "How about giving it a bit more thought?" he suggested, his eyes solicitous. "It's not good to rush to a decision."

"My mind's made up. I'm going," Hikozo said, the words more for himself than for Reed.

Reed said no more about the decision. Wiping the sweat from his forehead and neck with a handkerchief, he talked quietly with Hikozo.

This unstable situation in Japan, with one assassination after another, he said, couldn't last forever. Hikozo's career in Japan depended on finding a practical use for his fluency in English, and his knowledge of American politics, society, and economy. This was important for Japan, now that it had opened itself to the outside world, and would contribute to international relations between the two countries. Returning to America should be thought of not as a retreat from Japan but as an opportunity to grasp something new that he could make use of when he next came to Japan.

Reed also raised the idea of Hikozo working as a United States Navy storekeeper.

Whenever U.S. naval vessels called at Yokohama, they would stock up on coal, food, water, and firewood. A warehouse had been built to store these provisions, and an American in the navy had been appointed as manager of the warehouse, in charge of distributing provisions to the various vessels. But having to negotiate with Japanese merchants for the purchase of these provisions, he had run into the language barrier and was often unable to make the needed purchase. In fact, his work had ground to a halt, and complaints had come from ships. These complaints often found their way to the American consulate, causing Dorr quite a lot of trouble, with even Townsend Harris racking his brain for a solution.

"Now if you could only get qualified as a warehouse storekeeper...," Reed said.

It would be the ideal job for Hikozo. Bilingual, he should be able to respond in a timely fashion to the needs of the vessels.

"What do you think about going to America and getting certified to become a naval storekeeper?" Reed said, gazing intently at Hikozo.

Hikozo knew how the merchants in Yokohama delivered goods to the ships. He'd seen the drays haul goods from the warehouse to the dock, then load these onto boats and transport them out to the ships in the harbor.

"That's a wonderful idea," Hikozo said, brightening for the first time. "I'm glad I came to talk with you."

"If you become a storekeeper, you'll wear a naval uniform and a cap with gold insignia, and you'll be on an equal footing with the Japanese officials," Reed said with a smile.

That evening it rained, and the oppressive heat that had hung over the town dissipated a little.

The next day was cloudy, and Hikozo again went to the consulate and consulted with Reed about returning to America. Dorr was out, at the American legation in Azabu.

Hikozo said he'd like to go to San Francisco and enlist the aid of his old friend Cary, and Reed agreed that that was the best course of action to take. Cary was the manager of the Macondray Company that Hikozo used to work for. When Hikozo was about to return to Japan and was essentially penniless, Cary had arranged for his father to send funds to him, which allowed him to return to Japan.

"I'm sure Mr. Cary is interested in trade with Japan," Reed said, "so it would be a good idea to take some samples of Japanese goods with you to show him. When will you be leaving?" he added.

"As soon as possible," Hikozo replied. Reed consulted the shipping list of American ships coming in and out of port, and told Hikozo that the *Carrington* would be leaving for San Francisco in a week's time.

"The captain's a good friend of mine," Reed said. "I'll write a letter of introduction for you, and he'll see that you're taken care of." He immediately wrote out a letter of introduction.

Two days later Hikozo went to the local branch of the shipping company that the *Carrington* belonged to, showed the letter from

Reed, and obtained a ticket for passage. The ship was scheduled to depart on the morning of August 13.

The next few days were busy ones for Hikozo. He sold what little household goods he had, exchanged Japanese currency for dollars at the customhouse, and submitted documents to the commissioner's office for leaving the country. The officials agreed that it was a good idea that he go and were willing to expedite his departure.

He went around the town bidding farewell to Dorr and to all his friends among the foreign and Japanese merchants.

On the twelfth it rained, and in the afternoon, a large suitcase and umbrella in hand, he went to the shipping company's branch office. The foreign passengers were already assembled there, and together with them Hikozo took a boat out to the *Carrington* and boarded the ship.

He breathed a sigh of relief, knowing that he was out of danger now. On the ship only English was used, and Hikozo felt tears well up as he listened to this language of which he had such fond memories. He felt comforted, as if already enveloped by the vastness that was America.

CHAPTER TWENTY

THE NEXT MORNING Hikozo was awakened by the sound of engines, and he went out on deck to watch. The rain had stopped, and he was wrapped in the refreshing morning air.

The steamship had begun to move, the houses of Yokohama Village gradually fading in the distance. Unlike a year before, when he'd landed in Kanagawa, Yokohama was full of newly built houses, the white two-story foreign-style homes particularly conspicuous. The town now looked more like a harbor town in the United States than a Japanese community.

Hikozo reminded himself he wasn't running away but leaving in order to obtain the qualifications he needed to become a naval storekeeper. Having taken American citizenship and been baptized as a Christian, he could not live in Japan right now, until the situation changed. For the time being he was withdrawing to America.

The buildings in Yokohama blended into the green-covered slopes of the hills behind them.

The face of his stepbrother, Unomatsu, came to mind. With his stepfather now gone, Hikozo had no relatives. Not one person was sad he was going to America, and once more he felt how utterly alone he was in the world.

Out at sea he saw several Japanese vessels, their sails billowing as they passed nearby the steamship. Hikozo remembered how his stepbrother, now captain of a vessel like one of these, plied the waters between Hyogo (Kobe) and Edo.

Standing on the deck, Hikozo thought how odd his fate had been. If he hadn't been shipwrecked eleven years before, he'd no doubt now be a sailor on one of these ships. He'd be married, with children. That's the kind of life he should have had, yet here he was, hair cut short, dressed in Western clothes and boots, on the deck of a steamship leaving his native land. Being a castaway had turned his world upside down.

The steamship, a screw type, churned up a white wake astern. Seabirds flocked around the wake.

A man who appeared to be a foreign merchant was standing beside Hikozo, gazing out at the shore. He turned to Hikozo and said, "Japanese scenery is so beautiful."

"Yes, you're right ... ," Hikozo said, nodding.

The merchant didn't seem to consider him a Japanese. The ship sailed out toward the entrance of the harbor.

After a voyage of twenty-nine days across the Pacific, the *Carrington* arrived in San Francisco, on September 13—October 16 by the Western calendar.

As Hikozo went ashore and into the city, he felt his eyes welling up at all the familiar sights. The cobblestone roads, the wooden and stone houses along the streets, the carriages made him feel like calling out a greeting to everyone he passed on the street.

He checked in at a hotel and went to his room. Thin curtains hung over the glass windows, and when he turned the faucet, water gushed out. These were all things he'd grown used to living in the States, and he sat down in an armchair and looked around him.

He had dinner in the dining hall, then returned to his room and made himself a drink. As he gazed at the brightly shining gaslight on the wall, he realized he was truly back in America, and he felt a deep contentment.

The next day he paid a visit to Mr. Cary at the Macondray Company. As soon as he opened the door of his old place of employment and went inside, a middle-aged employee turned to look at him and got up from his seat in surprise.

"Hiko!" the man said, coming over to shake his hand.

The other employees followed suit, warmly shaking hands with their old friend. "We're so happy you're back!" one said. "You're looking well," said another. "And see what a gentleman you've become!"

When Hikozo said he'd come to see Cary, one of the employees led him to the second floor. The man knocked on the door and announced, "Sir, Hiko has come back."

Hikozo entered the room and saw Cary seated at a large desk by the window. Cary called out a greeting and came over to give Hikozo a big hug, patting him on the back. Hikozo was moved.

When they'd taken seats opposite each other, the American manager leaned forward and said, "Tell me what you've been up to. All the details."

Hikozo told him how he went from San Francisco to China, via Hawaii, how he landed in Shinagawa with the U.S. minister, Harris, how he worked for the consulate as an interpreter, and finally how he become a target of the faction samurai and returned to America because life had become dangerous for him.

"Yes, I've heard how frightening the samurai can be." Cary shook his head sympathetically. He told Hikozo how the San Francisco papers had widely reported the murders of the Russian sailors and Heusken, and the attack on the British legation. "Van Reed is well, I hope?" he asked. Reed had written earlier to Cary telling him he was employed as clerk at the American consulate.

"He's fine."

"I hope he doesn't become a target of the samurai," Cary said.

"I think he'll be all right. He's careful not to draw attention to himself...The reason I provoked the samurai was that I dressed like a foreigner."

Cary shook his head sadly.

Hikozo was silent for a time, then said, looking intently at his friend, "I have a favor to ask of you."

"Of course. I'll do my best to help you in any way I can."

"Van Reed suggested I ask your help in this matter," Hikozo began, and explained how he'd come back in order to qualify as a naval storekeeper. He told Cary how Van Reed had insisted that Hikozo would be perfect for the job and that with this position he'd have a comfortable, steady income.

"That's a wonderful idea Reed's come up with—doesn't surprise me, really, since he's quite clever when it comes to things like that. I'll consult with some of my friends what the best steps are to take. I'm sure there will be no problem." Cary nodded several times to emphasize the point.

Hikozo thanked the American manager, shook hands with him, and left.

After this he was busy for days making the rounds of old friends, giving them the presents he'd brought back from Japan—fans, things made from colorful Japanese paper, and other gifts. His friends invited him to dinner, and after he checked out of his hotel, he stayed at several friends' homes.

A message came from Cary on November 10, and Hikozo went again to the Macondray Company to see him. Cary told him he had spoken with friends of his who also ran businesses. They first thought of just sending a recommendation letter for Hikozo to the secretary of the navy but then all agreed that it would better if Hikozo went to Washington to make his case directly.

The recommendation letter was under the joint signatures of Cary's business associates, and he also planned to have the head of revenue and other leading citizens of San Francisco sign the letter as well.

"We should have the letter ready in three days," Cary said. "You take it to Washington and give it to the secretary of the navy."

Hikozo thanked Cary for all his kindness.

Two days later an employee of the customs appraiser's office called on Hikozo, who was staying at a friend's house, and asked him to accompany him to see the office head, Mr. Mudge, who was requesting his assistance. Hikozo agreed and went with the man to the appraiser's office.

Mudge was having difficulty determining the value of some Japanese antiques brought back by an American passenger on the

Carrington, the same ship Hikozo had taken to San Francisco. This passenger had taken his own ship to Japan but then, being completely smitten by Japanese antiques, had sold it for fifteen thousand dollars and used the money to purchase a great number of porcelain and lacquerware items. The appraiser, having never dealt with such items before, was at a loss as to their value. It was suspected, though, that they were of much higher value than what the passenger had stated in his declaration.

Mudge had one of his employees lay out the items on a table for Hikozo's inspection. Hikozo had no experience assessing the value of such things, but he could tell that they were all ordinary objects you could find anywhere in Japan. The passenger had bought them with the thought, undoubtedly, that Japanese goods would be valued abroad as antiques.

Hikozo believed the value of these goods was far below that stated on the declaration, but casually said, "I'd say this was about the price you'd find these items going for in Yokohama."

"I really appreciate your help," Mudge said, shaking his hand. Hikozo then left the appraiser's office.

Four days later a message came from the Macondray Company, and Hikozo went to see Cary.

"We've finished the recommendation letter, and I'd like you to read it." Cary took the letter from his desk and passed it to Hikozo. Hikozo sat and opened it.

San Francisco, November 13th, 1861. To Gideon Welles, Secretary of the Navy, the letter began. *Sir,* it went on, *We beg respectfully to recommend to your notice Mr. Joseph Heco as a suitable person to fill the office of U.S. Naval Storekeeper at Kanagawa, Japan.*

Hikozo felt a bit embarrassed by the fine words in his praise, but he was also grateful.

The letter told how, though a Japanese by birth, Hikozo was now a naturalized U.S. citizen who'd lived several years in the

States, was fluent in English, and had received extensive training in business practices in San Francisco. After returning to Japan, he had played an important role as interpreter for the consulate, but now he'd come back to the States to apply for the post of naval storekeeper. Such a post would allow him to serve the U.S. government and at the same time put him on an equal footing with Japanese officials.

We know Mr. Heco to be a person of worth and integrity, the letter ended, *and have no doubt he will be of great service to the U.S. Government if he is placed in a position where he can act directly with Japanese officials.*

The letter was signed by Cary, plus a number of business owners and bankers in San Francisco.

A second letter was appended, signed by the head of customs of San Francisco, the collector of customs, the navy agent, a navy officer, Mr. Mudge, the appraiser, the paymaster, and superintendent of the U.S. Branch Mint. Their letter stated:

The signers of the above memorial are merchants and bankers of the highest standing in San Francisco, and we entirely concur in their evaluation of Mr. Heco.... We have no doubt if Mr. Heco can be appointed as Naval Storekeeper this will be of great benefit to the United States.

This appended letter was entirely due to Cary's efforts, and Hikozo was deeply touched. Cary must have gone to each of the signatories, letter in hand, explaining the situation and urging them to sign.

"I don't have the words to express how grateful I am for all you've done for me," Hikozo said, his eyes glistening.

"If it makes you happy, then I'm happy. I'm sure all my friends who signed the letters are pleased as well." Cary nodded several times.

The next issue was how best to deliver this letter to the secretary of the navy. Cary told Hikozo that his mother and younger sister lived in Boston and that his sister's husband, Professor Agassiz, had a wide circle of acquaintances, and if he wrote a letter of introduction for Hikozo, Hikozo should be able to meet with the secretary of the navy.

Cary wrote down his mother's address and promised to telegraph ahead so they'd know Hikozo was coming.

Upon arriving in San Francisco, Hikozo had heard about how the southern states had seceded and formed the Confederacy and had, since this April, been at war with the North. Antagonism between two very different economic systems—the North's industrial, manufacturing system, the South with its slave-based agriculture—had led the country into civil war.

Hikozo learned that while the economic might of the North far surpassed that of the South, the Southern forces were led by the most skilled generals, which put the Northern army at a disadvantage. In fact, at the first battle, which took place only thirty miles southwest of Washington, the Northern troops were roundly defeated. Since then, though, the Northern army had gone on the offensive, and both sides were building up their military might. It appeared now that the war would be a long-drawn-out affair, and in light of this Cary urged Hikozo to hurry to Washington as soon as he could.

Hikozo followed his advice and sought out the first available ship; learning that a steamer was bound for Panama, he booked passage on it. The North's navy controlled the seas, and he was reassured that there was no fear of attack on the voyage to Panama.

Reaching Panama safely, Hikozo and the other passengers took a train across the isthmus, arriving at Aspinwall. In the harbor was the steamer *Champion*, bound for New York, which Hikozo boarded.

The ship left Aspinwall Harbor and headed north, and on December 14, when it was off the coast of Santo Domingo, they saw a steamship off their starboard. This was a part of the sea frequented by armed warships of the Confederacy, and the captain of the

Champion, sensing that this ship was one of them, opened his engines to full throttle and proceeded north.

The captain's intuition was good: the other ship turned out to be the armed *Sumter,* commanded by a Captain Sumner, which attempted to pursue the *Champion* in order to attack and sink it. With its superior speed, though, the *Champion* escaped unscathed.

This incident, though, unnerved the passengers. They'd read about the war in the newspapers, but San Francisco was so far from the front lines that until now it had seemed like a conflict that had nothing to do with them. But when they saw this armed ship puffing black smoke as it sped toward them, the reality of the war hit home.

The captain ordered his men to scan the horizon with spyglasses for the enemy. Hikozo, quite nervous, himself scanned the horizon.

Two days after being chased by the armed merchant ship, the *Champion* safely pulled into New York Harbor at two o'clock in the afternoon.

Two small pilot ships approached and tied up to their bow, and a harbor pilot and others came aboard. They were carrying a bundle of newspapers, which they distributed to the passengers. The passengers fell greedily on the papers for the latest news about the war. The headlines read: *The grand Army of the Potomac to move at an early date*; *A Great Battle Imminent*; *The Southern Army 100,000 strong marching on Washington.* Another headline read: *The British Government make a formal demand on Uncle Sam to deliver up Mason and Slidell.*

This article concerned something that had happened the previous month. The British merchant ship *Trenton* had left a Southern port on its way to Europe when a Union warship ordered it to halt, where it was boarded and inspected. The two diplomats to the Confederacy, Mason and Slidell, were on board, and they were taken into custody by the Union army and escorted to Boston. The British were incensed that one of their ships had been boarded this way, and, being sympathetic to the Southern cause, demanded that the two men be released at once.

The passengers on Hikozo's ship, their fear evident, discussed how if this incident was not resolved peacefully, it would lead to war with Britain. When Hikozo finally landed in New York, he found the town in a fever pitch.

Two days later he took a train to Boston, where Cary's mother lived. Upon arrival he paid a call on her at her home. Mrs. Cary, over seventy, warmly welcomed Hikozo. He thanked her for all her husband had done for him. Unfortunately the man had since passed away.

"Please come tomorrow at two to dine with us," she said. "I've invited Professor Agassiz, who'd like to meet you."

The next day Hikozo dined there with the professor and his wife, who was Cary's younger sister. Professor Agassiz read the letter of introduction from Cary and said, "I'll write a letter for you to Secretary of State Seward and to an influential senator I know. I'm sure this will help you." And right after dinner he wrote out several letters.

The letters weren't sealed, and Hikozo read through them. The informal tone of the writing told him that the professor was on intimate terms with these high officials.

Having finished what he planned to do in Boston, Hikozo headed back to New York. The date was January 1, 1862, but with the war in full swing, there were no celebrations in the city.

After two days in New York he planned to depart for Washington but couldn't pass through Baltimore, where his old mentor Mr. Sanders lived, without stopping to see him. He left New York by train, got off at Baltimore Station, and headed to Mr. Sanders's home.

Hikozo stood gazing at the house surrounded by trees, his mind's eye full of warm memories. When he knocked on the door, a black servant opened it, his eyes going wide, and ran back inside with a shout.

Mr. Sanders soon appeared and, without a word, gave Hikozo a hug. Mrs. Sanders followed suit.

"We're so happy to see you! We thought we'd never see you again." The tears trickled down Mr. Sanders's cheeks as he spoke. Tears came to Hikozo's eyes, too, as he clasped the old man's hand.

Three and half years had passed since he bade farewell to them, and in the interim Mr. Sanders had aged considerably. His face was lined with wrinkles, and he looked as if he'd lost weight. His wife, however, looked the same as always.

"We want you to stay with us. For as long as you like." Sanders looked at Hikozo affectionately. Hikozo thanked them and decided it wouldn't be a bad idea to rest for a few days with these warm-hearted friends.

Sanders wanted to hear all about what had taken place in Hikozo's life since he'd last seen him, and as they enjoyed tea after dinner, Hikozo told him all the details. Mrs. Sanders, too, listened carefully. The Baltimore papers had reported on the assassinations carried out by the faction samurai, and hearing that Hikozo had been one of their targets, she cried out and grimaced.

Hikozo went on to say that this unsettled and dangerous time would pass, and once things were settled again, he planned to return to Japan. Sanders lamented that it was their fault that Hikozo had been put in such danger, since Sanders was the one who recommended that he take American citizenship, and Mrs. Sanders had had him baptized. But Hikozo insisted this wasn't the case.

Hikozo told Sanders the reason he'd returned to the States, about wanting to obtain the post of naval storekeeper, and about the recommendation letter he received from Cary and other prominent citizens in San Francisco. Sanders nodded, read over the letter, and, after pondering the situation for a while, said, "Hiko, I'll go with you to Washington. I'll introduce you to Senator Latham. We can use his influence to help get you that appointment."

Eight years before, Sanders had introduced Hikozo to President Pierce. Hikozo was happy to accept his offer, knowing what a wide circle of acquaintances the man had in the political and bureaucratic worlds.

Early on the morning of January 7, in the rain, Hikozo and Sanders set off from Baltimore Station to Washington. A solid line of white tents was set up alongside the railroad tracks, temporary quarters for Union soldiers. Walking outside in the rain, the soldiers looked pitiful, like so many sick baby birds. These must have been the troops assigned to the defense of the capital.

Arriving at Washington Station, they went to the Willard Hotel, but it was full of officers, and there were no rooms available. Sanders talked things over with the manager, whom he knew, and the man told them, apologetically, that there was one room but they'd have to share it.

They went to the dining room for lunch and found it full of officers eating. The dining hall was noisy with their loud conversations about the war, which Hikozo and Sanders couldn't help but overhear as they ate in silence.

That evening Hikozo and Sanders took a carriage to the residence of Senator Latham. Sanders introduced Hikozo to the senator and said they'd come back again the following day to ask for help in a matter they'd discuss then. Latham agreed, and with a smile invited them to dine with him the next day.

Back at their hotel room, Sanders slumped in a chair, closed his eyes, and didn't say a word, but his face showed how tired he was. Hikozo felt guilty, realizing that the trip had been too much for the elderly gentleman.

The next morning as they ate breakfast in the dining hall, he said, "I'm so grateful to you for introducing me to Senator Latham." Drawing himself up, he said, more formally, that Sanders should leave the rest to him, that he could seek this appointment by himself.

"It's chilly out, and I'd hate to see you catch a cold," he went on. "Don't worry about me. Please go back home to Mrs. Sanders."

Sanders gave Hikozo a steady look. "But I want to do whatever I can to help you," he said.

Hikozo's expression softened. "I'm twenty-six—an adult. My English is fine, and now that you've introduced me, I think I can discuss things with Senator Latham and use his influence to obtain the post."

Sanders dropped his eyes and said, "I see. Twenty-six now, yes. In that case, I suppose I should go back home today." He sounded as if he were trying to convince himself that this was the best course of action.

A few years before, he would have dismissed Hikozo's words and spent days escorting him to see one official after another. Such quick assent only underscored how much the man had aged, and Hikozo felt sad at the thought.

He left the hotel with plans that day to visit some friends of his in Washington, as well as meet with a Mr. Wallace, president of one of the leading newspaper companies.

When he returned to the hotel after 3 PM, Sanders was nowhere to be seen. Hikozo, inquiring at the front desk, was told that Mr. Sanders had left the hotel in the morning and taken a carriage to Washington Station. Hikozo nodded and went back to his room. He could picture Sanders's wrinkled face as he rode back home on the train.

That evening Hikozo went to Senator Latham's home and was shown into the living room. He gave the senator the recommendation that Cary had prepared for him. After he read it, Latham said, "This is the best possible recommendation letter you could have. The signers are all the most prominent and influential people in San Francisco today. I'm sure you'll be appointed to the post. Come back tomorrow morning at nine with these documents. I'll go with you to see the secretary of the navy to discuss this with him."

Hikozo, overjoyed, expressed his deep appreciation.

The senator showed him into the dining room, where they dined with Mrs. Latham. Mrs. Latham was extremely interested in Japan and peppered Hikozo with questions, all of which he carefully answered. All the while the senator looked at the two of them with a happy smile.

Hikozo left their home at around 10 PM. As he walked back to the hotel, a soldier suddenly leaped out and challenged him, pointing his rifle at him. Hikozo knew that with the war the city was under martial law and that anyone on the streets after nine would be questioned like this by the military. He hurried on to his hotel.

The next morning he appeared at the senator's home at the appointed time, carrying his recommendation letter. The senator was dressed in formal wear and motioned Hikozo to get in the carriage that was waiting for them. With a calm face Latham said, "My wife found talking with you about Japan quite stimulating. Thank you for being so patient with her." Hikozo could sense how much the senator loved his wife.

Their carriage pulled up in front of the Department of the Navy, and Hikozo followed the senator inside. Latham had apparently already made an appointment, for a tall official led them, knocked at the door of the secretary, opened it, and announced in a spirited voice that the senator had arrived.

In the spacious room Hikozo saw a man in his fifties, wearing glasses, dressed in a navy-blue suit, seated behind a large desk and busily writing something.

The man looked up, got up, and approached Latham. Latham shook his hand, introduced Hikozo, and the man and Hikozo shook hands. This was the secretary of the navy, Gideon Welles.

The secretary invited them to sit, and they sat down across from him.

Latham explained the purpose of their visit, and Hikozo stood up and passed the letter of recommendation to Mr. Welles. The secretary opened the letter and read through it, then said, "Senator Latham, as you know, because of the present conflict the navy has put all its resources into the war. We recalled our warships that have been dispatched around the world back to America, leaving very few to dock at Yokohama. So there's no need to increase our quartermaster personnel in the Far East fleet. I'm quite sorry, but I can't accept your petition."

After a moment he spoke again. "How about this? Why don't

you go see Secretary of State Seward and show him this letter?...
The legation and consulates in Japan are under his jurisdiction."

Hikozo had no trouble accepting the secretary's explanation.
America was split in a civil war, which now looked like it would last
a long time. The secretary of the navy had to concentrate all the
Union naval forces he had in the fight against the Confederacy; he
couldn't very well appoint a new person to be naval storekeeper in
Kanagawa.

Hikozo rose, took back the letter of recommendation, and said,
"I understand completely. I'm very grateful you could take the time
from your busy schedule to meet with me." He bowed and shook
the secretary's hand.

As they exited the office, Latham said they should follow
Welles's suggestion and go see the secretary of state, so they headed
then and there for the State Department.

In the secretary's office they found Seward on his knees, sign-
ing passports spread out on the floor in front of him.

Latham shook hands with him, introduced Hikozo, and showed
the letter of recommendation. After Seward read this, Latham explained how the secretary of the navy had told them he didn't have
the resources to appoint a new storekeeper.

"I can understand the secretary of the navy had to take that position. He had no other choice." Seward nodded several times and
turned to Hikozo. "Your English is quite fluent. Just recently an official interpreter's post was established for the consulate in Kanagawa, so why not take that post? The appropriations for the
position haven't been finalized, but if you accept the post, I'll make
sure the budget is sent to Congress immediately."

When Hikozo had served as interpreter for the Kanagawa consulate, he'd been hired on a contingency basis. This post that
Seward mentioned was an official, full-time position under the
auspices of the Department of State. If being a naval storekeeper
was out of the question, then this was a stroke of good fortune.

Hikozo thanked the secretary and said he'd gladly accept the
post.

Seward said, "It's a wonderful thing for our government if you'll take the position. You're perfectly suited for it, and I'm very pleased you'll take the job." Again he shook Hikozo's hand.

Latham smiled broadly and said, "Well, it appears my duty here is done."

After they left the Department of State, Latham said he needed to go to Congress and left by carriage. Hikozo headed back to the hotel on foot. On the way he stopped by to visit Senator Summer, to whom Professor Agasszi had written a letter of introduction for him. He felt he should at least stop by and pay his respects.

After doing so, he returned to his hotel.

CHAPTER TWENTY-ONE

Hikozo sat in his hotel room, looking through the thin curtains at the frozen scene outside.

The country he left four years ago in September was a quiet, calm land where everyone he met was generous and kind, but coming to Washington now, he found an America not like the one he used to know. San Francisco still seemed unchanged, but because of the war everyone here was unsettled, eyes were bloodshot. People clamored over the latest newspapers, pored over the latest news. Hotels that used to cater to quiet travelers were now filled with army officers, and whenever Hikozo went to the dining hall, the loud voices and clatter of silverware as the officers ate disturbed him, and he couldn't enjoy his meals in peace.

He'd come to America hoping to obtain an appointment as naval storekeeper, but all he'd managed to get was a promise for an appointment as official interpreter at the Kanagawa consulate. Being promoted from part-time interpreter to full-time, official status should have pleased him, but after his meetings with the secretaries of the navy and state he felt that he'd exhausted all his possibilities in the United States.

The situation in Japan, too, was uncertain, but with their country torn apart by civil war, the American people were even more unsettled in their hearts. Denkichi had been assassinated because he worked as an interpreter for the British legation and dressed like

276

a Westerner, but ultimately the reason lay in his high-handed attitude, the way he flaunted the authority of the British behind him.
Hikozo had been warned by the commissioner's office that he was
also in danger, but there had never been any actual sign of this. As
long as he didn't draw attention to himself, he should be able to
avoid a similar fate.

I'll go back to Japan, he told himself.

The Civil War would drag on for a long time, and staying here
in the U.S. would not do him any good. Surrounded every day by
English and by Western food, he found himself longing to hear
Japanese, to eat familiar food.

Before returning to Japan, though, he'd have to stop in Baltimore and see Sanders again. Sanders was old now, and this might
very well be the last time he'd see him. In his mind Sanders *was*
America, and he couldn't leave without seeing the man's affection-
ate eyes one more time.

Two days later he left Washington, got off the train at Baltimore Station, and went to the Sanders home. The old man hugged
him again, his eyes teary.

Hikozo told him how he'd met with the secretary of the navy
but because of the war he couldn't be appointed as naval storekeeper, though he did win a promise from the secretary of state for
an appointment as official interpreter. "I'm leaving everything up
to Senator Latham, and am most grateful to him."

"Are you satisfied with the way things worked out?" Sanders
asked, worried.

"Yes, I am," Hikozo replied. "With the war on, it's the best I can
expect."

"I'm glad to hear it. I'm sure you'll be heading back to Japan
soon, but I'd like you to stay here with us as long as you can. Nothing could make me happier."

From that day on Hikozo stayed at the Sanders home.

Because of his age Sanders had given up all his business ventures and was living on his savings. He seemed to be in good health,

but he spent a lot of time napping in his chair and was unsteady on his feet. Hikozo had to support the old man as they took walks in the garden and talked.

Two weeks passed; it was February.

Several letters had come from a friend of Sanders, named Booth, a former captain of a merchant ship, asking Hikozo to visit him. Booth had often traveled by ship to China, had a great interest in Japan, and wanted to ask Hikozo about his native land.

"Would you go see him for me?" Sanders asked. "He's a friend of many years." Hikozo agreed to meet him.

Booth's home was in Alexandria. On February 6 Hikozo took a train to Washington and then the carriage Booth had sent for him.

Booth was over sixty but quite lively and jovial, as you'd expect of a former ship's captain. He warmly welcomed Hikozo to his home. Since Hikozo had been to China, they had much to talk about—Shanghai, Hong Kong, Canton, Macao, and other places they'd both visited, and Booth went on at length about the trips he'd made to the Far East.

He then asked Hikozo about Japan, and Hikozo answered in as much detail as he could. Booth's eyes sparkled with amazement at what he heard, and Hikozo enjoyed their conversation.

Three days after arriving at the Booths', Hikozo accompanied them to church on Sunday. There he prayed that the war would be over and peace would return, and that Mr. and Mrs. Sanders would stay healthy. On the way back from church he noticed that there was a disturbance in town—crowds of people had come out on the streets, some of them running. Booth, worried, stopped a passerby to ask what was happening. It turned out that soldiers had taken the pastor of the Saint Paul Church into custody.

The pastor in question had prayed publicly for the president of the Confederacy, but not for the president of the United States. When people demanded that he pray for President Lincoln, he ignored them and continued his prayer. Soldiers in the congregation, incensed at this, rushed the podium, grabbed the pastor by the arm, and dragged him outside. They took him away, no one knew where.

"What a frightening thing," Booth muttered as he walked along, Hikozo following him.

Hikozo fell into a dark mood. That such a thing could happen in a church meant that people's hearts were being corrupted by the war, he concluded.

After dinner Booth invited Hikozo to visit the home of his friend Mr. Bryant. Mr. Bryant ran a large dry-goods business and wanted to meet Hikozo and ask him about Japan. Hikozo agreed and set off with Booth for Bryant's home. The house was a solid building, and when they arrived, Mr. and Mrs. Bryant greeted them cordially.

Mrs. Bryant brought in wine for them, and they drank a toast. Just then the front gate clanged open, they heard footsteps, and a tall, young army lieutenant strode in. He looked at the assembled group and said, a severe expression on his face, "I'm sorry to barge in on you like this, but I'm under orders. Are you the only ones in the house?"

Bryant, dumbfounded, said yes.

"Then I must ask all the men here to come with me and the soldiers," the lieutenant insisted.

Bryant and Booth protested, asking what could be the reason for this, but the lieutenant motioned them to hurry. The three men, leaving the house, were shocked to find twenty armed soldiers waiting outside, their eyes grim. The three followed the lieutenant, and the soldiers wordlessly followed them, their boots making an ominous thud as they marched.

As they walked down the road at night, Hikozo was sure it must be some mistake. Booth was a former ship's captain, Bryant a businessman, and he a naturalized American citizen, so there was no reason for the soldiers to take them away like this. Hikozo imagined that when the lieutenant found out he'd made a mistake and arrested the wrong people, he'd have to apologize for his inexcusable behavior.

They arrived at the garrison, and the lieutenant ordered them inside. He opened the door to a room, where they found two captains seated, one by the fireplace reading a newspaper, the other at a desk writing. As Hikozo and the others entered, the captains shot them a sharp look.

The lieutenant came to attention and saluted, announcing he'd brought the men as ordered. The captain seated at the fireplace looked at all three of them, then pointed to Hikozo and barked out an order: "Lieutenant, this is the man we've been looking for. Escort him upstairs."

Hikozo, surprised, approached the captain, took out his passport to show him, and said, "You've obviously mistaken me for someone else. Please look at my passport." Booth and Bryant both explained Hikozo's background, vouching for his loyalty.

The captain merely glanced at the passport, then with a hard look turned to Hikozo and said, "I received a telegram from Washington to arrest one Joseph Heco. Lieutenant, take him upstairs!" His tone showed he'd tolerate no more protest, so Hikozo, glancing at Booth and Bryant, followed the lieutenant to the second floor.

The lieutenant came to a stop outside a room, took out a bunch of keys, unlocked the door, and wordlessly motioned Hikozo inside. Hikozo went in and heard the door being locked behind him. The room was rough in the lamplight. The bare floorboards were covered with dirt, and in one corner there were a couple of couches and sailcloth strewn about. The place was windowless, like a quarantine room. It also lacked a fireplace and was extremely cold. Hikozo stood rooted to the spot, unable to think.

He heard someone, then a bearded man emerged from the shadows.

Hikozo was shocked. The man was in his forties, but he was pale, with shunken cheeks and weirdly glistening eyes. Hikozo was greatly surprised to find another captive in the room.

"Why are you here?" he finally managed to ask.

"That's what I'd like to know. I have absolutely no idea why I'm being locked up like this." Anger showed in the man's face.

Hikozo was astonished. This man was in the same quandary.

"I was arrested two weeks ago," the man said, "and have been here since. When I ask them why I'm being held, they don't answer.

280

I ask them to let me see my family, but they won't listen." He looked thoroughly forlorn.

Maybe because he'd had no company, the man was very talkative. Waving his hands, shrugging his shoulders, he related how terrible life was in this room. The food was awful, he said, the kind of thing a charitable Christian wouldn't think of giving to a pig, but to stave off hunger he had to eat it. The room had no heat whatsoever, and at night it was like being in a freezer; without any blankets he had to make do with using the sailcloth for warmth.

"How can we get out of here? If I stay here any longer, it'll be the death of me for sure," the man grieved.

Hikozo stood there, numb.

The captain had said he'd received an order for his arrest from Washington, but Hikozo couldn't fathom the reason behind this. It had to be a mistake, and soon, when they understood they'd made an error, he'd be released. But this other man had been held for two weeks, shut up in this room, not being interrogated, not being allowed to contact his family. They might do the same with Hikozo, and he might very well be in for a long confinement.

Hikozo pictured the faces of the two captains downstairs. He'd never seen such cold, cruel faces in all his years in America, faces without a trace of human kindness. Until now all the Americans he'd met were warmhearted, reaching out to help a person like himself from a small, distant Asian country. There was never anything calculated in their behavior, making him wonder at times why they were so friendly to him. He'd returned to America hoping to find himself among such people again, but this captain's face revealed a new side of America. One telegram from an official, and the captain mercilessly took Hikozo into custody and threw him into this awful, freezing room. Hikozo had never seen such hard eyes.

He pondered the situation. Would he share the fate of this other man, spending endless days with no prospect of release, forced by hunger to eat dreadful food, wrapping himself in a sailcloth to fend off the cold? *If I stay here any longer, it'll be the death of me*—the man's words sunk like a lead weight into Hikozo's heart.

He stood there, not moving a muscle. The man sat back on one of the chairs in a corner of the room, his face buried in his hands, a picture of despair. Hikozo began to tremble because of the cold, his teeth rattling. Surely if he spent much time in this room, death would not be far off.

A dark object moved in fits and starts along the base of the wall—an amazingly huge rat. Another black object appeared near the opposite wall. Hikozo realized that the man had been sharing his quarters with rats. If the lamp ran out of oil and went out, the room thrown into darkness, the rats would take over. Hikozo felt his spine freeze with terror.

Steps sounded in the corridor, coming to a stop outside the door, and a key turned in the lock. The door swung open, and Hikozo turned around. The tall captain stood there. He looked at Hikozo and said sharply, "Out!"

Hikozo's feet were numb with the cold, and he stumbled, but braced himself and managed to walk through the open door. The captain locked the door again and headed down the corridor. Hikozo followed him, holding on to the banister as he descended the stairs.

In the room with the fireplace Hikozo saw Booth and Bryant standing. The captain seated in the chair turned his cold eyes on Hikozo and barked, "Leave!" Booth came over and took Hikozo's arm, while Bryant helped him out of the room.

They walked down the night street, Hikozo supported by Booth, and when they came to an intersection, Bryant said good night and left for his home. Booth and Hikozo continued walking, not saying a word.

Once ensconced again in the living room, Booth poured Hikozo a glass of wine, downing his own glass in a single gulp. He told what had happened after Hikozo's arrest. He and Bryant went immediately to the office of the head of the military police and pleaded for Hikozo's release. Finally they won his release by posting a twenty-five thousand dollar bond, on condition that he appear before the military if and when they called him in again . . .

Hikozo thanked Booth profusely for all that he had done. Americans still can be kind, he thought, unable, though, to shake the image of that captain's cold, cruel eyes. Try as he might, they would stay with him forever.

He still couldn't understand the reason for his arrest.

The next day Booth had to go into Washington on business, and Hikozo asked to accompany him. He wanted to meet with Secretary of State Seward and check on how his appointment as official interpreter to the Kanagawa consulate was going.

Since one of the conditions of his release was that Hikozo appear whenever the military called him in, he needed to notify them whenever he left Booth's house. So Booth went to the garrison first to obtain permission to take Hikozo with him to Washington.

"While you're there, please ask the commanding officer why I was arrested," Hikozo asked. "Since I've arrived in America, I only went to see the secretary of the navy and the secretary of state, and I don't remember doing anything criminal."

"I'll find out," Booth said and left.

While he was gone, Hikozo couldn't sit still. He'd sit for a while in the living room, then get up to pace the floor. What if the commanding officer of the soldiers ordered him not to go to Washington, or even set foot outside Booth's house?

Thirty minutes later Booth returned.

"Everything's cleared up now," he said, removing his overcoat and taking a seat in the living room.

Apparently the headquarters of the Union army in Washington had received a report that the Confederate army, in preparation for an attack on the capital, had sent a high-ranking Southern officer to the city to reconnoiter. Plainclothes police were dispatched everywhere to find this officer, and one of them reported that a man closely resembling an old photograph of the officer in question was in Alexandria. This turned out to be Hikozo, whom the detective followed; when he ascertained that Hikozo had gone to Bryant's house together with Booth, he informed the military police. That's when the lieutenant and twenty soldiers came to arrest and confine Hikozo.

The MPs sent a message to their Washington headquarters relaying the contents of Hikozo's passport, and the headquarters telegraphed them saying that Hikozo, far from being a Confederate officer, was an innocent bystander, and ordered them to release him at once.

"They learned this only this morning. The commander was very apologetic and said they'll return the bond we posted." There was a smile in Booth's eyes as he said this.

Someone knocked at the front door, and Booth went to see who it was. Hikozo heard voices at the entrance, then Booth came back and said brightly, "It was the lieutenant from last night. He came with a message from the captain expressing his profound apologies for their mistake. He said they know they've upset you, and begged your forgiveness."

The captain himself should come to apologize, Hikozo thought. The man's cold expression rose before his eyes, and he grew angry all over again.

Booth had a carriage waiting for them, which the two took to downtown Washington. Hikozo parted from Booth there and went to the State Department to see Secretary Seward. Seward reported that things were proceeding smoothly for his appointment. When Hikozo told him about the events of the previous night, Seward replied, "I'm afraid that in times like this mistakes happen."

Returning from Washington, Hikozo stayed in Booth's house.

Sensing how unsettled the town of Alexandria was, he couldn't relax. The evening after the day he returned, a newspaper company in Alexandria burned down. The fire was deliberately set by soldiers who'd been angered by a report in the paper on the abduction of the pastor who was sympathetic to the South. Many of the town's residents were Confederate sympathizers, and a tense standoff ensued between them and the Union troops. Hikozo worried that he might be arrested again.

Sleet had turned to snow the day Hikozo bid the Booths

farewell, thanking them for all their kindness. He rode in Booth's carriage to the station and took the train to Washington.

As he gazed at the snow swirling outside the train window, he again realized how much he wanted to return to Japan. The America he knew was no more, its people coarsened by the war. Japan was going through a turbulent period itself, with one assassination after another, but it was the only place where he could live.

The train pulled into Baltimore Station. The snow had turned to rain, and Hikozo hailed a carriage and rode to Sanders's home.

Life was quiet at the Sanderses', and he enjoyed dining with them and chatting over tea. He refrained from mentioning his arrest so as not to worry Mr. Sanders. On Sunday he went with them to church and prayed for their good health and that their lives would remain peaceful.

A letter arrived for him from Seward: his official appointment as interpreter for the Kanagawa consulate. He showed this to Sanders, who congratulated him. That evening Mrs. Sanders prepared a special dinner to celebrate the good news.

Late on the night of March 9 they heard the rumble of cannon firing in the distance; it continued for a long time. Awakened by the noise, Mr. and Mrs. Sanders went out into the garden, where they faced the roar and clasped their hands in prayer. Hikozo did the same.

The next day cannon fire echoed in the distance. There was a battle at Hampton Roads between the two armies, and a battle between the Confederate ship *Merrimac* and two Union ships, the *Cumberland* and the *Congress*, which it sunk.

Hikozo knew that this war that had torn America apart would only get worse. The citizens of Baltimore feared now that their city would become a battlefield. The Sanders themselves were uneasy and often went to church to pray. For his part Hikozo felt spurred on to hasten his departure for Japan.

On March 12, three days after they heard the cannon roaring, Hikozo left Baltimore for Washington. He wanted to see Seward to thank him for the appointment and to report on his plans to return to Japan.

He'd written ahead seeking a meeting, so as soon as he arrived at the State Department, he was shown into Seward's office. When Hikozo announced he was soon returning to Japan, Seward said, "So you're off to Japan, are you?" He was lost in thought for a while, then looked at Hikozo and said, "Before you go, we should have you meet our country's tycoon."

Hikozo knew that Americans called the Tokugawa shogun the tycoon, so "America's tycoon" had to mean the president.

Seward told him to wait and left his office. Sanders had introduced him to President Pierce, and Senator Gwin had had him meet President Buchanan. At the time Hikozo didn't feel that he was meeting an exalted personage, but now, back from Japan, he knew that the president was as eminent a figure as the Tokugawa shogun, being the leader of this vast nation. Even the daimyo, the local lords in Japan, were paid visits only by the highest-ranking samurai, and the shogun was so far above even this that he occupied a different world, one far removed from ordinary citizens.

It was nothing less than a miracle, then, that Hikozo had been able to meet two presidents, and now Seward was about to introduce him to a third. Hikozo felt so nervous he trembled.

The president's name was Lincoln. He'd been a lawyer and a member of Congress and had been elected as the Republican Party's candidate. He was held in high regard by many as a good-hearted man and was widely trusted and respected.

After fifteen minutes Seward was back and said, "Mr. Heco, let's go. I was able to get an appointment with the president," and went out of his office to the garden in the rear.

He held Hikozo's arm as they walked and said, cheerfully, "I have a cabinet meeting today, but I couldn't let you return to your country without meeting our great leader."

The presidential mansion was visible ahead, and when they arrived, Seward knocked at the door to the office. Inside Hikozo saw a man in a black frock coat seated in an armchair behind a large desk. The man was gaunt, with side-whiskers. He glanced in their direction, then turned back to listen to the army colonel standing in front of him with a sheaf of documents in his hands.

Seward told Hikozo to take a seat; he, too, sat down and began reading one of the newspapers on the table beside them. The colonel finally finished his business, saluted, and left the room. The other man stood up and came over to greet them. Hikozo was astonished at how tall he was. Hikozo stood up with Seward. The president greeted Seward warmly and shook his hand.

Seward looked at Hikozo and said, "I'd like to introduce my friend to you. He's Japanese."

The president held out his large hand and said, "You've come a long way, haven't you?" He shook Hikozo's hand and looked at him with gentle eyes.

The president took his seat again, and Seward and Hikozo sat down in front of him.

Seward gave the president a short summary of how Hikozo had been a castaway and how he became an American citizen. As he listened, the president turned often in amazement to Hikozo. Seward added that Hikozo had just been appointed official interpreter for the American consulate in Kanagawa and would be returning to Japan soon.

"I know we can count on things going well with a person like you working at the consulate," Lincoln said. "Please do your best, not just for America, but for the sake of Japan as well."

To Hikozo, Lincoln seemed less a president than a kindly old farmer.

As they were talking, Secretary of the Treasury Chase and Secretary of the Navy Welles had both come in to meet with the president, so Hikozo quickly expressed his gratitude to Lincoln for the appointment as interpreter, and he and Seward left the Oval Office. His meeting with the president had been a short one, but Hikozo felt a warm glow in his heart.

He stayed two days in Washington, then returned to the Sanderses in Baltimore. As Hikozo told Sanders all about his meeting with Lincoln, the old man nodded over and over. Sanders's eyes were always watery now.

Hikozo enjoyed several quiet days with the Sanderses and could sense that when he left their home for Japan, it would be his final farewell to them. Sanders may have thought the same way, for his eyes seemed to plead with Hikozo to delay his departure for as long as possible.

Hikozo found it hard to look into those eyes, and he extended his stay by a day. On the evening of March 26 he packed his bags in his bedroom.

The next morning after breakfast, he went upstairs to his bedroom and came down with his overcoat and suitcase. When he opened the door to the living room, he saw Sanders sitting there, his mouth slightly open, his eyes fixed on Hikozo.

Hikozo put his suitcase on the floor and his overcoat of top of it, walked over to Sanders, and put out his hand.

Sanders stood up with difficulty.

"I'm going back to Japan now. I can't tell you how very grateful I am for all you've done for me." Hikozo barely managed to get the words out.

Sanders's eyes filled with tears, and he hugged Hikozo weakly, leaning against the younger man for support. A sob broke from his throat, then he was sobbing loudly, his body heaving. Hikozo held the old man close and himself broke into tears.

Mrs. Sanders came and asked, "Are you really going back to Japan?" She clasped Hikozo's arm, her own eyes filling with tears.

The three of them stood there for a long while.

Finally Hikozo released Sanders and said, "I'll always be praying for your good health. Even in Japan I'm always your son. I'm sure I'll have a chance to come to America again, and when I do, please let me stay with you again."

Sanders nodded silently.

Hikozo picked up his suitcase and overcoat. "Good-bye, then," he said, pushed open the door of the living room, and left the house.

He put on his overcoat and began walking down the street. Turning to look back at the house, he saw Mrs. Sanders in the window, waving to him, Mr. Sanders beside her.

On April 1 Hikozo left New York Harbor on the *North Star.* As he watched the city fade into the distance, he had the feeling he would never see it again.

Because of the war, lookouts were posted on top of the mast and at various spots on deck, all of them scanning the horizon with spyglasses. At night all the portholes were shut to keep light from filtering out. The ship hugged the coast as it made its way south, arriving safely at Aspinwall. Hikozo and the other passengers then took a train across the isthmus. The *Sonora* was waiting for them, and they boarded it.

Now they were in a safer zone, and there was no need for lookouts. The ship plowed through the Pacific on a northwest course. Hikozo spent his time reading in his cabin or up on the deck gazing out at the ocean.

Several days later, on the day they arrived in San Francisco, there was a commotion on deck. A boy of fourteen or fifteen, sobbing aloud, was held tight by two sailors, who were dragging him. A strip of cloth hung around his neck all the way to his feet; the word THIEF was written on it in bold letters. A line of passengers watched, and Hikozo learned from them that the boy, the son of a second-class passenger, had stolen something from a first-class passenger, and the captain thought that having him hauled around in front of everyone like this would teach him a lesson.

Hikozo watched the sobbing boy being dragged across the deck and once again thought about how the America he knew was no more. During the time he'd lived there, not once had he witnessed this kind of scene. The war had put people on edge, and though it was well and good to scold the boy for stealing, they'd gone too far. Hikozo wondered what the boy's parents must be thinking. He couldn't stand watching anymore and went back to his cabin.

On the evening of April 26 their ship entered San Francisco Harbor, and Hikozo stayed at a hotel. The next morning he went to the Macondray Company and met with Cary. He told him how the secretary of the navy had refused to appoint him as a naval storekeeper, and how instead the secretary of state had made him official interpreter for the Kanagawa consulate.

"Ah, you weren't able to get the appointment as storekeeper, after all." Cary was discouraged, but Hikozo expressed his gratitude for all his efforts on his behalf.

Hikozo went on to say that now that he'd accomplished what he set out to do in America, he was heading back to Japan.

"So it's back to Japan for you, is it?" Cary's face was troubled. He said there'd been a drastic decrease in trade in America as a result of the Civil War; ships that normally carried goods and traders back and forth between America and the outside world were now transporting troops and armaments. Soon after Japan opened its doors to the world, trade had been brisk, but now it was nearly at a standstill, with barely a single ship bound for Japan.

"Occasionally a ship will go to China," Cary said apologetically. "I think the only thing for you to do is take one of those ships, go to China, and then search for a ship that will take you to Japan."

In Washington, New York, and Baltimore the war's effects were obvious, but they were being felt even here on the West Coast. Hikozo sighed. Unfortunately, what Cary said made perfect sense. The Union and Confederate armies were locked in such fierce conflict that most available ships had been mobilized in the war effort.

Hikozo asked Cary to let him know when he heard of any ship bound for China.

The harbor was filled with steamships and sailing vessels, but as Cary had said, these were all traveling between points within the United States; not one was a trade ship. Because of the war, too, the cotton fields were now battlefields, so production of the main export, cotton cloth, had practically ceased. There wasn't much business at Cary's company, either, just the supplying of the Union army with food and other provisions.

Hikozo spent his days hoping that a ship bound for China

would turn up. With nothing else to occupy his time, he often went to Cary's company to read newspaper reports on the war.

On May 5 he was there as usual, reading the papers, when an article caught his eye. It reported that eleven Japanese castaways had been picked up by a ship named the *Victor* and brought to San Francisco. The *Victor*, bound for San Francisco from China, discovered, at 33 degrees latitude, 161.2 degrees east longitude, a ship drifting without a mast. The *Victor* lowered a boat and rescued the eleven crew members, who turned out to be Japanese.

Hikozo got to his feet. All the hardships and sorrows he himself experienced twelve years before on the *Eiriki Maru* came rushing back. The Japanese sailors were surely happy to have been snatched from death, but just as surely they must long to return to Japan. Hikozo decided he'd do whatever he could to help them. Japan, open to the outside world now, would accept them back, so all that remained was the logistical problem of finding a ship that would take them there.

The consul, Mr. Brooks, in charge of U.S.-Japan relations, was permanently stationed in San Francisco, and as Hikozo knew him, he decided to seek his help. He hurried from Cary's offices.

Brooks had already received a report from the captain of the *Victor*, Crowell, and when Hikozo told him he wanted to help the castaways get home, Brooks agreed immediately and invited him to join him in going to the *Victor*. Seizing this opportunity, Hikozo went out with Brooks by boat to the ship.

The *Victor* was still going through the procedures necessary to formally enter the harbor and the passengers, the majority of whom were Chinese and still aboard. They met Captain Crowell, Brooks introduced Hikozo, and the two men shook hands. According to the captain, the ship had about three hundred Chinese passengers, both men and women.

The consul explained how they'd come to see to the Japanese castaways, and the captain ordered the Japanese brought to him. After a while a group of men, their short hair tied in the back, looking around fearfully, appeared at the cabin door. Their faces were pale and gaunt, and their party included a thirteen- or fourteen-year-old boy. None of them had the full chonmage hairstyle, which led Hikozo to conclude that, fearing they would sink, they'd all cut their hair and begged the gods to protect them.

He went over to them, smiling so they wouldn't be afraid, and said, "Do you know who I am?"

Surprised to be addressed in Japanese, the men stared at him. With his short hair and Western clothes he looked like an American, and the sailors cast suspicious eyes at him, none of them thinking he was Japanese.

One man spoke up hesitantly: "Begging your pardon, but who would you be?"

"I'm Hikozo from the province of Harima." Hearing this, the men all looked at each other. Hikozo briefly told them how he'd been a castaway twelve years before and was rescued by an American ship, and he asked them what had led to their rescue by the *Victor*.

"My name is Seigoro," the man said. "I'm the captain." He took a step forward and told their story.

The sailors were crew on a ship called the *Eiju Maru,* owned by a man named Iwakichi Hikotaro and based in Nakasu, Chita County, in Owari Province (modern-day Nakasu, Minami Chita Town, in Aichi Prefecture). On November 26 of the previous year, the first year of Bunkyu (1861), they'd left their home port bound for Edo. Their ship was carrying 437 ryo of gold and silver coins, plus a hundred straw bags of wheat flour.

On the way they stopped at Tobaura, and when they left that port, they ran into a violent storm. On the verge of sinking, the men chopped off their topknots and prayed to the gods to save them, and eventually they had no choice but to cut down their mast. They then drifted helplessly. After they ate all the rice on board, they made a mortar out of the mast and pounded the wheat flour and made dumplings; they caught various fish, too—sardines, tuna, and yellowtail—and managed to stave off starvation.

They encountered several more storms as they drifted and several times almost lost their lives, but finally on March 15 of the second year of Bunkyu (April 13, 1862), they were discovered by the American ship *Victor.*

One of the other sailors added, "When we transferred to the American ship, our captain refused to board the boat that came for us, saying he would share the fate of the *Eiju Maru.* We tried everything we could think of to persuade him, and finally he joined us."

On the *Victor* they were surprised to find so many Chinese passengers. These were all bound for the gold fields of California. Seigoro learned of this by communicating with them through writing. The Chinese passengers fed them rice and soup and even gave them tobacco to smoke.

When he'd heard all this, Hikozo consulted with Brooks, and they decided to take the men ashore and try to find a way for them to return to Japan. He told this to Seigoro, and the Japanese sailors were overjoyed. Hikozo and Brooks then left the *Victor.*

They found lodgings for the men and two days later escorted them off the ship to the place. Hikozo indicated Brooks to the men and said, "It's due to this man's good offices that you're able to stay here. Please thank him for what he's done."

Seigoro and the others got down on their knees and bowed deeply to Brooke many times.

In his diary Seigoro noted that the house they stayed in had faucets, something he'd never seen before. He expressed his surprise in these words: "They have metal fixtures that look like wisteria vines running along the wall. If you twist them at certain points, water gushes from them."

But could a ship be found going to China, if not Japan?

Only three days later, a message came from Brooks to the effect that an American ship was in port carrying cargo bound for Yokohama. Surprised, Hikozo hurried over and found that Brooks had already arranged with the captain of the vessel, the *Caroline E. Foote,* for the castaways to be passengers on it.

Hikozo also wanted to take the ship to Japan, but Brooks told him it was impossible. The ship didn't have room for any more passengers; in fact, it was only at Brooks's insistence that the captain cleared part of the hold to let the eleven castaways have a place to stay.

Hikozo decided this was for the best. He had helped these men, who had suffered enough already, to get home. He would wait for another day and another ship.

Thanking Brooks for all he'd done, he returned to the lodgings to tell the sailors the good news. They burst into smiles at the news, putting their hands together in a display of gratitude to him.

The *Caroline E. Foote* was scheduled to depart on May 14, but because of unfavorable winds they didn't leave until noon of the following day. The ship proceeded smoothly across the Pacific, along the way experiencing a lunar eclipse. On July 1 they sighted Hachijo Island, and the next day (June 6 by the Japanese calendar) they arrived off Yokohama.

Seigoro and his crew were handed over to officials from the commissioner's office, where they were questioned. By order of the commissioner, Seigoro wrote a document entitled *Record of the* Eiju Maru *and Its Castaways*. They had brought back with them the three hundred ryo and all the presents given them by Hikozo and various Americans, but these were confiscated.

It was decided that the men be handed over to the Owari Domain, where they were from, in early November, and on the nineteenth of that month one hundred ryo was returned to them. They were first taken to the residence of the Owari Domain in Tsukiji in Edo; then the following year, on January 2 of the third year of Bunkyu, they were escorted back to their hometown of Nakasu. Their relatives were beside themselves with joy when they were reunited, and people gathered from near and far to listen to the men's tales of their shipwreck and of their time in San Francisco.

In April of that year the Owari Domain had contracted in Yokohama to purchase a Western sailing ship, but since no one was able to pilot it, the domain thought of the sailors of the *Eiju Maru*.

The domain called in the former castaways and learned that, as sailors were wont to do, they had been fascinated by the Western sailing ship and had helped out on the voyage across the Pacific.

The domain decided to employ the five men in the crew who were able to read and write: Seigoro, Tsunekichi, Eisuke, Hikogoro, and Gonjiro.

The sailing ship was anchored in Uraga, so Seigoro and the others set out for the town, accompanied by samurai from the domain. The men carefully went over all the rigging and fittings of the ship, having the ones redone that weren't up to specification; when this was complete, the domain officially received the ship and christened it the *Jinriki Maru.*

The *Jinriki Maru* left for Owari with a crew of thirty, and Seigoro and his four companions in command. The ship made voyages to Osaka and Edo but five months later was damaged in a typhoon off Shimoda in Izu. There were no ship's carpenters to repair it, so the ship had to be abandoned.

Later, the domain purchased a British steamship, renaming it the *Chita Maru,* and Seigoro and his four companions were employed to command it. They were given a stipend as well as an allowance as crew members. At the time of the Meiji Restoration they were raised to the status of samurai.

Seigoro and three of the other men's lines died out, with only Gonjiro, who had been given the surname of Ishigaki, blessed with a family. On July 9 of the seventh year of Taisho (1918), he passed away at the age of eighty-nine on the island of Kyosai in Korea.

CHAPTER TWENTY-TWO

AFTER SEEING OFF THE castaways of the *Eiju Maru*, Hikozo stayed behind in San Francisco, waiting for a ship to take him home.

No ships were sailing to China, even, let alone Japan, but finally he learned that a ship bound for China by way of Hawaii had come into port, so he said good-bye to all his friends, took passage on the ship, and left San Francisco.

The ship was decrepit, old, and slow; it stayed for a long while in Honolulu after arriving there but finally lifted anchor and arrived in Hong Kong on September 5. In Hong Kong, Hikozo learned that the Civil War was still in full swing and that General McClellan's troops had engaged the Confederate Army at Richmond, losing twenty thousand soldiers in the battle before retreating in defeat. Britain, which was essentially in control of China, had a great antipathy for America at this time, issuing an order that American naval forces would be allowed in port for only twenty-four hours at any one time. American sea transport and trade were nearly at a standstill.

On September 11 Hikozo left Hong Kong on the British vessel *Rona*. The ship stopped in Amoi and Fuzhou, arriving in Shanghai on the twenty-seventh.

In Shanghai Hikozo searched for a ship to Japan, and took passage on the *Governor Wallace*, which was heading for Kanagawa. The ship stopped in Wusun and arrived in Kanagawa on October 13 (August 20, second year of Bunkyu).

Going ashore to Yokohama, he found the place in an uproar over the recent murder of foreigners at Namamugi Village. Three British merchants and the wife of one of them had been on horseback on the Tokaido Road heading for Kawasaki when, at Namamugi Village, they encountered a procession led by the head of the powerful Satsuma clan, Shimazu Hisamitsu. One of the merchants was killed, and two were gravely wounded. The British chargé d'affaires, Neil, had lodged strong protests with both the shogunate and the Satsuma Domain.

The attack reminded Hikozo of how the opening of Japan to the outside world was accompanied by bloody incidents like this.

Two days later he went to the American consulate in the Honkakuji Temple in Kanagawa, his appointment as official interpreter in hand. There'd been a personnel change in the consulate since Hikozo was last there. A half year before, Dorr had left his post, being replaced as consul by a Mr. Fisher; Van Reed had since resigned as chief clerk. Likewise, Townsend Harris had left his post as ambassador, replaced by a Mr. Pruyn.

The document appointing Hikozo as official interpreter had already arrived at Pruyn's desk, and the new consul was aware of this. Hikozo greeted Fisher, accepted the appointment, and officially took up his post. He was assigned a room in the Honkakuji Temple, where he took up residence.

He could sense the atmosphere around him growing more and more tense. After the Namamugi Village incident the foreign residents were extremely nervous, while the Kanagawa commissioner's office was overworked. Further incidents took place. On the night of December 12 the British legation building that was under construction in Gotenyama in Shinagawa was set on fire; Hikozo saw the night sky turn red with the blaze. Obviously this was an act of arson by faction samurai, so the shogunate, fearful that other foreign ministries might suffer a similar fate, increased the number of guards it assigned to them. At the American consulate where Hikozo lived and worked, guards were posted twenty-four hours a day.

As the New Year came, the third year of Bunkyu, assassinations of foreigners, dubbed *divine punishments* by the samurai who committed them, increased in number. Those targeted included Confucian scholars and shogunate ministers who supported the opening of the country, as well as merchants who had profited by the new foreign trade.

Repercussions from the Namamugi incident still were being felt. The shogunate paid reparations to the British, but the Satsuma Domain turned down this request, and relations between them worsened further.

On the afternoon of May 16 an urgent message reached the consulate from Ambassador Pruyn. That day a British mail boat arrived at Yokohama carrying a report addressed to Pruyn from the American consul in Shanghai. The U.S. steamship *Pembroke* had been anchored at the straits of Shimonoseki when it was suddenly fired upon by a warship of the Choshu Domain; the *Pembroke* turned around and took the Bungo Channel. The Choshu warship vigorously pursued the *Pembroke,* which was narrowly able to escape and continue its voyage, finally arriving in Shanghai. The captain of the ship reported this to the consul in Shanghai, who in turn reported the illegal attack to Pruyn.

A strong protest was lodged with the Kanagawa commissioner. Pruyn came to the consulate and sent out a messenger inviting the commissioner to come see him. Commodore McDougall of the U.S. warship *Wyoming,* anchored at this time in the waters off Yokohama, was also present at the meeting. The interpreter was Hikozo.

Pruyn first asked the commissioner whether he was aware of the incident. The commissioner said he had heard the news and that they believed that the cannon fire had come from a Choshu warship.

"Then the shogunal government must have allowed them to fire," Pruyn said, his tone quite harsh.

When Hikozo interpreted this, the commissioner replied, "This was a unilateral attack by the Choshu Domain, and the shogunate had nothing to do with it. We have friendly relations with the

United States, and the shogunate will do all within its power to bring the perpetrators to justice for firing on an American ship. However, this report only now reached Edo, and we need more time to consider our response..."

Pruyn, staring straight at the commissioner, said, "So you're saying people from Choshu attacked on their volition, and the shogunate had nothing to do with it. That being the case, I will direct one of our warships to proceed to Choshu to retaliate. I assume that the shogunate would have no objection to this."

As Hikozo interpreted these words, the commissioner's face stiffened.

"That won't do at all," he replied firmly. "Edo will quickly investigate the matter, and if it is determined that illegal acts were committed, punishment will be meted out according to our statutes. Therefore, I request that you refrain from dispatching a warship and wait for further communications from Edo."

Thus ended the meeting, and the commissioner left the consulate.

Hikozo listened as the ambassador discussed things further with the consul and Commodore McDougall. The ambassador said that if the commodore agreed, he would dispatch the *Wyoming* to the Shimonoseki Straits and have it seize the Choshu ship that fired on the *Pembroke* and bring it back to Yokohama. The ambassador himself would go with them.

The commodore had no objection, and it was decided that the *Wyoming* would depart the next morning, May 28.

"I'd like you to come with me," the ambassador said to Hikozo, and he returned to the legation.

The next morning Hikozo received a written directive from Fisher that read: "Board the *Wyoming* tomorrow morning at four."

The morning after this, before dawn, Hikozo took a boat from the docks out to the *Wyoming*. The time for departure arrived, but Pruyn had still not arrived, and the captain kept his spyglass aimed at the docks in the hope of catching a glimpse of him. The thought struck Hikozo that perhaps the ambassador was afraid to join them out of fear of the exchange of fire that would surely ensue between the *Wyoming* and the Satsuma forces. The ambassador did not show.

The captain gave up waiting, ordered the anchor raised, and they headed out toward Edo Bay. Two Japanese hired to help pilot the ship guided it to the Pacific, where it then turned west. Two days later, at dawn, they sailed past Murado Cape, part of the Toasa Domain.

In the captain's smoking room after breakfast Commodore McDougall asked Hikozo, "Do you think the Choshu people will fire on an American warship?"

"I think they'll fire on any ship, whether merchant or warship," Hikozo replied. "It's best to take all necessary precautions."

McDougall nodded.

The *Wyoming* continued west, at 3 PM entering Bungo Channel, coming to a stop and anchoring near Hime Island in the Suoonada. The captain assembled his officers and ordered that everyone man his battle station. All weapons were loaded, not just the cannons, but the rifles and pistols as well.

The next day dawned clear, without a cloud in the sky. They raised anchor just past 5 AM and cruised around the Suoonada in search of the Choshu ship that had fired on the *Pembroke.* There wasn't a breath of wind, and the sea was as smooth as glass.

No warships were sighted, and the captain, surmising they were near the Shimonoseki Straits, turned the bow in that direction. He ordered tarpaulins put over their cannons so they might appear to be a merchant vessel.

At around ten o'clock, as they neared the entrance to the strait, the first lieutenant at the forecastle called out that he spotted two armed sailing vessels and one steamship anchored before the town.

"Very well," the captain said. "We'll proceed between them and capture the steamer."

Hikozo noticed that the faces of the sailors were pale. Some wandered in a daze, their lips trembling. Having never been in actual combat before, they were frightened out of their wits.

As their ship neared the entrance to the straits, a cannon suddenly thundered. Smoke arose from a wooded area on the bluffs to their right. Hikozo ran over to the captain, who was at the bridge, and said, "I think this must be the signal to commence fighting."

Right after this a cannon boomed from a battery set up at the entrance to the straits, firing over and over. Columns of water spouted up here and there in the sea as the roaring echoed. The captain had the American flag run up the mast and yelled, "Battle stations!"

The crew hurriedly removed the tarps from their cannon and fired the sixty-four-pounders.

The *Wyoming* steamed straight for the three Choshu ships. The Choshu ships and batteries maintained a furious fusillade, but most of the shells exploded harmlessly over the ship, or fell short, sending up plumes of water.

High-ranking domain officials were no doubt aboard the steamship, for it flew a purple banner with the official family crest of the domain. The *Wyoming* cut in front of the steamer, all the while returning fire. Just then the steamer cut its cable and made off toward the inner harbor, trying to escape.

Commodore McDougall ordered the eleven-inch Dahlgren to fire. The sailor manning the gun, trembling and pale, didn't seem to hear the order and just stood there until the captain roared at him, when he finally got off a shot. The cannon roared, and the air was filled with gunpowder smoke. Hikozo saw a huge cloud of black smoke and white steam issue from the steamer's deck. Their cannon had made a direct hit on the steam boilers of the vessel.

The American sailors, till now shrinking in fear, gave a great cheer, their miraculous shot giving them the courage they'd lacked.

The Choshu steamer heeled over, gradually listing more and more until it sank beneath the waves. With this sight the sailors became more spirited and turned their cannon on the two sailing ships and let off some shots.

The two ships put up a good fight but suffered too many direct hits from the American cannons. Japanese crew members leaped into the sea like so many peas and then swam splashing to shore. The smaller of the two vessels caught fire and sank, while the larger ship sustained serious damage and lay still in the water. All the batteries on shore were now silent.

The captain gave the order to cease fire and turned the vessel around.

When they assessed their own damage, they found that they'd been hit by twenty shells, with four dead sailors and six wounded. The whole engagement had taken less than an hour.

The *Wyoming* left the straits and headed east, anchoring near Hime Island. They lowered a boat to inspect the damage to the hull; the damage was not severe enough to keep them from sailing on.

At five thirty in the afternoon the weather suddenly took a turn for the worse, and a heavy rain began to fall. Hikozo was invited to the captain's cabin, where he joined the officers in toasting their victory. He might be Japanese, but he felt no reservation about the great blow delivered to the Choshu Domain or about joining the others in their happiness at the victory.

At five the next morning the rain stopped, so they left Hime Island. They proceeded south down Bungo Channel, coming to a halt near the entrance to the channel at around nine thirty.

The previous night two of the wounded had succumbed, and the six dead sailors were wrapped in sailcloth and brought out on deck. Empty shell casings were attached to the cloths so the bodies would sink properly. Hikozo, the captain, and the entire crew lined up at attention, the officers saluted, the sailors presented arms. A rifle salute was fired into the air, and one by one the dead were committed to the sea.

The *Wyoming* continued east across the Pacific, entering Edo Bay and finally dropping anchor off Yokohama.

When Hikozo returned to the consulate, he asked Fisher, "Why didn't Ambassador Pruyn go with us on the *Wyoming* when he said he would? Captain McDougall waited two hours for him."

With a twinkle in his eyes the consul said, "I'm afraid the ambassador had a terrible case of indigestion."

Hikozo knew it wasn't true. This ambassador was quite different from his predecessor, Harris—he was calculating, concerned with personal gain, interested mainly in business ventures that would yield a healthy profit. The same thing could be said of the consul, Fisher, and Hikozo wasn't happy with either man.

News arrived at the consulate that, following an attack on the French warship *Kien Chang* in the Shimonoseki Straits, the Dutch ship *Medusa* had also been fired upon by Choshu forces and sustained considerable damage. The enraged French consul dispatched two warships, the *Semiramis* and the *Tancrède,* to the straits to exact revenge.

When he heard that these two ships had returned, Hikozo went down to Yokohama to see them. The French officers boasted that they'd routed the Choshu forces and had even sent a landing force that returned with various spoils of victory; they paid a price for this, though, for their smokestack had been broken, their mast sent flying, and several of their men had been killed and wounded.

The Namamugi incident was settled when the shogunate paid reparations of 110,000 pounds to the British government, but the Satsuma Domain rebuffed all compromise and several attempts at negotiations had broken down. The British chargé d'affaires decided it best to go to Kagoshima and settle things directly, so he joined a fleet of seven British ships under the command of Commodore Kupper and set off from Yokohama bound for Kagoshima.

The foreign community in Yokohama was convinced that at the imposing sight of such a fleet the Satsuma Domain would give in to all the demands made on it. Consul Fisher shared the same opinion. "When the Satsuma daimyo see this fleet in front of them, they'll tremble and beg for mercy," he said happily.

Hikozo's long years in America had shown him that the military power of Western countries and that of Japan were like day and night, and he was sure that if war broke out, even a major domain like Satsuma would immediately be overpowered.

Four days after the British fleet sailed, officials of the commissioner's office came to the consulate to speak with Hikozo. They all wore grave expressions. The man in the middle, clearly the senior official, related how two days previously a bloody severed head had been found tossed in the outhouse of a teahouse along the Tokaido Road. A notice was attached to the head that said it belonged to one of the men who'd been hired to help pilot the American warships from Yokohama to Shimonoseki. The note went on to say that there were two more men who'd been on the ship whose behavior was unpardonable and who would soon suffer the same fate.

"We believe these two are you and the other pilot." The official looked fixedly at Hikozo and told him that a large number of Choshu samurai had infiltrated the Kanagawajuku area.

Hikozo remembered the faces of the two men hired as pilots on the warship. These were sailors with much experience going through the Straits of Shimonoseki, and he recalled how they'd had them anchor at Hime Island and then proceed to the straits.

"You must avoid at all costs going near this part of Kanagawa. At all costs," the official said sternly, a hard look still on his face as he left the consulate.

Hikozo felt weak in the knees. That the Choshu Domain knew he was on board was proof of how well placed their informants were. They might have even known that he raised his glass with the captain in celebration of the victory.

The only reason he had been on the *Wyoming* in the first place was because Ambassador Pruyn had ordered him to. But then Pruyn himself feigned illness to avoid going on the mission, and Hikozo grew angry again at how low and mean this man was.

Fearing for his life, he wore a loaded pistol strapped to his waist at all times and stayed locked in his room at the consulate.

Three days after the officials' visit, news reached him that placards had appeared all over the Japanese part of Yokohama proclaiming that Japanese officials, one and all, would be cut down and their houses burned to the ground. As a consequence guards had been posted throughout the town, with checkpoints set up.

The next morning news came from the commissioner's office that a large group of Choshu samurai were heading toward the

Yokohama foreign settlement to attack it and that a large cache of weapons and ammunition had already been smuggled into the Japanese part of town. More guards were placed at the consulate out of fear that the consulate would come under attack.

Two days later another ominous report reached them. Several leading merchants in Kyoto had been attacked, their severed heads left at the foot of some of the main bridges in the city, with the following notice attached:

These lawless people have been doing business with foreign barbarians for their own profit, which has caused the price of all goods to rise and the people to suffer. Their actions are treasonous, and they've been punished accordingly.

News of this affair caused an enormous stir. The Japanese merchants who had shops in Yokohama and were doing business with foreigners now saw themselves labeled as traitors who deserved punishment. Fearful of an attack, some closed up shop early for the day.

When Hikozo learned of the great commotion among the merchants, he felt driven into a corner. It was well known that though he was a Japanese, he was employed by the American consulate as an interpreter, and he felt certain that if he stayed any longer at the consulate, he'd be cut down, his severed head put on gruesome display.

He made up his mind to leave the consulate. The faction would no longer target him if he quit his job as interpreter, would they? Besides, he was growing disgusted with his superiors. The former ambassador, Harris, and the former consul, Dorr, had been men with a sense of mission, trying their best to look after the interests of their country; in contrast, the present ambassador and consul were driven solely by the desire to line their pockets. Both were well paid, while Hikozo's salary was unreasonably low. He'd asked several times for a raise, only to be given the cold shoulder. He'd hoped that in his post as consular interpreter he'd be able to play a part in improving relations between the two countries but had now lost all hope of that.

After giving it careful thought, Hikozo wrote out a letter of resignation and handed it to Fisher. When Fisher read it, he just casually said, "I'll add a letter of my own requesting that this resignation be accepted and send it off to the States."

Normally one would have expected him at least to give a show of trying to dissuade Hikozo from resigning. Hikozo concluded that this was a most unfeeling person.

Until official notification of the acceptance of his resignation arrived from the State Department in Washington, Hikozo couldn't leave his job, so he stayed at the consulate working as interpreter, though his relations with Fisher were strained and he tried as much as possible to avoid seeing him.

Soon after this he read in an extra edition of a British-run newspaper reports on the British fleet that had sailed for Kagoshima. The British mail ship *Cormorant* had been on its way to Yokohama from Shanghai when it spied five British warships at anchor off the coast of Hyuga Province and stopped. A boat was let down from the flagship *Euryalus,* and a newspaper reporter came over to the *Cormorant.* According to the reporter a fierce battle had taken place between the fleet and the Satsuma Domain, and two warships were damaged and couldn't continue their voyage; they were waiting for them to rejoin the fleet.

The reporter entrusted his report on the battle to the captain, asking him to make sure it reached his newspaper company in Yokohama. Early that morning the *Cormorant* reached Yokohama, the report was immediately handed over to the newspaper company, and an extra edition was printed.

Hikozo was taken aback at the article on the engagement. The captain of the *Euryalus,* Captain Josling, as well as his second in command, Wilmot, had been killed in the battle, some sixty others had been killed or wounded, and every ship in the fleet had been damaged.

Hikozo had fully believed that this fleet from the British navy, which, after all, was one of the leading naval powers on earth, would crush the Satsuma Domain, but the newspaper article gave the distinct impression that the fleet had been defeated.

When he read the article, Fisher muttered to himself over and over, "I just can't believe it. This report must be mistaken."

Two days later an even more detailed report was in the newspaper. On that day the *Euryalus* pulled into Yokohama Harbor, and the reporter on board delivered his report to the newspaper company. It related how the Satsuma forces had been dealt a considerable blow, but at the same time the British fleet had suffered considerable damage.

The consulate heard reports of how the foreign community in Yokohama was upset by the news. In contrast, officials from the commissioner's office and local Japanese merchants were secretly delighted that the Japanese had held off the mighty British navy. Hikozo, though, couldn't rejoice, and realized that his sympathy lay with the foreigners.

Afterward many frightening reports reached him. There was a series of assassinations of Japanese merchants doing business with foreigners. In Kyoto, for instance, one of the leading merchants, named Hachimanya Uhei, had been cut down, his bloody head set on a stake at the foot of Sanjo Ohashi Bridge. A notice was attached to the stake that declared that trade with foreign countries had impoverished the people, that merchants seeking to profit and grow wealthy through such trade would not be tolerated and would be put to death. The notice also stated that four other leading merchants—Chojiya Ginzaburo, Nunoya Hikotaro, his father Ichijiro, and Yamatoya Shobei—had escaped death this time because they weren't at home, but would be "pursued and given divine punishment."

This incident threw the Yokohama merchants doing business with foreigners into a panic, and many of them shut their shops and left the town. Hikozo, too, was uneasy, and hoped he'd be able to leave the employ of the consulate as soon as possible.

Officials from the commissioner's office would sometimes

come to see him to warn him that Choshu samurai were lurking about and remind him to avoid going near the Tokaido Road. Whenever the officials visited him, he told them that he'd submitted his resignation letter to Washington and was just waiting for the reply that it was officially accepted. If the officials helped this news get out, he figured, the Choshu samurai might no longer single him out for attack.

He shuddered whenever he pictured that merchant's head stuck on a stake on that bridge in Kyoto. His own head might be lopped off at a single stroke of one of these razor-sharp swords. He stayed in his room at the consulate, a loaded pistol beside him at night when he went to bed. The slightest noise at night would have him leaping up to investigate, and he did not sleep well.

On August 18, a cloudy day, an American ship that had just come into harbor delivered the official notice from the State Department accepting Hikozo's resignation. As soon as he heard this from Consul Fisher, he reported to the commissioner that he no longer had any connection with the consulate.

He moved out of the consulate that very day, settling into an attached room of a Japanese merchant friend of his in the Japanese section of Yokohama. He felt relieved that things had been settled, though he still was fearful and avoided going out except when absolutely necessary.

A strange atmosphere had settled over Yokohama Village with its rows of Japanese shops engaged in foreign trade. Guards sent out by the commissioner's office were everywhere, while in the foreign settlement armed military from a number of countries patrolled the streets.

On the night of September 7 the Japanese settlement was thrown into even greater fear by a notice that had been pasted on the wall outside the commissioner's office. The notice listed the names of nineteen Japanese merchants involved in foreign trade and announced that they would receive divine punishment for their unpardonable actions.

As though anticipating this, six of the listed shops had already closed, and on that day three more joined them. Yokohama became deathly silent. Signs of shops for sale were posted all around the village.

In October a foreign newspaper in Yokohama reported that a peace conference was moving forward between the Satsuma Domain and the British chargé d'affaires. The two sides engaged in a productive exchange of views, gradually came to an understanding, and reached an agreement that the Satsuma Domain would pay reparations of twenty-five thousand pounds.

On November 1 Hikozo heard that this reparation money was transported by dray to the British legation, thus bringing an end to the Namamugi incident.

The New Year dawned, the fourth year of Bunkyu, and on February 10 the reign name was changed to Genji. The situation in Yokohama Village continued to be peaceful for the time being, but on April 23 a huge three-decked warship pulled into Yokohama Harbor, and the townspeople were thrown into confusion at its arrival. Its decks were filled with armed soldiers, and people feared that its arrival signaled the start of war with Japan.

The ship turned out to be the British ship *Conqueror* with a complement of 22 officers and 530 marines. The shogunate had agreed to having the troops stationed to protect the foreign residents of Yokohama and Kanagawa. The marines took up quarters in tents on the bluffs of the town, and the residents of the foreign settlements were joyous at the news, as was Hikozo, who felt that the danger had lessened.

The greatest obstacle for foreigners and Japanese wanting to do business with each other was the inability to communicate. Foreigners were able to speak a few words of Japanese, and the Japanese had a smattering of English, but for the most part they used hand signals and gestures. Naturally this led to many misunderstandings and much confusion. Thus there was a crying need for English interpreters. The only Japanese conversant in English were the shogunal interpreters assigned to the commissioner's office; their duties, however, focused on negotiations between the shogunate and foreign embassies. They didn't have time to interpret for merchants, and besides there was a strict ban on their doing so.

Hikozo stood out in Yokohama for his linguistic skills, and local merchants began to consider him as a possible interpreter. He'd already resigned his post as interpreter for the American consulate, so there were now no restrictions on his activities. Because he had lived for a long time in the United States and been educated there, his spoken English was far more fluent than that of the shogunal interpreters, and he read and wrote the language with ease. With his experience in business at the Macondray Company in San Francisco, he was also familiar with business practices, and they couldn't have asked for a better person to interpret between the foreign and Japanese merchants.

Therefore he was often asked to help with business negotiations and to translate and even write contracts; his ability to facilitate even the most complicated of business deals earned him honoraria in reward for his services. This work kept him busy, and when he wasn't interpreting, he tried his own hand at doing business.

The world cotton market was going through huge changes at the time. America was the largest producer of cotton, but with the Civil War, production had declined precipitously and export halted, thus leading to a steep rise in the price of cotton from other countries. Japanese merchants began buying up domestic Japanese cotton and selling it to foreign merchants at a healthy profit. Hikozo, too, took advantage of this trend and was now dealing in cotton himself.

Yokohama had started out as nothing more than an ordinary fishing village, but with foreign residences dotting the landscape, it had been transformed into a lively international port. British mail ships called regularly with the latest newspapers from abroad; foreign residents eagerly pored over these, and Hikozo made a habit of doing the same.

CHAPTER TWENTY-THREE

Hikozo found these foreign newspapers very helpful, for they contained the latest news on fluctuations in the world commodities market, including cotton.

Naturally the foreign merchants in Yokohama also monitored these market fluctuations in their own import and export businesses, but Hikozo's ability to read the market began to catch the attention of local Japanese merchants. They began approaching him, asking him to share the economic news he was reading.

He was happy to comply and would spread open a paper and translate aloud the latest article on trade. The Japanese merchants listened seriously as he read, taking notes on what various countries were importing and exporting, and often presented him with a good honorarium as they left.

Every time the mail ships arrived, these merchants would gather at Hikozo's home, which was fast becoming a popular place to socialize. Some asked him about other news, not just the economic. He told them about the Civil War, the disturbances in China, and all the latest political and social developments around the world—he even translated the advertisements. The merchants hung on every word, their eyes shining.

News that Hikozo was translating foreign newspapers and reading them aloud caused a stir. Samurai from the various domains visiting Yokohama began to stop by his house to attend these readings. At first he was frightened when these samurai, swords hanging from their belts, came calling, for he assumed they were members of the faction coming to cut him down. These samurai, though, turned out to be from a more progressive clique that approved of Japan's opening up to the outside world. They believed Japan must follow a path of peaceful coexistence with America and Europe, and felt it was imperative that the latest knowledge from the West in the fields of politics, law, and science be brought into the country. Burning with the desire to learn more about the world outside, these men began coming to his house to listen to him read from the latest English newspapers and learn whatever they could. Gradually he understood the reason for their visits and relaxed.

Hikozo first learned about newspapers when he landed in San Francisco. As he lived longer in the United States, he learned that not only the large cities such as Washington and New York but even smaller towns had newspapers, with reporters gathering material and writing stories. Newspapers were read by people at all levels of society, and were an indispensable part of American life, keeping everyone up-to-date not only on national news but also on what was happening around the globe. In a port city like San Francisco, newspapers listed the names, times of arrival, and persons of note on all the ships that arrived and gave information about the market and prices related to the goods offloaded from the ships.

In Japan, newspaper reporters dispatched by American and British newspapers lived in the foreign settlement in Yokohama and introduced newspaper articles sent from their parent companies; they also wrote their own articles based on reporting done locally on events within Japan. Local foreign residents relied on these newspapers to keep abreast of the world.

Hikozo felt it strange that nothing like a newspaper existed in Japan. Japanese relied on information relayed by word of mouth, which naturally enough led to many misunderstandings. This is why the shogunate, as well as each domain—not to mention the country's leading merchants—dispatched their own investigators to travel the length and breadth of the country to gather accurate information and reports. To learn about the outside world, until quite recently people were assigned to the sole open port of Nagasaki to read the printed matter brought in by the Dutch and Chinese ships that docked there, and talk with their crew members. But very little of this information was widely disseminated. If only there were a newspaper, a real Japanese newspaper, with accurate information printed in it, then everyone would have access to domestic and foreign news.

Hikozo pictured the faces of the merchants and samurai intently listening to him, taking notes as he translated articles from the foreign papers. What a wonderful contribution it would be if his translations were written down and published in a newspaper! Not just to the local merchants and a handful of samurai, but to the whole country. In America he'd learned to speak, read, and write English but had never really put these skills to great use; if only his talents could contribute to a newspaper, he'd be able to help enlighten the whole of Japan.

Then the thought struck him: Why don't *I* start a newspaper? In the paper he could include articles from the foreign newspapers that the mail ships brought in at regular intervals to Yokohama, and that way introduce world events. He could also excerpt articles from the British and American newspapers published in Yokohama for foreigners, articles dealing with domestic events in Japan. That way he'd be able to cover both international and domestic news.

But as he got to this point in his thinking, he realized there was one big problem, and he sighed deeply. These articles would have to be in Japanese, and written in polished prose, something quite impossible for him. His knowledge of written Japanese remained at the level he'd attained when he was thirteen and attending the local temple school. In other words, he could read hiragana, and could with difficulty make out Chinese characters, but could barely write. Not for the first time he realized that his writing abilities were out of balance.

English he could freely read and write, and people even praised his excellent penmanship. In contrast, his knowledge of his native language remained at the level of an adolescent. Now twenty-eight, more than ever he felt himself floating between two cultures, in some ways closer to being an American than a Japanese.

He recalled how when the captain of their ship, Manzo, had died in Hawaii on the way to China from San Francisco, one of the sailors, Kiyozo, had written the Chinese characters on Manzo's grave marker in an accomplished hand: *Praise Amida Buddha, here lies Manzo.* And when they were in China another sailor, Seitaro, had communicated with Chinese people through Chinese characters. In other words, even some sailors could read and write well.

This made Hikozo sad. As far as Japanese writing was concerned, he belonged to the realm of the illiterate.

On the bright side, he thought, when Thomas had taught the sailors English, he'd often said that Hikozo's ability in English far outshone everyone else's. This may have been due to the fact that Hikozo was so young at the time, his mind still supple and not filled with preconceived notions. But afterward, he, Jisaku, and Kamezo spent the same length of time in America, and though they were able to converse in broken English, they never learned how to read and write. Hikozo had been fortunate enough to receive some schooling while in the States, but Thomas must have been right—that he had an inborn talent for languages.

The interpreters hired by the shogunate were able to converse fairly well, but very few of them, he'd heard, could write English. Compared with them he was able to freely use English, even able to flawlessly draw up written business contracts. There could hardly be anyone in Japan who equaled his unique skills in English, so there was no need to lament over his inability to use Chinese characters.

Newspaper articles in Japanese obviously had to be written by someone who could write Chinese characters well, and he'd been mistaken to think that he should be the one to do it. Instead he set out to find someone who could write in excellent Japanese prose the newspaper articles he'd translate, someone with whom he could produce a newspaper. Hikozo suddenly felt relieved, as if all his problems had been solved.

The question remained, though: How was he to find such a partner?

Articles in foreign newspapers were written in an easy style, the explanations and descriptions appealing to readers in a straightforward way. A Japanese newspaper should do the same, a task that seemed easy but really wasn't. You couldn't use some narcissistic, flowery prose style that wouldn't appeal to the reader. Newspaper articles had to transmit the facts clearly and accurately and convey a sense of reality. They had to be written so that anyone would understand them if read aloud. Only a fine prose writer would be able to accomplish this, but was there anyone who fit the bill in Yokohama?

In Yokohama Village there was a foreigner who ran a laundry. When Hikozo lived in America, he sent his shirts and other clothes out to a laundry, and that became a regular part of his expenses. In Yokohama, too, foreigners relied on a laundry service, Hikozo among them, and would hand over their laundry to a young employee of the shop who came by regularly with a large cart. This man, going all over the foreign community, should know just about everyone. There were many Japanese who'd come to the community now to study English, and the man must have come in contact with them as well.

When the man came to his home a few days later, Hikozo asked him to introduce him to any Japanese he knew who was particularly skilled in writing. The man, a dubious look on his face, said he'd try to do that, then loaded Hikozo's laundry as usual into a basket on the cart and left.

Hikozo remembered a man named Kishida Ginko he'd met by chance at the home of an American by the name of Hepburn, who lived at lot 39 in the foreign community in Yokohama. Hepburn was a missionary and physician who'd come to Japan with his wife to spread the Gospel five years before, landing in Yokohama on September 23 of the sixth year of Ansei. This was about the same time Hikozo had returned to Japan and was hired as an interpreter at the American consulate.

Hepburn had visited the American consulate then to ask Dorr

315

for help in finding a place to live. At Dorr's direction, Hikozo had negotiated with the priest of the nearby Joubutsuji Temple, and the Hepburns were able to rent the main hall of the temple as their residence. Through this Hikozo became friends with the Hepburns, and they often consulted him about life in Japan.

Hikozo had heard that Hepburn treated the two British merchants who were badly wounded in the Namamugi attack. Hepburn was an eye doctor by specialty but he also did surgery and internal medicine and had become well known as a fine physician, with many foreign and Japanese patients coming to his free clinic for treatment. Patients often presented him with eggs and other food to express their thanks.

Kishida Ginko, suffering from eye problems, had paid a visit to Hepburn's clinic to be treated. Hepburn examined him and prescribed eyedrops, which proved quite effective; in a week Ginko's eyes had recovered.

Ginko was born in Haga Village, Kume County, in Mimasaka Province (Okayama Prefecture). Recognized as a child prodigy, he studied with the Confucian scholar Sayaka Seikei in the Tsuyama Domain, then went to Edo as a student in the school run by the chief of documents, Hayashi. He displayed enormous scholastic ability, even giving lectures in Hayashi's stead. Afterward he was taken into service with the Mikawakoromo Domain as an official Confucian teacher, but he left this service, returned to Edo, and fell on hard times, working as a bath attendant, a plaster's assistant, and finally as the manager of a brothel. The next year, though, a fire burned down the entire Yoshiwara brothel district, and Ginko was left to wander.

At this point Hepburn had begun researching the Japanese language and was editing a Japanese-English dictionary. As Ginko was being treated by him, he talked with him about his background, the Japanese writing system, and how kana are used. Hepburn realized that Ginko was an extraordinarily learned man and urged him to help him edit his Japanese-English dictionary.

Excited by this project, Ginko moved into the Hepburn home

and began making corrections to the words the doctor had translated into Japanese, finally making a copy of all this in a beautiful hand. The dictionary included words from all classes of Japanese society, and Ginko, with his experience working in many professions, was an invaluable aid.

Hikozo realized Ginko was the best man available to help him publish a newspaper.

The Japanese terms in Hepburn's dictionary had to be written in clear prose so that anyone could understand them, a principle that applied equally to a newspaper. Ginko, as a Sinologist of note as well as a person well versed in the Japanese classics, was quite able to write proper Japanese prose. Further, his work with Hepburn on the Japanese-English dictionary allowed him to acquire a great deal of knowledge about the West, which meant that he should be able to explain in accurate Japanese the events described in articles in foreign newspapers.

Hikozo went to Hepburn's house to meet Ginko. He explained to him how newspapers were found all over America and the role they played, that he intended to publish a newspaper in Japan and how he planned to do this. Ginko, intrigued by the idea of translating articles from foreign papers, immediately agreed to help Hikozo with his project.

Delighted to hear this, Hikozo was making preparations to publish his newspaper when a man named Honma Senzo suddenly appeared at his door. Honma was the son of the official physician of the Kakegawa Domain. He studied the Chinese classics in Sunpu (Shizuoka City), then came to Yokohama to learn English. He'd heard from the boy at the laundry that Hikozo was looking for a skilled writer to rewrite articles in foreign papers into Japanese, and thinking this was an excellent chance to improve his English, he'd come to ask for the job. Hikozo was much encouraged to have both Ginko and Senzo help him in his enterprise.

British mail ships arrived at Yokohama, and copies of London newspapers came ashore. Hikozo would take the papers, mark the lists of commodity prices and other articles of interest, and choose articles on domestic topics from the English newspapers published in Yokohama.

Ginko and Senzo began coming regularly to his home. First Hikozo would read the article aloud, translating it into Japanese, while the two men wrote down what he said. Then, following his instructions to write in the clearest prose, they would check each other's writing and make corrections. The finished product was re-copied and bound up with string.

"Let's call this *Shimbun Shi*," Ginko suggested, and Hikozo agreed that this translation of *newspaper* (literally, "record of the newly heard") was a perfect choice. Thus was born the modern Japanese term.

Word of their newspaper soon spread, and many people began to appear at Hikozo's door asking for copies. Local merchants were particularly interested in the lists of commodity prices, but the articles of events in the outside world were also of great interest to officials and samurai from various domains who'd come to Yokohama to study English, and all of them started to stop by his home.

Hikozo would give each a copy of the newspaper in Ginko and Senzo's hand, and soon a strange custom grew up around this. He knew that in America newspapers were sold to people for a set price and that many subscribed on a regular basis. Here, though, while some people left behind small gifts in payment, others just thanked him and left nothing. They didn't think of a newspaper as something that should be paid for, that all this was service Hikozo was providing out of kindness. He wasn't happy about it, but he hesitated to ask for payment for the paper and continued to hand it out free to whoever asked.

The newspaper came out on average twice a month, and people would drop by each time it appeared, receive their copy, thank Hikozo, and leave.

After consulting with Ginko and Senzo, he decided to switch from handwritten copies to woodblock printing. Since most of the news in the paper concerned foreign countries, they decided to rename it *Kaigai Shimbun*—"foreign newspaper"—the first edition of which came out in May of the following year. It was printed on several sheets of Japanese-size paper, folded in half, with a drawing on the masthead of a foreign steamer and sailing ship in the waters off Kanagawa, Mount Fuji rising in the background.

Kaigai Shimbun also came out twice a month and was distributed free of charge, though two samurai from Higo—Shomura Shozo and Nakamura Sukeoki—were paid subscribers.

The reign-era name changed on April 7 to Keio. Domestically there were great political upheavals, and the situation was unsettled. In July of the previous year, in Kyoto, the so-called Kinmon Incident took place, in which Choshu forces attacked near the imperial palace and were eventually defeated by the shogunate; the shogunate then issued an order to various domains to subjugate the Choshu Domain. Also a combined fleet of seventeen British, French, American, and Dutch ships attacked the Choshu Domain at the Shimonoseki Straits to retaliate for previous attacks on foreign ships there and dealt the domain a crushing defeat. The order to subjugate the Choshu Domain was settled for the time being when the domain officially submitted an apology and pledge of allegiance to the shogunate, and the problems arising from incidents at the Shimonoseki Straits, too, were settled through the payment of reparations.

Hikozo continued his trading business all the while, putting out the newspaper on the side. In July, though, he heard news of a shocking event that had taken place in America—President Lincoln had been assassinated. After years of fierce fighting, the Civil War finally came to an end with the surrender of General Lee on April 9 of that year, 1865, and only five days after the surrender the president was shot by the southern actor John Wilkes Booth while enjoying a play in the Ford Theater in Washington, and he died the next morning. At just about the same time, the home of Secretary of State Seward was attacked, and he was wounded, with some of his family members stabbed.

Hikozo couldn't believe it. He remembered shaking Lincoln's large, warm hand—and how the man had seemed less a politician than a kindly farmer smelling of straw. He remembered Seward, too, with his gentle eyes. Seward had been kind enough to appoint him as official interpreter for the Kanagawa consulate and had gone to the trouble of taking him to meet Lincoln.

Hikozo wrote a letter right away to Seward, inquiring how he was recovering. He also enclosed a note expressing his condolences to Lincoln's family, then entrusted the letter to a mail ship bound for the States. The reply to this letter from Seward, dated September 25, arrived at the consulate addressed to Mr. Joseph Heco. Seward wrote that he was so grateful to receive such a kind letter and that Hikozo was kind to keep him in his thoughts though so very far away. "We've gone through an unexpected tragedy," he wrote, "but the American people are standing up to the challenge and determined to forge ahead."

Hikozo reread the letter again and again and felt in his heart that the American people, who'd lost their spirit because of the war, would once again regain the openhearted, warm nature that he'd always loved.

The second year of Keio (1866) dawned, and with relations between the shogunate and the Choshu Domain taking another turn for the worse, the domestic situation in Japan grew difficult. Hikozo's trading business went into a decline, though he continued to publish the *Kaigai Shimbun.*

The shogunate issued its second directive to subdue the Choshu Domain, and on June 7 hostilities between the two began when shogunal warships shelled Oshima County in Suo Province. The situation turned in Choshu's favor, and with the death of the shogun Iemochi, who had accompanied his troops to the front, in Osaka, the shogunate negotiated an end to hostilities, and in September the shogunal forces and Choshu forces withdrew.

With Kishida Ginko's aid Hepburn completed his Japanese-English dictionary, which was then published in Shanghai. Hepburn, together with Ginko, set off for that city, and Hikozo, having lost his main writer, stopped publishing the *Kaigai Shimbun*—the very first newspaper in Japan.

CHAPTER TWENTY-FOUR

Soon after ginko left for Shanghai, in the morning of October 25, a fire broke out in Yokohama near the swampy area of the Minatosaki District. Fanned by a strong westerly wind, the fire spread and soon became a major conflagration. Hikozo hurriedly threw some belongings in a suitcase and trunk and, like many others, escaped toward Kanagawa. Rising sparks glittered in the sunlight against the backdrop of the blue sky.

Houses continued to burn, but in the evening the wind stopped, and by 11 PM the fire had died down. Half the Japanese section of town and a quarter of the foreign settlement had burned to the ground. The merchant's house that Hikozo lived in was fortunately spared, and at dawn he was able to return home. Yokohama presented a horrible spectacle, and with a gloomy look on his face Hikozo walked around the charred ruins of the town.

Eight days later, at dawn, another fire broke out, in the Ota District. Though it didn't turn into a major fire, in the confusion caused by it groups of thieves broke into a number of merchants' homes, throwing people into a panic. With all the damage caused by the successive fires, business in Yokohama ground to a halt, and Hikozo, left with little to do, spent his days in vague idleness.

Around this time a letter arrived from a man named Frasier doing business in Nagasaki, who wrote that he was returning to America and wondered if Hikozo would be interested in taking over his business. Frasier had earlier done business with the Walsh brothers in Yokohama, and all three were old friends of Hikozo. They had left Yokohama to start businesses in Nagasaki after that port was opened. The older Walsh brother, John, in addition to running a trading business, was honorary U.S. consul in Nagasaki.

After Yokohama was reduced to ashes, Hikozo lost all hope for the place and thought he'd best accept Frasier's offer. Being the honorary consul, John should be able to smooth the way for him, and besides this Hikozo had a desire to see the lovely port town again, the first place he'd seen upon his return to Japan—aboard the *Mississippi* with Townsend Harris.

He wrote a reply to Frasier accepting his proposal and saying he would come to Nagasaki. As he was making preparations for the journey, he learned that a British steamship hired by the shogunate was about to leave for Nagasaki. He went to the Kanagawa commissioner's office to ask for permission to take that ship, and with the goodwill he'd built up during his tenure as official interpreter for the American consulate he was afforded special treatment, the officials allowing him free passage on the vessel.

On November 19 he boarded the ship. The sky was clear and sunny. The ship weighed anchor and headed toward Edo Bay. Hikozo stood on deck watching the charred ruins of Yokohama slip by. The ship headed west, stopping in Hyogo, through the Inland Sea and the Shimonoseki Straits, arriving in Nagasaki on November 28.

Frasier took a small boat out to greet him, and together they went to the foreign settlement in Oura and dined at Fraiser's house. Fraiser explained to him how, even though it was an open port like Yokohama and Hakodate, Nagasaki was quite different—the reason being that the chief imports were warships and weapons.

The main customers for these were the shogunate and the various domains, and demand had shot up with the growing political tensions. The Satsuma and Choshu domains, whose relations with the shogunate had grown especially strained, were the two buying the most ships and laying in a huge supply of guns. Nagasaki had become an arms capital because it was far from Edo and not under the watchful eye of the shogunate. The shogunate was actually quite liberal on this point, encouraging the domains to arm themselves in order to resist pressure from foreign countries, though it insisted that this be done after application at the customs office set up in Nagasaki.

Thus the town overflowed with samurai from various domains negotiating these purchases with foreign merchants. The central figure in this business was the Englishman Thomas Glover, who had such a close relationship with the Satsuma Domain that no one else could squeeze in.

"Weapons are the only thing being traded here," Frasier said. "During the Civil War we made a good profit exporting cotton, but once the war was over, that trade dried up. Lately I've been exporting tea and coal, and importing textiles."

Frasier's words made Hikozo realize how trade in Nagasaki was essentially under the control of one man, this Englishman named Glover.

After the Namamugi incident, in which British merchants were attacked by samurai of the Satsuma Domain, the British had dispatched seven warships to Kagoshima, and a violent conflict ensued. Eventually peace between the two was established, and these two enemies did an about-face and became friends.

The close relationship between Satsuma and Glover was a manifestation of this, and Hikozo was filled with apprehension hearing how Satsuma was building up considerable military might through large-scale purchases of ships and guns from Glover.

Being so close to Edo, Yokohama was always under the watchful eye of the shogunate, but the power of the shogunate didn't extend to distant Nagasaki, so it was a much freer and more open port. Hikozo was certain that Nagasaki would play a vital role in the Japan's future.

Frasier explained the workings of his business, going into all the financial figures. From his frequent shrugs Hikozo sensed that business hadn't been that good, which explained Frasier's eagerness to return to the United States, but Hikozo wasn't upset at having this business forced upon him. He was sure he'd succeed no matter where he went and what sort of work he did. Confidence came naturally to him in the light of all the hardships he'd endured since his time as a castaway. His life to this point had been much like that of a ship without a mast, drifting here and there across the ocean. But all the experience he'd gained through this life gave him the resolve to put a failing business like Frasier's back on its legs.

He accepted Frasier's offer and took up residence in a room in his house. Two days later Frasier took him to No. 3 Oura to see Mr. Walsh. Those with American citizenship were required to register with the consul, and Hikozo, as a naturalized citizen, was duly registered as Joseph Heco and officially given permission to live within the foreign settlement.

He began his duties running the business and soon got to know many foreign merchants. Frasier had only to introduce him, and these men looked kindly on him as they grasped his hand in a firm handshake. They all had heard of Hikozo's background—how he arrived in America as a castaway, then became naturalized and took the post of interpreter at the Kanagawa consulate. Many invited him to dinner, where he regaled them, to their utter amazement, with stories of his time as a castaway and his experiences meeting Lincoln and two other presidents.

Samurai sent by their domains to Nagasaki to purchase weapons soon heard about Hikozo, and on December 17 Motono Shuzo of the Saga Domain came to visit him, along with his retainers. Motono was here on orders of the former head of the domain, Nabeshima Naomasa, who had directed Motono to bring Hikozo to Saga so he could hear from Hikozo all about the situation in foreign countries.

Naomasa was greatly intent on gaining as much knowledge as he could from foreign countries, and had built an arms factory, almost an armament ministry, where he had cannons and other weapons made. Hikozo, thinking it would be useful to meet such an important man and tell him about America, agreed to do so. Naomasa, though, was about to set out on a trip to Kyoto, and in the end Hikozo wasn't able to visit him, though through this connection he was able to have close relations with Saga samurai thereafter.

New Year, 1868, came, and the streets of Nagasaki were lively, filled with the sounds of flutes, gongs, and drums. Frasier continued to make preparations for his voyage home, and in order for Hikozo's business to go smoothly he continued to introduce him to various foreign businessmen in town. At the time 224 foreigners resided in Nagasaki, including 66 British citizens, 36 Americans, and 38 Dutch, the majority of whom were businessmen.

Thomas Glover stood head and shoulders above the others. His company, which dealt primarily with the import of ships and rifles, had the highest volume of any trading firm in Nagasaki. Glover had a virtual monopoly on sales of weapons to the Satsuma Domain, and rumor had it that he was also secretly selling to the Choshu Domain. After the two times the shogunate had to subdue Choshu, it kept careful watch over its affairs, instructing the customs office in Nagasaki that Choshu alone was forbidden to buy imported weapons. The Satsuma Domain, though, indicated to Glover that it was willing to pretend to be importing weapons for itself while allowing him actually to funnel the weapons to Choshu, a suggestion that Glover enthusiastically embraced. Through this importing of weapons the two domains, Satsuma and Choshu, grew close, forging a secret alliance that strengthened their opposition to the shogunate.

Great quantities of firearms that were not needed now that the Civil War was over were imported to Nagasaki by Glover by way of Shanghai, and selling them to the Satsuma-Choshu alliance earned him a healthy profit. Glover took notice of Hikozo, because of his abilities in English and his knowledge of business practices, and often asked him to be present during negotiations with the various domains over arms sales.

On March 8 Frasier turned over his entire business to Hikozo and left Nagasaki on the *Feelong*. Hikozo lived in Frasier's trading house along with his chief clerk, Shojiro.

Not long after Frasier returned to America, a Mr. Mackenzie, head of the Osaka branch of Glover's firm, came calling with an unexpected proposal. The coal mine of Takashima Island outside Nagasaki Harbor belonged to the chief retainer of the Saga Domain, he said, and produced some of the finest quality coal around at a price far below that of the world market. Since steamship traffic was increasing in Shanghai, the demand for coal had increased dramatically, and the Glover Company wished to purchase this island and export the coal to Shanghai.

"A six-thousand-dollar investment in the latest European engine and pumps would let us mine three times the yield they're getting now," Mackenzie said, explaining that Glover wanted to run the Takashima Mine as a joint venture with the Saga Domain and wanted Hikozo to act as go-between.

"Do you have any friends in the Saga Domain?" Mackenzie asked, looking closely at Hikozo.

The first person who sprang to mind was Motono Shuzo. Through Motono's introduction Hikozo had became friendly with samurai from the Saga Domain, among them one Matsubayashi Genzo, who'd been living for some time in Nagasaki conducting business for the domain.

"I have several friends among them," Hikozo replied. "There's one man, an agent of theirs named Matsubayashi, I know well."

"That's excellent," Mackenzie replied. He took some documents out of his case and showed them to Hikozo. Hikozo ran through the English text, which read as follows:

1. The Takashima Mine will be run jointly by the Saga Domain and the Glover Company, each paying half the expenses and receiving half the profits. However, the investment funds of the Saga Domain will be borne by the Glover Company, which will be paid back to the Glover Company as profits from the sale of coal rise.
2. The Glover Company will pay the Saga Domain a royalty of $1 for use of the mine for each ton of coal produced.

3. Export of coal taken from the mine will be done solely by the Glover Company, and it will pay a 5% commission for this.
4. The length of the contract will be seven and a half years.

Hikozo felt that the terms of the contract were reasonable. The British had the reputation of being not entirely straightforward when it came to business dealings, but in this proposed contract it was clear that both sides would profit.

"Why don't I show this proposed contract to my friend from Saga? I'll do my best to help the contract get drawn up." As he said this, Hikozo could picture Glover standing there behind his agent Mackenzie.

"Thank you so much for any help you can lend us," Mackenzie said, shook Hikozo's hand, and left.

Hikozo ordered Shojiro to ask Matsubayashi Genzo, who was staying in the official residence of the Saga Domain in Nagasaki, to visit him. Shojiro changed clothes and quickly left.

Matsubayashi showed up that same evening. Hikozo explained Mackenzie's proposal and showed him the contract.

"As far as I can tell," Hikozo said, "there's nothing in it that runs counter to the interests of the domain, and I think you should accept it. It should be translated into Japanese, and I'm embarrassed to say that I can't write Chinese characters well, so allow me to translate it aloud while you write it down, if you don't mind." Blushing a little at this admission, he took up the contract and slowly translated it aloud into Japanese. Matsubayashi took the inkstone and paper Shojiro had prepared and wrote as Hikozo dictated. He wrote in a skilled hand.

After Hikozo finished translating into Japanese, he asked Matusbayashi to read aloud what he'd written.

"That's exactly right, every word," he said.

Matsubayashi read over the contract once more, then looked up and said, "It's rather sudden, so I can't give a reply right now, but I'll return to Saga and ask the retired nobleman, Naomasa, to look at this proposal. I think he's the kind of person who could see the advantages of such a plan."

"Please do whatever you can," Hikozo said, handing over the English contract.

"I leave for Saga tomorrow," Matsubayashi said with a bow and then withdrew from the room.

That evening Hikozo visited Mackenzie to report on his meeting with Matsubayashi and what he'd asked him to do.

After carefully considering the matter, the Saga Domain signed the agreement, with Hikozo acting as witness. Several people from the domain, including Matsubayashi, were assigned as directors of the joint operation, with the understanding that the actual management of operations would be left to the Glover Company.

Mining technicians were hired and brought over from England, the very latest steam-operated conveyors were installed, as well as water extraction and ventilation systems, and mining operations began. Hikozo was involved in overseeing this operation and drew a salary for his efforts. Through this joint venture at the Takashima coal mines, he became very close to the Glover Company.

Frasier had left his business in Hikozo's charge, but Hikozo soon realized that trade in Nagasaki was mainly focused on the Glover Company and that his own efforts at trading would not pay off. Some of the foreign trading firms in Nagasaki had already become subsidiaries of the Glover Company, and Hikozo began to think that it would be best if his company, too, was absorbed by Glover.

Hikozo went to see Glover himself to suggest this, and the Englishman agreed. What he needed most was an interpreter fluent in both Japanese and English, which would allow him to negotiate business deals. Hikozo, with his knowledge of business, was the perfect person for the job, and they decided that while Hikozo would continue to run his own business, he would be an employee of the Glover Company.

As such an employee, in July he moved into a Western-style house at No. 16 Higashi Yamate, which Glover was renting from the commissioner's office.

At the end of July two Satsuma samurai calling themselves Kido Junichiro and Itoh Shunsuke (Itoh Hirobumi) came calling and questioned Hikozo, who still kept up with world news by reading foreign newspapers, about the situation abroad.

Hikozo politely answered all their questions, but after they left, his clerk told him that these men, supposedly Satsuma samurai, had no trace of a Satsuma accent; he recognized the man calling himself Kido Junichiro as a Choshu samurai named Katsura Kogoro.

A few days later, when the men came to visit again, Hikozo questioned them about this, and the men, surprised, admitted they were from Choshu. As the shogunate was hostile toward their domain, the customhouse wouldn't permit them to purchase ships and weapons from the Glover Company and other trading firms, so they were forced to obtain weapons quietly by pretending to be purchasing them for the Satsuma Domain. They revealed this secret to Hikozo because they thought that they could rely on him, as an employee of the Glover Company, to be discreet. They went on to explain how they believed the shogunate's power was illegitimate and that Choshu was supporting the restoration of imperial power. They hoped, they added, that this position could be widely understood among the foreign community.

They began casually dropping by to see Hikozo, urging him to become a special trade representative for Choshu. When Hikozo agreed, they wrote out an agreement, which read: *On behalf of the Prince of Choshu we agree on this date to appoint Mr. Joseph Heco, a citizen of the United States, as the prince's special agent for the port of Nagasaki.* The men handed this document to Hikozo, with their names affixed to it.

Through this association Hikozo later met men who became famous in Japanese history, such as the Choshu samurai Inoue Monta (Kaoru), and the Satsuma samurai Godai Saisuke (later renamed Tomoatsu). He also had visits from the interpreter at the British legation, Ernest Satow.

According to Motono Shuzo of the Saga Domain, the Satsuma and Choshu domains had formed a secret alliance that seemed bent on toppling the shogunate; proof of this could be found in how samurai from both domains were in and out of Nagasaki constantly to purchase rifles.

Both Nagasaki and Hikozo felt uneasy about what the future held.

On November 6 a messenger from Kyoto arrived at the Nagasaki commissioner's office with news that on October 14 the shogun, Tokugawa Yoshinobu, had petitioned the throne for a restoration of imperial rule, and the petition had been accepted. Also, at the end of the month the imperial household announced the restoration, and Hikozo knew a major upheaval in political power had just taken place.

This busy year drew to a close, and the fourth year of Keio dawned.

On the seventh of the year, as the townspeople of Nagasaki enjoyed the traditional herbal broth, they learned that the shogun had resigned his position and retired to Osaka. Further, fighting had broken out in Fushimi between the Satsuma-Choshu forces and the shogunal army, with rumors that the shogunal forces had been routed, followed shortly by news brought in by a foreign ship that docked in Nagasaki that the shogunate's army had been defeated.

On the night of January 9 a fire broke out in the Furukawa-cho part of town, and a strong wind soon spread it to Enogizu, Yorozuya, and Higashihama. The rumor was that secret agents of the shogunate had set the fire, and the townspeople were anxious.

Reports came in about more shogunate defeats, and that Yoshinobu had escaped to Edo on a warship, with the imperial forces in hot pursuit. In Nagasaki antishogunate forces and shogunate forces (soldiers attached to the commissioner's office) squared off, and there were fears that hostilities would break out. However, the commissioner, Kawazu Izunokami Sukekuni, in order to avoid this confrontation, at 11 PM on the night of the fourteenth surreptitiously boarded a British ship and slipped out of Nagasaki with only one retainer.

Kawazu left things in Nagasaki up to the head of the Fukuoka and Shimabara domains, and the Nagasaki commissioner's office was abolished, with a Nagasaki council office set up in its place. A Nagasaki court was established as well, and finally the tension was resolved.

Glover, who'd been back in England for a while, returned, and when he heard of the defeat of the shogunate, excitedly declared, "The Japanese have succeeded in their revolution! A new path has opened up for them."

News continued to filter into Nagasaki through ships that called on the port. The large imperial army that had been marching to Edo had conquered the city without a drop of blood being shed and were even now setting out to subdue the domains in the northeast part of the country.

Every time he heard about these new developments, Glover wondered how as a businessman he could best respond to the quickly evolving political situation. "Nagasaki is too removed from the center of events, and we can't do much here," he maintained, and hurriedly set off for his branch office in Osaka. As the war continued, he planned to supply the imperial army with whatever weapons it might need.

Soon after the beginning of the intercalary month of April a mail ship arrived carrying a letter for Hikozo from Glover, requesting him to come to Osaka as soon as he could. Thus Hikozo set off from Nagasaki on April 8 on the steamship *Nicaragua*.

As Nagasaki faded in the distance, he suddenly thought of the castaway Rikimatsu whom he'd last seen sixteen years ago in Hong Kong. He thought of how former Japanese castaways were now living in China, how they had tried to return to Japan, only to be fired at by shogunate forces under orders to drive away all foreign ships.

Of course, the situation had changed. The shogunate had opened the country to the outside world, and now even the shogunate itself was no more. Castaways were now free to return home, but the fear and grief they'd felt when driven away from their own country by cannon fire must have been branded on their memories, and they might now not want to return.

Sixteen years had passed, and maybe none of them were even alive. They'd settled comfortably into life in China, but maybe they never really got used to the different food, the different customs, before they passed away. Hikozo gazed out at the broad expanse of sea at the mouth of the harbor. He could picture the sad, lonely grave markers of these men, far off in China.

The steamship passed through the Shimonoseki Straits and into the Inland Sea, two days later anchoring in Hyogo at the port of Kobe. Hyogo was where, at age thirteen, Hikozo had first boarded the *Sumiyoshi Maru* and set off on his first voyage. Now it had been made an open port and was completely transformed. The harbor was filled with ships of all sizes, newly constructed Western-style houses dotted the landscape, and the streets were crowded with foreigners. It was a much livelier place than Nagasaki.

Japanese merchants were obviously busy as well, bringing cargo on carts to the wharf. These were then loaded onto boats, which made countless trips back and forth between the wharf and the ships in port. The supplies were clearly military, and Hikozo was impressed by the huge amount of them needed in wartime. He stayed overnight in a hotel and then set out for Osaka.

The Glover Company branch in Osaka was extremely busy, though Glover himself was gone on a business trip to Edo. There were numerous negotiations with the new government for arms sales, all of which Hikozo attended, and he had no rest.

Several days after Hikozo arrived in Osaka, a Satsuma samurai, Godai Saisuke, paid a call at the branch office. Godai had a close relationship with Glover through numerous previous purchases of ships and arms. He told Hikozo that the Glover Company Shanghai branch manager, Francis Groom, was in Osaka, and Godai wanted Hikozo to go with him to Yokohama right away.

The shogunate had signed a contract to purchase the American ironclad *Stonewall* (1,358 tons), which had just arrived off Shinagawa. The naval power of the new government was much inferior to that of the shogunate, and if a mighty warship such as the *Stonewall* fell into the shogunate force's hands, the discrepancy in naval power would be overwhelming—the new government's forces were superior on land, but their opponents would rule the seas. The new government thus wanted at all costs to block this ship from falling into the hands of the shogunate and obtain it for itself. Thus the call to Hikozo to come to Yokohama to help with the negotiations.

Groom, experienced in Shanghai in importing ships, agreed, and he and Hikozo set out on the Glover Company vessel *Kyushu* for Yokohama. They arrived in Yokohama on June 8, and Hikozo and Groom split up to look into the disposition of the *Stonewall.* Groom went to meet the British ambassador, while Hikozo went to speak with Terajima Munenori, the commissioner of foreign affairs. Hikozo told Terajima that he wanted to negotiate with the American ambassador in order for the new government to obtain the *Stonewall.*

"That's out of the question," Terajima immediately replied.

The American ambassador had declared that he would hand over the ship neither to the shogunate army nor to the new government. If the ship were given to one side, he said, that would call into question America's stance of neutrality, so he declared the ship a possession of the American embassy.

"It's pointless to meet the ambassador," Terajima insisted.

His tone told Hikozo it was meaningless to ask anymore, so he left. Groom finally returned from the British embassy, reporting that he'd been told the same thing. Thus the mission Godai entrusted them with failed, and they returned to Osaka and reported to him on what had taken place.

CHAPTER TWENTY-FIVE

THE WAR MOVED TO THE northeast part of Japan, battles between the new government's forces and the shogunate forces breaking out here and there.

The trade in weapons naturally expanded, and Hikozo took on the role of interpreter at the Glover Company Osaka office all by himself. Before long, at the request of the Saga Domain samurai Motono Shuzo, he brought an American physician assigned to a warship, Dr. Boyer, to treat the former head of the domain, Naomasa, who was suffering from rheumatism. Happily Naomasa recovered to the point where he could return to Saga, and to express his gratitude he presented Boyer with three pieces of embroidered silk and fifty silver coins, while Hikozo received seventy ryo of gold.

Officials and merchants often dropped by the branch office, and on the evening of June 16, Itoh Hirobumi, appointed governor of Hyogo Prefecture on the twenty-third of the previous month, came. Hikozo stared at him for a moment, since he had changed so much in appearance. Itoh, under the name of Hayashi Uichi, had frequently visited the Glover Company in Nagasaki as he went around town trying to purchase guns. It was rumored that he had been involved with Takasugi Shinsaku and others in burning down the British embassy being built in Gotenzan in Shinagawa, and he always had a frenzied, piercing look about him.

The year after the burning of the embassy, Itoh stowed away in a ship and spent four months in London. There he picked up the rudiments of English and in Nagasaki took the opportunity to get to know Hikozo. He would speak to him in English and occasionally send a letter written in simple English. Itoh was constantly on guard against attack, looking around him sharply.

The Itoh who stood before him now, though, was relaxed and had gentle eyes. He must be able to sit back a bit, Hikozo surmised, now that his efforts to oust the shogunate have succeeded and he's been given a high post in the new government.

"How about going out for some fun on the river with me?" Itoh asked. "I have a boat." Hikozo was sure he'd come on business, but instead Itoh was proposing they enjoy some time in a pleasure boat on the Yodogawa River.

Hikozo smiled and agreed. Itoh's being able to go out like this to enjoy a little time on the river, with only a single retainer with him, was proof that he no longer felt himself in danger.

Hikozo, Itoh, and the retainer left the office, walked through the town in the gathering evening darkness, and arrived at the Yodogawa. A pleasure boat was tied up at the shore, and Hikozo followed Itoh down the stone steps and took a seat in the middle of the boat. In the lantern light Hikozo saw there were two geisha aboard, who bowed politely to them.

The man at the bow pushed off with his pole, while another man at the stern began rowing. Hikozo and Itoh took up sake cups, and the geisha poured for them. The pleasure boat, hugging the shore, slowly made its way upstream. Stars were just coming out in the night sky.

Itoh told him how at Toba and Fushimi the imperial forces of Satsuma and Choshu, outnumbered ten to one by the shogunate army, were able to soundly defeat them due to the new types of guns and cannons they possessed. "We can thank the Glover Company, which helped us purchase these, for the victory," he said. The shogunate forces possessed only old weapons—swords, lances, and matchlock muskets. He added in a calm voice, "The fighting in the north should be over soon, I expect."

Itoh lay down, his arms pillowing his head, and smoked a pipe.

335

It had been a long while since Hikozo could relax like this, and he indulged himself in the sake, and enjoyed chatting with Itoh. A cool breeze blew along the water.

He suddenly found himself thinking of his hometown, Hamada in Honjo Village. When he was a castaway, he wanted nothing more than once again to stand before the sea in front of his village, and after returning to Japan he often pictured his hometown. Since he'd taken American citizenship, though, he knew it was impossible for him to travel there. The treaties Japan had concluded with foreign countries specified that foreigners were limited to travel within a fifteen-mile radius of the open ports. The distance from Hyogo to Honjo Village far exceeded this limit, so it was off-limits to him. Besides, there continued to be a danger of attack from those in the antiforeigner faction, so it wasn't safe to venture outside the foreign settlements.

As Hyogo prefectural governor, Itoh had a lot of influence, Hikozo knew, and might be able to help him visit his home.

"There's something you can help me with," Hikozo said, placing his cup on the tray.

Itoh sat up, looked at Hikozo, and asked, "What would that be?'

"In 1850 (Kaei 3)," Hikozo said, "I left my hometown of Honjo Village for the first time on a ship. I became a castaway and was rescued, but in the eighteen years since I haven't been home once."

Itoh listened, a sympathetic look on his face.

"Since I took U.S. citizenship, I'm forbidden to go to my hometown, which is beyond the prescribed limits, so I was wondering if there's some safe way I could travel there."

"That's easy," Itoh replied. "We've purchased a small steamboat, the *Orphan,* for use by the government, and you could take that to your hometown. Foreigners are limited in where they can travel on land, but movement by sea is unrestricted. Tomorrow I'm planning to take the *Orphan* back to Hyogo, so why don't you go with me as far as Hyogo, then take the ship yourself to your hometown? That much I can do for you."

One of the geisha filled the cup Itoh had in his hand.

Hikozo felt a warmth swelling in his chest. He'd always dreamed of returning to his birthplace. Taking a ship, he could have them lower a boat and could go ashore on the village beach. He remembered his meeting with his stepbrother and learning that his stepfather was dead. He longed to see the beautiful sea of his hometown, but with his mother dead so many years, he wondered if there would be anybody in his village who would welcome his return.

"We'd better be getting back," Itoh said to his retainer.

Hearing this, the captain of the boat slowly brought the bow about, and the boat rode the current back downstream.

Hikozo felt pleasantly drunk and thought how fortunate it was he'd met Itoh and enjoyed this evening on the river with him. A nostalgia for the houses, cotton fields, and sea of his village came over him, and a burning desire to visit the graves of his mother and stepfather. Tears welled in his eyes.

The next morning, when Hikozo went to work, he told Mackenzie that he'd asked Itoh to help him get back to his hometown and that Itoh had agreed, and then asked for some time off to do this.

"That's no problem at all. I imagine your village is quite lovely?" Mackenzie said with a smile.

"Of course," Hikozo said emphatically. "It's a wonderful village."

One of Itoh's assistants came and told Hikozo to be at the Yodogawa dock at 3 PM. Godai Saisuke, who'd been appointed judge for Osaka, together with his wife, would be traveling on the same ship as far as Kobe.

Hikozo changed into a travel outfit and went to the dock at the appointed time. A pleasure boat was already there, with Godai and his wife on board. Hikozo joined them, and before long Itoh and his retainer came too. The boat began to move downstream.

When they reached the mouth of the Yodogawa, they saw a small steamship, which turned out to be the *Orphan*. A rising-sun flag flew from the stern, and wispy smoke trailed from the smokestack. The pleasure boat pulled up alongside, and Hikozo followed Godai and his wife and Itoh on board the steamship.

337

They soon weighed anchor, and black smoke billowed out of the smokestack. Off their bow they saw several small cargo boats, their sails catching the wind, which they passed. Were these on their way to the Aji River in Osaka? Or headed via the Kitan Straits to Edo? Hikozo remembered how, eighteen years before, he'd ridden the *Eiriki Maru* on this very same route.

Godai and Itoh became engrossed in discussing the importing of warships and arms.

As they neared Kobe, the ship's engine suddenly died, and the ship came to a halt. They thought it strange, and the captain came to tell them there was a problem with the engine. It was already growing dark, so they'd have to spend the night on the ship.

A full moon came out. Hikozo went on deck to gaze at it. He'd dreamed about returning to his hometown, and now he was on his way, and he couldn't have been happier. He was too excited to sleep much that night.

The next morning they transferred to a small boat that had come out for them, and landed at the wharf in Kobe. Saying goodbye to the Godais, Hikozo and Itoh proceeded to the Hyogo prefectural office. With the *Orphan*'s engine needing repair, Hikozo would have to go by land to Honjo Village.

Itoh had a wry smile on his face as he instructed the staff. First of all, being a foreigner, Hikozo would need official approval to travel beyond the prescribed boundaries, and Itoh ordered the paperwork prepared. Lest there be attack, he also ordered that armed guards accompany Hikozo.

"The departure's set for tomorrow, and the prefectural office will make all the necessary preparations by then," Itoh said.

Hikozo thanked Itoh for his kindness and went to the foreign settlement, where he took a room in a hotel for the night.

News of Hikozo's plan to travel to his hometown soon spread through the foreign community, and an unexpected proposal arose among the foreign merchants. When these merchants, like all foreigners prohibited from traveling outside the foreign settlements, heard about Hikozo's trip, they declared that they wanted to accompany him, and went to see Itoh to ask that he issue travel passes for them also. These were men whom Itoh knew well through the arms business, and he couldn't easily turn them down, so he promised to issue passes for four of them.

Hikozo welcomed the news. If he returned to his hometown alone, surrounded by armed guards, he knew he'd feel constrained: it would look like he was a convict being escorted somewhere. Going with these other men would make for a much more lively and enjoyable journey. Besides, he wanted to show off the beautiful sea near his village.

The next morning he ate breakfast, left the hotel, and went to the prefectural office. He found the merchants already assembled there, suitcases in hand, and they happily shook his hand. They were all men he was acquainted with, and included the head of the Kobe branch of an American trading company.

Itoh handed them the travel passes and in English explained that he'd issued an order to the lodgings they'd be staying at to afford them all possible courtesies and not overcharge for whatever purchases the group might find necessary to make. He added that he'd also informed the heads of Hikozo's home village of his arrival, directing them to prepare a warm welcome.

"Well, I hope you have a very pleasant journey," Itoh said in English, and the men all shook his hand. Outside the prefectural office they found a line of palanquins waiting for them, and officials armed with rifles. One of the palanquins was quite large, prepared especially for the American branch head, who was heavy.

They all climbed into their palanquins, the bearers lifted them up, and the company set off.

Hikozo felt embarrassed to be escorted in this way back to his hometown, surrounded by armed guards, in a line of palanquins bearing foreign merchants. *Returning home in glory,* the phrase went.

They left Hyogo and went west on the Sanindo Highway. To their left the sea sparkled. Ordinary people along the road turned in surprise at the procession of palanquins, and other travelers stopped and gawked. They'd never before seen foreigners riding in palanquins, and were utterly amazed as the procession filed by. There wasn't a cloud in the sky, and the hot sun beat down. Hikozo felt sweat beading on his forehead.

They stopped to rest at Shiotani Village, the palanquin bearers squatting and wiping off the sweat with towels. They then shouldered the palanquins once more and set off down the dusty road. The town of Akashi lay before them. When they were about 6 ri (14.5 miles) from Hyogo, the road was lined with many houses. They stopped at a roadside inn for lunch, then got into the palanquins again and continued west.

They entered Tsuchiyama Village and there left the highway and took the road that led to Hikozo's hometown. They passed fields overgrown with weeds. His heart beat in anticipation.

As they approached Hamada, they saw people lining both sides of the road, so they stopped their palanquins. The armed guards walked over to an elderly man dressed in a half-length Japanese coat, who appeared to be a village official, exchanged a few words, and came back to Hikozo. "They're villagers who've come out to welcome you," he reported.

Hikozo turned his gaze to the villagers. They seemed nervous as they stood together, watching the procession, some of them stealthily exchanging a word or two. They'd never seen foreigners before and also weren't sure which of the five men dressed in Western clothes in the palanquins was Hikozo.

As the procession again moved, the villagers, flustered, to a man bowed their head. When the palanquins neared the entrance to the village, the travelers saw several men standing in formal dress. One of the officials with the travelers went over to speak with the men and returned to say that these were the village elders. At their direction the procession moved on to the village, coming to a stop in front of the imposing gate outside the home of the head of the village. Hikozo and the others alighted from their palanquins. The short, squat village head, escorted by the guards, came over to stand in front of Hikozo.

Hikozo introduced himself, saying, "I'm the stepson of the ship's captain Kichizaemon. My childhood name was Hikotaro, which I've changed to Hikozo."

The village head silently bowed and then unsteadily withdrew.

Hikozo looked around him. Ever since the procession entered the village, his heart was in his mouth. The village looked different from what he remembered from the first thirteen years of his life spent in it. The houses that had seemed huge and wonderful to him then were now small and miserable, the road he'd thought was broad was now narrow and cramped—the memories etched in his mind when he was a small boy now betrayed.

He looked around again. The village was shabby, the houses tilted, some of them clearly abandoned. From the shadows men and women peered out at Hikozo; only children appearing on the road to stare at him, their clothes shabby, their thin arms and legs dirty.

He felt a chill run through him.

He went into the village head's home. They were shown into a sitting room, where the four foreign merchants, looking around uneasily, sat on the tatami with arms around their knees or with their legs stretched out.

Hikozo listened while the prefectural officials who'd accompanied them as guards questioned the village head and other prominent members of the community about conditions in the village. The village had many cotton fields, and with the monopoly on cotton sales by the Himeji Domain, it was a vital source of income for the farmers; unfortunately, though, the price of cotton had dropped drastically, reducing the farmers' income. Moreover, the Himeji Domain, loyal to the shogunate, had exacted heavy levies from the village to help finance its campaign against the Choshu Domain in the battles at Toba and Fushimi. Several years of poor harvests on top of this, and the village was destitute. Many people had had to give up their family farms and become homeless, with the sixty-two households in the village now down to thirty.

Hikozo listened to all this silently and understood now why there were so many abandoned houses and why the people looked gaunt. He felt embarrassed in front of the foreign merchants. On the way to the village he'd described it in glowing terms. But now they found the place dilapidated, and all spark of life gone from the villagers' eyes.

The merchants didn't say a word.

Hikozo spoke to the village head. On the way back to Japan, in Shanghai he'd heard from a castaway named Otokichi that the sailors from the *Eiriki Maru* had been taken back to Nagasaki on a Chinese ship. Among these were four men from Hikozo's home area—Seitaro, Asauemon, Jinpachi, and Kiyozo—and they should have all made it home. Hikozo wanted to see them and asked the village head to bring them.

The village head answered in a low voice. Jinpachi had died of illness after returning home, while the remaining three had been hired by the Himeji Domain so they could make use of the men's experience on Western sailing vessels. They now lived in Himeji and weren't in the village. Hikozo again looked at the faces of the prominent men of the village around him. He must have seen them as a child, but they were all strangers to him now. If his stepbrother were here, he'd run to see him; Unomatsu's absence could only mean that he was out at sea captaining a cargo ship. Relatives of Kichizaemon were surely around, and the fact that they didn't come to see Hikozo must mean that either they didn't want to or they'd lost their farms and were among the homeless.

Hikozo wondered when his stepfather passed away, and decided he'd have to go to the Rengeji Temple, part of the Bodaiji Temple, to find out.

"I'd like to go to the temple," he told the village head. The village head nodded and exchanged a few words in a low voice with the other prominent villagers there, and two stood up. Hikozo followed them from the house. A large number of men and women were gathered outside, but when they saw Hikozo, they scattered, some running off into the cotton fields.

Hikozo walked down the road with the men. A crowd tentatively followed behind—not just local villagers, but people from

342

nearby villages as well. Since Itoh had issued a notice to afford Hikozo and his party all proper courtesies, the news of his return must have spread far.

They took a narrow path and soon saw the entrance gate to the temple. Cicadas called out shrilly from trees in the temple compound. They passed through the gate and came to the priests' living quarters. One of the men who'd escorted him here went inside, and soon a priest in his fifties emerged.

Hikozo bowed to him and said, "I'm Hikozo, stepson of Kichizaemon of Honjo Village. I've just returned home and would like to know when my stepfather passed away."

The priest nodded and urged him to come inside. Hikozo removed his boots on the dirt floor of the entrance and stepped up into the building. He followed the priest to the main hall, sat down in formal style there, and bowed to the statue of Buddha on the altar.

The priest brought over the death register, sat, and turned the pages. "This is it," he said, placing the register in front of Hikozo and pointing to an entry.

Hikozo looked. Below the posthumous Buddhist name— Koukaku Jisho Shinshi—was his stepfather's name, and Ansei 3 as the year of death. That would make it twelve years ago, meaning his stepfather died six years after Hikozo became a castaway. His stepfather had always been a brawny, vigorous man, but perhaps he'd lost his vitality after his wife, Hikozo's mother, passed away.

Hikozo stared at his stepfather's posthumous name.

He glanced to the side of this and hurriedly read what was written there: *Hoto Joben Shinshi, son of Kichizaemon, died at sea on the* Eiriki Maru *of Daiishi, Nada.*

The characters used for *Eiriki Maru* were an alternate way of writing the name, but Hikozo knew that the *Eiriki Maru* had been owned by Matsuya Hachisaburo of Daiishi Village in Nada, so the ship described here had to be the same one he'd been a crew member on.

Died at sea. He couldn't keep his eyes off these words.

343

"Is something the matter?" the priest asked.

Hikozo looked up and said, "This part...," and pointed to where the register listed him as dead.

"Oh, that's Kichizaemon's stepson..." The priest suddenly stopped, looked at Hikozo, and froze.

"That would seem to be me—no, it *is* me. And they even gave me a posthumous name," Hikozo said in a low voice.

The priest paled as he stared at the name of the dead.

A long silence ensued. Finally the priest stood up, went to sit in front of the Buddhist altar, put his hands together, and prayed. He then returned to Hikozo, put his hands together reverently, and said, "It's through the mercy of the Buddha that you have returned alive." He bowed deeply.

Hikozo again looked at the death register.

"I'm the one who gave you the posthumous name," the priest said quietly.

In the seventh year of Kiei (1854) an official from the Himeji Domain came to the village to report that four sailors from the *Eiriki Maru,* which had been lost at sea—Seitaro, Asauemon, Jinpachi, and Kiyozo—had, according to the Nagasaki commissioner's office, arrived safely in Nagasaki aboard a Chinese merchant ship. Seitaro's family, overjoyed at his safe return, planned a huge feast to celebrate, but then, out of consideration for the families of Hikozo, Jisaku, and Kamezo, called the celebration off. According to the copy of the report from the Nagasaki commissioner's office, Hikozo and the other two were taken back by a ship to America, their whereabouts unknown, the implication being that they had died afterward.

Kichizaemon had grieved terribly and came many times to the temple to pray. Before long he asked the priest to give his stepson a posthumous name and hold a memorial service for him. Kichizaemon held on to a faint hope that Hikozo was still alive somewhere, but four years had passed and there was no news, so the boy must be dead.

"He told me to hold a memorial service so your poor spirit

wouldn't continue to wander. This is what a father should do for his child, so I went ahead and gave the posthumous name and held the service. Kichizaemon cried terribly, as I recall." The priest's face was mournful as he said this.

As he listened, Hikozo could feel the great affection Kichizaemon had had for him, and tears began to well in his eyes. He thanked the priest, gave him a fee to hold memorial services for his stepfather, and stood up.

As he left the priest's quarters, Hikozo could sense curious eyes on him. He went with the two men from the village who were waiting for him, took the path back to the village, and returned to the village head's house.

At twilight, lanterns were lit. Mosquitoes buzzed incessantly, special incense sticks were lit to keep them away. Dinner was brought in and set down on trays before Hikozo and the four foreign merchants. As the prefectural officials instructed, the rice bowls were filled with rice; the merchants awkwardly took up their chopsticks but soon put them down. Hikozo, too, more used to Western food now, shuddered at how coarse the food was in his hometown.

"Where is the toilet, may I ask?" one of the merchants said in typically accented Japanese.

A villager showed him the way.

Hikozo grimaced. The toilet was behind the house, so at night you had to feel your way there to take care of your needs. Foreign toilets had a seat on them, but Japanese ones required you to squat. Hikozo could picture the confusion the man must be experiencing, and he was thoroughly embarrassed.

Futons were laid out for them in three rooms, and mosquito netting was spread. Hikozo undressed to his undershirt and lay down on the moldy-smelling futon. His body felt as if it were sinking, he was so disappointed. His hometown had once had neat houses all in a row and a wide, well-cared-for road. Fields full of puffy white cotton flowers, plum blossoms that came out in spring, and sudden showers in the summer. The villagers had been well off, and on New Year they would all, men and women, dress up to pay their respects at the local shrine and temple, and the men would end up happily drinking sake. But the village he'd seen this day was poor in every respect, the fields gone wild with no sign that anyone was growing cotton.

He found it strange that people even lived here anymore, and knew he could no longer stand to live here himself. Even a single day had been painful, and he wanted to leave tomorrow as soon as he could.

He couldn't get the words he'd seen in the death register out of his mind: *Died at sea.* He'd come back to his village excited and happy, only to find that, as far as the village was concerned, he was dead. The thirteen-year-old he'd been—the boy for whom this was home—had passed away, and the real Hikozo, the one here now, maybe was no longer even a Japanese.

The foreign merchants with him had left most of their dinner untouched, and likewise Hikozo had found it hard to eat. He wanted to place a napkin in his lap, have some soup, and tuck into a slice of beef. He also found it unpleasant that the locals were staring at them as if they were part of a sightseeing tour. To the people tagging along on the way to and from the temple, Hikozo with his Western attire and boots must have looked like some strange animal in their midst.

He was sure that the merchant sharing his room, used to a bed, wouldn't be able to sleep in the futon, but the man was soon snoring away. Hikozo closed his eyes and finally fell asleep.

The next morning he woke to the sound of roosters crowing far off and nearby. He got up and dressed. The merchant was still curled up asleep. Hikozo went to the dirt-floored entrance, put on his boots, and went outside. Dawn was just breaking, and the houses and fields were still misty.

As he relieved himself by the side of the road, tears suddenly sprang to his eyes. The refreshing morning air carried with it the faint fragrance of the sea, the smell he remembered as that of his hometown. The thin, pale face of his mother came to his eyes.

346

But these fond emotions soon died. He could never get used to this place again; it was disagreeable. The posthumous name he'd been given meant he was no longer in this world—appearing suddenly before the villagers as he'd done must have convinced them they were seeing a ghost. His home wasn't this village anymore; perhaps it was—America.

That's all right, he told himself. Fate has made me what I am, and if people think I'm American, so be it. I'll live my life as I see fit, as an American.

He thought about breakfast, which they'd soon be eating. He had no problem enjoying a heaping bowl of steamed rice, miso soup, and pickled vegetables, but his foreign companions, even if they were able to get down the rice and vegetables, no doubt would find it hard to stomach the soup.

The crow of the roosters made him think they should serve the men some eggs, something they were used to for breakfast. A few eggs ought to whet their appetite. He went back in the house and found the prefectural officials in the room near the entrance, some of them smoking pipes. Hikozo asked them to prepare three eggs apiece for the foreign merchants' breakfast.

"Raw eggs are fine, I assume?" one of the officials asked.

"No, they must be *boiled*," Hikozo answered, using the English term.

"*Boirudo*? What does that mean?" the official asked, perplexed.

Hikozo stared at the man. How did you say *boiled* in Japanese? For a moment he was at a loss, then explained haltingly that you put the eggs in hot water until the inside was hard.

"Oh, you mean *yuderu*," one of the younger officials said.

Hikozo suddenly remembered the word. "That's right," he nodded, "*yuderu*. Boiled."

Breakfast was finally brought into the parlor, and sure enough three boiled eggs were on each person's tray. As he peeled away the eggshell, Hikozo felt small and miserable. It made him both embarrassed and sad that he'd forgotten such an ordinary word. Was English his first language now and Japanese his second?

After breakfast he quickly told the officials that they'd be returning soon to Hyogo. He wanted to be back in the foreign settlement, among foreigners again.

The senior official had a doubtful expression on his face. Wouldn't Hikozo, who'd been thrilled at finally returning home, want to stay at least a few days in the village?

"We'll be setting out very soon," Hikozo said in a commanding tone.

None of the merchants objected. They'd had quite enough of life in the village.

Hurried preparations were made to leave; Hikozo and the others climbed into their palanquins, and they departed from the village head's house. A great many villagers trailed after the line of palanquins. Hikozo found their presence irksome and wanted to shout at them to disperse.

But he confined himself to a frown as his palanquin bounced down the road.

CHAPTER TWENTY-SIX

AFTER HIKOZO RETURNED to Osaka from Hyogo, he left Kobe on the *Costa Rica,* arriving back in Nagasaki on June 27.

On July 17, Edo was officially renamed Tokyo, and news reached Nagasaki that on September 8 (1868) the era name was changed to Meiji. The Aizu Domain continued obstinately to fight against the new government, but on September 22 they gave up, and the Restoration was complete.

Every time Hikozo recalled his visit to Honjo Village, he felt empty inside. The shock at seeing himself listed as dead continued to haunt him. He'd always believed his roots lay in that little village, but it proved to be an illusion. He was like a sad little bit of seaweed, rootless, carried along by the tide.

In a melancholy mood he went about his duties for the Glover Company.

The following year, at the direction of the new government the Glover Company imported a minting machine from Shanghai, and Hikozo was put in charge of it. The machine was sent to Osaka on September 10, and the Osaka Mint was established.

On December 3 the latest model of steamship from England, commanded by J. M. James, entered Nagasaki Harbor. This ship had been specially ordered by the head of the Kumamoto Domain, Hosokawa Yoshikuni, and was christened the *Ryujo*. Hikozo was asked by the councillor to the domain, Mizoguchi Koun, to handle the negotiations with James, and on September 9 the ship was inspected and officially handed over to the domain. Hikozo received a generous honorarium for his services.

The New Year came, and Hikozo continued as always to work for the Glover Company, but on July 26 the company suddenly took advantage of the bankruptcy laws and declared bankruptcy. It had made tremendous profits selling arms, but with the Treaty of Hakodate orders had dried up.

Hikozo was out of a job but managed to occupy his days helping various businesses with their negotiations. He often thought of his trip back to his hometown. The memory was thoroughly unpleasant, but he regretted that he hadn't paid a visit to his mother's grave. At the time all he could think of was getting out of the village as soon as possible, and he didn't want to spare the time to make the visit. Also, he had been afraid to visit her grave.

A stone had been placed to mark the spot where they'd buried his mother, but by now it might be impossible to locate. Even if Kichizaemon had erected a nice headstone, it was no doubt a simple, coarse affair. With each passing day the desire grew in Hikozo to erect a new headstone over his mother's grave—his duty as her son.

Finally he couldn't contain these feelings anymore, and on October 1 he boarded the American steamship *New York* and left Nagasaki, planning to travel from Hyogo to his village once more. The ship passed through the Shimonoseki Straits, sailed through the Inland Sea, and two days later arrived in Hyogo.

He'd need another special pass for foreigners to travel to his village, but when he arrived at the foreign settlement, he was disappointed to learn that his friend Itoh Hirobumi, the prefectural governor, had been transferred to an important post in the central government in Tokyo and that the post here was now occupied by a high councillor standing in as his proxy. Regulations governing foreigners were still quite strict, so Hikozo imagined his request for a pass would be turned down, but his strong desire to return to his hometown drove him to submit a request anyway.

The next day he set off for the prefectural office to ask how his request was going and was surprised to find it had already been issued and was waiting for him. The councillor in charge apparently couldn't refuse such a request, seeing as how Itoh, the governor, had issued one before. Hikozo was overjoyed, and impressed again at the major role Itoh now played in the new government.

Hikozo was staying in a hotel in the foreign settlement. He wrote a letter to the village head at Honjo Village, informing him that he would be visiting again, and entrusted it to a messenger service. Three days later he left Hyogo in a palanquin. This time he had no guards with him, but he did have a pistol strapped to his belt, and as he traveled he guardedly scanned the road outside through the screen.

The palanquin traveled west down the Sanyo Road, and Hikozo finally arrived at the village. No one was about along the road, and he had the palanquin stop in front of the village head's house. He stood at the front door and announced himself, and the village head soon appeared and showed him inside to the parlor.

After exchanging greetings, an elderly woman came in from the corridor, placed her hands on the tatami, and bowed deeply. When she raised her head, Hikozo couldn't help but give a small cry of surprise. It was his aunt on his mother's side—she'd apparently been waiting for his arrival in the village head's house and had changed into her best clothes to greet him. At the time of his mother's death she'd been the one who tried to cheer him up, and who was in charge of the funeral and burial. A wave of nostalgia struck him when he saw her. His aunt, though, found him so changed she was confused, and sat hunched over in a corner of the room.

Hikozo stood up, went over, sat down in front of her, and took her rough hand in his. The feeling finally struck him that yes, this was his own flesh and blood, and he really was back home. In a low voice that could barely be heard, her head still bowed, his aunt explained how the previous year, when he visited the village, there'd been an unfortunate occurrence in her parent's former home and she couldn't leave her village.

Hikozo nodded silently, tearful.

He told her that he'd come to erect a headstone for his mother's grave, and asked her what the condition of the grave was now. There was only one stone marking it now, she said, and Hikozo understood it was as he'd imagined. He remembered how he and his mother had lived for a time, just the two of them, and was more determined than ever to honor her with a handsome headstone.

He consulted with the village head and then set off with his aunt to the Rengeji Temple. The head priest was at home and invited them into his parlor. The last time Hikozo had visited, accompanied by officials, with Governor Itoh commanding the village to welcome him, the head priest had got the decided impression that Hikozo was a man of importance, and he was most gracious in his reception this time as well.

Hikozo told him his intention to erect a gravestone for his mother and asked his advice. The priest meekly replied, "That is laudable. I will do what I can to help you."

"I'm my mother's only child, and even now I dream about her," Hikozo went on. "They say that by the time you want to be a good child to your parents, they're gone. I'd like to make a decent grave for her. It's the least I can do to honor her memory..." He mentioned the amount of money he planned to use for the stone. The priest stared at him, amazed at how much Hikozo was willing to spend.

After pondering for a time, the priest rose and asked Hikozo and his aunt to follow him, and they left his quarters. He walked toward the main temple gate and stopped just inside it. "You can place the memorial stone right here," he said. This was clearly the best spot within the temple compound, and Hikozo thanked the priest for his kindness.

After they returned to the parlor, Hikozo and the priest discussed the practical aspects involved. The priest told him that the best stonecutter around, named Ishitora, lived in Futami Village (present-day Akashi City), and urged Hikozo to make use of his services; Hikozo said he'd leave this entirely up to the priest. He said he'd like his stepfather's posthumous name carved on the memorial as well, an idea the priest heartily endorsed; he suggested that they carve all the names of Hikozo's ancestors on the memorial.

The head priest promised he'd get in touch with Ishitora right away, and Hikozo left the temple and spent that night in his aunt's house.

The next morning Ishitora and his assistants visited. The stone-cutter was a man in his fifties, of sturdy build, and with bright, alert eyes. After Hikozo explain his plan for the memorial, Ishitora said that the best design would a be a three-tiered memorial, and gave an estimate of the cost. Hikozo agreed immediately, directing him to carve on the front of the memorial his mother's and stepfather's posthumous names, and those of his ancestors.

"And on the back . . . ," he said, taking out a sheet from his case. On it was written, in English, *Erected in memory of his parents by Joseph Heco.*

Ishitora stared in amazement at these English words. He'd not only never carved such writing, he'd never laid eyes on it before. He traced the shape of the letters over and over with his finger, finally appearing to be satisfied.

Hikozo handed Ishitora an advance, and Ishitora gave him an estimate of the time it would take to erect the memorial. Ishitora carefully folded up the paper with the English writing on it and left. Hikozo asked his aunt to handle communications between Ishitora and the Rengeji Temple, then went to say good-bye to the village head; he called for a palanquin and left the village in high spirits.

Back in Hyogo, Hikozo boarded a ship to Nagasaki. Although he'd lost his job after the collapse of the Glover Company, Nagasaki was still a busy trading port, and he had much to do helping various merchants with their negotiations.

Motoki Shozo had by this time started a letterpress printing plant in Nagasaki and was making movable type. Hikozo heard that he'd gone to the capital in December and founded a daily news-paper, the *Yokohama Shimbun*. Hikozo had lost his enthusiasm for publishing a newspaper, but this news convinced him further that newspapers were indispensable for Japanese in this modern age.

In June of the fourth year of Meiji, telegraph communication began in Nagasaki between Japan and foreign countries. Telegrams were sent between Nagasaki and Shanghai, Vladivostok, Hong Kong, and Singapore. Ordinary letters between Nagasaki and Yokohama, even with the fleetest messengers, took seven to nine days, so more and more people began using the new telegraph system. Hikozo could feel how Japan, following America's lead, was benefiting from the blessings of modern science.

In a monumental step, on July 14 the Imperial Rescript was issued abolishing the old domain system and replacing it with the modern-day prefectures.

On September 12, as signs of autumn grew more evident, Hikozo received an unexpected letter from a former samurai of the Himeji Domain, now prefectural governor, Sakai Tadakuni. Hikozo was suspicious, and extremely nervous, to get a letter from a former samurai of the domain that had counted Honjo Village as part of his realm. He opened the letter, and though it was written using many Chinese characters, he was able to grasp the general point.

Tadakuni had taken note of Hikozo, who was well known because of his time in America, and was surprised to learn he was from the same domain as himself. He'd written, he said, because he wanted very much to meet Hikozo. He would be waiting in the former domain residence in Kobe, he added, asking Hikozo to take a steamship as soon as he could to come see him. Hikozo could sense from the letter that Tadakuni was a kind and friendly man, and he was greatly impressed.

Hikozo had no job at this time, so when he learned that the British steamship *Costa Rica* would be sailing for Kobe in two days, he went to secure passage. He made preparations for the trip, boarded the ship, and left Nagasaki.

On the morning of September 16 the *Costa Rica* docked in Kobe. Hikozo took one of the palanquins waiting for debarking passengers and headed for the former Himeji Domain's residence. He announced himself to the man who appeared at the front door; the man bade Hikozo follow him into the guest room.

Footsteps sounded in the corridor, then Tadakuni, accompanied by some servants, appeared. "Sorry to have kept you waiting," he said, settling down on a thick cushion.

Hikozo had assumed that Tadakuni, as a former samurai, must be a man of mature years, and was startled to find that he was only eighteen.

Tadakuni told him of his great interest in Western civilization, and without much ado began questioning Hikozo, paying careful attention to the replies. The questions were pointed, and Hikozo knew he was dealing with a brilliant young man.

They eventually stopped, and Tadakuni thanked Hikozo for coming all the way to Kobe and for the valuable things he'd learned from talking with him. He ordered his servants to bring in a haori kimono with the family crest of the domain daimyo, as well as twenty-five ryo in gold, which he presented to Hikozo. A haori with the family crest was given only for the most meritorious service, like an honorary decoration, and Hikozo received these presents with gratitude and great humility.

Tadakuni was on his way to Tokyo and had to depart soon. Learning from Hikozo that the ship that he'd taken, the *Costa Rica*, was bound for Yokohama, he had his retainers book passage on it for him.

Tadakuni then turned to him and said seriously, "Could you come to Himeji?" Prefectural officials, he said, former Himeji samurai, knew very little of the outside world, and he wanted them to hear about foreign countries and have a firmer sense that they'd turned a new page in the history of their country. It was just the kind of bold request Hikozo might expect of Tadakuni, and he assented.

Tadakuni left Kobe on the *Costa Rica* at three that afternoon. Hikozo stayed at the former Himeji Domain's residence.

The retainers pressed ahead with plans for him to travel to Himeji, and on the morning of September 20 Hikozo left Kobe in a procession of retainers aboard palanquins. The party traveled west down the Sanyo Road. To the left the sea sparkled, to the right the foliage on the hills was just changing color.

As he bounced along in his palanquin, he thought he'd like to stop by his home village, which lay halfway on the road to Himeji. The memorial to his parents should be done by this time, and he wanted to see if it had been. When the memorial was completed, he thought of stopping at the village on his way back from Himeji and holding a banquet to celebrate with the villagers. At the banquet he'd wear the special haori with its family crest he'd received from Tadakuni, for he wanted the villagers to know he was the kind of person who received such honors.

As they rested in a roadside inn, Hikozo told the retainer in charge that he wanted to take a detour and stop by his home village. The retainer had no objection, so the procession of palanquins turned left at the Tsuchiyama Inn. Along the way farmers in the fields stopped and stared curiously at the procession, at the sight of a line of palanquins bearing samurai and, among them, Hikozo in Western garb.

The procession entered Honjo Village and came to a halt in front of Hikozo's aunt's house. His aunt came out. "How is the memorial progressing?" he asked. She replied that it was finished two days before and that Hikozo's mother and stepfather's bones had been transferred to it.

"Thank you for all the trouble you took," Hikozo said, and quickly told her why he was traveling to Himeji. He told her his plans for a celebratory banquet after his return from Himeji and asked her to make the necessary preparations.

"I'll consult with the village head about this," his aunt said, bowing.

"Well, we'd better be going..." Hikozo bowed and got back into his palanquin.

As the palanquins set off, a number of villagers followed the procession for a while. From Tsuchiyama Inn the procession continued west on the Sanyo Road, passed the Kakogawa Inn, forded a river, passed Yamawaki Village, and went across the Ichi River on boats. They arrived in Himeji in the evening.

Hikozo was excited to arrive in the castle town of the domain that controlled his home village. The town was lively, with lines of large inns lit by lanterns. He was shown to one of these inns in the Uomachi section of town. The owner of the inn took him to a first-class guest room. Hikozo removed his boots and sat down, throwing his legs out in front of him.

Soon after dinner an envoy arrived from the governor's representative, the former domain councillor Honda Iki; the man told Hikozo to please let him know if there was anything he could do for him, adding that three officials with him—Kondo, Igarashi, and Haruyama—had been assigned to help him in any way they could.

After greeting Kondo and the others, Hikozo asked them about his former shipmates Seitaro and the other two who had been hired by the domain to pilot Western-style sailing vessels. He wanted very much to see these men, who had been castaways with him. He learned, however, that they were at the moment piloting ships owned by the domain and not in town. Hikozo was disappointed at the news but encouraged to hear that they were able to make good use of their skills as sailors.

The next morning he was warmly entertained and received. He was ushered into a large reception hall, where a great number of officials were seated awaiting him, and proceeded to tell them what he had learned while living in America—about ships, telegraphs, the way trains were constructed, and much more. The officials listened intently, took notes, and asked one question after another, all of which Hikozo carefully answered. When he saw how their eyes shone with interest, he was reassured that with his knowledge of the West he was indeed a very special person, and felt happy and satisfied.

He was amazed by how magnificent the castle was. Its nickname was the White Heron Castle, and it certainly did have the elegance of a crane with its wings spread wide. Hikozo could also see how solidly built it was, an altogether wonderful structure.

They showed him the interior of the castle as well. He passed through the main gate, then several smaller gates, then went upstairs to the parlor on the upper floor. The room was spacious, the view from the windows outstanding. To the east he could see the Ichi River and gentle undulating hills, while to the south lay the sea dotted with islands. He stood there for some time, enchanted.

At the invitation of the prefectural government he attended a military review held in the outer precincts of the castle, was invited also to the mansion of the former councillor Kawai Heizan, and saw a display of rickshaws of a type he'd never seen, even in Kobe. Kawai seemed to have a taste for the very latest and unusual things.

On September 23 a large banquet was held by Honda Iki, to which Hikozo was invited. All the highest officials were present, and after Honda thanked Hikozo for coming to Himeji, he asked him to take the seat of honor nearest the tokonoma alcove. Hizozo was flustered. How could the mere son of a sailor possibly sit in the seat of honor above the highest former samurai of the clan?

Honda, however, saying that Hikozo was a very important guest of the prefectural governor, insisted. Hikozo was both embarrassed and happy.

His enjoyable stay in Himeji drew to a close, and on September 29 he left the town. The prefectural government had several officials travel with Hikozo. On the way back, they stopped as planned at his hometown.

Hikozo's aunt took him to the Rengeji Temple to see the memorial. The gravestone was a splendid monument, three-tiered, just over a meter in height, and set, as the head priest had directed, to the right inside the main gate. On the face of the memorial were carved the posthumous Buddhist names given to his mother and stepfather—Shuzen Sokuto Shinyo and Kokaku Jisho Shinshi, respectively.

Hikozo walked around the back of the monument, where he found the English he'd ordered carved done without a single mistake. Ishitora was indeed a skilled carver.

The head priest donned his priestly raiment and chanted sutras in front of the memorial. With this, Hikozo felt he'd finally done his duty as a son toward his mother and stepfather, and left money with the head priest so that services could be conducted in perpetuity.

That evening he borrowed the village head's spacious guest room and held a banquet. Prominent villagers were all there, as were the officials who had accompanied him. Hikozo stood and expressed his thanks for the completion of the memorial, then took out the special haori he'd been given by the former head of the domain and displayed it for all to see. The village head and the other villagers hesitantly approached the garment, with its family crest on it, bowing deeply before it, many of them even bringing their hands together in prayer.

Food and drink were brought out, and Hikozo toasted the officials sitting near him. The prominent villagers came up, one after the other, and, sitting formally, poured him a drink; once they'd withdrawn, though, they didn't approach again.

The villagers' faces remained stiff, and though as they drank, they occasionally stole a glance in Hikozo's direction, they soon looked away. Some whispered among themselves.

The more he watched them, the less he enjoyed himself. He'd held the banquet to get to know the villagers in a more relaxed atmosphere, but they'd placed a barrier between themselves and him. Some even seemed to grow more distant as the evening wore on. This village was his hometown, but the villagers would not permit him to be one of them. Dressed as he was in Western clothes and boots, he must have seemed a foreigner to them, an outsider now and always.

A sadness swept Hikozo like a cold wind. *I have no home,* he muttered to himself.

The next morning, with vacant eyes, he left the village.

CHAPTER TWENTY-SEVEN

In AUGUST OF THE FIFTH YEAR of Meiji (1872), Hikozo went to Tokyo, and, at the recommendation of Inoue Kaoru (also known as Inoue Monta), the vice minister of finance, he joined the accounting division of the Finance Ministry. On November 9 of that year the old Japanese lunar calendar was replaced by the solar calendar, with December 3 becoming January 1 of the sixth year of Meiji (1873).

It was around this time that Hikozo noticed that people were referring to him in private as America Hikozo, then realized how this had become almost an official name for himself. It was common practice now for commoners to use last names, and he felt that, having become an American citizen, it made some sense for him to use the word *America* as his last name. His strong point, he told himself, lay in the fact that he'd been educated in America and could read and write English, so using America as a kind of substitute last name wasn't such a bad idea.

But as the years passed, he felt his value in Japanese society begin to fade. With the rapid spread of English-language education after the Meiji Restoration, there were now many people able to read, write, and speak English nearly as fluently as any foreigner. In the Finance Ministry, too, there were many of these people employed, and they freely associated with foreigners.

Hikozo had been studying Chinese characters for some time now, taking up his brush in the evenings and practicing calligraphy.

Though he was able with great effort to read official documents, written as they were with many Chinese character compounds, he found it difficult to write the characters, which he knew disqualified him from ever becoming a civil servant. He stopped coming to the ministry and effectively resigned.

Unsure what path to take now, he left Tokyo for Kobe, where he had many foreign friends. He was happy to be able to speak English again, and while meeting these foreigners engaged in trade, he made the acquaintance of a wealthy businessman named Kitakaze Shouemon, who helped him get into the tea business. Business went smoothly, and Hikozo was able to settle down in Kobe.

In February of the tenth year of Meiji (1877), the Satsuma Rebellion broke out, but in September the leader, Saigo Takamori, committed suicide, and the rebellion ended.

Hikozo turned forty, and married an eighteen-year-old woman named Choko, daughter of Matsumoto Shichijuro. Since he'd taken U.S. citizenship, he had no family register, so his wife succeeded to the Hamada family line, relations of Hikozo's whose line had died out, and he took on the last name of Hamada, becoming Hamada Hikozo.

His tea business continued apace, but he was swindled by an unscrupulous businessman. He took the man to court in Kobe and won the case, but the whole affair made him disgusted with business, and he closed up his shop. Having property of his own, he was able to live a quiet life with his wife in Kobe.

He spent much time looking back over his life. After returning to Japan, he had been so busy and hurried it sometimes seemed to him that he was still afloat on the sea like a castaway. He'd always treasured his ability to speak English but saw now that he'd spent his years at the beck and call of various foreigners and Japanese, like a ship without a mast, adrift.

Thoughts like these made him feel his life had been wasted, and he spent much of his time gazing at the sky. He began suffering from neuralgia, began seeing a doctor.

He still read English newspapers, and having learned to read

Chinese characters, he read Japanese papers as well. On June 18, as he looked through the paper, he called out in surprise at one particular article. The headline read: *Son of Yamamoto Otokichi, who Was Shipwrecked Forty Years Ago, Returns to Japan and Requests to Be Added to Family Register.*

This had to be the Otokichi he met in Shanghai twenty years before, in the sixth year of Ansei (1859), the man who'd been a castaway on the *Hojun Maru*. Giving up on the idea of returning to Japan, Otokichi had settled permanently in Shanghai. He helped Hikozo's fellow shipmates from the *Eiriki Maru* sail to Nagasaki on a Chinese merchant vessel. There had been many times over the years that Hikozo recalled this kind man with gentle eyes.

Hikozo hurriedly read through the article. It began: "John W. Watson, the son of Yamamoto Otokichi of Chita County, Bishu, who was shipwrecked in America forty years ago, has arrived in Japan recently and made application to Kanagawa Prefecture to be added to the family register." Included was the text of the application submitted to Nomura Yasushi, head of the Kanagawa Prefecture government. Otokichi was known in Shanghai as Watson, and apparently his son had also taken the name.

"My father," the application read, "is originally a Japanese citizen named Yamamoto Otokichi." Becoming a castaway, he "eventually drifted to America, where he and two others were rescued by American Indians." The other two men were named Iwakichi and Hisakichi, all of which fit exactly what Hikozo had heard from Otokichi long ago. The article went on to describe how Otokichi returned to Japan on the *Morrison*, only to be fired on and driven away. In 1863 (Bunkyu 3) he left Shanghai and went to Singapore, "and there he joined the ranks of the dead," the article said.

Joined the ranks of the dead—the phrase sent a chill up Hikozo's spine.

Otokichi had said that the *Morrison* affair made him resigned never to return home, though of course the desire to once more tread his native soil must have remained strong within him. After

Japan opened itself to the outside world, he still didn't return, less because of the fear that he'd be executed for breaking the law than because he'd settled down abroad already, with a wife and children, and couldn't very well return home.

John W. Watson, the son, must have come to Japan to register in order to fulfill the wishes that his father was never able to. Hikozo read the papers carefully after this to see what became of the application, but there was nothing more about it. Hikozo sent a letter to the Kanagawa prefectural government to inquire into the case.

Hikozo's name was widely known, so the prefecture responded immediately with a report on the outcome of the application. At the prefecture office Watson was questioned in detail about his background. They learned he was Otokichi's eldest son, aged twenty-two, and had two younger sisters, each of whom had married Englishmen and taken British citizenship. Watson looked just like any Japanese, so they believed his report must be genuine, and the prefecture official put him in the family register. Nomura Yasushi, head of Kanagawa Prefecture, reported this to his superior, Itoh Hirobumi, head of the Ministry of Home Affairs.

Hikozo felt sure this report would bring some measure of comfort to Otokichi's soul. Three years later, however, he learned that Watson, who'd taken the name Yamamoto Otokichi and was now employed in an ironworks in Kobe, had submitted an application to the Kanagawa Prefecture office to have his name removed from the family register.

According to the application, Watson only recently learned that his father had become a British citizen in Singapore under the name John M. Watson, and the son wanted to join his father in taking British citizenship. This application was forwarded by the head of Kanagawa Prefecture, Oki Morikata, to Inoue Kaoru, minister for foreign affairs, and to the minister for home affairs, Yamada Akiyoshi, and after considerable deliberation it was decided that the law allowed Japanese to take foreign citizenship only in the case of marriage. Watson had, after all, applied himself for

Japanese citizenship, and now to ask to be removed from the register was too capricious, they concluded. His application was rejected.

Hikozo had mixed feelings when he heard this. After he came to Japan, Watson must have learned in what high regard the British were held, and decided to take the same citizenship his father had. In all likelihood Watson had spoken English from childhood and knew no Japanese, making life for him in Japan very difficult, and he must have decided he wanted to live again in Singapore, an English-speaking environment.

Watson was as much a castaway as his father had been, Hikozo decided. He, too, was like a bit of seaweed floating aimlessly on the sea of fate. Just like himself, a person with no home to return to, a dead person as far as his hometown was concerned. He felt sorry for Watson, who would no doubt end up dying in Japan.

Hikozo's hair had begun to turn white, and his neuralgia made one of his cheeks twitch. On February 1 of the twenty-first year of Meiji (1888), he and his wife left Kobe, where they'd lived all this time, and took the *Yamashiro Maru* to move to Tokyo. His doctor had recommended a change of climate to help his neuralgia. They landed in Yokohama and then went to Tokyo, where they settled in a house in Negishi, near Ueno Park. It was a quiet area favored by scholars and artists.

At the end of that year Hikozo saw some notices in the newspaper that made him frown. These were personal announcements placed by a wealthy official, a banker, and a businessman. The content of each was essentially the same, namely, that they would be at hot-springs resorts until January 4, thus not at home and unable to receive any New Year callers. Hikozo felt sad reading this, seeing how traditional Japanese customs were coming undone. The New Year was a time when people paid visits to shrines and temples, cooked and enjoyed special dishes. One rang in the New Year by receiving the first guest of the year. Neglecting these customs and going off to some hot springs was a deplorable, egotistical act, brought on by the harmful influences of foreign culture. And the audacity, to publish this in a newspaper!

After this Hikozo abandoned Western clothes and spent each day in a kimono, seated on tatami in Japanese style, earnestly practicing his brush calligraphy. Japan had beautiful traditions not found in foreign countries, he felt strongly, and as a Japanese that's what he needed to follow. He was still an American citizen, but when the proper time came, he was determined to take Japanese citizenship.

In May of the twenty-second year of Meiji (1889) he built a new house in the Hara District, near the former residence of the Himeji Domain, and moved there. He was fifty-two now and spent his time in idleness, feeling a physical weariness creeping up on him.

He continued to keep up with the newspapers in order to follow current events. He learned, for instance, that the old custom of married women shaving their eyebrows and blackening their teeth had been discontinued, and he saw more and more men with short hair and wearing Western clothes. Telegraphs had spread throughout the country, and ordinary citizens—not just high officials—were beginning to use telephones. Riding on trains, too, had become commonplace.

More and more newspaper companies were founded, and Hikozo often saw the name of his partner in the *Kaigai Shimbun*, Kishida Ginko, mentioned. Ginko had been hired by the *Tokyo Nichinichi* newspaper and was able to make good use of his talents as a reporter, being the first reporter to join the Japanese military at the front in their conquest of Taiwan. Afterward he quit reporting and started a pharmacy on the Ginza called the Rakuzendo Yakuho and sold a brand of eyedrops that was advertised in the newspapers.

Hikozo felt nostalgia as he followed Ginko's career, but his association with the man was in the distant past, and he didn't feel like going to see him.

Hikozo moved again, this time to the Yokoami District. This area, along the Sumida River, he thought would be perfect for him now that his health was not good.

He spent much of his time seated on the banks, gazing out at the river. Riverboats—rowed ones and ones with white sails—plied the waters. As he watched them, the smell of the rigging of the *Eiriki Maru* came back to him. From the thick reeds on the opposite bank a flock of white cranes flew off like snowflakes swirling in the air.

The crowded streets of Hong Kong, carriages clopping down the streets of San Francisco, scenes in New York and Washington—hazy memories came back to him. He found it strange that he'd actually lived in those distant places.

He'd visited Honjo Village a total of three times, but never again after that. He was dead to that village, and all that was left was the memorial, with English carved on it, to his mother and stepfather and to his ancestors. His aunt had died of illness, and not a single relative remained.

But sometimes thoughts of the village came to him. It was a dreary place, but he missed the smell of the sea, and tears came to him whenever he remembered this. In all the world that little village was the only place he could call home.

Reports reaching him from the village told him that the survivors of his crew who'd been hired by the Himeji Domain—Seitaro, Kiyozo, and Asauemon—had all, one after the other, passed away, so he was the only one of the original crew from his hometown still alive. He wondered how the other sailors of the *Eiriki Maru* were doing. Maybe all of them had passed away by now.

In his travels he'd met many other Japanese castaways in China and America, many of whom had, like Otokichi, ended their days in foreign lands. Those lucky enough to have made their way back to Japan mostly lived aimless lives, a race of castaways, and then finally breathed their last.

Hikozo drifted through the days himself, intent only on his calligraphy.

In the thirtieth year of Meiji (1897) he found himself too out of breath to go to the banks of the Sumida River anymore. It was quite rainy from June until autumn, but the weather improved in November.

On December 11 a terribly strong wind blew from the west, but it died down in the afternoon, and the next day was fair. That evening Hikozo felt a sharp pain in his chest and collapsed, and though a doctor was soon summoned, he never regained consciousness and breathed his last. He was sixty-one.

His death was reported in the newspaper with the following headline: *America Hikozo Has Died; Founder of the First Newspaper in Japan.*

In December of the following year a gravestone was erected in the foreign cemetery in Aoyama by his wife, Choko. The top of the marker, in English, stated that this was the grave of Hikozo. Below that, in Japanese, it read: *Here lies Joseph Heco.*